DEAL ME A [...]

"Airborne All the Way!"
David Drake

"Look out below!" is the only cry you *won't* hear when the Goblin Balloon Brigade fires up its derigibles and heads for the skies.

"The Lament"
S. M. Stirling

When the Hurloon Minotaur cries, its song rings through the hills, with grief and rage . . . and a wish for revenge.

"What's in a Name?"
Michael A. Stackpole

Pull up a chair, hear a tall tale, and get yourself into a world of trouble with a Benalish hero at Grover's, a pub run by one of the Ironroot Treefolk and a magnet for mischief of every kind.

"Animal Trap"
M. C. Sumner

Whether you're a trapper, a thief, or a seller of skins, there are some deep secrets better left unknown.

Look for these
MAGIC: The Gathering™ Novels

Arena
Whispering Woods
Shattered Chains
Final Sacrifice
The Cursed Land*
The Prodigal Sorcerer*

Available from HarperPrism

*coming soon

ATTENTION: ORGANIZATIONS AND CORPORATIONS

Most HarperPaperbacks are available at special quantity dis-
counts for bulk purchases for sales promotions, premiums, or
fund-raising. For information, please call or write:
Special Markets Department, HarperCollins*Publishers*,
10 East 53rd Street, New York, N.Y. 10022.
Telephone: (212) 207-7528. Fax: (212) 207-7222.

MAGIC
The Gathering ™

TAPESTRIES

AN ANTHOLOGY

Edited by Kathy Ice

Foreword by Richard Garfield,
creator of Magic: The Gathering ™

HarperPrism
An Imprint of HarperPaperbacks

If you purchased this book without a cover, you should be aware that this book is stolen property. It was reported as "unsold and destroyed" to the publisher and neither the author nor the publisher has received any payment for this "stripped book."

This is a work of fiction. The characters, incidents, and dialogues are products of the author's imagination and are not to be construed as real. Any resemblance to actual events or persons, living or dead, is entirely coincidental.

HarperPaperbacks*A Division of* HarperCollins*Publishers*
10 East 53rd Street, New York, N.Y. 10022

Copyright © 1995 by Wizards of the Coast, Inc.
All rights reserved. No part of this book may be used or reproduced in any manner whatsoever without written permission of the publisher, except in the case of brief quotations embodied in critical articles and reviews. For information address HarperCollins*Publishers*, 10 East 53rd Street, New York, N.Y. 10022.

First HarperPaperbacks printing: July 1995

Printed in the United States of America

HarperPrism is an imprint of HarperPaperbacks.
HarperPaperbacks, HarperPrism, and colophon are trademarks of HarperCollins*Publishers.*

Library of Congress Cataloging-in-Publication Data
    Tapestries: an anthology/edited by Kathy Ice; foreword by Richard Garfield.
        p.   cm.—(Magic, the gathering)
    ISBN 0-06-105308-2
    I. Fantastic fiction, American. 2. Imaginary places—Ficiton. 3. Card games—fiction. I. Ice, Kathy. II. Series.
PS648.F3T38   1995
813´.0876608—dc20   95-9986
                                                 CIP

❖ 10 9 8 7 6 5 4 3 2 1

Acknowledgments

I would like to acknowledge the help of several support teams at Wizards of the Coast.

My "slush-pile readers:" Julie Campbell, Shaw Michaels, Sue Mohn, Gene Romaine, and JoAnn Wonderly.

My "anthology commandos:" Casey Brebberman, Maria Cabardo, Ellie Haguel, Beverly Marshall Saling, and Vic Wertz.

And, of course, Janna Silverstein—colleague, mentor, and Editing Goddess.

Thanks, guys. I couldn't have done it without you!

Introduction

Kathy Ice

In the summer of 1993, I was introduced to a weird little card game called *Magic: The Gathering*. Like so many since then, I was immediately hooked—not only by the game, but of the fascinating glimpses into a strange place called Dominia. In bringing together these stories, I hoped to expand a little on these glimpses, giving *Magic* fans and fantasy readers alike a clearer picture of the worlds of Dominia.

The response to this project from authors has been overwhelming, and the resulting anthology exceeds all our expectations. Each story presents a unique vision of the people, creatures, and magic of Dominia.

Our intention here is not to replay one *Magic* game after another. We have no stories that feature wizards' duels, although the effects of those duels are often evident. These are fantasy stories, so even people who haven't yet tried *Magic* will be able to read and enjoy them.

I'm proud to have played a part in creating such a terrific book. I hope you'll enjoy reading these stories as much as I did.

Foreword

"Take a world and put the key elements on cards; shuffle the deck and deal it out to the players," was one of the first descriptions I gave to Peter Adkison of the concept of trading-card games. This is a collection of stories that take place in the first such world. This is backwards from the way things usually go, where a world is explored through stories and perhaps later made into a game.

Dominia is not actually a world, but a set of loosely connected worlds. This makes it a good environment for story writing, because as long as one understands the global rules, those things that are true for all of the worlds of Dominia, a world can be created for a story. This makes the story environment mimic the card game environment in a rather pleasant way; there are an abundance of places and characters, and writers can choose to use the ones they like. In the long run, the loved elements will stay and the disliked ones will be relegated to the graveyard.

The workings of magic in Dominia are detailed enough to really get some involved and interesting stories. I am not referring to casting lich and then playing Sheherezade and in the subgame using Ring of Maruf to retrieve the lich from the outer game, or any other particular game combinations. I am referring to the relationship between the magics; there is not just good versus evil, but also life versus death, order versus chaos, artifice versus nature, and mind versus matter. These dichotomies are classic, and the characteristics of the magics give us a fresh method to explore them.

My personal preference in reading tends to favor science fiction over fantasy, particularly in the case of the short story. I think the primary reason for this is that the shared world the authors have in science fiction—usually our world—is one rich with detail that I can identify with quickly. I find the ones used in fantasy are often too ill-defined to be appealing. I get the feeling the author can pull anything out of his or her hat, so it feels kind of flabby. In fact, my favorite fantasy short stories are Niven's *The Magic Goes Away* series of stories (for which I made Nevinyrral's Disk). I believe this is because he laid down reasonably simple rules for his world and worked it in many ways like one of his science fiction stories.

At least the mechanics of magic in Dominia are pretty well understood. This is a good start on the way to really understanding a fantasy world. The alternative to really simple rules is a world many people build together. This is the sort of work that leads to a movement, like cyberpunk, being created. I have a lot of faith in the concept of authors building a world together, drawing on each others details to produce a convincing whole.

The idea of stories in a world based on a card game doesn't seem particularly strange to me, at least not as strange as it probably should seem. Perhaps that is because the game was already somewhat based on a world. Perhaps it is because the range of emotion and drama I see in games played with good players exceeds that in many stories. By good players I mean people who play well, people who play with life and enthusiasm, not necessarily those who win all the time.

My guess is that a reader of this book is one of the better players by this standard. The talents of a reader and that of a good game player are actually similar in my mind. Both will be able to internalize a world and its rules. Both will be good at identifying with other characters or players. Both will be able to reason in this artificial environment.

Perhaps another reason fiction based on a game doesn't seem strange to me is that I believe that games are a microcosm for life. What happens in games reflects something primal from real life, from the *Survival of the Fittest Game* (Registered Trademark of Darwin) that has been played since the beginning of time (at least our time), to the *Cooperation Game* that has probably been around nearly as long.

Give us feedback if you really like a story, or really dislike one. Ideally, stories that the readers love to read and the writers love to write will come about. I hope you enjoy watching the worlds of Dominia being created as much as I, the most biased of readers, do.

Richard △ Garfield

Contents

Thief's Flight

Carla Montgomery

The bitter wind sliced through the mountain pass like a sharpened blade as Kyree rounded yet another turn of the narrow trail. Larut, sure-footed steppe horse that he was, nickered in protest and stopped in his tracks.

"Look, I know it's colder than Jyr's moon out and we've been climbing since dawn," Kyree explained to her mount as she eyed the black chasm yawning on their right, "but even if this pathetic excuse for a road were wide enough to turn around on, there's no going back now and you know it."

The young woman shivered, pulling her worn cloak closer around her shoulders, and stared with yellow-green eyes into the growing darkness ahead. The fortified walls of Indorin's tomb straddled the pass at the summit, twin turrets glowing like polished teeth in the last evening light.

"If we don't get what we were sent for, there's no return—ever," Kyree reminded herself as well as the balking horse.

The wind howled down the mountainside, yanking the hood off her head and sending her wild, brown hair whipping behind her. She didn't bother to pull it back up again.

"Come on, Larut," she said, digging her heels into the shaggy horse's sides, "let's get this over with before we both freeze to death."

Larut stamped his hoof, then continued up the winding trail as darkness filled the valley behind them. Kyree fell into silent thought.

The two had traveled together since late summer, when Kyree's masters had at last revealed to her the Task. Born to the Haari, the feral tribe of warrior thieves who called the high desert of Mirab home, Kyree had trained all her young life for that journey, the chance to prove herself worthy of the Hunt. Her earliest memories as a fledge were of the Clan preparing for it—the smell of her mother's freshly oiled leathers and of the thick, orange dye she laughingly used to paint the rays of a rising sun across her father's face, the jingle of gaudy jewelry against armor, the excited voices as the members of the Pack gathered in their places within the Form. Then, the faraway look that came over their painted features as the low humming began, the lithe grace of their half-naked bodies as they performed the movements of the Form and sank deeper into the trance. The rising wail. The ring of drawn steel. The whirling and spinning. The bright crimson streaks as the bloodprice was given, and the glorious cry of the Hunt as they rose as one into the sky and became the very wind.

Even in this desolate place, Kyree's bones ached with joy at the memory of it.

She yearned for the day when she would join them.

It was said the Haari were human kin to the great raptors that flew in ages past. No outsider knew for sure. The secrets of the Aerie, ancestral home of the Haari, lay with it deep in the heart of the Mirab. From that inassailable cliff-dwelling where the young were left in the watchful charge of the Masters, the hunting members of the Clan ranged the surrounding countryside in migratory packs, searching for provisions, treasure, and glory. There were many outsiders who sought their skill as allies and hired thieves, and more who feared to hear their bloodcurdling warscream. But to the Haari-born, it was neither grand cause nor promise of rich reward that brought them diving with eyes bright and swords drawn into the thick of the battlefield, or sent them deep into wizard's vaults and dragon's lairs for treasure. It was only the thrill of the Hunt itself. To use all—mind, body, sword, wind—and risk all for the honor and greater good of the Clan. That was what it meant to be Haari. That was what it meant to be alive.

And that was why the Old Ones had granted the Haari the Task so long ago. For if a young hunter could not return from the trials of a Lone Flight with an appointed object safe in hand, how could they be trusted with the lives of bloodkin in the heat of the Hunt? To succeed was to earn a place in the Pack and a seat at High Council.

To fail was to be cast out from the Clan for all time.

It was Kyree's Task that had led her to this lonesome pass on the verge of winter. Her Masters had decreed she must brave the walls of the tomb and bring back something from within for the glory of the Clan. She had no intentions of failing.

Abruptly, the horse stopped swaying, snapping Kyree back to attention.

Before her, the monument to the fallen knight loomed in the darkness like the silent, bleached bones of something long dead.

"Not going to do either of us any good thinking of home at a time like this," she whispered to her snuffling mount. "Time for me to take over."

Kyree dismounted quickly and led the horse toward the cover of a stand of pine and scrub oak. With growing excitement, she eyed the fortress tomb. The Masters had said it was built long ago by the Order of the Silverstar to mark the place where their fallen comrade, Indorin, had died battling a demon or some such monster. Its curved outer walls had no entrances or windows, and it was rumored that the members of the order still met there in secret from time to time. That was all she'd been told; even the Masters did not know for sure what lay inside.

She had no other plan but to scale the outer wall near one of the turrets, drop, hopefully unnoticed, into a dark corner of the inner courtyard, and see what she could find. It would all be much simpler, of course, if she could just fly over and be done with it. But flight by the uninitiated was generally frowned upon by the Masters except as a last resort. Besides, since every flight cost a bloodprice, it was downright foolish to fly too often. Far better to rely on a cunning mind and a body honed to the agile strength of a bird of prey.

They had almost reached the grove of trees when Kyree felt the ground shift slightly beneath her feet.

"Get back, Larut! It's a trap!" she hissed through clenched teeth.

But before the horse could move, the ground under her feet opened with a metallic grating that echoed deep within the mountain. Kyree lept sideways, but not far enough. She fell.

In an instant, her cloak flipped over her head, gone fluttering into empty space below, and her right arm was nearly wrenched from its socket. Stunned, she slowly realized she was hanging suspended over a black pit with no visible bottom, Larut's reins wrapped tightly around her right forearm. A half dozen squeaking bats flew out of the depths, flickering past her into freedom and the night. The dank smell of ancient decay rose up to her from somewhere far below.

"Oh, this is just great—I haven't even started yet," Kyree cursed under her breath as she swung above the gaping pit. "Okay, Larut, now's when you prove that the year's worth of nimzer pelts I paid for you was a bargain. Pull!"

The stocky horse, eyes white with fear, nearly sat on its haunches as it strained backward. Its front hooves loosened clods of earth that pelted Kyree as she planted her feet against the dirt side of the pit and struggled upward. Leather harness creaked as the horse took one unsteady step back, then another.

"Come on, come on . . . you can do it," Kyree wheezed as she placed one boot on the ledge, slipped, and tried again.

Then, she was over the edge, panting heavily on the bare ground where she lay. Larut snorted in her ear.

"All right, all right, thanks," she said quietly, sitting up and scratching the winter whiskers beneath the horse's chin. "What do you say we head to those rocks over there instead, just in case someone decides to see what their trap has caught?"

In answer, Larut blew a cloud of frosty breath in her face.

Quickly, the two companions skirted the edge of the pit and headed uphill, ducking behind several large boulders for protection. For long minutes, Kyree searched for signs of movement below them. She could make out no signs of imminent danger; nothing shifted except the branches of the trees tossed by the wind. Yet, something intangible had changed, as if now an invisible presence were watching her from somewhere inside those white walls.

Despite its deserted appearance, it was possible that a sorcerer or even some nastier entity had taken up residence in the tomb without the Masters' knowledge. Certainly, her encounter with the pit trap would have announced her arrival to anyone lurking inside. It may have just been her thief's sense working overtime, but Kyree didn't like the increasingly tense feel of the place.

"Well, if they know I'm here already, I might as well get on with it and see what they send out to greet me," she said resolutely. "And, if by some small chance I find them still fast asleep in their beds, it'll be a nice little surprise for us both."

The icy wind whistled among the rocks as Kyree prepared for the culmination of her Task. It took some effort, but she quieted the excited fluttering in her stomach by reciting the words of the Masters as she stripped to nothing but her metal breastplate, belted leather breeches, embroidered thief's pouch, and the double scabbard that held her windswords on her back. She smiled slightly as she tied the hawk feathers her mother had given her into her tangled hair for good luck. Then, she dipped a tremulous finger into the vial of red pigment she'd carried hundreds of miles and carefully traced the scarlet lightning bolt of the initiate across her face. Finally, with a practiced motion, she drew her weapons—the solid cutlass of human warrior, the fine-bladed scimitar of hawkish thief—and knelt to recite the invocation to the Great Ones. It was the sacred prayer for balance: the balance that kept earth and sky, human and hawk, body and soul, bound together. For it was balance that gave the Haari the gift of flight, and only through perfect balance could Kyree complete her Task.

The ritual completed, Kyree rose, eyes glittering like a wild thing in the frosty night and stretched her lean body. Below her, the sheer walls of the tomb stood in stark relief against the night. It wasn't going to be an easy climb, but, after all, no one ever said a Lone Flight was easy.

Larut shifted uneasily, tossing his head.

"Don't worry, I won't be long," she said as she sheathed her swords.

Then, Kyree was off at a crouching sprint, her bare feet scarcely touching the ground.

Two-thirds of the way up the cleft between turret and wall, Kyree paused to let herself wish for her cloak. Her fingers and toes were numb from clenching to the tiny crevices between ice-cold blocks of white stone. The relentless wind froze the sweat to her skin. With a final push from her legs, she scrambled upward and caught hold of the top of the wall with her fingertips. Every muscle in her arms quivered and strained as she heaved herself up. Then, without daring to stop and catch her breath, she swung her legs over the far side and dropped, rolling to absorb the impact of the landing.

At last, she was inside.

The greater of the two moons had risen in a crescent over the mountain peaks and lit the inner courtyard with a pale light. The grounds were completely barren except for great black scorch-marks, some traced eerily along in the dirt like oily smoke, others blasted deep into the earth at random. Kyree wondered if the sheer outer wall had been built to preserve those signs of Indorin's great battle of an age past. Was it possible that the demon had returned? The back of Kyree's neck tingled and she shuddered as the feeling of being "watched" crept over her again. Her keen senses strained for any sign of another's presence. But there was only silence and moonlight. Not even the wind dared disturb this place.

At the center of the courtyard stood a domed structure, unim-posing but striking in its simplicity: Indorin's tomb.

Something scuttled behind her. Kyree spun. On this side, the turret had a doorway opening onto the courtyard. The noise had come from there. She pressed her back against the wall, drew her cutlass, and glanced inside. Kyree let out a sigh of relief as she spotted a small furry creature scurrying across the dusty floor on tiny feet and into a cobwebbed corner. Rusting spears and tar-nished bits of armor lay strewn about the otherwise empty room. That was all; nothing of real importance, or danger. The real glory would come from the tomb itself.

With that thought, Kyree turned and darted across the open courtyard, avoiding the burned streaks as she ran toward the gleaming tomb. She lept up the steps in one fluid motion, took a deep breath to quiet her pounding heart, and stepped inside the arched doorway.

Despite all her training, Kyree gasped in wonder as the dark-ened inner chamber of the tomb filled with amber-colored light at the touch of her foot on the floor. The room was circular, smaller than she'd expected from its outward appearance, almost a private chapel. Yet, it was breathtaking, carved entirely of pure, white marble.

The golden glow illuminating the chamber arose from large orbs like giant pearls suspended above a dozen alcoves along the perimeter of the room. Slender columns cut to resemble the trunks of birch trees supported the domed ceiling with their gracefully chiselled branches. In the alcoves stood alabaster statues of unicorns and saints, pilgrims and prophets, all poised as if in silent prayer. Between them were draped curtains of fine white silk.

At the very center of the pristine room, beneath the winged effigy of a sculpted angel that hung from the ceiling, rested the sarcophagus of Indorin on a raised dais. The likeness of the knight was flawlessly carved out of the heavy stone that housed his coffin. And, there, in long-fingered hands of snow-white marble, it clasped an ivory cup to its breast.

Kyree's breath escaped in a low whistle.

Here was a prize that was worthy of the Clan, an object that would grant her the title of Hunter. Here it was at last, in reach of any who would risk the taking.

Kyree crept forward, bare feet silent on the cold, marble floor that shone smooth as a frozen pool. The back of her head itched as she inched her way toward the center of the chamber. Statues seemed to glare viciously from their pedestals, as if readying to pounce upon her for disturbing their meditations. Her heartbeat rang in her ears and filled her chest with its rapid drumming as she approached the glistening sarcophagus. She mounted the steps of the dais.

An inscription carved around the lid in bold letters read:

Here Lies Indorin, Protector of Dominia,
Who Died That Evil Should Not Walk This Plane,
May His Body Rest As His Soul Travels Onward

Kyree glanced quickly over her shoulder, then up into the stern, alabaster face of the angel hanging above her with its sword upraised. She steeled herself, held her breath, and gingerly lifted the cup from Indorin's marble hands.

Nothing happened.

Slowly, Kyree grinned, then giggled lightly to herself as she twirled the exquisite chalice in her hand. Her thief's eye told her it was priceless, carved out of a single piece of flawless ivory by hands whose skill knew no equal.

"That was not so very difficult, after all." She laughed, raising the cup in salute to the fallen knight. "I shall drink a toast to you, great Indorin, first town I come to on my journey home."

She was tucking the cup into the pouch on her belt when the glowing orbs dimmed and went out. Kyree spun around to face the entrance to the tomb in the sudden darkness, drawing her swords. There had been no sound.

"Hardly a decent way to welcome a visitor." Her voice echoed through the cavernous room as she tried desperately to adjust her eyes to the conjured darkness.

Kyree's body tensed for action. This was a wizard's doing, like as not.

"I hate to disturb you any further at this hour, so I'll just be on my way. Wouldn't want to overextend my welcome," she added, stalling, hoping for some hint of which direction the attack would come from.

In answer, the silk draperies along the walls of the chamber began to rustle and flap like a flock of great white swans. Then, a sharp crack sounded behind her.

Fearing the worst, Kyree turned back around to face Indorin's sarcophagus. It appeared unchanged. Yet, the area around the dais was becoming steadily brighter, the blackness turning into blue, then gray. Another snapping sound drew her eyes upward. With growing dread, she watched in spellbound fascination as a tendril-like fissure ran down the carved angel's face. A flake of stone fell from the statue's cheekbone and a piercing shaft of white light shot from within it across the darkened tomb.

The angel was awakening.

Kyree ran. She was nearly to the entrance of the tomb when a frigid wind from outside ripped into the room, setting the statues rocking on their pedestals and crashing to the floor. The force of the blast slammed Kyree sideways into a wall. She struggled to regain her footing on the smooth marble as yards of white cloth reached searchingly toward her, grabbing at her like pale tentacles. Biting her lip, she slashed at the rippling silk with her swords, shredding it to jagged ribbons before it could entangle her limbs. Then, she sprinted through the entranceway. Behind her, the entire figure of the angel was beginning to glow.

Outside, it was as if the north wind itself had descended upon the dead knight's tomb. Rushing air tore the breath from Kyree's throat and the fine dirt of the courtyard whipped around her, stinging her bare arms and legs. Strangely, the dark stains on the ground remained untouched by the rising gale.

They seemed to leer knowingly at her, laughing silently to themselves at her act of disrespect. From somewhere beyond the walls, Larut's panicked whinnying rose faintly above the din.

There was no time.

"If this isn't an emergency, I don't know what is," Kyree growled to herself.

She closed her eyes and began to hum softly. At first, she was worried the trance would not come quickly enough, that her movements, her song, would be too hurried. Her awareness of the stirring statue behind her threatened to erase all memory of her training and send her fleeing like a mindless rabbit for cover. But gradually as she began to move, carefully sidestepping the blasted places on the ground, her body tracing the familiar outlines of the Form with limb and sword, all other thought, even the clamor of the rasping winds about her, died away.

Time stretched out before her like a shining thread as she dove inward through the Form to find the knife's edge that was balance. Deeper and deeper within she danced as flashing windswords sliced through the summoned storm and her body leapt and spun about the courtyard to become thought itself. She was not aware of the streaks of pulsing light that spilled out from the entrance to Indorin's tomb behind her, or of her own voice rising in a banshee wail above the wild winds that buffeted the courtyard. There was only the reaching for that bright point, that infinitesimal, needlesharp speck where earth and air, body and mind, walker and soarer focused and became one. For an instant, she glimpsed it, shining in the darkness within her like a star.

Now.

Kyree, eyes glazed with concentration, raised her windswords high above her head. In one swift motion, she slashed the blades diagonally across the tops of her feet, cutting them cleanly, severing their tie to the land. Then, with a tremendous leap and the cry of the Hunter, she threw herself into the air and was lifted up into the sky like a leaf in a cyclone. Below her, Indorin's tomb glowed white-hot as though a sun had come to rest within its walls.

Distantly as she rose, Kyree heard her own voice shout to Larut to run. A vague, dreamlike image of the horse careening in terror down the mountain path filtered into the back of her focused mind and was gone. She allowed no other distractions, imagining herself an arrow as the Masters had taught her, and sprang away into the night.

Behind her, a flash brighter than a hundred lightning bolts turned the night momentarily into day, and with it came a deafening, unbearably beautiful sound as if all the world's raindrops had each been granted a single note to sing for one instant. Light and music exploded outward as the Serra angel burst into the world.

Kyree flew.

Faster than she had ever willed herself to go before, she plunged straight down the mountain's gaping chasm and sped through the night. She became a silver meteor, windswords vibrating with their high-pitched keening, hair streaming behind like the tail of a comet, face furrowed in concentration, its scarlet paint matching the blood that dripped from her toes. Narrowly missing jagged rocks and the tops of trees, she swept past in a blur, keeping as close as she dared to for cover. She did not let herself look back.

Behind her, with stately grace of such beauty and fluidity it was painful to gaze upon, the angel strode through Indorin's tomb. Shattered statues and tattered curtains were made whole and restored to their places as she passed. And, at the touch of her golden sandal, the maelstrom in the courtyard subsided, the ancient blackened marks in the earth were retraced in glowing, iridescent white.

She stood to her full height, great wings unfurling and twitching in growing anger.

"Who has disturbed the sanctity of this place?" she shouted to the stars. "Who has stolen what is not rightfully theirs?"

Eyes like diamonds scoured the scene before her, coming to rest on the ruby-red prints where Kyree had taken flight. Face ablaze with fury, the angel gazed heavenward and raised its fiery sword.

"I am Adriel, guardian of hallowed ground. Those who defile it face my WRATH!"

With a beat of her shining wings that echoed down the mountain like thunder, the angel rose from the courtyard and gave chase.

The thunderclap that rolled over her told Kyree she hadn't much time. With another burst of concentration, she reached the end of the chasm. Her thoughts flew ahead of her. The chasm opened onto a flat river valley at the base of the mountains. She'd be an easy target out there on the plain. Better to keep to the rough terrain of the foothills where she might find a cave to hide in before her strength gave out. Quickly, she veered north to fly parallel to the mountain range.

She glanced over her shoulder.

In the distance, a thing like a brilliant firefly bobbed and danced, flooding the mountain crevice beneath it with light. It was rapidly growing larger and brighter as it came shooting down the pass toward her.

Kyree felt a sharp twinge of panic and her body dipped dangerously close to the rocky hillsides as she struggled to regain control. Surely, the Masters had never imagined she'd end up half-frozen in the middle of nowhere, trying to outfly an angel. A Lone Flight was a test, not a suicide mission. She must believe they had taught her well, prepared her even for this. Grimly, she sought her balance again, recentered, and flew onward.

Low clouds driven like wooly sheep before the dying wind began to cloak the peaks as the angel neared her quarry. Between them, the indigo sky was filled with stars that shimmered like her sisters' and brothers' eyes. It had been long since last she was called. She had forgotten how striking this world could be despite its raw, chaotic nature and its infuriatingly misguided inhabitants. Manifestation on this plane definitely had its drawbacks—the bittersweet pull of mortal existence, the limitations of physical form—but with it there was also a certain kind of rapture. The freedom of absolute, righteous fury filled Adriel's wings as she sighted the fleeing intruder and began to close in.

Kyree dodged and darted up narrow gulleys and under low bridges of stone, desperately trying to elude her pursuer. Her eyes streamed tears and her breath began to come in ragged gasps as the ground flew past beneath her in a smeared, gray blur. It was no use. The angel was gaining. She was caught in the inescapable white glow that spread before its mighty wings, like a silver fish in a net. The faster she flew, the more she struggled and twisted in the air, the more entangled by unearthly light she became. The angel was closing.

"No!" Kyree screamed to the being behind her. "I will not give up!"

Abruptly, the mountain range she followed ended and Kyree found herself shooting over the lapping waters of a great inland lake like a skipping stone scant inches above the surface. On the far side, she could just make out a jumble of pitched roofs and lit windows that told of a small village. She sprinted for it. Behind her, the waters of the lake ignited in a myriad of sparkling, golden reflections as the angel plunged after her. It, she, was close enough now that Kyree could hear the rustling of her wings and a sound like hundreds of tiny bells that filled the air around its shining body. She almost prayed for strength, but caught herself, remembering who it was that followed her like a fox on a hare. Even the Great Ones could not help her in this. Silently, Kyree pressed her weakening body onward.

The thief and the angel dodged among the masts of sailing boats tied to docks at the shore, then past them and up the cobbled streets and alleyways of the village, deserted in the lonely hours before dawn. They tore through the town, Kyree's windswords howling as she fled. The blazing Adriel was at her heels, filling the night village with a strident song of triumph and threatening to set the roofs on fire with her sword as she passed. Shutters flew open. Tavern signs were spun on their hinges. Horses screamed in their stalls as Kyree swooped through the inn's stable, and the temple pigeons tumbled from their midnight roosts in confusion when she momentarily hovered behind the highest spire in a vain attempt to escape the angel's flaring gaze.

There were villagers who, wakened from their sleep by a roar and a flash, wandered wearily to their windows and swore ever after that two comets—one of silver and one of gold—had landed that night and chased each other around the fountain in the square singing a song of such beauty that the fountain hums it still on cold, clear nights.

Kyree's lungs burned, her windswords felt as if they were made of lead and began to quiver in her grasp as her outflung arms screamed with pain. There was no escaping her shining, relentless pursuer. With a hopeless, hunted cry, she abandoned the village square and flew straight upward like a silver javelin into the sky above the lake. She crashed, unseeing, through a squawking chevron of a flock of wintering geese, her cutlass sending one of the birds careening far below with a severed wingtip. Higher and higher she flew, higher than the nearby mountains, above the scattered clouds, until the air was so thin and cold it froze in her mouth and she could almost reach out and touch the crescent moon.

It was then, as she shot through the rarefied night, that Kyree remembered.

She was not bred to be a defenseless, cowardly creature that fled in terror before danger. She was not shaped to value life over honor. She was Haari. If she must die, she would choose to die as Hunter, not Hunted.

Kyree turned and threw her head back to give the piercing warscream of the Clan. Then, painted face set in resolve, she dove straight toward the angel.

They closed with a clash of swords that shook the lake valley below. Kyree's scimitar thrust was blocked easily by the angel's flashing sword and countered with a stroke like a lightning bolt that sent her reeling backward as it glanced off her cutlass.

"Give up, mortal!" Adriel demanded. "Return the cup you have stolen!"

The voice rang in Kyree's head, a deafening trumpet blast. She felt herself slip downward in the air. She was losing altitude. Her exhausted mind struggled to maintain her flight, but the effort she needed to focus on her opponent threatened to tax her to the limit.

"I told you once, I won't give it back," Kyree snarled into the perfect countenance of the golden being hovering before her. "Maybe you need to learn how to take no for an answer."

Kyree laughed out loud as the angel's eyes of fire widened momentarily in shock at her arrogance, then narrowed with renewed outrage.

"And, perhaps, you need to learn respect for those who are far beyond your understanding," the angel said dangerously, lips widening in a radiant smile.

Again, they closed in a silver and gold flurry of great wings of light and whirling steel. Every grating clash of their swords boomed and sent pulses of white light flashing like lightning, until the mountains rumbled and shook in violent echo and the lake boiled and frothed below. Kyree fought like a trapped animal, furious and wild. The angel, her expression almost joyous, countered each stroke with a surety and power that did not fade. As the battling figures sank lower and lower in the sky, Kyree felt her strength ebbing. Soon, her bloody feet touched a cool, wet bank of cloud, then she was up to her waist in a swelling sea of fog. Her swinging arms felt as if they were made of stone. She was losing her edge, the balance was eluding her grasp. She must regain it; she must rest.

Suddenly, Kyree broke free and dove headfirst into the thick blanket of mist like a seal into the sea. She wrapped herself in muffling cloud, feeling her body drift downward into the dense center of the cloud as she desperately fought for control.

Above her, the angel shouted in fury.

Kyree closed her eyes in the clammy grayness, but balance would not come, and the harder she tried, the more rapidly she sank in the damp, murky air.

Suddenly, a graceful, glowing hand shot out of the mist and clamped like a white-hot vice onto her wrist. Kyree screamed. The smell of singed flesh filled her nostrils as her hand opened reflexively. She watched in shock as her scimitar fell and was lost in the swirling mists below, taking all possibility of flight with it. Then, the water vapor around her erupted into millions of droplets of molten gold and was blasted away into nothingness. The cloud bank was gone. The night was filled with white-gold light and deafening music. She found herself, wrist burning, eyes nearly blinded by the brilliance, staring directly into the angel's face.

"You are foolish to not return the cup willingly," Adriel said chidingly, almost gently, in a voice like liquid sunlight. Her arched, golden brows drew together in pity as Kyree struggled in her grasp.

"I do not wish to harm you further, only to return what is not yours to its rightful place," she said, her tone growing more forceful, her molten grip tightening on Kyree's wrist. "Do not defy me."

Kyree could feel her bare skin blistering, her armor breastplate heating up from the intensity of the angel's nearness. She could not see. It was as if she'd flown straight into the sun. Dizzy from pain and loss of blood, at the point of exhausted despair, Kyree felt her body go limp.

For an instant, she hung in the sky from the angel's powerful grasp.

Then, with her last strength, Kyree slashed blindly upward with her cutlass, kicking out at the same time. She missed. But the surprised angel released her burning hold. With a strangled shout of triumph, Kyree and the ivory cup plummeted into the darkness below.

The air roared past as she tumbled end over end toward the earth. It was strange how, now that all hope of flight was gone and death was looming up to meet her, Kyree's mind found clarity once again. True, her first Flight would prove to be her last, but at least she would die as a Hunter, her prize still in hand. Eyes still dazzled by angel light, Kyree felt for the chalice in the pouch on her belt as she fell, found it, and grasped its delicate stem underneath the fabric.

With a tremendous splash that sent a white plume into the air behind her, she plunged into the icy waters of the mountain lake. Liquid darkness covered her head and filled her lungs. She was sinking still, but in her blind confusion and pain, she could not tell which way to turn in the utter blackness. Her armor crushed inward on her chest as she struggled and fought for a surface she could not find.

Her limbs moved awkwardly, nightmarishly slowed by the frigid, unfamiliar thickness of water.

Arms and legs seized up rigidly as overtaxed muscles finally succumbed to exhaustion, and the waters of the lake closed in hungrily around the fallen Hunter.

"Hawks were never meant to swim," a dreamy voice whispered inside her head as the last bubble of air escaped her lips and she became one with the black depths.

Her last memory was of reaching for the crescent moon.

Two distorted but familiar faces loomed above her like strange reflections in a cavern pool. Someone called her name.

Kyree blinked and sat up.

It took a few moments for her vision to clear and the sense of falling to stop.

Somehow, she realized, she was dripping wet, shivering in a puddle on the High Ledge above the Aerie. On either side of her crouched two of her Masters, genuine concern etched into their angular, lifeworn features. To the east, the sky was turning lavender and rose. The trill of a fading trumpet rang deep in her mind.

"There was a flash like a star had fallen and struck the Ledge," snapped Oria, disturbed that something had penetrated her carefully chosen night watch.

"And a music that pierced me like an arrow it was so pure," whispered Pyrin in his gentle, singer's voice. "Then, it was gone . . . and here you were."

Kyree shook her head in disbelief. She was dead, wasn't she?

"The rest of the Masters, and your parents, will be here soon, little fledgling," said Pyrin.

"Yes, and after such a grand entrance, I am quite curious to see what you have brought us from your Lone Flight," Oria added, turning her needle-sharp gaze toward her.

Still stunned, Kyree patted the drenched pouch at her side. It was empty.

But, just as she numbly registered the thought and started to panic, Oria and Pyrin gave a startled gasp and drew back a bit from her in wonder.

The ivory cup was gone. But in her hand, its wrist marked forever with the throbbing brand of the angel, was a single feather that shone as if it were made of sunlight itself. Dimly, a watery memory washed through her as she stared at the feather in her hand. Yes, with her last gasp, she had turned and grasped toward the light. And, in that instant, she had clasped an angel's wing.

Here, then, was her Gift to the Clan. Her Task was done. She had given all and learned in return that, perhaps, there were some things best left untouched.

And, she had been granted another chance.

With trembling fingers, she raised the feather in salute to the first rays of the rising sun. Faintly, like an echo, it was answered by a shimmering chorus of crystal bells that faded and disappeared like the stars overhead.

What's in a Name?

Michael A. Stackpole

For reasons I have yet to figure out, or just can't remember, the Benalish heroes always choose to talk to me before they make their run. This phenomena has puzzled me for as long as I've been around at Grover's. Benalish heroes, the men anyway, all tend toward tall and muscular, with chiseled good looks—though most have noses that look like the chisel slipped a few times. And tall, I suppose, is a relative judgment. Since I'm not afflicted with that condition I tend to overestimate height.

And the Benalkin tend to overestimate their good looks and charm.

This particular one—he shall remain nameless on the off chance he learns to read and stumbles across this account—sidled up to me at Grover's and leaned forward on the hardwood bar. His forearms hit the bartop with the impact of a warhammer on a skull, making my beer dance and my head begin to ache. The hero didn't seem to notice, but I imagine it takes a long time for nerve impulses to actually search out a contact point in such a small brain.

"I was wondering if I . . ." he began in a deep, rich baritone voice.

"Don't. You won't like it and the scars won't heal for a month."

Nameless gave me that low chuckle which meant we could certainly come to an understanding. "I heal quickly."

"It's not the speed of your metabolism, it's the size of the wounds." I closed the condensed version of the *Sarpadian Chronicles*, fighting to memorize the fact that I'd been on page "wolf chasing cat up a mountain"—and, no, you don't want to even think about Sarpadian math texts. I sighed. "Trust me on this, friend. She's an attractive nuisance. You don't want to trouble yourself."

He looked from me toward Kyyrao and back again. "Attractive, yes; nuisance, not even if her claws are razor sharp."

I was about to tell him that her claws were the least of his worries when he stepped aside so I got a good look at her, too. Kyyrao Grrenmw is a rarity among the race known commonly as Cat Warriors. Lithe and tall as are most of her race, she did not bear the more familiar markings of a tiger or leopard. Her coat ran from an almost blue-gray to a yellow-brown, with dark rosettes decorating her haunches, flanks, and forearms and angular black markings breaking up most of the rest of her coat. White fur covered her throat and breast, though the black leather halter she wore obscured most of it. She wore the traditional green loincloth of a Cat Warrior, and the jeweled golden greaves, but the cut of the garment and the armor did nothing to detract from the beauty of her long legs.

I could tell by the way her tail twitched she knew we were watching her standing over there. Her black ears flattened back as she raised her chin and laughed at a joke told by the Argivian archeologist from whom I'd borrowed my book. After he laughed, she leaned forward and rested her elbows on the table, stretching her legs. She flashed her canines in our direction and her amber eyes widened invitingly.

At least the Benalish hero took that as an invitation, but few of them have had experience being prey, so the mistake seemed reasonable. The hero looked at me and saw I'd been giving Kyyrao the eye as well. "Sorry, little man, but I saw her first. Wish me luck."

"Look, let me buy you a drink. Let me buy you several. That way you'll get drunk, fall down, and wake up with a colossal headache, which will be worlds away better than what you'll get if you decide she's a sex kitten and you're her scratching post." I looked up at our Ironroot Treehost. "Grover, something that will put our friend here out cold."

"Cold, I'm not interested in, friend."

I sighed.

Grover lowered a bough and swept the book up. "Wolf chases cat up a mountain."

"Yeah, and I chase a fool away from a cat." I slid off my stool and grabbed the hero by the elbow. "I've tried to warn you nicely."

Nameless pulled his elbow out of my grasp and snarled at me. "Go away little man, or I'll make you into kibble and give you to her as a snack."

"Fighting over me?" Kyyrao licked her lips as she slunk toward us. Most all the eyes in this section of the tavern watched her approach, including those belonging to the big guy. A quick sucker punch would have ended it all there, but then there would be one of those blood-vendettas and whenever possible, I've learned, angering a whole nation through one easily misinterpreted act of kindness is not a good idea.

The Benalkin nodded solemnly. "We will if he does not understand he's already beaten. I'll give him scars to match that crow's-foot on his forehead and not break a sweat doing it."

"And I get the winner?" Her ears flicked forward, all full of interest.

"It would be my pleasure."

I shook my head. "No, it wouldn't." I pointed a finger at Kyyrao and followed it with a glare. "You stay out of this for a second. My friend, the *Khyyiani* are a fierce tribe of warrior people, and they wish their kittens to all be strong. The right to mate is one that is fought over . . ."

"Like we're going to be doing . . ."

"*No*, not like we're going to be doing." I tapped my own chest. "I'm not interested in snuggling up with you."

"Nor I with you."

"Yeah, but you've got to win your right to mate with the object of your desire. Now among the *Khyyiani*—with their thick pelts—wrestling, love nips, and rib-tickling doesn't do permanent damage. You, on the other hand, will look like you've been plowed and planted with nettles, but you won't feel nearly so good. And that's if you make it past me first."

The hero's eyes narrowed and I thought, for the briefest of moments, I saw a spark of intelligence in their brown depths. "And why am I fighting you?"

Kyyrao purred delightfully. "To win the right to fight me, you must defeat my current mate."

That brought Nameless up short, and even abnormally short in his thought processes. Physically the surprise caused him to rise up to his full height, which bumped his head against one of the rafters. He looked at her and then me, and her again and then me again. His mouth opened and he wanted to ask how, but then he knew it was impossible for me to have beaten her in a fight. Then he began to wonder if he could beat me in a fight.

Just once I'd like one of these Benalkin to decide he couldn't beat me in a fight. It will never happen, of course, as much as it would do wonders for my ego. Walking away from me would make Nameless's ego shrivel up and go away. Of course, losing a fight to me would do worse things to his ego, but all the dreams of glory Benalish heroes stuff into their brains leaves little room for self-doubt.

Or a serious sense of self-preservation.

Then again, not many folks feel they need to be preserved against someone they intend to pound into the ground like a tent stake.

The look of surprise slowly blossoming on his face meant he didn't expect me to move so quickly from beneath the melon-sized fist arcing down toward my head. The fact was, of course, that I'd started to move the moment he began his turn away from Kyyrao and back toward me, with his fist rising up like a cobra's head. I moved with him, stepping right into the energy flow of his punch. Twisting around, I even turned my back on him, so the punch came in over my right shoulder. I grabbed his thick wrist and tugged ever so slightly. As I did that, I ducked low and guided him straight over my back.

He hit hard enough that some floorboards creaked and others cracked. I released his wrist and he rolled up into a ball against the bar. The stool that got trapped between him and the bar exploded, broken legs and crosspieces skittling all over the place. He looked up at me from the floor, since he'd come to rest with his buttocks in the air and his body supported by his shoulders.

Nameless clearly expected me to kick him in the head, and we both knew that even with his thick skull the blow could kill him.

Instead I dropped to one knee and poked my index finger against the spot in the center of his forehead that should have been clear of eyebrow. It hurt him a bit, which it didn't need to, but the pain helped cover the effect as I cast a spell. His eyes went quickly in and out of focus, with his pupils dilating and contracting out of sync with each other. The one time I'd been hit with the spell it made the world ripple around me, as if I was looking at the world through a wall of water, and the effect wasn't all that pleasant.

He rolled over and vomited.

"Well, my work's done here." I glowered at Kyyrao. "Isn't it?"

She delicately leaped over the Benalkin's lunch puddle and purred at me. "It is. You still care."

I sighed. "You know, if you want signs of my caring, you don't need to entice these guys into fighting with me. I can go out and pick some flowers for you."

Kyyrao frowned, which included a cautionary flashing of sharp teeth. "While the thought of you presenting me the heads of your conquests as a token of affection excites me, I'm afraid you're overmatched against flowers."

I gave her a sidelong glance since she was missing the point, but her return glance told me I was missing the point. Since she did know the customs of her people and I didn't know the customs of my people, we defaulted to her way of doing things. I mean, I knew humans provided flowers and gems and other valuables to their lovers as signs of affection, but I couldn't confirm that was the custom in my home nation since, even here in Grover's, there *weren*'t any others from my home nation—nor was there anyone who knew what that nation was.

A dwarf came walking over, smoothing his long gray beard with a hand as he approached. He looked at me and her, then down at the Benalish hero who, on his hands and knees, was still as tall as the dwarf. The dwarf looked back up at me. "You would be Lute."

The Benalkin hung his head in shame. "I was beaten up by a bard."

"That's *Loot*—L-O-O-T." Both of them looked quizzically at

me. "Well, it beats *precious,* which was her idea."

Kyyrao caressed my cheek with the back of her hand, then flicked her tail against the back of my legs. "*Precious* flows so easily from the mouth, and you are precious."

I snarled at her, and she retaliated with a melodic yodel of delight. I chose to ignore her from that point forward, and I was as good at that as she was at ignoring me when she wanted to. I extended my hand to the dwarf. "Loot Niptil, at your service."

He shook my hand. "Corsen Mon Duur. I am fair new to these lands. I and mine were summoned three moons back, give or take. Ours lost the fight and we were left."

I nodded. Everyone in Grover's could tell a variation on that tale. Planeswalkers—which is what I started calling them since I think I'm an atheist, so I can't let myself believe in gods and all—summon up people, from dwarves and Benalkin to Cat Warriors, merfolk and the various vilekith, to fight their battles for them. At some point, one or the other decides he's had enough, so he concedes and vanishes. The victor, being a sport, usually returns his champions to wherever he plucked them from. The loser seldom does, leaving lots of displaced folks to wander the world.

Many of those wanderers end up at Grover's.

The dwarf continued. "About a week back we were detained by a whole brood of kobolds—Crookshanks, by the look of them—who were holed up in what appeared to be the ruins of an old monastery."

I nodded. "You came in from the west?"

"I did. They detained us for a day or so before we could break out. There was fighting. I alone escaped. I was a might rushed in my departure, but in hiding while a search party went past I met a woman prisoner who called herself Anaytha. She looked a fair bit like you—black hair, green eyes, sharp cheekbones, the lot. I was speaking of the experience to Sular the Merlord, and he said I should mention her to you. Is she kin of yours?"

"Anaytha?" I tried the word on my tongue, then let it play around in my head. *Anaytha, Anaytha.* It resonated fine and let me build up a picture of a petite woman with hair as dark as mine and four times as long. Her emerald eyes were bright and bones as fine as sculpted ivory. I could see her clearly.

But know her?

"I don't know."

The Benalkin wiped his mouth on the back of his hand. "I was beaten by a bard so feeble-minded he doesn't even know who his kin are."

Kyyrao hissed at the man and would have given him a slap that would have scattered most of his face over half the room, but I caught her wrist. "He's not making fun of me—he does not know."

"Ignorance should be painful."

I rubbed at my temples. "It is, love, very much so."

The dwarf frowned at me. "You don't know if she's kin, or don't know if you know she's kin?"

I pointed toward the table where the archeologist sat. "Why don't we sit down and I might be able to explain some of this." I slapped the Benalkin on the back. "You may join us if you wish."

As we sat down I introduced the dwarf to Malkean Feorr, the archeologist, and the Benalkin. I smiled at the dwarf. "Like you, as nearly as I can tell, I was summoned from somewhere and fought for a planeswalker who presumably lost, since I'm here and not where I came from." I touched the three-legged scar on the right side of my forehead. "Having been bashed on the head, I remember nothing of who I am or where I came from."

The dwarf nodded solemnly. "This condition is not unknown among my people. Sometimes another blow to the head will restore the memory."

I glanced sourly at Kyyrao. "That's the cure among her people, too, but it hasn't taken."

"You should let me try again, love. I might get it right this time."

Corsen raised an eyebrow. "So you weren't fighting her when you cracked your skull?"

Kyyrao idly flicked out a claw and started carving an arcane sigil in the tabletop. "I and some pride-friends were refugees from a godspat. We were coming in this direction, to Grover's, when we found him. One of us tried to kill him—Shinra was a bold kitten, but thought my precious here was little more than a mouse. Even dazed as he was, my precious dealt with Shinra. I claimed him next, and I, too, was put down. Still, the exertion

was too much and my precious collapsed. I fended the others off
him."

In this telling she made it sound like a minor incident. Even
though I don't remember more than fits and snatches of the fight,
what does come to me is frightening. Kyyrao is all claws and
fangs, with a soul-piercing scream and a quickness that makes
every move a blur. She says I put her down, but I have no recol-
lection of doing so. Still and all, to this day Shinra acts as if he's
dancing on razors around me.

What I do remember is the aftermath. Kyyrao and the four
other Cat Warriors who were all that remained of her squad—
what she called a pride—stayed with me, caught food for me,
and brought me back to my senses. They adopted me, in
essence and fact, which is not a bad thing to have happen in the
long run, and named me.

Or made an attempt at naming me. Kyyrao likes the sound of
precious, both in her tongue and the common argot spoken by
most folks. Other candidates were treasure and spoils, which I
had no use for. I settled on Loot and contracted the surname
Nippedtail down into Niptil. Kyyrao usually respects my choices
and calls me Loot.

The exceptions are when she's mad at me—something that
happens for reasons I have no hope of figuring out—or, more
commonly, when she's bored. Like now.

I shrugged. "So, the head injury is why I don't know who I am
or if this Anaytha is my kin or not."

Nameless sat down as I spoke. "In Benalia we know another
blow to the head will restore the memory of those who have lost it."

"Yeah, well you tried that and it didn't work, did it?"

"But my punch never landed."

"Right, and if you find yourself forgetting why, I can thump
you on the head again and remind you."

The Benalish hero blushed in silence.

Kyyrao laid a hand against the dwarf's arm. "This monastery,
it is five days from here, west by northwest?"

"It is."

Her amber eyes flicked toward the archeologist. "Do you
know this place?"

Deep thought furrowed Malkean's brow for a moment. "It is

probably the Peregrinator Complex. It fell to ruin two centuries ago, or so legend has it. There were supposed to be extensive catacombs and burial chambers under the building, so any manner of vilekith could have taken up residence there."

The archeologist shrugged. "I've not been there, but one night Grover told me the story behind it. Two hundred and fifty years ago, perhaps more or even a little less, a number of wanderers who treat planeswalkers as gods—no offense intended to your worship of Lord Windgrace, Kyyrao—decided they had not been returned to their homes because their patrons found them unworthy. They created the monastery and surrounding community to give constant prayer and sacrifices to their god so he would come and return them to their homes. The wanderers waited, and after a third generation they believed their prayers were answered.

"A god showed, and may, in fact, have been the planeswalker who summoned some or all of their ancestors, but the peregrinators had woven a complex theology that carefully defined questions and answers that would sort false gods from the true god. Those questions had been conceived by new generations based on the recollections of the traditions of the founders of the monastery, and therefore had no connection to the planeswalker. They decided his answers indicated he was false and they attacked him. He summoned help and the peregrinators were destroyed."

I rubbed my jaw. "Weren't you telling me there are rumors of great treasure in that place?"

He nodded. "Yes, and a curse as well. Given how short-lived the culture there was, I doubt any of those stories. Then again, those who have gone out seeking treasure haven't come back this way, so I could be wrong."

"But you probably aren't." I stroked Kyyrao's back. "You want to head out, yes?"

She nodded. "This place is closing in on me, and we cannot have someone from your pride left in the hands of kobolds, can we?"

"Corsen, will you lead us back there?"

The dwarf looked at the two of us and laughed. "There are at least forty kobolds there, maybe more. The three of us would get slaughtered."

"Perhaps if we had a great and strong warrior to go with us."

Nameless didn't take the bait.

"Shinra will join us." Kyyrao leaped to her feet, threw her head back and let out an ear-piercing shriek. I heard it echoed seconds later from further around the bend in the place, then saw a flash of orange and black as the male Cat Warrior leaped from rafter to rafter toward us.

"Shinra will be good, but forty kobolds is something only a *hero* could handle, not a *banal* threat at all."

Nameless nibbled on a thumbnail.

I sighed. "Would my Lord Benalkin like to join us?"

He smiled. "All you had to do was ask."

"You're smarter than you look, aren't you?"

"If I said yes to that, Loot, I'd not be going with you, would I?"

I smiled to let him know I'd gotten his point. "Malkean?"

The archeologist shook his head. "A small expedition went out to search through what they believe to be the ruins of a Sarpadian outpost only a fortnight's ride from here. I expect them back in the next couple of days and would hate to miss the chance to examine any artifacts they bring back. The same goes for anything you find, of course."

"Of course." I nodded to him, then to Shinra as the tiger-striped Cat Warrior lighted on Nameless's shadow. "Let's head out. The sooner we get there, the sooner we can be back telling lies about our bravery."

Grover had no words of wisdom for us—he offers such advice or recollections only when the mood strikes — but he gave us enough jerked mammoth and three-league biscuits to see us out and back again. The warriors drew their weapons from storage. Grover doesn't require folks to check their weapons, but he provides a place for them to be stored. The wayhouse tends to be fairly crowded, so hauling a halberd or greatsword around really does become a bother.

I don't carry a sword. I didn't have one when Kyyrao found me, and even though I have shown some aptitude for using a rapier, I don't like the weight on my hip. More importantly, being as small as I am, I surrender a good half-foot of reach on most normal-sized foes. Since a half-foot is more than the distance between my outside and vital parts of my inside, wearing an invitation to sword duels strapped around my waist seems decidedly foolish.

My facility to defend myself while unarmed, and my meager ability to cast spells, has Kyyrao thinking I am a member of some secret sorcerous assassin cult, though no one we've spoken to knows of such a group. Of course, depending upon how secret they are, no one would have heard of them, so ruling that possibility out is functionally impossible. Even so, I consider it highly improbable.

I learned I could cast spells by accident. At Grover's I met a hedge-wizard who could light candles with a spell. After drinking too much one night he used the spell to ignite the shot of liquor dwarves favor. Unfortunately for him, a dwarf was consuming the shot at the time. The dwarf vomited fire all over the wizard, then the two of them raced over table and chair to get to the canal room at Grover's and douse themselves. The dwarf survived, but the wizard did not—presumably because, in his state of inebriation, he forgot he could not breathe water.

In recounting the story of this incident I aped the hand motions and said the same words as the wizard. After we put the fire out, Kyyrao decided we had discovered something that made me even more precious. Since then I've learned a few spells from magickers at Grover's, or remembered how to cast them. While I've got no spells with suitable martial applications—few foes march into battle swilling raw grain alcohol—my magical ability can be useful for staunching wounds and providing heat on a cold night.

We looked quite the odd company as we headed out. We borrowed a pony for Corsen and a massive draft-beast for Nameless. The two Cat Warriors—serving their preferences and those of the horses in Grover's stables—traveled on foot. I walked, too, for the most part, leading a packhorse. I rode occasionally, but only to catch up with Kyyrao or Shinra when they scouted ahead and indicated they'd found something interesting.

The distance to the monastery had been reckoned at five days, but those were dwarven foot-days, so we neared our target only three days out. We agreed to camp one valley shy of the monastery, then head in on foot in the morning.

While the rest of us prepared to bed down, Corsen picked up his ax and shield. "I am of a mind to scout ahead, just to make sure they've not arranged any surprises along the lines of my previous retreat."

I frowned. "Is that wise?"

He looked surprised. "What do you mean? I can see in the dark, you know."

"Not my point."

"What is?"

"The kobolds can see in the dark, too. They tend toward being active at night, especially early in the evening, like now." The image of bandy-legged little red imps came far too readily to mind. "Crookshanks, save perhaps one of the broodlords, don't have enough brains to think about ambushes. You didn't see a broodlord among them, did you?"

Corsen shook his head and sat down. "There had to be one, of course, but I didn't see him." The dwarf scratched at his beard. "You never said you've dealt with kobolds before."

I shrugged. "Why speak ill of the dead?"

Corsen smiled and let the firelight play along the edge of his ax. "Harvested a few in my day, too."

I glanced over at Kyyrao and Shinra. "Then you have more experience than we do. About a year ago a bunch of kobolds started frequenting Grover's and eating him out of everything. He told their leader, a snaggle-toothed broodlord who called himself Dreadfang, that his brood had run out of credit and they needed to provide a service to the wayhouse. He told them to round up pirquelberries. The kobolds left and waylaid an incoming caravan, so Grover told a bunch of us it was last call until the kobolds were scattered."

Nameless poked the fire with a stick, raising a column of sparks that swirled up into the sky. "What happened to Dreadfang?"

I tapped Kyyrao lightly on the snout and she made a lazy attempt to bite my finger off. "Lady Grrenmw gave him a case of fangdread." The fire snapped and I nodded. "His neck sounded something like that in her jaws. With the broodlord down, the others broke and ran. Corsen's report from the monastery is the first sign of trouble since then."

Nameless nodded solemnly. "Then I, Anonymous Nameless of

Clan Nameless, avow that after tomorrow, these kobolds shall worry no one forever more."

Yes, in reality his little proclamation was far more stirring and heartwarming than it might read here. The firelight splashed red and gold highlights along his jawline, and enough shadow hid the irregularities in his nose that his profile seemed suited to a new-minted gold coin. After his declaration he even set whetstone to the edge of his greatsword with impressive gusto. The dwarf and the Cats followed suit, and I drifted off to sleep amid strains of a steel and stone symphony.

The next morning we set out. The sun had gotten well up and away in the sky so its rays warmed us and blunted the sense of fear we should have had going in. The fact that the wind came from behind us bothered Kyyrao and Shinra, but I was not as worried as they were. Kobolds were not known for their sense of smell, and the only likely spot for an ambush, if Corsen had told us about the monastery correctly, came where the walls of the valley narrowed to a slender pass.

Which was right where we found the kobolds. They were arrayed in ranks four across and at least five deep. They bore sharp little spears and square shields. Dirty rags wrapped their loins and their helmets ran from dented pots to chipped bits of crockery. A feral light burned in their little piggy eyes and gaped jaws gave us a view of yellowed teeth.

Before I could even begin to think of what we might do, Nameless shoved me aside and charged toward the kobolds. His greatsword whirled into a silver disk as he ran, quickly shrinking the distance between himself and the red horde. As he shouted his war cry, the kobolds answered and countercharged. I winced and felt Kyyrao's breath hot and moist with anticipation on my neck.

I was less worried about Nameless getting killed than being spattered and battered with kobold blood and limb-bits.

I think Kyyrao was actually looking forward to what I feared.

Nameless rushed onward, his voice counterpointing the whistling of his sword. The kobolds' voices rose in one martial scream. Sunlight glinted from the rusty edges of their spear points. Gold flashed on the hilt of Nameless's weapon. Bare inches separated the lethal arc of his blade from the kobolds, and I braced for the sound of shields splintering, bones breaking and the gentle patter of blood-drops raining down.

Then Nameless vanished.

Not vanished beneath a snarling, snapping horde of impish tormentors.

Not vanished in a scarlet haze, impaled on countless spears.

He just vanished.

Summoned.

Away.

While Nameless apparently had faced the idea of a kobold charge without much in the way of trepidation or, I might add, forethought, I had plenty of the former and not a little of the latter in store. The little buggers had boiled themselves up into a truly frothing rage. With their charge unchecked by our Benalish hero-shield, they came at us quickly. Kyyrao and Shinra both snarled in delight and frustration, aware, as I was, that they'd get their fill of killing just about at the same time they'd get their fill of kobold spears. While the former would delight them no end, the latter would end them far from delightfully.

Corsen Mon Duur shouldered his way between Kyyrao and me and flung his arms open wide. I sensed no magic, but the effect of his gesture seemed enchanting in the extreme. The kobold ranks split right down the middle as if Corsen had driven an invisible wedge through them. I expected to see a look of triumph in his eyes as he turned to face us, but instead I read worry and sadness.

"Go around. Surround them. He wants the small one alive, remember that, alive."

The Cat Warriors both looked at me as the kobolds followed Corsen's command and surrounded us. Neither one of them wanted to die, and the dwarf's order to the kobolds left that a distinct possibility. Because, in rescuing and adopting me, they had taken responsibility for my life, they awaited my direction. Either of them could have leaped the line of kobolds and escaped, but in abandoning me, they would have surrendered their responsibility and they would not do that without my orders.

I looked at Corsen. "They have your compatriots hostage?"

The dwarf hung his head. "My brother and nephew."

"And there was no woman of my coloring?"

The dwarf shook his head.

From beyond him a voice echoed from the dark recesses of the pass: "I gave him the telling to tell." The voice had odd pops and cracks in it, but still seemed faintly recognizable.

Kyyrao bared her teeth and began to hiss.

A kobold broodlord stepped from the shadows. Bigger than his compatriots and even the dwarf, he wore bracers and greaves made of bone and had the bared skull of some great cat perched on his head as a helmet. As he opened his arms I recognized the expansiveness of the gesture, and that allowed me to identify him even though he had changed.

"Dreadfang."

"Again, again."

His flesh seemed more purple than scarlet—closer to the color of old blood than new. His neck seemed odd, though the problem with it was hard to see. A latticework of bones bound with sinew sat perched on his shoulders and rose up to support both the cat-skull cap he wore and the head beneath it. The bone-derrick had an opening in the front through which I could see more of Dreadfang's face than I wanted, and his ears poked through smaller holes on the sides of his head.

He turned to the right and left, moving his shoulders so he could see all of his people. "Inside, gather them." He turned carefully and headed toward the monastery as the kobold cordon tightened around us.

I frowned at Kyyrao. "I thought you killed him."

"I did. You can see where I broke his neck, precious." Her fang-flash made me shy a step. "You were the one who told me you didn't want his head delivered to you as a sign of affection."

"My mistake, clearly." I'd heard tales of people being resurrected from the dead, but they were always told about a friend of a friend, so I doubted them. Invariably the story involved planeswalkers and the tremendous magics they wielded. It was possible, of course, that some sort of inferior reanimation attempt had been used on Dreadfang—one that made him alive again without repairing the damage done.

Even allowing that was what had happened to Dreadfang, it did not explain why he had sent Corsen to Grover's to bring me to the monastery. Had his aim been revenge he would have lured Kyyrao out here and would likely have slain her where we stood. While at Grover's, Dreadfang had learned enough about me to know that the story he gave Corsen would lure me to the monastery, but there was no guarantee Kyyrao would come along.

He wanted me, but I had no idea why.

Dreadfang himself solved that mystery when his kobolds finally conducted us to a chamber deep beneath the monastery. The tunnels had all been man-sized, so I knew the kobolds had not done the digging. Granite monument stones imbedded in the walls suggested that some of the peregrinators' more famous founders had been entombed down here. While I never got a good chance to read any of the inscriptions on the gravestones, the script and the words I did catch got more menacing the deeper we went, making me more and more mindful of the rumors about curses that Malkean had mentioned.

Torches ringed the walls of the large chamber below the monastery. I mentally subtracted two centuries of neglect and a year's worth of kobold-lairing from the room and could see it had once been an elaborate mausoleum. The few freestanding biers were topped with effigies of the people they housed. Even in the wan torchlight I caught hints of color, suggesting the figures had once been painted so the stone simulacra would seem more lifelike.

Dreadfang pointed toward a stone slab set in the chamber wall. I could see all manner of writing on the gray stone surface, but I could not make sense of any of it. This struck me as odd because I could identify the letters used, but it was as if I was trying to read it in a dream. I knew the words existed, but I could not make sense of them, even if I took them a letter at a time.

"Step closer, closer and read, *Loo-ooo-oot*."

I gave Dreadfang a Khyyiani growl that brought a smile to Kyyrao's face. I hated the way the kobold always added extra syllables to my name. With my friends ringed by spearwielding kobolds, a snarl was all I could do in way of protest, so I capped it with a nasty glare, then turned and approached the stone as if it had been my intention to do so anyway.

As I stepped to within a foot of it, I felt the tingle of magic wash over me. It had two effects on me, both of which should have been pleasurable, but neither of which was particularly. First off the stone's color faded, bringing to it a crystalline clarity that allowed me to see straight through it. Beyond the stone I saw all manner of riches—gems, coins, bits of jewelry and other finery. I also saw magical weapons and, quite near the front, a robust suit of armor that fairly crackled with etheric energy. As I stared at it for a moment, I realized that donning it would heal Dreadfang of his injuries and make him quite invincible.

That realization solved half the mystery of why he wanted me at the monastery.

The second bit of magic closed the circle and provided me the other half of the reason Dreadfang wanted me there. The letters, which had been all ajumble before, resolved themselves into fiery golden words that burned without being consumed and ringed the edge of the stone. Even the words that seemed archaic at first glance resolved themselves into more modern verbiage, and the message shifted around to convey its full import to me.

> *Wary must be he who steps yet closer*
> *To this treasury filled with things of fame.*
> *Enter here and steal just one,*
> *And Cursed will be all of your name!*

Not being a scholar of prophetic poetry, I wasn't certain how it stacked up in comparison to other curses. I thought the words lacked menace in and of themselves, but as I read along the fire-letters turned red and ran like blood. The words may not have been sufficient to convey the intended threat, but the medium of delivery did leave little in the way of ambiguity concerning the message. In this case, I decided, the medium was the message.

I took a giant step backward.

The broodlord grunted. "You have seen what you saw."

"I have, and I have no intention of triggering that curse."

"You will not."

I had expected those words from Dreadfang, but more in the form of a question instead of a statement. I shelved my sharply and wittily worded denial for later use and blinked. "What do you mean?"

The broodlord gave me the look I expect I had often given Nameless on our journey. "Cursed will be all of your name."

"I read that."

Dreadfang smiled, which was almost more menacing than the curse. "You have no name."

I stopped for a moment and thought. Because I didn't know who I was, I didn't have a name. In a number of discussions Malkean and others had argued that I probably couldn't be summoned again by a planeswalker because my amnesia meant the person I had been really no longer existed. While I knew enough magical theory to know possessing the name of a creature greatly enhanced your ability to summon or enchant it, I had no proof that my lack of memory would insulate me from the curse.

"Nice theory, Dreadfang, but I don't want to test it."

"I have theory that my broodspears are sharp. Shall I test it?"

I could have told him the spears were not sharp at all, but even dull, the little monsters on the other ends could easily shove the spears through my friends. "I'm still not liking this at all."

Corsen rose from where he had been crouched over two bedraggled and chain-fettered dwarves. "What did you see when you neared the stone?"

"The gold, jewels, treasure."

"What else?"

I shook my head. "Nothing."

"I saw my son dying, my family being torn apart in a civil war. My home was shattered and overgrown with nettles and venomweed."

That vision *was* substantially different from mine. I tugged the sleeves of my tunic back up past my elbows. I winked at Kyyrao, then turned back toward the treasury. Feeling my throat tighten, I stepped up to where the rock cleared to glass, then I plunged forward.

I passed through the stone as if it hadn't existed. Looking back I saw the blood from the words leach out to fill the opening with a crimson curtain, but I could still see through it. I heard Dreadfang yell "steelskin," so I started tossing the armor out in pieces. The kobolds who had not been pressed into guard duty responded to his new shouts. They gathered up the pieces of the armor and approached him with the reverence of acolytes bearing vestments for a hierophant.

Kicking the helmet back out through the red opening, I turned and bent over. Like a dog digging to uncover a buried treasure, I started scooping handfuls of gold and silver coins back out between my legs. I tried to make the spray of treasure as chaotic as possible. Some of the larger gems, I thought, might have been sufficient to crack a kobold's skull, but I wasn't aiming and they were moving, so that idea died without serious inquiry.

The other effect I'd hoped for didn't take place. Had things gone the way I wanted, the kobolds would have gone mad for the gold and jewels and trinkets, making them leave off their guarding of Kyyrao and Shinra. The problem with kobolds is, of course, that their heads can only hold one thought at a time, and for the ones given guard duty, the thought transfixing them was of transfixing my friends, so things began to look very grim.

Then I uncovered the sword's hilt. As I pulled the blade free from the pile of coins, I could tell by its weight it was just what I needed to return Dreadfang to his grave. I turned and darted back out of the trove, bringing the sword up and around in a cut intended to bob both of Dreadfang's ears right about at eye level.

Then a ruby rolled beneath my left foot, twisting me off balance. The blade turned and the flat of it struck the kobold's rising forearm. Dreadfang came up off the bier that had served as his throne and lashed out with his gauntleted fist. The backhand blow caught me in the side of the head and lifted me clean off my feet. I spun through the air, then bounced hard off the chamber floor. My head smacked against another bier and I blacked out for a split second.

Consciousness returned, bringing pain, fear and bewilderment with it. *Where am I? Who am I? Why am I here?* I shook my head to clear it, then Dreadfang's gravelly voice filled my ears and it all came flooding back.

The broodlord brandished the sword with which I had tried to kill him and clawed the last of the bone lattice away from his head. "No more do I need you, little man."

I snarled a bit more loudly than I had before and pulled myself to my feet. "You fool," I spat at him, "do you have any idea what you have done?" Pure malevolence filled my voice as I swiped away a trickle of blood from my forehead. I rubbed the blood into nothingness between my thumb and fingers, then smiled. "The blow to my head. My memory."

A chuckle, all sinister and buzzing, rolled from my throat. "I am a planeswalker. Tremble in my presence, vilekith!"

"You lie!"

I opened my hands and spread my arms wide. "Come to me and I will show you the depth of your stupidity!"

With both hands wrapped firmly around the hilt, the broodlord whipped the sword up and back for the blow that would split me crown to toes. A feral glee burned in his eyes, yet, even as the sword's straight blade reached the point where it should have reversed direction, the expression on his face began to shift. Fear entered it, then pain. I couldn't tell why until the tip of the sword burst out through the armor breastplate, then curled back in on itself and pierced the broodlord's heart.

Dreadfang fell on his spine and rockered back and forth a couple of times before a twitch pitched him onto his side. The other kobolds looked from him to me and back again. Just as they turned toward me, I gestured at the closest one. His shield and spear immediately combusted. His shriek, plus the stink of his sizzling hide, unnerved the rest of the leaderless kobolds. They scattered out every corridor and crack they could find, leaving me alone with the dwarves and the Cats.

They sank to their knees before me. Kyyrao looked enraptured, while Shinra and Corsen looked dazed. His companions stared at me fearfully.

"Get up."

"As you command, Most Wise," Corsen breathed reverently.

Shinra sank to the ground, pressing his chin against the stone, then rolled over on his back and exposed his belly to me. "Please, Lord Windgrace, forgive my presumption of opposing you when we first met."

I held my hands up before anyone else started in. "Wait, hold it, stop. I'm not a planeswalker."

Kyyrao sniffed and sat back on her haunches. "We heard what you said."

"It was for the kobolds alone."

Corsen nodded. "Yes, of course, but we each heard it and understood it. Speaking with the alltongue is a planeswalker gift."

"Ah, no, you understood because I spoke in argot, not kobold. I don't know kobold." I sat down and crossed my legs. "I'm not a planeswalker."

"But you must be." Corsen pointed at Dreadfang's body. "What you did with the sword. Only a planeswalker could do that."

"Agreed," I said. "A planeswalker did."

"And that's you, my *pre . . .* lord."

"Not me." I dabbed at the blood from my forehead with a strip torn from my sleeve. "It was the planeswalker who gathered all that stuff into the treasury and laid that curse down."

They stared at me as if I were either a god or insane. "Look, it all fit together when I hit my head, or when it cleared. The legend reads, in part, 'Cursed will be all of your name.' We assumed the curse would have no effect because I have no name."

Corsen nodded. "Of course."

I smiled. "But I *do* have a name: Loot." I pointed to the armor and the sword. "That stuff is *loot*. Where you saw your family being destroyed, I saw the armor and knew it would make Dreadfang invincible. That was a curse as far as I was concerned. Then the sword didn't kill him and I slipped on a ruby—the loot was all cursed."

Kyyrao purred. "And when Dreadfang sought to kill you, his cursed items betrayed him."

"As the peregrinators betrayed and attacked the planeswalker for whom they had built this monastery." I shrugged. "So, you see, I am not a planeswalker. I am as much subject to planeswalker magic and curses as anyone else."

Shinra rolled over onto his belly. "So you are cursed now?"

"I don't think so. Corsen, in your vision were you hurt?"

"Except by what I saw? No."

"If I were going to be cursed, I think the line would have been, 'Cursed will be *you* and all of your name.' This planeswalker was subtle and wanted the progenitor to live through the pain caused by the curse."

Kyyrao slunk over to Dreadfang's body. With a slash of her claws and a wrenching twist, she popped his head free of his body. "To be sure."

"Agreed." I stood. "Shall we be going?"

Shinra leaped toward the tunnel through which we'd been brought into the mausoleum. "The air is clearing of kobold spoor."

Kyyrao crossed to the tunnel mouth and screamed a *Khyyiani* challenge up into the darkness. She sniffed as the echoes died. "The air is *clear* of kobold spoor."

I smiled and looked back toward where the dwarves were moving slowly, delicately picking their way over the carpet of coins strewn from the trove. "Corsen, do your kin need help?"

The dwarf blushed. "No, it is merely our way. We reluctantly leave the presence of such great wealth without taking any with us." He held his little hands up. "And I know, with planeswalker magic guarding it, taking anything would be a mistake."

"Perhaps, someday, another planeswalker will defeat the magic here and the treasure will go to those who appreciate its true value," offered another of the dwarves.

"Perhaps." I took a deep breath and let out a sigh. "Of course, the only loot here was the sword, the armor, and that ruby that rolled beneath my foot. The rest of it is just *trash*."

Corsen's eyes brightened. "Not *loot*?"

"No. Anyone can see that." I looked around. "In fact, someone might want to tidy this place up."

Kyyrao yodeled a half-laugh. "And take the trash out?"

"Far away from here," I smiled.

"Far, far away?" asked the younger of the dwarves.

"At least."

Corsen rubbed his hand together and reached for a large emerald, then stopped and looked back at me. "Do you really think it's safe now?"

"Quite safe, Corsen." I squatted down and plucked a plum-sized tigereye from a pile of coins. "In fact, I'd stake my name on it."

The Brass Man Who Would Sink

Hanovi Braddock

In olden times, when the sun was whiter and the stars
were brighter and but one moon hung in the sky, there lived a
miller whose son was as handsome as his mother was poor.
And poor the miller was indeed, for the stream that drove her
mill had little by little and year by year dried up. Now it was
only a trickle, and far from the flow needed to turn the great
grinding wheel. The miller's neighbors carted their harvest far
away to have it milled. The miller grew so poor that soon all that
was left to her were the mill and the cherry tree behind it.

Though she was poor, the miller wanted the best for her son.
Only a rich suitor would do for him. When a farm girl came
courting with her family and a bouquet of wildflowers, the
miller and her husband drove them off.

"But Mother, I know of her," said the miller's son, picking up
the flowers the young woman had dropped. "All say she has an
honest heart, a quick mind, and a gentle hand. With her I might
know the Delight of Two Hearts." For he was a pious lad, and
the Delights of the Prophets were more in his mind than were
any thoughts of riches.

But the miller would not be moved. Her son would live in a
rich house, not some farmhouse. Her husband was not quite so
sure. There was much to be said for the Delight of Two Hearts.

Had not he and the miller found such happiness? But though he had some say in the matter, her word was final.

One day, as the miller's husband was walking home from the forest with a load of wood on his back, he met a party of hunters. Among them were the lady of the nearby lands and an even more richly dressed woman whom the miller had never before seen.

"Cutting wood. There's a labor I'm happy never to have done," said the lady, making a sour face.

"Would that I never had to do it again, madam," said the miller's husband. "I must cut wood these days to earn our bread. I'd give anything to be free of such toil."

"You're the miller's husband, are you not? Do you speak with the voice of your household? If you mean what you say, I can see to it that you need never labor so again. I'll exchange these rings on my fingers and a heavy bag of gold for what's behind your mill."

What could the lady mean but the cherry tree? The miller's husband eagerly agreed, the bargain was written and signed, and the lady dropped her heavy gold rings with their heavy great jewels, *plop, plop, plop* into the husband's hands.

To the husband, the lady said, "In a month, I'll bring the gold and come for what's mine." Then, to the richly dressed stranger, she added, "Justiciar, you have born witness."

"I have," said the justiciar, adjusting her robes, "and the weight of the law seals this bargain."

The husband arrived home rejoicing, and the miller sang out in delight when she saw the rings with their great gems. "But what did you give in exchange?" she said.

"The lady asked only for what's behind our mill. That cherry tree is certainly something we can do without!"

The miller laughed. "What would she want with a cherry tree? Husband, she can't have meant that! Our son was behind the mill, airing out the bedclothes."

The husband went white with this news.

"Come, come," said the miller. "It's a good bargain after all. Our son will live a rich life as the lady's consort. We've provided for him well."

"For his body, perhaps, but not for his heart," said the husband, who knew his son.

He was right. The son, upon hearing the news that he would

be a lady's keepling, flew into a rage. He stormed out of the mill house and into the forest, and none of his father's commands or entreaties would bring him back.

The son marched deep into the forest, and then deeper still, further than he had ever gone before. At last he came to a clearing where there sat a pile of stones and a great clump of bushes. The young man was tired of walking by then, but he was still full of fury. One by one, he picked up the stones and hurled them at the bushes.

Whoosh! went the first stone as it scattered green leaves. *Whoosh!* went the second. *Clang!* went the third.

Now there's a mystery, the young man thought, and curiosity overcame his anger. He parted the branches of the bushes, and what should he find but a man of brass? The metal figure stood at attention like a soldier, and had stood so long that it was sinking into the earth. Everything below the knees was already underground.

"A little enchantment might make a great warrior of you," the young man said, "but I don't see what use a warrior is to me." And he walked slowly homeward, his anger spent, but his sorrow enduring.

He did not come out of the forest in quite the same place he'd gone in, so found himself crossing ground he'd never walked before. As night fell, he lost his way, but he saw a little square of yellow light and made for it. It was the window of a woodswoman's hut. I'll ask directions here, he thought, and he opened the door.

Inside was a very, very old woman, whose head bobbed constantly up and down and whose hands shook like leaves in the wind. She was tending a fire that did not smoke.

"Many pardons," the young man said. "Do you know the way to the mill house?"

"The mill house?" said the old woman. "The family that turned my granddaughter out when she came courting?"

"The same," the young man said. "But refusing your granddaughter was no wish of mine." And he told her the story of how he'd been pledged against his desires.

"You poor child," she said. "The lady of these lands keeps her consorts brightly jeweled and richly dressed, but before long their hearts turn to ice and they die."

"What can I do?" he asked her. "If I run away, I'll be a pledge thief and outlaw."

"Think on this riddle," said the old woman. "What is yours that you might not give whole? When you have the answer, give a measure to my granddaughter and to her alone. From this very moment speak no word to anyone before you have done this." Then she took up a knife, reached into the unsmoking fire, and snipped off a little flame as if it were a bit of wool from a sheep's haunch. The old woman put the flame in a tinderbox, put the tinderbox into a breadbasket, and put the basket under her cot. Only then did she point the way to the mill.

The miller's son nodded his thanks and departed. He spoke no word during the days that followed, which his father took as a sign of grief and his mother as a sign of stubbornness. But all the while his thoughts were on the riddle.

When the time was up and the lady arrived with her bag of gold, her huntsmen and the justiciar came with her. No sooner had they appeared at the miller's door than the farm girl, with her brothers and father and mother, also came into the miller's yard. "We've a stake in this matter," said the girl's mother, "for we made a prior suit which was not answered."

"Not answered!" said the miller. "Why, I drove you from this very ground."

"Before you heard our suit," said the farmer. And her daughter added, "If we made any suit, let your son now repeat the terms of it."

But the miller's son was silent. He still puzzled over the riddle.

"A suit not heard is a suit not refused," said the justiciar. "It is no prior claim, but they've a right to be heard now. So stands the weight of the law."

"Well, let them say what they will," said the lady. "It's a small matter. I have a contract."

"A contract for what stands behind the mill, and what stands there now is a cherry tree," said the farm girl.

"The contract's well understood," said the lady, "or why are we arguing?"

"Not clear, not clear," said the justiciar, clicking her tongue. "A vague contract might not hold. So stands the weight of the law."

"But you, justiciar, were witness!" said the lady. And then she threw the bag of gold at the miller's feet, hoping this would seal the matter. "Miller, is that not the gold as promised?"

The miller hefted the bag and smiled. But her husband took the bag from her, and though it was indeed heavy, he shook it as if it were a bag of eggshells. "Not so heavy as I thought was promised," he said.

The miller glared at him. "Heavy enough," she said, taking the bag again. "He's my son, so it's my judgment that matters."

"But the contract was agreed to by his father," said the farm girl.

"'Tis so, 'tis so," said the justiciar.

The miller and the lady both glared at the justiciar. "Do you mean to say that this contract would not stand?"

"Well," said the justiciar, and she leaned one way and told one side of the question. Then she leaned the other way and told the other side, as lawyers are wont to do. In the end, her answer said nothing at all.

"The law is slow and uncertain," said the farm girl. "Let us agree to some other test of the contract."

The lady smiled at this. "Fine, fine," she said. "Yon wheatfield is in need of harvesting. If all the wheat is cut and sheaved by dawn tomorrow, the contract shall be void. But if there is the smallest scratch or blister on the young man's hands, he shall be mine."

With that she reclaimed her bag of gold and rode off, with her huntsmen and the justiciar close behind. The miller was so angry that she marched into the mill house without a word, husband at her heels. The farm girl's family started away, too, but the girl herself lingered for a moment.

"Have you anything to say to me?" she asked the miller's son.

"Memory is mine, but I might not give it whole," he said, for he had solved the riddle. "Here is a thing I remember—deep in the forest is a clearing. In the center and overgrown with bushes stands a brass man so ancient that he sinks into the ground."

"Well answered," said the farm girl. "You must meet me in that place by moonlight, but touch no tool and do no work before then."

The miller's son did as she said. When the moon was high, he met her in the clearing where the brass man was. The farm girl chopped down the bushes and dug free the brass man's legs and feet. Then she opened a tinderbox and out jumped the flame of the unsmoking fire. She spoke a word to the flame, and the fire went out as the brass man opened his eyes.

"Command him," said the farm girl. So the miller's son told the brass man to harvest the wheat. The brass man was off quick as lightning, and by the time the miller's son and farmer's daughter had found their way out of the woods, the sky was just growing light in the east and every stalk of wheat was cut and every sheaf bound up.

The brass man, who had done all the work with his metal hands, now bowed before them. A sparrow lighted on his shoulder and said, "*Cheap, cheap, cheap!* Though I've served queens and wizards well, I'll not find rest till I find hell, so let me sink." Then the brass man's head nodded, his eyes closed, and the sparrow flew away.

"We should release him," said the miller's son. "He has served us well."

"Not yet," said the farmer's daughter, and she covered the brass man with branches to hide him.

When the lady, her huntsman and the justiciar returned, they were quite surprised to see the wheat all cut and bound into sheaves, but what surprised them even more was the condition of the young man's hands. There was no scratch, or blister, or even blemish upon them. The miller herself was no less amazed.

"Let me see again," the lady insisted, and this time when the miller's son held out his hands, she marked the palm of his hand with a pin. "I see a scratch," she said.

"Where none was before!" said the miller's son.

"A scratch is a scratch," said the miller, eyeing the bag of gold.

"Justiciar?" said the lady.

Once again, the justiciar leaned to the left and considered the matter in one view, then leaned to the right and considered it another way.

"Enough!" said the lady. "We'll settle it thus: The wheat needs to be threshed. If he brings in all the sheaves and threshes the grain before tomorrow morning, then the contract shall be void. But if there is any fleck of chaff or straw upon him, then the young man is mine." With that, she clutched her bag of gold and rode off with her huntsmen and the justiciar. As before, the miller was so upset that she went into her house without a word, and her husband went close behind her.

"Touch no stalk of straw, but meet me by moonlight where we left the brass man," said the farm girl.

The miller's son did as she said. When the moon was high, he found her already removing the branches that hid the brass man. To the young man's surprise, the brass man had sunk into the soft earth a little ways, so that the farm girl had to dig free his ankles.

Then she opened her tinderbox and out jumped the flame of unsmoking fire. She spoke the word, the flame went out, and the brass man opened his eyes.

"Command him," said the farm girl. So the miller's son told the brass man to bring in the sheaves and thresh them. "And winnow as well," said the farm girl. The brass man was off in a glint of moonlight. Almost faster than the eye could follow, he carried the sheaves to the mill house, threshed the seed from the stalks with his metal hands, and tossed the seed into the night breeze to winnow it. He stacked the straw as well. By the time the sky was turning pink in the east, the miller's yard was covered by a great mound of finished grain, a breeze-blown carpet of chaff, and a haystack.

The brass man now bowed before them. A robin lighted on his shoulder and said, "*Cheeryup! Cheeryup! Chereep!* Though I've served queens and wizards well, I'll not find rest till I find hell, so let me sink." Then the brass man's head nodded, his eyes closed, and the robin flew away.

"Truly, we should do as he asks," said the miller's son. "He has served us well."

"Not yet," said the farmer's daughter, and she again hid the brass man with branches.

Imagine the surprise of the lady, her huntsmen, and the justiciar when they returned. Not only was the grain threshed, but winnowed, too! The lady dismounted and sifted the grain in her hands, and it was clean. She sifted the chaff, and there was no grain in it. Even more amazingly, there was no speck of chaff on the young man's clothes, no sliver of straw in his hair. The miller, too, was amazed.

"Let me see again," the lady insisted, and this time when the miller's son bowed his head before her, she flicked a bit of chaff from her fingers into his hair. "I see chaff," she said.

"Where none was before!" said the miller's son.

"Chaff is chaff," said the miller, looking at the lady's saddlebags where the bag of gold must be.

"Justiciar?" said the lady.

Once again, the justiciar leaned to the left and considered the matter in one view, then leaned to the right and considered it another way.

"Enough!" said the lady. She put her hands on her hips, and she looked high and low. At last she spied the stream with its meager trickle, too little to drive the grinding wheel. "We'll settle it thus: The grain must be milled. If he makes flour of all this wheat before tomorrow morning, then the contract shall be void. But if there is any trace of dust or flour upon him, then the young man is mine." With that, she climbed into her saddle and rode off with her huntsmen and the justiciar. As they went, she leaned toward one of her huntsmen and said, "There's more to this than we know." So the huntsman rode into the woods and hid himself to see what he might see.

The miller was again upset, but this time she stayed in the yard. "Are you mad?" she asked her son. "Here a fine lady will have you, and you'll not be hers?"

So her son told her what he knew of the lady, that the lady kept her consorts brightly jeweled and richly dressed. "But before long, Mother, their hearts turn to ice and they die."

Now at last the miller understood, but she feared it was too late. "The stream will never drive the grinding wheel," she said. "My son, my son, you are lost!"

"Not so," said the farm girl. And she told the miller's son to bathe and to wash his clothes, so that there would be no trace of dust upon him to begin with. "Then meet me by moonlight again," she said.

The miller's son did as she said. When the moon was high, he helped her to remove the branches that hid the brass man. This time the brass man had sunk into the soft earth half the distance to his knees, so that the farm girl had to dig him free again. Then she opened her tinderbox and out jumped the flame of unsmoking fire. She spoke the word, the flame went out, and the brass man opened his eyes.

"Command him," said the farm girl. So the miller's son told the brass man to grind the wheat into flour. "And put it into bags as well," said the farm girl. The brass man did not even go inside the mill, but did all the grinding with his metal hands and let the flour fall into bags. The farm girl tied the bags when they were full, but the miller's son stayed well away, so that he'd not be dusted with the flour. By the time the first cock was crowing, the miller's yard was stacked with bags of flour.

The brass man bowed before them. A kestrel lighted on his shoulder and said, "*Killy, killy, killy!* Though I've served queens and wizards well, I'll not find rest till I find hell, so let me sink." Then the brass man's head nodded, his eyes closed, and the bright-feathered kestrel flew away.

"Let us do as he asks," said the miller's son. "Has he not served us well?"

"Not quite yet," said the farmer's daughter, and she again hid the brass man with branches.

Now all this was seen by the huntsman who had stayed behind, and he rode forth to meet the lady as she approached with the rest of the huntsmen and the justiciar. The lady smiled when she heard what the huntsman had to say. She ordered him to return to her estate to bring the carriage.

In the miller's yard, the lady made a great show of carefully inspecting the quality of each bag's flour. She sifted it with her fingers. When the miller's son stepped forward for the justiciar to see that there was no trace of dust upon him, he was careful not to let the lady dust him with her floury fingers. But the lady did not even try. Instead she said, "The bargain was that the young man would harvest the sheaves, thresh the grain, and grind the flour. But he has not done so. A brass man has done it all!"

"By my command, it was done," said the young man. "If you command your tenants to build a road, do you not say that the road was your doing?"

The justiciar cleared her throat and began to lean first one way in her saddle, but the lady waved at her impatiently. "I don't care about the finer points!" she said. "I made an agreement, and I was tricked!" She flung her bag of gold at the miller's feet.

"No," said the miller. "I don't consent. Take back your gold."

"Too late," said the lady. "Your word was given and the young man was pledged to me. What's more, I'm claiming the means by which you have tricked me. The brass man is mine as well."

Just then, the huntsman drove up with the carriage and pointed out for his lady the place where the brass man was hidden. The brass man had already sunk as far as his ankles again, so that the huntsmen had to dig him out before they could load him into the carriage.

"I tell you," said the miller, "there is no bargain for my son."

"And I tell you that I am a lady, mistress of a great house. You are only a miller."

"Well, before the law—"

"Shut up, justiciar," the lady said. She told her huntsmen to draw their long hunting knives so that no one should stop what she next commanded. She had the miller's son tied hand and foot and thrown over her saddle like a great bag of flour, and her horse was tied behind the carriage. The carriage set out then, with the brass man and the lady riding inside.

When the huntsmen put away their knives and rode off, the farm girl ran after the carriage. She ran until her breath burned in her chest, but she could not keep the carriage in sight. Still she ran. Even as her heart might burst, she ran, but the carriage went on and on.

The miller's son, on the back of the lady's horse, was half dead with despair. When he heard the rush of wings sweeping past him, he did not even raise his head until the third time the bird passed overhead.

A crow circled the carriage and the horse. At last the great black bird settled on the roof of the carriage, and it called, "*Caw, caw, caw!* Though I've served queens and wizards well, I'll not find rest till I find hell, so let me sink." Then the crow flew away.

Now the young man had troubles of his own to worry about, so he did not say anything at first. But as the carriage was passing a graveyard, he said in a loud voice, "Brass man, though you saved me not, you served me well, so let you find your rest in hell. Now may you sink."

At that, the wheels of the carriage began to rattle and slow. The carriage grew so heavy that the horses could no longer pull it, though the huntsman in the driver's seat whipped them furiously.

When the ground began to shake, the horse carrying the young man reared and threw him to the ground.

The carriage axles strained and broke. The road cracked open, and the whole carriage, with the brass man, the lady, the huntsman driver, the team of horses before and the lady's horse behind, all sank into the depths of the earth. The remaining huntsmen fled in terror. The ground closed again, and only the justiciar on her horse and the miller's son remained.

The justiciar cleared her throat. "When one party to a bargain is swallowed up by the earth," she said, "the contract is undone. So stands the weight of the law." Then she turned her horse and slowly rode away.

It is said that the farm girl found the miller's son sitting in the middle of the road, wriggling out of the ropes that had bound him. It is further said that they were soon married and lived their lives in the Delight of Two Hearts.

And that, any woman of the law can tell you, is hearsay. You might lean one way in your saddle and consider it a lie. You might lean the other, and say that it is so.

Inheritance

S. D. Perry

This was my dream:

I am an infant, unable to speak except in sounds and simple motions, and my eyes are heavy with sleep. I can see high, dirty walls and dimly familiar objects that I do not know the uses of. I see my mother looking down at me; her face bears no lines and her hair is not yet lightened with age, but she frowns with anxiety or fear as she mouths soft words to me. I recognize her because the worry makes her into the woman she will become. There is a scent through the air that should be pleasing but is not, an incense like ashes and star-flower bloom. Beneath that is something heavier, an odor of decay, perhaps; I associate it now with great age and mold.

My mother starts at a noise from beyond my vision, a sudden thunder of movement that is followed by silence. She looks away from me and then back again, smiling but still afraid, and the words she speaks now are full of promise, of things to come. I wish to comfort her but cannot. She lifts me, and—

She lifts me up and now I am no longer a child. I stand, looking down as she shrinks, wailing, to the floor of dirt. She is still my mother. I know it even as she gazes up at me with terror shadowing her young features, but I know too that things have

changed. Because she is my mother, part of me cries with her.
But the part she sees begins to laugh, and I feel the power of
what I am, and everything turns to swirling black, chased by her
tears and my own echoes of screaming mirth.

I grew up in the woods near the Bade Mountains, the farthest
one from the sea, or so I was told. As early as I can remember,
my mother and I lived with the others peacefully and without
ordeal. Since there was no blood between any of us, I suppose
we were really a tribe, although I called them Family. All of us
did; we were taught that Family was the term for those who lived
together in harmony.

By "we" I mean the other children; there were eleven that I
remember clearly, all of us similar in age, and seventeen grown
women. For many years I thought that all children grew to be
females; it was not until perhaps my seventh winter that I realized I was different than the rest—that I was the only girl-child
in the Family.

Leen, Scio and I were play-hunting in the snow just outside of the
big grove when they beckoned me to join them in a new game. Scio
was a season or so older, I remember, and he said that we could make
images in the fallen ice by relieving ourselves. Intrigued at first, I was
quickly horrified when they pulled flesh quills from beneath their
coats and proceeded to draw steaming pictures of mountain creatures
with their water. I remember running to our small dwelling, crying
with fear because I had no such writing utensil.

My mother calmed me, fed me sweet milk, and dried my tears
with the song that she always sang to rest my heart. The song
was from her native language of Brip'dei, the song that she had
named me by, "Mita." It meant hope. Then she explained to me
how very special I was, being the only young woman in the
Family. I know that she meant to ease the awareness, but I could
not help my sense of separateness from then on, my difference
from the other children. A feeling was seeded inside of me then,
a thing that grew and bloomed miserably—I didn't know to
name it as loneliness until many seasons later.

That is not to say that my life was entirely unhappy. There was
a closeness in our Family that meant as much as blood does to
many. Everyone had strengths and abilities that were called upon

to serve the whole of us, and the fruits of the hunt and garden were shared by all. I remember Seran, the leader of the hunt, teaching me how to move silently through thick brush and how to track a wounded creature. She also knew the skies, and sometimes in the warm seasons we would all gather after nightfall and she would tell of the moons, or the great warriors made up of stars. Mother once told me that Seran was from a clan of brave fighters who lived in the trees, far away from the Bades. I asked my mother why Seran had no child, and she told me Seran's son had been killed, although she would not tell me how; the sadness in her eyes was enough to stunt my questions.

All of the women were from different clans and tribes; Leen told me that his mother was from a people called Samites, which was why she was the healer. He said that many of the Samites were healers, although he had no ability to mend bones or flesh; he said that sometimes the power did not pass on.

Katlya was the tale-spinner, and the wisest of all of us; she and her son, Shaim, lived beyond the big grove where the rest of us dwelled. Our homes circled, facing each other within the trees, but not Katlya's; my mother told me that it was because Shaim was ill, and that the healer could not mend him. I don't remember Shaim very well, except that he was older than the rest of us by two or three seasons, the oldest of all the children. Shaim had been a great playmate to me in my earliest memories and had inherited his mother's skills, although his stories were nothing like her gentle legends and fictions. Shaim used to spin bloody, frightening tales (well away from grown ears) of monsters and dark places, thrilling me and the others into night terrors, all the time claiming that they were as real as himself. I best recall the horrid marsh goblins, spawned from mud and mysteriously deviant in their practices. Or the dreaded Ragman, of the bony fingers and empty eyes, whose very touch could take your soul.

Not long after the realization of my sex, I asked Mother why there were boys and why there were girls, and if there were other kinds. She was planing a table behind our home, as that was her special ability; Mother knew all of the ways to form wood, from vats and furnishings to almost all of the dwellings in our Family, always sturdy and level. The table was for a meeting place, a room big enough for the whole Family to come together in poor weather, with fresh clearstone windows and a stone hearth; it would be finished by summer and would practically close the circle of the grove homes.

She looked up from the wood-dusted planks and smiled, laying down the shaving tool and coming to me. She sat down on one of the stump chairs she had made and motioned for me to sit beside her. And though she still smiled, there was a studied wariness in her eyes that I had not seen before.

"There are many different things and creatures in the world, Mita," she said. "So many that I don't know them all, though Katlya would be able to tell you—"

"But *why?*"

Mother opened her mouth and then closed it again, thoughtful. Her brow creased with the thoughts, and she stared off into the deep woods as if there was an answer for me there. The ice had all gone, and there were light green shoots on most of the trees, soft and new. The comforting scent of fresh-cut wood floated sweetly through the air, and I waited, eager for the words that took her so long to find.

She took me by the hand, then, and told me about how babies were made. Her words were chosen carefully, I knew that by how slowly she spoke, and she explained that all creatures had different methods—but that for me and the other children of the Family, there had been counterparts to the mothers. Grown male counterparts. Men.

"Then where are they? Where are the men who planted the seeds?"

At that, Mother looked away again, and her fingers tightened around mine. "That is a question for another day, Mita. I will tell you only that there are some things you should not know at so young an age, and I ask that you be patient with me."

When she met my eyes again, her own had welled with tears, and she took me in her arms and held me for a long time. I cried then, for causing her such unhappiness, and vowed to myself that I would not ask about such things ever again.

I remember clearly the day that Katlya came into the grove and told us that Shaim had left the Family. I was leaving my thirteenth cycle of seasons, and the trees had turned their faces toward winter, changing their colors to deep reds and golds.

My mother and Seran and a few others had left early in the morning to bring home kindling for the coming cold, and we had been taught how to make wooden whistles by one of the women watching us; the cooling air was filled with the bright, piping sounds of our efforts. I don't think any of the other children paid mind when Katlya walked through the fallen leaves to join us, although I remember watching her closely; no one had seen Shaim for many seasons. The storyteller did not seem herself; her wide, round eyes, usually deep with secret words, were red and swollen, and her hair looked knotted and dirty.

Katlya took a deep breath and addressed us. "You all know that my son, Shaim, has not been well for some time now. I am here to tell you that he has passed on in the night from his illness."

Katlya started to cry, the tears finding new tracks down her lined face. There were a few heavy sighs from the children, and several of us found our own tears; we had all been taught that the passage from one plane to another was not a sadness, but Shaim had been the teller of our favorite stories, the ones we weren't supposed to know, and he had left us.

Katlya went to the open arms of the women watching, standing near where I sat, my new whistle forgotten in my lap. One stepped forward, smiling gently in spite of the sadness in her eyes, and encouraged us to talk about Shaim, and all of the good things we remembered about him.

I watched for a long time as the boy children sniffled and talked about Shaim, but my thoughts were elsewhere as they shared their grief. Because when Katlya had passed me, I had overheard her muffled, sorrowful words to the other mothers, and I didn't understand what was meant by them. Not then.

She had said, "There is no hope. I cannot bear it, all of them."

When my mother came home that evening, she wanted to know if I was all right; I told her that I was fine and did not feel like discussing it. I believe it was the first time I had ever kept anything from her purposely; I longed to know the significance of

Katlya's whispered statement, and although I felt that Mother would know, I also felt that it was a question not to be asked.

We went to bed early. In the morning, Shaim would be burnt in proper ceremony at the lake, which was almost an hour's distance from the Family grove. It had been over ten seasons since the last ceremony, which I couldn't recall, and I was looking forward to seeing the ritual.

Mother tucked me snugly into bed and sat with me awhile, her face still and drawn by the wick's bobbing flame. She did that sometimes, watching me as I fell to sleep, and the comfort of her loving gaze followed me downward to the land of dreams.

And I dreamed, the awful dream that felt so real I still screamed as I jerked awake, terrified and guilt-stricken—certain that I would find my mother on the floor at my feet, her heart broken by what I had become.

What I found instead, as Mother lit the lamp and came to me, frightened and sleepy, was that my bed was full of blood.

Mother and I did not attend Shaim's farewell as I slept long into the next day. She had told me of the woman's cycle before and the role it played in bearing children; I knew that she and many of the Family adults shared the passing of blood as the right of the Life-Bearers and were proud of the responsibilities that came with it.

I didn't tell her of the dream, except that I had suffered a nightmare about Shaim leaving us. I had no real motive for the untruth, except that she seemed terribly upset and I wanted her to be at ease.

She talked for a long time that morning about the joy of passing blood, but her words were hollow. The supposed pleasure of a girl's first cycle did not explain her worried brow or her empty smiles, but I did not question; even then, I think I knew that there was something wrong in our Family, and I knew that I would have to find the answers for myself. The loneliness that had been growing inside of me had become a young tree, spreading its wretched fingers through my thoughts; my bloody womb seemed to be just the nourishment it needed to strengthen its grasp.

*   *   *

It was Seran who brought the new woman into the grove later that winter. The hunter had taken her pack and arrows and gone off alone to seek fresh meat, tired of jerky and dried fruit stews. Seran often took solitary trips, lasting days at a time; Mother said that this was her nature.

Mother had gone to make the healer new containers for her herbs; some of the old ones had splintered and chipped, and apparently there was need for more of them, for Scio. I had not seen my playmate for many days, and only the night before, his mother had come to our home to tell us—Scio had taken ill, and they were going to move into Katlya's dwelling, beyond the grove. Katlya would exchange homes with them now that Shaim was gone.

So I was home alone, laboring over some mending and worrying about Scio, when I heard Seran call from outside, her deep voice commanding and firm.

"Sisters! Healer! Come, quickly!"

I barely paused to snatch up my cloak before running out into the dying snow, to see what had caused Seran to shout so.

She stood in the center of the grove, supporting a thin woman dressed in rags. The stranger seemed barely alive, leaning so heavily on Seran that I was sure they would both topple, but I could see her breath, frost-white against the bitter air. Her bare head lolled, crowned with dark dirty locks that framed a face too pale.

The healer ran forward, calling instructions over her shoulder for my mother to boil water and gather blankets. She and Seran half-dragged the strange woman into her home, followed by the whole rest of the Family—and at the door, Leen was pushed out with his coat to join us.

The other adults led us to the meeting place, where a fire was quickly built and our eager questions went unanswered; the women were tense, exchanging glances of hidden meaning, and the children amused themselves out of necessity. I spent much of those long hours thinking of my dream, which I had suffered randomly again and again since the first time—although I had ceased waking my mother with my screams. It was still far from pleasant, but the guilt and fear associated with the vision had strangely, slowly dwindled, and I had found myself turning it over in my mind on more than one occasion.

Night was setting in when my mother came to address us with the news: the woman would live.

"She does not know the Family's language, but her name seems to be 'Keil'," Mother said, "and we know that she has not eaten well for quite some time, and that she . . . the healer, she cured her of snow bite."

Mother trailed off and dropped her gaze to the wooden floor. I was surprised at her fumbling announcement; my mother was not one to stumble over words. When she looked up, she met only the pensive stares of the adult women, and her next words, though simple, were spoken as if they held great consequence.

"Keil is with child; now is the time to watch."

I saw it in her eyes then. My mother was very, very afraid.

We had all been taught to stay close to the grove, to never stray farther than calling distance from the circle of homes—the lesson deeply instilled from farther back than my memories can recall. There were also occasional tales of great, crashing beasts in the dark forest that could swallow you up whole—stories that reaffirmed the teaching and kept all of the children afraid of roaming.

But for the next few days we were told over and again, as if we had somehow forgotten: never, and especially for the rest of the winter, ever were we supposed to be out of sight. For any cause. The lectures started that night and continued, the warnings clear but the reasons cloudy.

We all knew it was because of Keil. My friends and I whispered it secretly to each other, the stories strange and wild and made-up: she was being hunted by the Scarwood goblins. She had stolen gold and jewels from a royal queen who wanted her head and had sent assassins after her. She was a witch, sought by demons who needed her craft to make a special potion for their dying master. The children all tried, but the women were in a state of anxiety that bled the color from our fantasies.

We got no help from our mothers, who said only that because she was a stranger, we could not know who might come—perhaps members of her clan, who would be confused by our Family and our intentions. And we might have accepted that, I think, but the aura of fear was too dense around the grove, and the trappings of caution too obvious. All of them watched, even as they smiled and laughed and went about their simple chores; watched and listened for things they wouldn't name.

The boy children went about their games and play-battles as if they did not notice the underlying apprehensions in the Family, avoiding the feelings or simply not feeling it at all—that is, that our mothers and grown sisters were hiding something from us. I believe they enjoyed the mystery of it all and stopped there, and still I wonder how they couldn't see the truth of it. I could see it on every lined face, and in the way my own mother would not look me in the eye—we were being lied to.

Almost a week had passed since the stranger's arrival when I finally decided to ask for the truth. Although I had been surrounded by my Family for every waking moment of those days, I had really been inside myself, lost in my fears of betrayal and my half-formed conclusions of deceit. And feeling more alone than I had thought possible.

I sat on my bed after supper and waited to find the courage. Our home was warm and snug, the rich smell of root stew still in the air. Mother was whittling some bit of decorative trim by our fire, her skilled hands moving slowly and methodically, her dark hair pulled back from her shining face. I looked at the deeply etched lines on her skin that had been laid there by seasons of worry, and I thought of my dream once again. And I realized that if I did not ask, or if she would not tell, we would be lost.

"Who is she, Mother?"

She didn't look up from her work, but her hands paused for the barest second. "Who is who?" Her tone was even, but careful.

"Keil. Who is she really? And why are you all so afraid?"

She laid down the wood and the knife and turned toward me, slipping on a mask of exasperation. I could actually see her do it, the way her mouth set and her eyes shaded, and even then, it hurt to see her wear that fakeness for me, her child.

"I've told you, Mita, more than once—we don't know anything about her, not yet. After Katlya teaches her our language we can find out more about who she is. And what do you mean, *afraid*? No one is afraid, we're just being careful, that's all. Now why don't you—"

"No, you are afraid, all of you, I can see it, and I don't know why you're lying to me!" I heard my own voice rising, and still I hurt, but even more, I was angry. "It has to do with Keil, and who is after her, and you know, I can see it! You act as if—a, a tribe of ghouls, or a scourge of death or, as if the *Ragman* were coming!"

At my last words, she stood so quickly that her chair over-turned. I opened my mouth to say more, but stopped when I saw what had happened. My mother had lost her mask, and I saw the fear in the open for the first time. Her tanned skin had blanched to a deadly white, and her gaze had filled with a dread so great and deep that I was certain, in that moment, she would die from it. My anger fled with my accusations as I looked into those awful eyes, staring into my own, so in pain and so frightened that I did not know them. The seconds stretched on, impossibly long, and still she exposed herself to me, naked and defenseless in her horror.

"Mother . . . ?"

She turned then, and broke the hideous spell with the simple act of uprighting her chair, though she did so as if in a daze. She walked toward me, and then past, to the door, where she lifted her coat from its peg.

Not looking at me, she spoke, her voice without inflection. "Go to bed now. I will be back later."

In a rush of cold air, she was gone.

Time passed, although I did not feel it. The fire slowly dwindled to embers, but I didn't put on a lamp, just sat in the gathering shadows and tried to think of nothing. After a time, I cried, and after more, my tears dried and went away. I even slept awhile: dreamless and sudden sleep, overtaking me as if my conscious-ness simply left my body. The embers were still lit when I fell back into myself. She had not come back.

I'm not certain what I was thinking to do as I slipped into my boots and coat, other than to find her. I had no feelings, no thoughts except that I would dress warmly and go, get away from the strange deadness in my heart.

I walked out into the dark and into the circle of our Family's houses, not knowing where to begin. The night was clear and brisk, the only sound that of the snow crunching dully beneath my feet. I looked up and saw a million stars shining down, surrounding the big moon like so many tiny candles.

The homes were all silent and black, shadows against shadows, except for one: Katlya's. I could see the flickering mist, cast from her frosted window, and the shapes that sat inside.

I walked closer, and as I neared the doorstep, I heard their muted voices. My mother and Katlya were speaking softly, but their words carried easily through the stillness. My mother had been crying.

" . . . know what we should do. There will be others."

"Yes. And each one brings a risk." Katlya sounded like she had the day that Shaim left us, full of grief and exhausted from her own life. "He may be coming now."

"I know, don't you think I know?"

They paused, and I stepped away to catch a glimpse of their hazy forms through the polished and dirty clearstone. I held quite still, my breath sending tendrils of steam into the darkness.

When my mother spoke again, I heard a strange and forlorn hope in her voice. "None of the others are female . . . isn't there a chance that—"

Katlya rested her arm around my mother's shoulders. "Already she knows his name."

They were talking about me. My cheeks burned with it, and I wanted to run, to get away from their words that already cut into my heart. But I could not move; my body, my entire *being* was frozen in place, and the storyteller went on to seal my fate.

"She will change. He . . ." A deep, shaking breath. "My son changed. And now Scio, and she may be the next. Perhaps she already dreams."

Mother's head dropped down into her hands. "No, not yet! I can't, I'm not ready, *she's* not ready!"

There was a long silence, and then Katlya continued. "There is nothing we can do for our own, except release them, as I released Shaim. After we grow to love them, and pray that it won't happen, and then watch as they change into their fathers . . ."

My mother raised her head slowly, and the last words I heard her speak are these:

"My Mita, my beautiful hope. The Ragman's daughter."

I turned and fled.

I ran for as long and far as my legs would carry me, until my skin dripped with sweat and I could breathe no more. Into the blackness of the deepest woods, far from the only home I had ever known, I ran and ran.

At last I stumbled and fell, landing hard against the solid base of a gnarled tree. Curled into a ball, eyes squeezed shut, praying that the thoughts would not come and helpless to stop them.

The Ragman's daughter. The Ragman's family. Keil's unborn child, spawned by my childhood's vision of purest evil.

Me. Me. Me.

My breathing slowed, bit by bit, and the cold of the winter night seeped into my bones as the truth gnawed through the rest of me. It did not matter where I ran, the change would come as it had for Shaim—and I would die by the hands of my loved ones, die or create death for others.

Abomination. I would become the wretch that stole life, and I hugged myself tighter and damned the Family that had brought me to this; damned my mother, who had given me the destiny of damnation.

Sleep.

The thought bloomed into my mind like a beacon of hope. The night was too cold for me to reawaken, too bitter for my life to go on; I would sleep.

I did not bid farewell to the sky above. I had no second thoughts; I waited for the slumber that I knew would be my last, praying only that I should never rise again.

The darkness is warm and the trees move closer, shadowing me with their kind arms. I awake, sit up, and find that I am still where I fell so long ago—and there is a figure here, crouching down to look at me.

There is no fear as a stray shaft of moonlight illuminates the dark face. It has the features of a boy, but lined and grown; this is a man, then, and still there is no fear. For this man smiles at me, and his eyes are kind.

Not empty at all. Only black like mine.

"Are you my father?" A whisper, so timid that it is almost lost.

"Yes," he says, a voice of softest leather.

"You are the Ragman?"

"Yes," he says again, and I see that there is no breath in the chilled night, no wisps of life between us—yet I am not afraid.

"Are we dead?"

The Ragman, my father, laughs and shakes his lovely head. "We are dreaming, my child. I have come to help you find your way."

My child.

"I thought that you were a bad man," I whisper, and the glint in his eye tells me that he laughs inside.

"There are many who think so," he says, "but they fear what they do not comprehend. I am but a part of the world that must be, the same as the skies and the seas."

He reaches out to me, and shyly, I slip my pale fingers between his slender bony ones. As we touch, my soul flutters inside like an autumn leaf, a soft chill inside that is anything but wrong. I feel it go into him as the loneliness of my young life melts and dwindles, the branches of the wretched tree releasing my heart to fill with love.

"I have come for you, my child," he says. "You are the flower of my heart, and my only daughter; your fate lies with me."

This, then, is the destiny that I feared, that the Family struggled to deny. For the first time in my life, I feel complete inside; is my soul such a cost? Not when his hand is warm with mine, and not with the knowledge that great awakenings lay ahead.

We stand, my father and I, and a strange thing, a wonderful thing happens. We rise, high above the woods. And I see that my body is no more. High above the mountains that reach nobly toward the stars, I see the grove of trees where once I lived, where fear still shadows life. Soon, I know, we will go there together and welcome my brothers to the truth.

* . * . *

My dream now:

*My mother stands over me, anxious and full of fear, desperate
to steal me from my father's home and my rightful inheritance.
She lifts me up and I stand, becoming the creature that she
shrinks from. I am part of the Ragman and part of her, but also
my own being, strong and proud of all I can possess. I laugh, but
only because she does not understand. And I cry inside, because
she is my mother—but there is no guilt, never again.*

I no longer sleep, but dream whenever I please. I dwell in
many places and seek truth in the souls of men and women,
always learning new paths and gathering strength from those
who would shun me.

I am the Ragman's daughter.

Finally, I am whole.

Gathering the Taradomnu

Mark Shepherd

1

"**Y**ou may see your father now," the healer's assistant said icily as he opened the door of the king's bedchamber. Though bowing in deference to Terena, she saw clearly that she was far from welcome.

The door widened, but only darkness greeted her as she stepped inside. The stuffy, cloying odor of sickness greeted her nostrils as she peered inside. A huge canopied bed occupied the far corner, and within its layers of silk and satin lay the once robust figure of King Aedhan, ruler of Elfhame Ruadach of the Llanowar line.

"Still, he sleeps," the healer hissed from somewhere behind her, but she paid him no attention. Her father seemed grayer and more ashen than he had the last time she visited. He lay quietly with his hands at his side, his mouth open and pointed toward the ceiling. Had his chest not marked his breathing, he would have looked quite dead and lying in state.

"He sleeps," Terena spat. "For four days now, he sleeps," she said, glaring down at the assistant. He relented only with a slight cower, then dared to return a gaze longer than was polite. "And still, you know *nothing*?"

The assistant shrugged noncommittally. "Macha has clues. He has gone to find a solution. But," he sniffed, looking away dramatically, "he tells me nothing."

Her eyes brightened at this news. *So, Macha is off looking for a cure. That means the healer must have an idea, some idea, of the cause of the sickness.*

Terena turned back to her father, feeling her frustration turn to anger. "Father, can you not hear me?" she shouted at the still form. The assistant scurried to the bedside, wincing visibly, wringing his thin hands, acting as if the king were made of frail crystal that would shatter at the slightest vibration. She touched the king's hand, then shook it. Her only reply was his steady breathing. Terena fought back tears as she contemplated her father's face, for a moment seeing the ghost of the elven king she once knew, the tall and strong leader of Ruadach. He was tall and broad of shoulder, even for a Llanowar. In his not so long-ago youth he had defeated ten other elves in sword battle, without injury. But now he looked like a wilted flower, waiting to go to seed, waiting to die.

No, thought Terena, as she leaned closer. *The gods have not given their permission for you to die! Not . . . yet.* Touching his wrist again, she closed her eyes and reached for his soul, the very root of his being. Something thick and muddied veiled his mind from anything and anyone trying to reach it; she found no spark of awareness, not even the edge of a dream. Her gentle probe revealed only the mysterious barrier which shielded the king's mind and soul absolutely.

She'd detected the veil before and discussed it with Macha, who agreed that some foe had placed it with medicine, or renegade magic, or both. The magic's mana was distinctively dark and elusive, but no one they knew in Elfhame Ruadach used such magic. The magic was powerful, to say the least, and such power could easily be used for either good or evil. *Who, then, has reached for this mana? And who among us has that capability?* Terena had no idea, and she seriously doubted anyone of their court, or the royal family, had such abilities.

The king's sickness had fallen upon him suddenly, after an evening meal; the food was immediately suspect, but no poison was found. His tea had contained an additional herb Macha could not easily identify, but this was not particularly suspicious. The king was an accomplished herbalist and usually mixed his own tea, often improvising combinations at a moment's notice. That he might use an obscure but benign herb in his tea was not only possible but likely.

She withdrew from the king's mind, then turned away from his bed. *I must know what Macha has found,* she thought feverishly as she stormed out of the bedchamber.

2

Macha Mac Aonghus, Healer and Head Mage of the Tuatha de Ruadach, solemnly rode a black steed onto the palace grounds. A thick white blanket of fog covered the land and smothered the sun so that only a pale, yellow light shone through.

Terena knew that somewhere beyond the fog, past the palace walls, lay the hills on which the city of Scoria was built. Beyond that, to the northwest, stood the Ath Mountains. But all was shrouded in the deep mist, out of which the healer rode in his cloak of black, and with a posture that reflected a mood just as dark.

Macha pulled his steed to a stop beside Terena and regarded her with sad, old eyes.

"How is the king?" Macha asked, without much apparent hope.

"Alive, but still sleeping," she replied, studying him closer, sensing about him an air of hope, which faded to disappointment, then to grief. "You know what ails him, don't you, Macha the Healer?" she asked, already knowing the answer.

He nodded only slightly, shutting his eyes against his sudden yawn. "Come with me to my workshop," Macha said, urging his steed forward. "We have much to discuss."

In the tower that served as his laboratory, Macha built a roaring fire against the chill outside. Once the flames subsided, and the fire became warm with coals, the healer sat in a chair carved from an enormous trunk of oak amid a forest of vials and flasks, some older than the palace itself.

"Your father has been poisoned with a root known as Forever Sleep," he said finally, but he didn't seem altogether grateful for the discovery.

Forever Sleep. She knew the herb well, even though she had just begun her studies in herbology. The herb was the only plant outlawed in Ruadach, and most elves of the land knew it to be

extinct. It was a plant used by assassins, and had been brought
into the elfhame by foreign mercenaries who needed to keep a
cache in hiding. Though it had been a century since the last
known crop of Forever Sleep had been burned, evidently not all
of that cache had been destroyed.

"I know," Macha continued, arranging the cloak so that it draped
down the sides of the huge oak chair. "It was supposed to have been
eliminated from this land, but as any warrior will tell you, something as powerful as the Sleep will find its way back to our world."

"Others will find a use for it," she said. "Perhaps Beothach
had found use for it, himself."

Macha cringed at the mention of Beothach, and the name itself
had tasted bitter when she mentioned it. Beothach, her older brother,
was next in line for the Ruadach crown. Though he had been traveling throughout the kingdom lately, he had loyal followers here at
home who would gladly do his unpleasant work for him. Word had
recently reached the king that Beothach had attacked a colony of
humans, a place called Summertown, up the Moen River. Beothach
had killed all the adults and had sold the children into slavery. The
slaughter was senseless, as the humans worshiped peace, ate no meat,
grew crops for sustenance, and had no weapons to speak of. They
had even entered into an agreement with King Aedhan, in which permission for the humans to colonize had been clearly granted.

But there were some in the kingdom who saw the humans as a
poison to their land. Historically humans had been the aggres-
sors, taking elven lands in times past, but these new humans of
Summertown were nothing of the sort. There were also the elven
purists, of which Beothach was an outspoken member, who saw
the humans as a possible contaminant to their race. Terena never
understood the fear, but was well aware that the elders of the
court, Macha included, did not look favorably on any contact
with the humans, peaceful or not. But King Aedham knew that
contact with the humans was inevitable, and it would be better to
introduce his subjects to this peaceful lot, where the possibility of
violent conflict was very slim. Terena had only seen humans at a
distance and had found their appearance disagreeable, even disgusting, though she knew there was no real reason for her to feel
that way, except that perhaps she and all other elves were taught
this prejudice by elders who had suffered at the hands of the

humans. With her father's guidance she began opening her mind to this, which she knew very little about, and tried to find ways they were alike, instead of focusing on their differences.

Therefore it was no real surprise to hear of Beothach's slaughter of Summertown's inhabitants. The news had arrived several nights before, and upon hearing it the king had told those in his confidence that he would disown and banish his son for his actions. But in order to do so, officially and by the ancient laws of the Ruadach, the proclamation had to be made in public, with witnesses, and a scribe to record his words. This the king would have done in his court the next day. Had he not fallen ill.

"Aie, yes," Macha admitted. "Undoubtedly, Beothach has put Forever Sleep to use." He leaned forward and whispered softly, "But be careful who you confide in, young one. I don't know who to trust anymore, save Lord Erko. And I am among the oldest of the elfhame."

But to poison the king, so blatantly. Only a fool wouldn't see Beothach's motives. He must be certain of his influence to attempt to kill his own father in such a cowardly manner.

Terena shook her head at the boldness of the act; as they were growing up the king had favored Beothach over herself, and as a young elven adult she now understood, after years of resentment, why father had shown so much more attention to her older brother. She didn't love her father any less and remained at his side through the years as Beothach seemed to drift away from him emotionally and, lately, physically. Beothach spent little time around the palace, and the king had written this off as his son "sowing his royal oats." Now, Terena thought in retrospect, it was clear that while out sowing he was really fortifying his position among the lords.

It was no secret that of the three elven lords of Ruadach, two were in favor of Beothach and were very likely plotting with him to overthrow the king. Ruadach law required any heir to have his or her own heir already conceived to assure the lineage of the clan. Beothach had not one but two young sons at Lord Roech's castle, thus satisfying the law. Her brother might be conspiring to kill their father, Terena mused bitterly, but he was going about seizing the crown within every other law of the clan.

Lord Roech and Lord Fergus, whose holdings lay to the north and south of the capital, had made no secret of their alliance with

Beothach; it was the latter's holdings that the murdered human colony bordered.

But Lord Erko, whose holdings lay to the east, had joined the priesthood early in life and, at the demise of his father, had only recently assumed his title. Though on permanent leave from the priesthood, whose objects of worship included the Eye of Emer, the smaller of the two moons, Erko adhered to his principles of peace, much as the humans of Summertown had. Erko's officials had informed the king of the human slaughter, having watched from a hillside as Beothach and his soldiers committed the atrocity. Lord Erko had remained loyal to the king and had reasserted this loyalty by turning informant on the prince.

Erko is on our side, Terena thought. *But how much help would he and his lands be in a war? Probably not much.*

" . . . Terena?"

She looked up, startled. Her thoughts had wandered so far that she had ceased hearing the healer. "Yes, Macha. Forgive me."

"Has your brother, Beothach, taken up the study of sorcery?" he asked with an expression of innocence that chilled her blood.

"No," she said. "No, certainly not. I would have known, I would have felt . . ."

"Would you, now?" Macha asked. "Does he tell you everything?"

She didn't like the direction the conversation was going and let her tone tell him so. "He tells me nothing," she replied coldly, "but I would have known by the blood. That he cannot hide."

"And what if he could?" Mach said, his eyes cast downward, the flare of a twig catching fire lighting his ancient face. "The use of Forever Sleep comes with risks to the user as well. Only the skillful use of mana can contain it to keep it from killing the one using the herb. Certainly you knew that much from your studies."

She had, but didn't want to admit that just yet. To do so would admit that a direct relative of hers was using mana to cause harm, an act which carried severe penalties in Ruadach. If Beothach were thus guilty, it would look unfavorable on her, to her entire family, including the king. Such use of mana represented everything her clan had opposed since the beginning of time; to embrace it now would renounce all good that had come out of Ruadach for the last thousand years.

Would Beothach betray what his father, his entire line of ancestors, had spent millennium building?

When she could not answer herself immediately, she became quite concerned for Ruadach's future.

Macha shrugged, held his hands up to the warm fire. "There is a cure for the king. It is a plant known as taradomnu, a vine that favors the large trunk of oak trees. Taradomnu is also not native to this area. It comes from the far north and does not fare well in warm lands, except in sheltered valleys." He didn't seem at all relieved that an antidote existed. *Does it grow in our land?* she wondered frantically.

"The vine is not good for much else, so we haven't kept it in stock. There was a bit growing a short distance from here, in a small valley formed by a branch of the Fors River. I have just returned from there."

Macha paused, took a metal poker and rearranged some of the logs. Sparks jumped, leaped up the chimney. A wave of heat filled the room as the fire came to new life.

"And?" Terena asked when her patience ran out.

"It was all gone. Every last vine. It was uprooted and then piled onto a bonfire. I found absolutely none of it left."

Terena stared at him. "Someone knew what it was, and where it was?"

"Obviously," Macha replied. "Its location wasn't a secret. I take all my apprentices there to show them what taradomnu looked like, and where it could grow, should they travel to other lands."

Terena groaned and buried her head in her hands. "Then all is lost," she mumbled.

"Not exactly," Macha replied. He stood and shuffled over to a tall bookcase, reached up to a pile of parchment and withdrew a scroll. "I have more of it growing elsewhere."

She looked up, alight with hope. "Where? I will go find it!"

Macha gave her the scroll, a small affair with a leather pouch attached. When she unrolled it she discovered a map, which trailed up the Fors River going north from Scoria. It wound up toward the Ath Mountains.

"Look for a rocky cliff," Macha said. "Then the river branches. It leads to another valley marked by three large boulders."

She gazed at the map, her hands shaking with excitement.

"Yes, yes, I know this trail," she said. "But it goes through the lands of Fergus."

"That it does," Macha said, returning to his chair. "But Lord Fergus doesn't know where this patch of taradomnu is growing. In fact, no one knows. I've kept it a secret, just in case something like this came up."

Terena leaped from her seat and threw her arms around Macha, giving him a big kiss in the center of his forehead. "Gods, child, what have I done to deserve such gratitude?" Macha cried out, but Terena saw he was blushing. "Take note of the drawing of the taradomnu vine." She looked at another parchment, attached to the scroll. On it was a carefully drawn picture of a vine, which had four distinctive leaves to a cluster. "Obtain enough to fill a good-sized pouch. Root, stem, and leaf. But do not take it all, for it is our law to leave some for nature to resupply itself. That is nature's share."

As she studied the drawing, she also contemplated her mission and everything that depended on it. *The elfhame. The court. The king. . . my father.* She didn't feel worthy, but there was no on else to trust.

"If harmful mana is involved," she said, "will I not need magic to combat it?" It was an old argument, one they had had for some time. To harness protective mana she needed the sigils, but to have so much power was, in Macha's estimation, too much responsibility for one so young. She had accepted her place as a nonmagical student for some time now, but as her hormones had become restless, so had her aspirations to become a full magician's apprentice.

Macha shook his head smugly, as he often did when he knew he had the secret she so desired; it was enough to make her slap that smug grin off the old elf's face, if she would ever dare such a thing in this incarnation and expect to live.

"What a clumsy way to attempt to trick me," the healer said, and Terena opened her mouth to object. "No, no, no objections, I don't want to hear it," he said good-naturedly, which told her he was in a half-playful mood this afternoon, despite the seriousness of their conversation. "We have been over this a number of times, young lady. You will know the sigil for protective mana when you are ready for it to be presented to you." Macha folded his arms resolutely. "And not before. It was the rule I learned, and there is no reason to alter the rules for you, in spite of your lineage." Behind the rough words, however, she caught a sly twinkle in his old eyes, telling her that he was baiting her. And she was not about to give him the pleasure of a childish outburst.

"And what if I must deal with a magical attack?" she asked, trying to keep the sarcasm out of her voice.

"Never worry," Macha said, "you will be protected. Swords and arrows, however, you must deal with yourself."

"So be it," she said, purposefully changing her tone to a lighter one and regarding the drawing of the taradomnu leaf with just a touch of awe. "You just may have saved my father's life," she added, tucking the scroll away in its pouch. "I ride today."

3

Terena insisted she needed no one to go with her, that to travel in numbers would only attract unwanted attention. Macha strongly suggested she take a contingent of guards, as she would be traveling in hostile lands, the lord of whom would unlikely allow her to pass. Her plan was to penetrate Fergus's holdings secretly, without detection, a difficult feat with fifty guards at her heels. After all, if the lord knew she were passing through they would either challenge her, or have her watched. And if the other source of taradomnu were discovered, all would be lost.

They reached a compromise. Two guards, expert archers from the elfhame's elite fighting force, would ride with her for protection. She estimated that three could travel the road along the Fors River without much notice. Her brother Beothach was still traveling somewhere, having yet to return to the capital. If he were between Scoria and what was left of Summertown, then her path would take her away from him; Beothach would return to find Father dying, as planned, and would likely as not rest on his laurels and wait for the Sleep to complete its work. But if he were traveling to Roech's palace to visit his sons, their paths would intersect. She tried not to consider this too much when preparing for her trip.

The two archers were subdued as they left the palace grounds. Either they were awed by the presence of royalty, or just tired; they were young, their pointed ears small and nearly rounded, the sign of youth. Macha's ears had been rather long and pointed, with a slight curl at the tip of one, these being the common traits of age in elves.

The Ath Mountains remained shrouded in mist as they began their journey up the For's River road. Their destination lay at the foothills, and Macha had estimated the trip would take a day to reach the crop of taradomnu and another to return. Time was of the essence, so they departed immediately without waiting for the cover of darkness. In three days, the healer estimated, the king would die.

By midday they had encountered only a handful of merchants with their mule-drawn carts: no one who looked official, who might alert Fergus of their presence. The sun rose, only to be blotted out by rain clouds, which delivered a fine mist to the land. Terena had stowed the map and drawing in an oilskin bag, which should keep it bone-dry, and she remembered enough of the map that she didn't have to refer to it.

The mist turned out to be a mixed blessing. While it helped to keep them hidden, it also transformed their road into a river of mud. Her horse had some difficulty negotiating the less than level sections, and hesitated at stretches of high water which flowed across their path. While crossing one of these obstacles, Terena heard one of the guards cry out sharply.

She whirled around in time to see him staring ahead in terror as an arrow protruded from the center of his chest. He clutched at it as he doubled over and fell off the horse. The other guard pulled his bow and nocked an arrow, but seemed to have no idea where the attack came from.

All around them, silence. Terena knew they were next. Then, a *twang* from somewhere to her right, and the deadly hiss of an arrow sailing past her head.

"Ride!" she shouted, and kicked her horse into action. They were all sitting ducks if they stayed where they were, Terena knew, and she urged the horse into a gallop. She heard the other guard behind her, but he was lagging. Perhaps he had second thoughts about leaving his comrade behind.

Terena knew only that if she died here, her father would surely follow her in death, so she concentrated on the uncertain road before them. It turned sharply, which nearly caused her to fall off, but the horse handled it with ease. Moments later, she looked back and saw that she was alone.

She felt like a coward, running from an attack like that, and she tried to convince herself that she had no choice, they were likely outnumbered. Then she heard shouts, and a cry that might have been the other guard, followed by the thunder of many hoofbeats.

They're after me, she knew, focusing on her horse, considering tactics which might aid her. She could dismount and hide, sending her horse on without her. The sounds of the attackers would likely keep her steed moving and lead them away from her. But then she would have no transportation, save her own feet, and she didn't think she could thus accomplish her task in time to save her father. So she rode, as hard and fast as she ever had, praying to the gods that her horse was faster then theirs.

The attackers were most likely a group of Fergus's soldiers, but she couldn't be certain. Bandits were known to travel this road, particularly when the weather was foul. But for some reason this attack didn't feel like bandits; that arrow had been fired by an expert, and the bandits in these areas were not known for their bowmanship. *Only the military would have men that skilled. . . .*

After rounding another bend, two soldiers on horseback intercepted her suddenly; Terena's horse reared, throwing her backward. She rolled as she landed and reached for her sword.

Not in time. A sword tip met her throat as she stood, and she looked up into the face of a soldier, wearing the red-and-black Fergus livery.

"So it *is* the princess," he said softly. "If you wish to live I suggest you stay where you are. What reasons have you for being on our land?" The sword remained at the soft spot just under her chin as she glared silently back at him.

They're all traitors, they're all under Beothach, she realized, though it wasn't a particularly new revelation. This soldier's willingness to threaten the life of the princess implied only one thing: a coup was indeed in progress, and he was on the side of the enemy—Beothach.

Her horse's hoofbeats receded into the mist. The other soldier dismounted and came up behind her, seizing her arms and pulling them back.

Terena saw something move in the tree above the mounted soldier, but in the fog she couldn't be certain. The three of them stood silently as she debated on which lie to tell them. *I've come to seek an alliance with Fergus.* Or, *There is an army of orcs at our border, we need Fergus. . . .* The lies danced briefly in her head, but none of them sounded convincing even to herself.

Then the something leaped from the tree onto the soldier's back with a spine-chilling scream that could *not* have come from an elf. The creature was all arms, legs, and hair.

The soldier drew back as he struggled against whatever had descended on him. Terena seized the opportunity by stomping on the soldier's right foot with her boot heel. The soldier screamed; a sound which was quickly cut off when she turned and slammed her palm upward, into the center of his face. He fell backward, the bridge of his nose now located somewhere in his brain.

She saw only a shadow of her other foe. The mounted soldier still struggled against whatever had landed on him, the horse turning backward in panic.

Her horse gone, her only escape lay with her feet. She wanted to help whatever had landed on the other one, but she had no idea if it was going to be friendly to her. The decision was made for her when she heard the rest of her pursuers splash across the high water, mere paces away.

Quick like a bunny, Terena crept off into the mist, putting as much distance between her and Fergus's men as possible. As she ran into what soon became a thick forest, she couldn't help but wonder what in hell's name the gods had sent to attack that soldier.

4

The rain had dampened the ground thoroughly, making her movement away from the battle as silent as she needed. Terena's first task was to get away from her attackers, but at the same time she didn't want to lose track of the road. She still intended to fulfill her mission, with or without a horse.

Angry, confused shouts receded behind her as she stole through the forest, taking a path which she guessed ran parallel to the river road. She had only her sense of direction to guide her, these being unfamiliar lands. As near as she could tell, nobody was pursuing her.

Her pouch with the map and drawings remained tucked at her side, alongside her sword, which she had yet to draw during this strange journey. As long as it was, it was not very good defense in close quarters. Indeed, the palm of her hand had proven to be an effective killing device. Her dagger remained sheathed at her side, and had her reflexes not acted on their own she would have used it instead of her palm. She was tired from the battle, and some of the fear was starting to wear off, leaving her feeling shaky. But she had to move on, had to keep moving. Fergus's men would not give up yet, particularly when they knew they had the advantage. She was on foot.

A rustle in the brush caught her attention, and she stood firm, drawing her sword.

A young human, riding on one of Fergus's steeds, moved into view. He was tall and wiry, with a huge crown of unkempt, curly hair, his knees sticking out from the steed's sides like elbows. At first she thought he was naked, then saw the loincloth, and the boots, but that was all.

He wore a dagger at his side, but made no move to draw it. They regarded each other for several long moments before Terena put away her blade, having determined he was no real threat. Then she realized this was the wild creature which had leapt onto her attackers from the tree and had evidently won a horse for his trouble.

Behind her, the attackers shouted again, this time closer. The young human looked up, alarmed. Then he glanced down at her, and without a word motioned for her to get on the horse with him. With one jump she was positioned behind him, and a moment later they were off, flying through the forest on the captured steed.

5

"North," she said into his ear as they came back onto the river road. "Take us north, please. I have urgent business to tend to."

Though she didn't know if he understood her or not, they did take the northern direction alongside the Fors River. She heard no sign of the others and had come to believe they had lost them.

During their escape her thoughts turned to the young human who had become her unlikely savior. While at first she thought him a young man, he was little more than a boy, though a large, lanky one, with the soft beginnings of a beard and fine, sculptured shoulder muscles. He knew how to ride, quite well in fact, and she found herself admiring him in spite of the fact he smelled like a goat.

They exchanged no more words until they stopped for a rest, since their horse was beginning to show signs of fatigue. She felt vulnerable on the rocky riverbed, but there was no other way to the water. As the horse drank deeply from the Fors River, Terena cast frequent looks downstream, listening for Lord Fergus's soldiers. The fog had cleared, and now it was a warm late afternoon, the sun beginning to touch the peaks of the Ath Mountains.

"So who *are* you?" she asked pointedly, assuming they spoke the same tongue. "Humans don't live here, at least that I know of. These are *elven* lands." As soon as she uttered the last, she felt immediately silly. *As if anyone can own the earth.*

The boy glared at her before he knelt and took his own drink from the river, still saying nothing.

"I suppose I should thank you," she said softly. "I think they would have killed me, if you hadn't leaped on that soldier."

Though dirty, and a bit rough around the edges, and in dire need of grooming, the human youth was not unattractive. His rounded ears made him look less intelligent, more animal-like, and his lack of clothing didn't help him look any more civilized. She realized she was judging him by elven standards, and elven prejudices, which her father had warned her about. *Humans are no less wise and intelligent than we,* she thought, remembering her father's kind admonishments. Terena felt a kindness emanating from the boy, a gentle demeanor he was desperately trying to hide with feigned anger.

"Do we speak the same language?" she asked, feeling like he was ignoring her. "Where are you from?"

"Summertown," he said suddenly with a soft, weary voice, and faced her squarely.

She opened her mouth to speak, but no words came. *Good gods,* she thought, suddenly afraid, her hand itching for her blade. *The human colony Beothach attacked.*

"Summertown . . ." she replied distantly, and her voice trailed away. She felt sad for the murdered humans and made no attempt to hide her feelings.

"So you know," the boy said, stepping closer, but not threateningly. "Why are they trying to kill you?"

"The one who killed your people," Terena said, hoping she made sense. "The leader. He is the prince, and he's trying to take the crown of Ruadach before his time. This elfhame," she said,

daring to meet his eyes again. Though she tried to convince herself otherwise, she still felt guilty. *My brother killed his people.
Perhaps even his family.* "The king is dying. If he dies, this beast
who killed your people will become the new king."

. At first his expression was unreadable, then she saw that he
was mulling her words over. After a moment he said, "So he was
not the king of this land. We were led to believe he was."

She shook her head violently. "No, no, absolutely *not*," she
said urgently. "He is plotting to overthrow King Aedhan, and
may well do so if I fail in my task."

"Your task?" he asked, rubbing his face, looking suddenly tired.
"What is so important in the north that you risk your life to go there?"

Terena told him of the poisoning by Forever Sleep and her
mission to obtain enough taradomnu to cure him. "Those soldiers
who are following us, they belong to a lord who is aiding
Beothach. All will be lost if my father dies," she blurted out,
realizing too late her mistake.

"Your father is the king?" the boy said. "Then, it was your
brother who attacked Summertown."

She couldn't deny it, not now. "Yes, Beothach is my brother,
damn his soul. I would as soon see him disowned, or even dead after
what he did. And so would the king, if he lives." She glanced back
at the road, seeing nothing coming toward them, but feeling nervous
nevertheless. "We must keep going."At first he seemed uncertain, as
if debating her character, or looking for faults in her story. Then he
extended his hand. "You can call me Grenfher," he said, clasping her
firmly. "Where do we go to find this antidote of yours?"

6

At Terena's suggestion they removed the decorative tack that
would indicate the horse's owner, namely Fergus. Still, most of
the local folk, if they encountered them, would likely recognize
the horse for what it was after careful scrutiny. At least they
weren't waving a banner anymore.

As they made tracks for the Ath mountains, Gren explained
himself a little more, apparently having relaxed enough around
Terena to reveal some of his secrets.

The raid on Summertown had resulted in the deaths of the adults only; several hundred children were sold into prostitution after the town had been sacked. A group of orcs had been waiting to buy the children long before the raid began, and they were well on their way to whatever destination had been planned for them.

Grenfher had been sold specially to an unknown buyer, who had a contact waiting for him at the other end of the Ruadach lands, along with a large amount of gold. A group of Fergus's men had been taking him there when they encountered Terena and her former bodyguards. Gren had escaped while the soldiers were attacking her and had hidden in a tree for lack of a better place to go. When he saw his former captors attacking Terena, he went into action.

Damn Beothach to hell, she seethed. *Is nothing sacred to him anymore? It is tradition of the Llanowar to protect children, all children, no matter what race they belong to. Instead, he sells them off as whores!*

She asked him about the secretive buyer, and at first it looked like he didn't want to talk about it. Then he said, with a touch of anger, "All I know is he has a harem of boys. I'm only sixteen. I would have been the youngest."

They rode in silence after that, and Terena wondered if she had probed too deeply. His mood seemed to lift, though, when they came across a branch in the river in which flowed pure, spring water.

"Summertown was like this," Gren said distantly. "We built our homes on the edge of a creek, which ran down from the mountains."

Terena wasn't paying much attention, as something else had caught her eye. Towering over the creek was a rocky bluff with small trees sprouting at its top.

"Hold a moment," she said, then pulled out the map of the area that Macha had given her. "This is it. This must be . . ." She looked upstream past a group of three white boulders. "That way," she said. "We've found it!"

Gren led the horse up the shallow stream toward the boulders, then onto the rocky bank. Terena dismounted and ran over to a grove of oaks.

Growing profusely up the trunks of the massive trees were layers of green vines, each of the mature leaves having clusters of four.

"Taradomnu," she whispered gratefully as she began pulling up the vines.

7

Gren solved the problem of where to stow the plants by tying them in bundles, using the vines themselves. Nothing remained on their steed that would serve as a pouch, but they did find a way to bind the bundles to the horse's side, using leather thongs on the saddle.

The boy had started to act peculiarly, though, as they gathered the vines. When Terena asked if anything was wrong, he said, "This whole area . . . I feel like we're being watched. Something is . . ."

As if on cue, a heinous laughter rippled from somewhere just behind her; she spun around, seeing nothing there that could have made the sound.

But she recognized the sound itself, having heard that obscene laughter more than once during her upbringing.

Beothach.

But where was he? It sounded like he was standing right behind her, but no one, and nothing, stood there.

Apparently sensing some unseen danger, Gren pulled his dagger and rushed to her side, looking about warily.

Then, just a few paces away, the air shimmered like a mirage. A breath of heat passed by her, and the image within the mirage focused, until she saw her brother Prince Beothach of Ruadach, sitting atop a black stallion.

The prince had grown his straight, black hair out until it draped over the black leather armor. He wore a single ceremonial eyeguard, a black orb strapped across his face with silver chain. About him dripped a thick aura of pain and suffering, a pent-up force of terror that he was evidently preparing to unleash on her. It was the dark mana, purposefully collected and stored somewhere in the several pendants and talismans he wore around his neck. One crystal in particular, which hung from a silver setting, seemed especially rich with the forbidden force. With a black gloved hand, he reached up and stroked the crystal lovingly with a single finger. Mana swept off of it in wisps, like fog from the surface of a cold lake, confirming her suspicions.

Macha was right, she thought dismally. *He has turned to*

harmful sorcery. The revelation angered her. *If he knew, then why didn't he give me the secret of the forces before I left?*

Terena drew her sword, but as soon as she had it out, four other warriors on steeds appeared in a semicircle around her. Gren looked stunned, and whatever fight he might have had visibly drained away. The hand clutching the dagger fell to his side.

"It has been most interesting, this merry chase you've been leading us on," Beothach said haughtily, casually folding his hands over the reins. "And fortunate, for me, that I would bother. What is this strange vine you're harvesting, young sister? Taradomnu, perhaps?"

Terena said nothing as she feverishly calculated her chances of escaping this situation with their prize. Even Gren, with his pathetic little dagger, would not be worth much against a sword. She glanced to the left and saw, just beyond the bank of the stream, a cluster of rocks that Beothach's horses would have trouble negotiating. But the chance of making those rocks before the horses outran them didn't look promising, and she didn't care for the prospect of dying with a sword in her back.

"As you should well know," Terena seethed, testing the rocky ground beneath her for stability. "Did you really think you could kill our father and expect to inherit the crown?"

"Oh, young sister, I do, and I shall," he said. "As it does not look like you can stop me." His eyes narrowed as he scrutinized Grenfher. "Who is this young beggar? Isn't he the little whore from Summertown we sold to the orc traders?"

Gren didn't reply. His gaze was wandering toward the bank of the stream as well, and he was perhaps considering the same plan of making a run for it. *Given the odds,* Terena thought dismally, *that may be our only option.*

The other warriors stirred restlessly, but didn't appear to be ready for any kind of attack; they were obviously waiting for the prince to give the command.

For the moment, Terena decided to delay any attack with the only weapon that might be effective: her tongue.

"So it is true, then, that you have been working dark magic. It is what made you invisible."

"'Tis only a matter of perspective," Beothach said, and for a moment he looked ready to yawn. "It will help me attain what is rightfully mine. Tell me, how is our father doing? Is he still alive?"

"Oh, quite," Terena replied. "The taradomnu Macha had in stock revived him immediately," she said, wondering what information he might already have that would contradict her bluff. "He has sent me to replenish the supply, in case some other dog tries to poison him again."

Beothach's face darkened, and tensions between her, Beothach, and his men became tangible.

"How dare you address your future king with such words?" he said.

"And like a fool," she replied handily, "you convict yourself with your own tongue."

While carrying on her conversation, Terena became aware of something happening in the space surrounding them. It seemed to be related to mana, but it was not the mana her brother wielded. She sensed rather than felt the power growing around her. *But I am not a wizard,* she thought briefly, keeping her eyes on her brother. *I am not an apprentice. Unless . . .* At her feet lay a bundle of taradomnu, bound by itself, having a strong, spicy smell that reminded her of the great feasts held quarterly at the palace. Five of the bundles lay scattered at their feet, more or less equally spaced apart in a circle.

Time ceased to have meaning; Beothach spoke, but his words never reached her, and when he moved, it was with such slowness that she thought some drug might be affecting him.

Around her the bundles of taradomnu emitted a light along with the powerful smell. Dim at first, the light flowed from the bundles as if they were on fire. She pulled Gren closer to her, suddenly aware of what was happening.

"Get in the circle," she said, knowing that a circle of protection was indeed forming, though by what forces she didn't know. With no apparent comprehension Gren did as he was told.

Macha's words repeated in her mind, so strongly that she thought he might have been standing next to her:

You will know the sigil for protective mana when you are ready for it to be presented to you.

Before her a ball of white light formed, and within the ball was a pentacle with a long, hook-shaped symbol piercing it. Then the pentacle faded, leaving only the hook, which looked very much like a seed sprouting, reaching for sunlight.

And then you will make your shield, Macha had said. *It is the only defense you will need.*

She did as instructed, operating mostly by instinct. The mana was malleable, like clay, but still retained a will of its own. It seemed to assist her in forming a thin layer of mist around her and Gren, spinning it around until it formed the shape of an egg.

Once the shield was complete, the time and space within her shield joined with that of the world outside.

Beothach looked worried.

"So," the prince said, one hand on his blade and the other on the crystal. "Macha has taught you more than I thought."

Around her whirled the mist, retaining its shape and, she assumed, its effectiveness. Gren moved closer to her and put his arms around her, but it seemed to be more reassuring to him than to her, who, strangely, didn't feel threatened any longer by her brother.

This new confidence seemed to disturb him. Anger darkened his face a deep purple. She glanced at the others behind her and saw to her amusement they had backed off a number of paces.

"You cowards!" Beothach spat toward his minions. "She is no wizard, you fools! I am the wizard of this land, and I will soon be the king of this land. Do you dare doubt me?"

They didn't answer, and that sounded like doubt to Terena. During his tirade she had sensed a growing power within his own shields, which she recognized as a blast of energy in the making. Gren remained quiet, wisely, Terena thought. She would need all of her concentration to deal with her brother.

When the force lashed out from Beothach, it came as a surprise even though she had expected it. She had only heard of power used in this way and had never seen it in action; certainly her brother had been studying under a mage, or perhaps even a planeswalker. When the blast came, it was a wall of darkness that reeked of death itself. *He is not holding back,* she thought, strangely unalarmed. She knew that what surrounded her and Gren would protect them.

The force connected with their shield, blocking all light momentarily. Gren clutched her tighter, whimpering a bit, then the darkness was gone. Their shield of mist likewise dissipated, but Terena didn't find this disturbing. She knew, instinctively, that it was no longer needed.

When the light returned, Terena pulled out her sword, ready for an attack. On seeing the scene around her, she sucked in her breath in surprise.

Beothach lay on the ground, facing the sky. His steed stood a short distance away, nibbling on weeds. The others were likewise sprawled on the ground, their steeds nowhere in sight. She approached her brother and prodded him with the sword. Getting no reaction, she leaned over him with her dagger pulled, and with the other hand touched his neck. Terena recoiled from the cooling skin.

My brother is most assuredly dead, she thought. *And by his own hand.*

The only burial Terena could provide for her brother and his fallen minions was a simple cairn of stones. Grenfher stated this was more than they deserved, and Terena was inclined to agree. But Beothach had been a member of the royal family, and even though he was a traitor to their clan, he deserved at least a pauper's grave. That they were burying her brother left her feeling unmoved. It was what he had become, not what he had been in his youth, which stood out clearly in her mind.

From her brother's hand she pried a gold ring inscribed with the family's coat of arms, her proof that Beothach had died.

8

Night had brought with it a hard, cold rain. In the wet twilight Terena and Grenfher gathered Beothach's steed and the one Grenfher had appropriated earlier. The others had vanished; they probably had fled in terror at whatever had bounced off her shield when Beothach attacked. She was grateful his power hadn't killed them as well.

They led their steeds uphill to a mound of boulders, under which they found a cave formed by collapsed rock. Gren explored it thoroughly to make certain nothing already lived there, and satisfied it was empty, declared it safe for the night. They tied the horses in a clearing beyond the boulders and found in one of Beothach's saddlebags a blanket, a flask of wine, and a chunk of dried meat. They also brought the five bundles of taradomnu in with them for safekeeping.

A lingering ray of dusk illuminated the cave as they took shelter from the rain, giving a murky light to see by. As soon as she had spread the blanket, Terena collapsed on it, her body finally giving itself permission to go off duty. Grenfher carved off a huge chunk of the jerky and tossed it to her, then turned to devour his own meager strip.

"I will stay up and guard," Grenfher offered. "Those others, who shot your comrades with arrows, are still out there."

"If you must," she said, though she didn't feel like they were much of a threat anymore. With Beothach dead, she suspected that would take the fight out of his minions, once the news got around.

The wine was bitter and potent, the way her brother had liked it, she remembered, allowing herself a fleeting thought about Beothach. *When had he turned?* she wondered, taking another drink from the flask. *What had possessed him to turn so hateful, when he had the kingdom in his pocket?*

She would probably never have an answer to that, and would have to satisfy herself with the knowledge that she stopped him from becoming king. *As king, the gods only know what terror would have reigned. . . .*

If they rode fast, and didn't encounter any trouble along the way, she figured that with two horses they could make Scoria in a day or less. She had even considered making the trip at night, in this downpour, but with no moon to see by she doubted they would make much progress. If they rested now and began at daybreak, she estimated they would arrive in plenty of time for Macha to administer the antidote.

She passed the flask to Gren. His hand closed gently around hers, lingering for a moment before he taking the wine.

Their eyes met, and Terena knew that look. *They all look the same way, when boys are feeling randy. Like hungry puppies,* she thought, but didn't find it as annoying as she normally would. Gren smiled faintly, as he seemed to take in her uncertainty. He lay down beside her on the blanket, his raw human smell radiating from his thin, wet body in spite of the natural shower they had both just had outside. Without a word she grabbed his arm and pulled him closer.

As he began kissing her neck and shoulder with rising passion, something that could not have been his knee jabbed her in the leg.

When the heat between their bodies threatened to ignite the air, her reasoning screamed at her. *Why are you doing this with a disgusting human? Are you mad?*

But somehow, this far from home, in a cave during a heavy downpour, and after a long hiatus from male companionship, it didn't seem disgusting at all.

9

Good gods, she thought, as a smile threatened to close her eyes shut. *What have I done?*

Riding swiftly a few paces behind her, Grenfher sang, at the top of his lungs, the dirtiest tavern song she had ever heard. It didn't matter; she didn't find the song as insulting as she might have a day earlier, and she certainly wasn't concerned about being attacked. Nothing really concerned her, except for getting the taradomnu to her father.

The weather had cleared by dawn, and they were on their way back to Scoria before the sun had risen. When the city walls loomed into view, her mind filled with dark thoughts as she considered different ways to let Macha know that she had been consorting with a human boy.

But when they reached the gate, she knew that something was horribly wrong in the capital.

Black flags hung from every window. No shops were open, and the few elves she saw were wearing the black cloak of mourning and therefore could not speak.

Father, she thought, in panic. She kicked her horse into action and rode as fast as she could, leaving Grenfher far behind.

At the palace, her fears were more or less confirmed. From these gates hung the black banners of mourning, indicating the death of a royal family member. And since the king was the only royalty left at Scoria, that would have to mean him.

Or would it? *What if news of Beothach's death had reached the palace before I did?* She didn't see how that was possible, but it was a hope. Terena felt better, but not completely relieved.

The guards at the gate waved for her to stop, then stepped

aside when she saw that she wouldn't. "It's the princess," one of
them murmured as she rode past. "Let her through."

She dismounted and left the horse to graze on the grounds,
and ran into the palace. More black banners lined the halls. She
went to the great hall, where the court was likely gathered at this
hour. Terena rushed into the room without regard to protocol,
which required her name to be announced before entering.
Looking as she did, mud-streaked, wet and road-tired, she didn't
feel particularly royal at the moment anyway.

She stood on a snowy white carpet, dripping mud and dirt, and
cleared her throat loudly. A dozen noblemen, seated at a round
table, looked up.

"Good heavens child!" Macha shouted from the table, and
rushed over to her.

"Greetings, healer," she sniffed, and regarded still more black banners hanging in the great hall. "Whose loss are we grieving this day?"

She recognized Lord Erko, who stood and joined Macha at his
side. He, too, was wearing riding clothes, but was nowhere as
dirty as she. A thin beard framed his gentle face, but where she
would usually see bemusement in his green eyes, she saw only
grief. Her heart fell. He would grieve only for Father.

"Terena," Erko said softly, putting a fragile hand on her shoulder, "your father was assassinated this morning."

She stared at him for what seemed like an eternity. "No!" she
cried out, and felt her knees buckle. Macha caught her before she
fell to the floor, and another nobleman rushed over with a chair.

"No, into the king's chambers," Macha said. "We must discuss
this in private."

10

When Lord Erko closed the huge double doors behind them,
the great hall erupted in frantic, raucous chatter.

Terena stood by the bay window, which overlooked the garden. Beyond the sculptured trees and rose bushes stood the
palace gates. *Father loved that garden,* she thought distantly.
That's why he had these windows put in.

"Princess, you must understand the predicament the kingdom
is in now," Lord Erko began, standing by the doors, apparently

trying to catch whatever stray bits of conversation drifted his way. "Word reached the palace that the prince had been slain. It wasn't certain by whom, or under whatever circumstance. One of Lord Roech's guards discovered the grave and rode all night through the weather to reach us this morning."

Terena turned to the lord as she reached into her pouch, trying hard to keep the smugness out of her expression, knowing that she was probably failing. She found the ring she had taken from Beothach and tossed it casually toward Lord Erko, who caught it easily with one hand.

The lord stared at the ring for a long while, while absently looking for a place to sit down. Once positioned in a massive marble chair, he looked up at the princess with a gleam of admiration.

"You?" Lord Erko said with a grin.

"The same," she said. "Though not in the way you probably think." The lightness of her mood didn't last. *"Who killed my father?"* Terena insisted.

Macha stepped closer to her. Terena saw how tired the elf was and realized he had not slept the whole night.

"When you left, we doubled the guards on your father's bed-chamber. I thought for certain no harm would come to him, provided you returned in time with the taradomnu."

Terena nodded and pulled a bundle of the vines from the pouch. "For naught," she whispered. "And?"

"Semion, my assistant, heard that Beothach had died when Roech's guard arrived. He . . . closed himself in the bedchamber and cut your father's throat." Terena looked away, choking back the pain that rose up from her chest. "He tried to escape through the window, then later tried to blame one of the guards. The blood on his hands convicted him. He was executed a mere candlemark ago."

She turned away from Macha, uncertain if she should hate him for allowing a traitor so close to her father. "I'm sorry, Terena. Had I any idea he was a part of the conspiracy, I would have had him in shackles long ago."

Terena half-listened to Macha's explanation, while a scuffle of some sort was taking place at the edge of the garden, just inside the gates. She heard yelling and screaming which sounded familiar, but could not see what precisely was going on. It looked as if

someone was trying to get into the palace, and the guards were
not allowing him in.

"The king is dead. The prince is dead. I, however, am alive,"
she said, as the full implications of what had transpired began to
sink in. *"Am I the new ruler?"*

Lord Erko sighed. "If it were that easy, Terena. Beothach left
sons, who are as we speak being sent word of their father's
death. The nobles, out there," the lord said, jerking a thumb in
the great hall's direction, "are inclined to abide by our laws. They
would very much like to see you become queen. But they fear
that if you were to become ruler, without fulfilling the proper
requirements, the situation in the other lord's holdings would
only worsen, and the elfhame would certainly rip apart."

"Lord Fergus? Lord Roech?" She frowned, trying to remember if she saw them when she first marched into the great hall.
"Are they not here? What situation?"

"No, my child, they are not," Macha said. "They are busy . . .
dealing with uprisings in their own lands. A counterrevolution is
underway."

The shouts from the garden became louder, and a quick glance
down there told her what she needed to know. Grenfher was
struggling to get past the guards who, thankfully, had drawn no
weapons. They seemed to find the incident amusing, evidenced
by the laughter that found its way to the bay window.

I don't believe today, Terena thought, and turned her attention
back to Lord Erko.

"It is no secret that those two lords were planning to back
Beothach in his coup. They had fortified the support in their own
courts to do so, with the promise of more power and more land.
They were planning on dividing my holdings among themselves.
With the king out of the way, nothing would have stopped them."

"So now, with Beothach gone . . ."

"Now that he's gone," Macha continued, "the plan has fallen
apart. I would suppose those nobles who back Roech and Fergus
might feel a little betrayed. I wouldn't be surprised if one or both
of them were hanging from a long rope right about now."

Terena glanced outside again to check on Grenfher's
progress. They had his arms pinned behind him and were dragging him back toward the gate. But sometime during the strug-

gle, he had lost his loincloth and was naked save for his boots. Terena giggled.

"Child, what has you so fascinated out there?" Lord Erko asked. He and Macha joined her at the window.

"What a little barbarian," Macha exclaimed. "A disgusting naked *human,* no less!"

"How did the gods even let him into the city?" Lord Erko asked, morbidly fascinated by what was going on below.

"Terena, I LOVE YOU!!" Gren shouted, with such volume and clarity that there was obviously no doubt as to what he said.

"He rode in with me," Terena said simply. "He saved my life and helped me to collect the taradomnu."

Lord Erko was visibly appalled. "That human *boy*? What does he mean, he 'loves' you?"

"Fitting, don't you think," Terena continued. "He was a survivor of Summertown. And he helped me defeat Beothach."

"TERENA!"Gren shouted. *"PLEASE!"*

She turned to Lord Erko and met his eyes with the fiercest expression she could manage. *"I owe him my life."*

"I see. Well," Lord Erko said, turning pale. "Well, I suppose I should go down there and . . . see that he is properly admitted."

"And give him some proper clothes," Macha said. "It will not do to have him running around the palace like *that*."

Lord Erko groaned as he left the room, and closed the doors firmly behind him.

"What a fine mess this day has turned into," Macha said wearily. "But I am grateful to see that not all of Summertown was murdered. Yes, we do indeed owe him."

What Erko said earlier was still nagging at her. "Beothach's eldest son is to be the new king?"

"According to the laws, yes," he replied. "You see, even though you are the next heir, you must have conceived an heir yourself to assume the crown. It is the law. And at this point the only thing that will keep the kingdom together is strict adherence to the law."

When Macha said *conceived,* Terena felt something twitch in her abdomen.

"Macha," she said glowingly. "What if I were *pregnant*?"

The healer stared at her. *"What?"*

"Just suppose," she said. "How could you tell?"

"My young lady, you don't think you are pregnant, do you?" The concept seemed completely alien to him. In that moment, she had ceased to be the little girl elf the healer knew and had become a young woman. "I could tell you right now," Macha said hesitantly. "May I?"

"Certainly," she replied. Macha bent over and placed a single hand on her abdomen, then closed his eyes. She felt something tickle across her skin before it reached down, past her tummy, to somewhere in the middle of her pelvis. It was the thought touch Macha was known for, through which he could discern disease beneath the skin without surgery. It was also a method he used to monitor the unborn, though he hadn't had much use for that talent. Until now.

When he stood up, his eyes were on fire.

"My young lady," he said, sounding short of breath. "You *are* pregnant! When did this enchanted event take place?"

"Last night," she said.

Macha nodded, satisfied with the answer. "While the king still lived. That would indeed satisfy the Law. Tell me, *who is the father?*"

She looked down at Grenfher, who was being treated a little more civilly now that Lord Erko had arrived on the scene. "The young human man down there."

After a rather long *pregnant* pause, Macha Mac Aonghus, Healer and Head Mage of the Tuatha de Ruadach, hissed loudly as he recoiled from the window.

"There is no law in our Elfhame regarding the race of the heir's father, is there?" Terena asked, though she already knew the answer.

"Aie, no . . . " Macha said weakly, turning an alarming shade of white.

"Need we be wed, either?"

"Preferably," he said, his voice becoming a whisper. "But not by the strict letter of the law. No."

"Then it would seem," Terena said, feeling a tad giddy, "that I am now the ruler of Elfhame Ruadach."

"Aie. Indeed . . . " Macha said, and fainted on the chamber floor.

Smoke and Mirrors

Ben Ohlander

Captain Grinstable stepped outside her soggy command tent and into the cold drizzle. Her boots squelched in the sticky, ankle-deep mud. She snuffled her nose on her damp sleeve and looked up at the sky, just as she had for the past four days. She saw nothing but gray, not even a glimmer of blue to break the monotony overhead. She hunched her collar, trying vainly to ward off the tiny droplets that crept underneath her greasy cloak and inside her woolen breeches. She shivered as drips trailed underneath her floppy hat and ran chilly fingers down the nape of her neck. Her morale broke under the onslaught and she turned back toward her tent, eager to flee to the relative comfort inside.

At that moment she heard the banging *whang* of a catapult as its lever arm hurled a stone skyward. She squeezed her eyes shut against the painful squeak as the weapon's crew began tugging on the stiff, rusty windlass. She heard grunts and strains as they pulled the arm earthward for another shot while the attached sack of rocks lifted out of the mud with a sullen, sucking sound.

She opened the tent flaps. The shelter's damp, fusty smell assailed her nose, which by some miracle was relatively clear. She stood a moment, feeling guilty about seeking shelter when her troops toiled in the miserable outdoors. The time honored

mantra of "Rank Hath Its Privileges" warred with her conscience. Her sense of guilt won out, barely.

She turned away from her shelter as the catapult fired again.
She watched the machine rock back and forth on its board foundation as the heavy timbers absorbed the arm's recoil. The tops
of the foundation pilings splayed, opening gaps in the flooring. A
barrel tipped, followed by a small pile of ammunition stones. She
shook her head as the crew jumped to fix the boards. She noticed
the catapult's hurling arm had bent under the load, losing
mechanical advantage as it acquired a distinct frown. She heard
the desultory *clack* a moment later as the 'pult's stone struck
something on the turtle-shell keep, probably the outer battlement.

Grinstable shook her head in dismay. The catapult was prov-
ing to be the single most useless piece of equipment they'd
brought for the siege. The animal sinews normally used to wind
the arms wouldn't hold torsion in the rain, no matter how much
wax was poured on them. They wetted and stretched to useless-
ness within minutes. Then, the pawl-arms rusted almost solid
each night, regardless of how much horse grease was slathered
on them. They had to be broken free with mallets, damaging the
winding springs and teeth. The dried and seasoned timbers
they'd brought to assemble the weapons had begun to soak and
swell the first day, in many cases splitting the frames. The
replacements they'd cut from the nearby woods were still green
and springy. They warped and flexed, bollixing accuracy and
reducing throw weight.

The engineers had managed to get about half of the siege
weapons operational by lengthening the casting arms and attach-
ing sacks of rocks to the lower end. Range and payload had been
cut in half, but at least rocks were being thrown at the defenders.
Another stone hit the keep. *Clack.* Not the sound of a war being
won.

The only glimmer in an otherwise grim picture was that the
core of the castle's defenses relied on archers whose bowstrings
fared no better in the rain than catapults. Arrows wouldn't be a
factor until the rain stopped. If it stopped. Ever.

She looked from the catapult along the siege line and felt her
already waterlogged spirits sink another notch. *None* of her siege
equipment seemed to be working. The shovel, customarily even

more the soldier's friend than the sword, was more bane than boon. The troops had been set to building defensive trenches, fire pits, and convellations to ring the small castle. The rain softened the alluvial deposits and underlying clay, turning the valley floor into layers that alternately ran like custard and clung like glue. Trench walls required reinforcement to function properly, so more soldiers trudged off to the nearby woods to cut and hew logs. Four days of miserable, back-breaking work, all to get one day's siegework done.

The wicker baskets designed to make earthworks and palisades functioned no better. Water collected in them, soaking and softening the reeds until the baskets burst. In other places the mud simply ran out between the loose weave. Picks were pointless in ground whose single most charming aspect was an affection so great it desired to cling to horses' hooves and soldiers' boots, and occasionally sought ownership of contested footgear. A hundred tiny battles for sole-possession could be fought simply crossing from tent to latrine.

The obligatory tunnel, designed to undermine and collapse the wall, hadn't made it more than a quarter furlong before it came glorping down. The cave-ins, by some small mercy, weren't lethal. The troops caught inside merely had to worm to the surface to be rescued.

She sighed. She should have guessed that it would be her flank of the "Big Push" that bogged down. Her regiment should have already undertaken the cheerful battery of the keep. The siege plan noted that the engineering troops were supposed to have been sitting on their wicker baskets today, watching the walls fall in. The assaulting forces should have been sharpening their swords and readying themselves for a half-day's light work rather than squatting on their haunches and picking their running noses.

She looked across the miserable, gluey plain. She'd planned for the keep's investment to take three days, followed by a battery lasting two more. Her engineers had agreed that she'd allowed enough time to punch enough holes for the infantry to pour through. She'd thought to play it safe and allow herself a few extra days in case of setbacks. Her Lordship Amberly had chafed at even that small delay.

The thought of Her Lor'ship made her shiver. She recalled Amberly, resplendent in furs and gold, smiling as she promised a fiefdom to the first commander to break through vile Isely's defensive line. Grinstable had salivated at the size of the reward, and had so fully expected that plum to land in her lap she had almost missed what followed. Lord Amberly's smile had changed, becoming feral as she described the rewards that would accrue to those who failed her. The skulls from the last batch of object lessons were still drying on Her Lor'ship's mantlepiece.

Grinstable's planning for the unexpected hadn't included uncooperative weather, a fact that Amberly would accept as both true and irrelevant. Grinstable knew now that she'd have to wait for the rains to stop and *then* for the plain to dry out enough that the assault party didn't bog down. Only then could she knock the damned walls down and maybe win the prize. Until then . . .

A sudden squall accented her thoughts, an evil gust of cold breath pelting drizzle *up* under her hat. She sneezed. She had three days left to produce one captured keep and a reasonably healthy advance, or be the guest of honor at one of Her Lor'ship's motivational dinners. Not at all a fate she relished.

She cursed the castle, shaking her fist and mouthing obscenities. The tower stood mockingly defiant. The irony was that the castle that blocked her egress from the valley like a cork in a bottle was a cheesy battlemented wall surrounding a moss-backed, sag-shingled donjon. It couldn't mass enough population to make up a decent-sized nuptial feast, much less a credible defense. Yet, so far it hadn't had to. She pounded her fist against her rusty thigh. It was *so* unfair.

A slapping roar drew her eye to the right. She saw a flurry of motion from the encircling trench and shouts of dismay. "Call the commander," she heard. She sighed and turned toward the disturbance. She navigated carefully around the worst puddles and stepped past a dispirited clot of troopers trying to feed wet hay to wet horses.

She came around the low hillock made from tunnel spoil and saw mud-covered engineers emerging from a soggy hole like half-drowned rats from a sewer.

Engineer Krebbel was the last to surface, covered from head to toe in brown sludge, yet still carrying his pickax and lantern. He sat on the inside of the trench and began digging mud out of his ears. Grinstable, fearing the worst, crossed to him.

"How long?" she demanded.

Krebbel continued to peel mud out of his short, scraggly beard. "Well, we're gettin' there," he replied. "We had a pump to draw the water out 'an we were usin' sand to stabilize the floor. It seemed to work. We just have to shore it up better."

"How long?" she repeated, her patience fraying as another tunnel of water found its way underneath her scarf and down her back.

He threw a clot of mud across the ditch. "Assumin' this keeps up," he said with a vague gesture skyward, "it'll be mebbe' two or three weeks to get a shaft all the way under the keep. Another week to undermine and drop the wall."

"Three weeks?" she repeated, appalled. "You told me yesterday that it would be a week at the most."

"That was then," Krebbel said. "I thought we could dry it out enough to work with it. There's so much water in the ground that it stays the consistency of oatmeal."

Grinstable looked grim. "Her Lor'ship wants the Big Push started in two days. We're supposed to have this reduced by then."

Krebbel shrugged. "Call off the weather. Then I'll get you inside. Until then?" He shrugged just as she heard another roar from inside the tunnel. A breeze like a wet breath *whuffed* past her cheek a moment later.

"There she goes." Krebbel sighed morosely.

Grinstable walked away. She knew it wasn't fair to blame Krebbel. He had done his best and continued to pursue the original siege plan long past the point where it showed lack of any promise. Krebbel was her fault, too. She'd selected him as the chief engineer precisely as a result of his reputation for being loathe to let go of an idea once he'd sunk his teeth into it. Grinstable suspected that the engineer could only handle one thought at a time and hated change. She sighed. She'd wanted a numb-wit who wouldn't upstage her with innovations. "Be careful about what you wish for," she grumbled to herself, "you just might get it."

She glanced at the low hills, wondering if she could bypass the whole damned rock pile and press her forces into the vales beyond. Her Lor'ship was big on resource denial. She could leave a small force to keep the defenders bottled up and run her supply convoys through the narrow channels on each side of the keep.

She shook her head. The narrow valley floor was entirely within bowshot of the battlement. She knew with grinding certainty that the moment she moved past the castle, the rain would stop, the sun would shine, and she'd be cut off. The castle's archers would mince anything crossing in the open.

She had no choice: the damn thing had to be taken. She looked up and down the valley, considering an assault along a narrow front. Grinstable knew the one thing Her Lor'ship disliked more than blundering commanders was blundering commanders hiding mistakes under piles of bodies. She rubbed her chin. Successful commanders, however, had considerably more latitude. She looked again at the churned field between the siege lines and the castle. Perhaps the mud didn't look *that* bad.

She sent a messenger to gather her battle leaders. They met her near the collapsed tunnel, glumly aware of why they had been summoned. They cobbled together an assault for that afternoon and soon had the expected outcome: fifteen hundred men and women bogged down in the mud, slogging painfully toward the castle. The assault had a chance until the troops' way was blocked with a lambent green barrier. Grinstable cursed and stormed, tossed her helmet on the ground, and pled for a counterspell. All to no avail. Her muddy troops pushed and prodded against the faintly glowing barrier but had no success in breaching it. The attack fizzled and the soldiers trudged wearily back to their lines. The castle's defenders never fired a shot.

She watched the lines passing her, heads down and expressions glum. The siege was a failure. She saw no choice but to write a letter to Her Lordship admitting her inability to accomplish her mission. Lord Karin Amberley wasn't likely to take the news with a philosophic shrug.

She sat at her desk as afternoon faded into evening, surrounded by crumpled pieces of paper and listening to the drizzle fall on her tent. Big, fat drops leaked through the sodden material to spatter onto everything: her map, her bed, and her rust-speck-led armor. She'd long since considered and discarded the idea of putting out catch basins; that would have required flooring the place with tin.

She looked at her wrinkle-tipped fingers, blew on them to warm them, and picked up her pen to start again. "Less whiney," she said to herself, "try to beg more coherently." She was careful not to let the nib dig into the damp paper. It would tear easily.

She heard the *squit-squish* of hard infantry boots through the mud as someone approached her tent. She quickly sat up and brushed back her long hair from her face. It simply wouldn't do for her subordinates to see her brought so low.

The sentry entered her tent and stood to attention, water dripping solidly onto Grinstable's sodden carpets.

"There's two dwarfs out 'ere to see you ma'arm," he shouted.

"That would be dwar-*ves,* trooper," she answered, "and *ma-am,* not ma-arm. Carry on."

"Yes, *ma-am,*" he shouted, "carry'in on, *ma-am.*" He did a clashing about-turn and stamped out, leaving brown footprints, several clumps of brownish gray earth, and a rusty puddle in his wake. "If I live to be a hundred," Grinstable muttered, "I'll never understand the soldiering mentality." She raised her voice to the trooper outside. "Bring them here to me."

She heard the soldier's muffled voice above the *stamp-squish* of his boots. "*Yes, ma-am.* Bringin' 'em 'ere to you, *ma-am*!" He stomped away.

She stood to compose herself for her guests, putting on her cloak of rank and tidying her hair. She wondered what in the hell the dwarves wanted. Her Lor'ship's dwarven units were mostly in the center or on the left, so it was unlikely these two were messengers or emissaries. She'd made herself so obnoxious at the commanders' call that the odds approached zero that another leader was sending her quiet help or a back-channel message. She hopped pensively from one cold foot to the other while strange voices approached the command tent.

The tent flap jerked back and the dwarves entered. They looked *dense* and compact with their dour features, broad shoulders, and heavy armor. The leader swept off her low helm and met Grinstable's eye. The captain felt the dwarf's measuring stare. She'd have given her eyeteeth to know what was going on behind that still expression.

"May I ask what you think you are doing?" the lead dwarf said, her voice short and irritable.

"I am conducting a siege," Grinstable replied, as though the fiasco outside deserved the name. "Why?"

"Is that what you call this?" the dwarf-lady scoffed. "Who gave you permission to cut trees from our woods, trample our brickyard, pollute our picturesque stream, and shout and clatter all day and all night?"

"I," Grinstable said, drawing herself up to her full height, "am Captain Grinstable, of Lord Karin Amberly's service. We are besieging the keep of the evil malefactor, Lord Dane Isely."

"Your evil malefactor asks permission before cutting our trees," the dwarf replied dryly, "and doesn't let his horses eat our posies."

"I'm afraid we're going to be here awhile," Grinstable said, trying desperately to keep her voice neutral, "with all that entails for your streams and flowerbeds. Unless you know some way to bring this siege to a hasty conclusion."

The dwarf gave her a measuring look. "That, Cap'n Barnstubble, is what we unwashed call a 'leading question.'" The dwarf rubbed her chin. "Still, if it will get you off our land . . ." The dwarf looked up decisively. "If your siege were to be concluded, would you go?"

"Yes," Grinstable said, "all except for our supply convoys."

The dwarf made a rude face. "I knew there'd be an 'except' worked in there. We'll accept your wagons *if* they roll through without stopping." She smiled. "*And* you pay an indemnity."

"Done," said Grinstable, fully aware that such an agreement was beyond her authority. "Who are you, anyway?"

"I'm Glemp, lead factor of the Posied Hill Dwarves. At least we had posies until you lot came along." She pointed over her shoulder to the second dwarf, who grinned at her with a mouth full of broad, yellow teeth. "This amulet-covered fool beside me is Eod, my master of Smoke and Mirrors. He'll take care of your castle for you." Grinstable looked at the second dwarf. His armor seemed entirely covered with talismans and charms. Eod held up a hand in a friendly gesture. Grinstable noticed that he was missing two of his fingers.

Glemp saw her frown. "Captain Brimstample, Eod here commands the Dwarven Demolition Corps, Third Squad."

"Umm, that's Grinstable," Krebbel supplied from behind the dwarves.

"Whatever," Glemp answered. "And who might you be?"

Krebbel tapped himself on the chest. "I'm the right flank's engineering chief."

Glemp made a noncommittal sound, something between a grunt and a snort.

"Umm, are you here to replace me?" Krebbel asked mournfully.

"They're from the local government; they're here to help," Grinstable interjected.

"Oh, good," Krebbel said. "We've tried everything we can to reduce this castle. Mining, trenches, battery. It'll work, but it'll take time." He looked around at the ring of silent faces. "It's the mud, you see," he added lamely.

Glemp gave him a long look. Krebbel subsided into silence. "Now that we've gotten past that," Glemp said, "shall we get started?"

"Don't you need tents and a camp, or something?" Grinstable asked.

"No," Glemp replied, "we won't be here that long."

Grinstable tried hard to suppress her disbelief. "How many are you?"

Glemp shrugged, her shoulders clashing up and down. "Eight. One squad."

Krebbel made a rude noise. "Eight? That's it?"

Glemp looked nonplussed. "One squad, one castle. No big deal."

"When do you think you'll be through?" Grinstable asked disingeniously.

Glemp fixed her with a long gaze. "About this time tomorrow, I should think."

Grinstable tried hard not to show any reaction, even though inside she was cavorting and whooping. "That would be fine," she said evenly. "Let me know if there is anything you desire."

Glemp took a long, measuring look at Krebbel. "Just stay out of our way."

Krebbel opened his mouth to speak. Grinstable leapt into the breach. "Of course we will." She fixed the engineer with a glare she hoped would keep him silent. "Won't we, engineer?"

Krebbel yawned and dug into his ear with one grubby fingertip.

"Thank you, Captain Bramstoker," Glemp said.

"That's Barnstubble," the Captain replied. "Oh, never mind."

"What?" Eod asked.

"In case I forgot to mention it, Eod is a little hard of hearing," Glemp supplied.

"Peachy," Grinstable grumbled.

"What?" Eod asked again.

Glemp turned to leave. Eod stood there grinning.

"Eod," she said. He didn't respond. "E-O-D," she repeated, slowly and loudly. He turned toward her. She made sweeping gestures with her hands. He grinned and followed her out.

Grinstable collapsed back into her chair and pinched herself. She simply couldn't believe the rate at which her fortune had turned. She pulled a fresh piece of parchment out of her camp desk and began to compose a long letter to Her Lor'ship, advising her that while things had begun slowly, they were now moving along splendidly. She anticipated no difficulties in making her prong of the assault on time.

Captain Grinstable took her evening meal of vegetable stew inside her tent, desperately trying to ignore the squeaking and creaking that pervaded the evening camp. The rain continued its interminable fall, made worse by the loss of the sun's meager warmth. She was chilled already, and night was hardly begun.

She hadn't the slightest idea of what to make of the dwarves. Within hours they had set up a long pulley system with buckets suspended beneath, attached to a pedaled paddle wheel. The buckets would snake out of the enlarged tunnel hole, cross the open space to the paddle wheel, then tip into rectangular troughs mounted in the beds of the carts that they used in place of wagons. The mud was then hauled away to some dwarfish mystery.

The excavation was being carried out with a device they called a "screw-auger." The machine looked something like a giant metal rutabaga with grooves and channels cut in its face. Two dwarves behind a heavy shield pedaled the thing while another pair pushed the whole assembly into the shaft. Mud cut from the tunnel's face flowed down the channels and into the buckets which then creaked away to be emptied. The return pulley in turn fed fresh pails to be filled. She found the whole device fascinating and incomprehensible.

Other dwarves worked close behind the screw-auger, hammering together arches to support the soft mud ceiling and laying boards along the floors. Krebbel openly scoffed at the process, then gave Grinstable a black look as she reminded him that in two hours they'd surpassed his best two-day tunneling effort. He stormed away in a huff.

The squealing from the pedal-bucket contraption was driving her crazy. She stood up from her lukewarm stew bowl and emerged from her tent. She was about to rudely suggest the bucket-pedaler put some grease on the gears when she saw Eod riding a donkey and leading a two-wheeled cart up toward the tunnel mouth. The cart appeared to be completely filled by a bulbous iron sphere.

Grinstable noticed that both the horse's hooves and the cart wheels were shod in felt. Eod led the animal with exaggerated care. "What's all this in aid of?" she demanded.

Eod got down from his pony after kissing one of the dozen amulets he wore around his neck.

"It contains the Magic Smoke," he said in the too-loud manner of the nearly deaf.

"Is it like an air poison?" she asked, worried about the effect on her troops that such a thing might have in the capricious valley winds.

"No," he replied as conspiratorially as his booming voice would allow, "it's the Big Damage." He pointed toward the tunnel. "Once we've dug the shaft, we'll pour the Magic Smoke down the hole and let it seep toward the end. Then, when we're ready . . ." He made a billowing gesture with his hands.

Grinstable looked long and hard at the sphere. "That will drop the wall?" she asked quietly.

"Hum?" Eod answered. "Yeah, it'll do the trick." He squelched over to the cylinder and tapped it lightly. Grinstable expected to hear a hollow sound emanate and was surprised at the solid *thunk* it made. She walked over and put her own palm on the metal. It was warm to the touch—body warm. She jerked her hand away, as though burned. Eod laughed.

"How does it work?" she demanded.

"Eh?" Eod answered. She repeated her question, this time more loudly. "Well," he answered, "once we've got it poured into the hole, we'll focus the sun's rays with the aid of a pair of curved mirrors. That'll set it off."

Grinstable felt her stomach lurch. "But it's been raining; there hasn't been any sun."

"Yeah," Eod agreed, looking up into the cloud-covered night sky, "that could be a problem." He grinned at her. "But I've been lucky so far." He waved his half-hand at her. She wondered what constituted luck to a dwarf with two missing fingers.

She sat the night away, looking hopefully up at the sky and imagining she could see patches of stars through the milk-colored clouds. Her letter predicting victory weighed heavily on her mind. The dwarves worked all night as well, clanking and squeaking as they moved toward the keep's wall. Grinstable thought she could see a barely perceptible hump in the ground, like the path of a giant mole, as the dwarves' machine chewed through the mud. The wagons appeared like clockwork to take the spoil away while the pedalers worked without rest or relief.

Just before dawn she saw them pull the soil-caked machine out of the hole and start to push it back to the woods that marked the dwarven frontier.

Eod appeared as the clouds in the east lightened, carrying a stub of candle and a curved and polished bronze shield. He walked purposefully toward the tunnel mouth. She pursed her lips as he stepped past. "What are you doing?" she asked him.

He looked up at the east. "About daybreak, I should think," he answered.

She rolled her eyes. "May I watch?" she said again, considerably more loudly.

He made a face. "Well, you don't have to shout. I don't mind if you come along. Just don't get in the way and try not to knock any supports down." He touched his finger to his nose. "Cave-ins, you know."

She looked toward the tunnel mouth. "I'm not afraid."

"Suit yourself," he said, then went down the hole as smoothly as a terrier after a rat.

She followed him, stooping where he walked upright. The tunnel was round with a flattened floor, except where roots poked through. She followed him into the murk, grimly aware that his tiny mining lamp didn't provide enough illumination for a bat, much less a person.

She grew increasingly aware of the damp, heavy pressure overhead and the creaking of the supporting arches. She wanted to beg him to stop, to take her back into the light where tons of mud didn't threaten to smother her. She nearly reached out to him twice, stilling herself only when she remembered that she'd essentially forced herself on him.

She almost blundered into him when they reached the end. The tip of the shaft was barely wider that the tunnel itself, just enough to turn the machine around and pedal it away.

She looked around in confusion. "This is it?" she demanded. "Where are the galleries running under the walls? Where are the timbers holding things up until they get burned away? Where is the kindling to set the place on fire?"

Eod winced as her voice rose an octave in the confined space. "Shoosh," he said, making calming gestures with his hands. "You keep that caterwauling up 'an you'll drop the roof for sure."

"What about the galleries?" she repeated.

"Don't need 'em," he replied. "The Magic Smoke'll do it."

He began to position the bronze mirror with the concave side pointing toward the distant exit. He sighted through a tiny hole cut in its center and back toward the pinprick of daylight at the far end of the tunnel. Once he had it perfectly aligned, he wedged it into the mud and took a small stand and ball of twine from his pockets. He wet his thumb and forefinger, twirled the end of the string into a point, and fed it though the hole. He stretched the string to its full length and carefully placed the stand at the right distance, pounding it into the mud to give it the right relative height. He then took the candle stub and set it on the stand. Grinstable watched the whole process with a baffled expression.

"Now what?" she asked.

"Now we leave," he answered.

Her perplexed expression only grew as she followed him back up the shaft.

She emerged into the light, hoping to see blue sky and sunlight. Dreary clouds greeted her instead. Eod didn't seemed fazed in the least. He carefully backed the placid cart horse up to the hole and positioned the wagon so that a small stopcock in the bottom of the cylinder was oriented directly over the maw. He then placed a coiled piece of wood beneath the stopcock and opened it. Gray smoke began to slowly emerge and worm its way down the wood. Grinstable stepped back, alarmed, as did those of her command who had gathered to gawk. The smoke moved sluggishly, like cold gravy, rather than wafting as honest smoke should. She stood, rooted in fascination as it drifted slowly into the cave mouth and deeper under the earth.

"What makes it creep like that?" she asked in a strangled voice.

"The tunnel's cut at an angle," Eod replied. "It's seeking the lowest level."

He waited until the last of the smoke had trickled out, then closed the stopcock and led the horse and cart away. He then positioned a mirror, identical in all respects to the one deep underground, in front of the tunnel mouth.

She looked curiously at him. "Now what?" she asked when he was finished.

"We wait," he replied.

"For what?" she asked.

He made a vague gesture at the sky. "For me to get lucky," he said.

She puttered away the morning, readying her assault troops and taking meetings with her subordinates. She wrote a flurry of letters, tidied her tent, and began drawing battle plans for the victorious advance. None of this stopped her from running outside every few minutes to see if the sky showed any signs of clearing.

Her sandglass suggested the approach of the noon hour. She glanced outside to peer upward as a messenger rode up, bearing a sealed scroll and an officious air.

"For you," he said, handing her the document without any show of courtesy.

She broke the seal and unrolled it, ignoring the drizzle that blurred the ink even as she read it.

From Her Most Puissant Lord, Karin Amberly,
To Her Brave Commanders,

It has come to our attention that the rude and imprudent weather has conspired to rob us of our timetable. We have graciously extended the planned assault for a week, to permit the base and insubordinate clouds to clear and the mud to dry. Should any leader manage success in despite of this unruliness, then our rewards shall be commensurate with your success.

Signed,
X
(Her Mark)

Grinstable tapped the scroll against her teeth. The messenger sighed loudly to draw her attention.

"Yes," she said absently.

"Well," he said, "have you any reply?"

She frowned and looked skyward. A small patch of blue, touched with golden yellow, appeared almost directly overhead. "Tell Her Lordship that 'We persevere.' "

The courier looked skeptical. " 'We persevere?' That's it?"

She walked away, heading back toward the tunnel mouth. "That's it," she said. She heard him turn his horse and ride away.

Krebbel, still in his muddy clothes, looked at her as she rejoined the group. Eod pranced around, carrying a third mirror that he pointed this way and that. A shaft of sunlight broke through, startling Grinstable with its intensity. Eod leapt into its yellow wash, angled the mirror and caught the light. A clean beam connected the two mirrors, then plunged underground.

"It'll only be a few seconds now," Eod cried.

"Damn," Grinstable cursed. "Krebbel, call the assault parties forward!"

Glemp appeared from around the troopers' clustered legs. "Assault parties? Whatever for?"

Grinstable looked at her. "Why, to capture the keep, of course."

Glemp looked puzzled. "There isn't going to be any keep to capture, Captain Renstimple."

"But," Grinstable said, "we *have* to capture it. It's part of the plan."

"*Now* you tell us," Glemp said irritably. "Yesterday, all you said was that you wanted the siege ended as soon as possible. You didn't say anything about leaving it intact."

Grinstable's mouth made a tiny "O." She turned toward Eod just as he dropped the shield and ran. A tongue of flame shot out of the cave mouth like a dragon's breath. A deep bass rumble shook the earth. She turned, horrified, toward the keep. The entire body of it seemed engulfed in a gray haze that mushroomed upward. A rocking shockwave swept over them, blowing everyone off their feet. Boulders, debris, and rubble rained down.

Grinstable sat up and stared, open-mouthed and stunned, as the stone hail slowly subsided. A crater, as deep as three men were tall, stretched from one side of the narrow valley to the other.

The blue hole in the clouds closed. A steady rain began to fall. The steep crater began at once to fill with water, blocking the valley even more completely than the keep had previously done.

The Light in the Forest

Michael Scott

Once it had stood taller than a tall man, a beautiful, elegant pillar of stone, incised with swirls of script that were older than the land. The first orcs had worshiped around it, and later dwarves and the hill giants had claimed it in turn and had fought over it, until the cause of their dispute had been forgotten and only the enmity remained.

Time and the elements conspired to bury the pillar beneath a covering of earth, and though scholars of many races had sought its location, it was never found. Eventually the Pillar of Stone was relegated to scattered legends and finally dismissed as nothing more than an amalgamation of a score of similar myths.

But at the heart of every myth there is a grain of truth.

"I thought I saw something." Dolena reined in her mount and stood in the stirrups, shading her eyes against the setting sun. "In the valley," she added.

"It's nothing," Brons snapped. He tugged at the reins of the lead ox, urging it forward. "Let's move on. The light is fading and I don't want to be out on the mountains after dark."

"I saw something," Dolena insisted. She raised her hand, and the six guards she had employed in Skerry reined in their

mounts and reached for their weapons. Dolena's reputation as a
trail guard was respected throughout the north lands.

The warrior walked her mount to the edge of the trail and
peered into the shadowed valley below. There was a hollow
emptiness in the pit of her stomach, a creeping chill on the back
of her neck that she had come to know and fear. It had kept her
alive through too many campaigns and skirmishes along the borders and during the Island Wars. Staring into the valley, the
woman allowed her gaze to roam over the dense covering of trees,
not looking for anything, simply waiting for something to impress
itself on her consciousness. When she realized she was squinting,
she forced herself to relax and open her eyes wide. She was two
and thirty summers now and her eyesight was beginning to fade;
she could no longer make out far distances, and at night her sight
deteriorated dramatically. There would come a time when she
could no longer earn her keep as a paid mercenary, a bodyguard
or, like now, as a trail guard. She wasn't sure what she could do
then. Her options were limited; she had no tradable skills other
than her weaponscraft, she had never been pretty, and the vivid
white scar—the result of a brief encounter with an Erg raider—
across the deeply tanned flesh of her forehead didn't help.

There!

A flash of color, indistinct, fragmentary against the gloom.

Deliberately not turning her head, aware of the object at the
very periphery of her vision, Dolena tried to work out what could
be prowling through these dark northern forests at this time of
year. The list was depressingly large.

The crippled dwarf, known only as Crane, urged the shaggy
mountain pony across to her. Her mount whickered nervously
and pranced sideways, breaking her concentration.

"What is is?" Crane snapped, voice rasping and labored.

Dolena pulled off her leather cap and ran her fingers through
close-cropped hair. "There's something in the valley."

"Let's move," Brons called, voice echoing flatly off the stones.

The dwarf ignored him. "What do you see?"

"More a feeling," Dolena murmured.

Brons clambered down off the wagon and strode up, sour
sweat mingled with the rich odor of oxen enveloping him in an
almost tangible miasma. Dolena suspected that there was orc

blood in the stinking wagon leader; she had never see a man so ugly and with such an ill-temper. "I'll not delay here because this *hruptch*i has a feeling . . ." he began.

The dwarf turned his head, one white blind eye fixing on the wagon master's bald skull. His remaining eye was black as pitch, without any white. "You I hired to lead this wagon across the mountains," he said, every word a rasping effort, "because you came highly recommended. Dolena I hired as guard because she too was as highly regarded."

"I heard Dolena was killed by a vampire," Brons muttered. "This is probably some deserter taken her name. Who recommended her anyway? Some rogue . . ."

"The same rogue recommended you both," Crane snapped.

Brons backed away, glaring at Dolena, who hadn't even glanced at him during the exchange. The big man started down the wagon train, checking each ox, running a callused hand over the large wooden wheels of the eight wagons. Only when he was sure neither Crane nor Dolena could see him did he spit his disgust into the dirt.

"Something down there troubles me," Dolena said quietly, leaning forward on the pommel of her saddle.

Crane looked into the shadows. "I can see nothing," he admitted, "but I've lived this long because I've learned to trust the opinions of those I respect."

"I've done nothing to earn your respect," Dolena said, glancing sidelong at him. "But you are held in high esteem by those I respect . . . and that is good enough for me," Crane said, lips moving in what might have passed for a smile. He nodded toward the valley. "Are we in any danger?"

"I'm not sure. I feel . . . uneasy."

"What would you do?"

"We should make a secure camp for the night, double the guards, keep the fires burning all night. I'll go and investigate."

"Is that wise?"

"It is always wise to know your fears."

"And then face them?"

"Facing them is not always wise," Dolena said grimly.

*   *   *

They made camp for the night in the gutted shell of a barbaric temple. At some time in the ancient past, fire had raged through the heart of the building, blackening the walls, coating the ceiling with a thick covering of soot, obscuring the ornate and beautiful frescoes and patterns incised into it. Later, the forest had crept in and claimed the temple, body-thick vines snaking through windows and gaping doors, cracking walls, uprooting the tiny intricate tilework. Then, for some obscure reason, the encroaching forest had died back, withered away in an almost circular pattern around the building, leaving dead vines, like skeletal fingers, clutching the walls and splayed across the floors.

Although Dolena had no time for the arrogant wagon master, she had to admit that he knew his job. Ignoring the larger buildings, which offered shelter of sorts to men and wagons, but which would have been impossible to defend, he had brought the wagons into the central courtyard and had them surround a tiny stone hut which housed nothing more than the tumbled remains of a well. Brons had directed Crane to the hut, and although he had offered to carry some of the bags, the dwarf had refused. Dolena noticed that some of them were sealed with expensive amulets. Even if the bags were stolen, they could not be opened without the appropriately matched amulet. Any attempt to force them would reduce the contents to cinders. Not for the first time, she wondered what cargo was so precious that it required six guards in addition to herself. She had encountered Crane in the town on several occasions; the crippled dwarf came down from the highlands two or three times a season to buy supplies for the community of dwarves who worked in the abandoned lava mines. The dwarf's reputation usually protected him, though she had heard the stories that Crane was perfectly capable of defending himself from those who would either mock him or steal from him. She had been one of the troop who had investigated travelers' tales of a group of flayed bodies lying in a field off the highway half a year previously.

The five identifiable bodies turned out to be remains of a party of army deserters who had been terrorizing the road for the best part of a season. The local judge had decided that they had been killed by werewolves; Dolena had discovered that Crane had ridden the road on the day the bodies had been discovered. When she had returned to the scene of the butchery, she had discovered the evidence of the dwarf's misshapen footprints in the soft earth. They were overlaid by the prints of distinctive pointed-toed army boots. Reading the signs, she had decided that Crane had been taken by two of the deserters, who had marched him into the clearing where he had been surrounded by three men. Crane had then done something which had turned five ruthless brigands into bloody meat. But if he was skilled in magic, why did he need someone like her to guard the wagons?

Crane appeared out of the well house and looked around, the gestures quick, almost birdlike. Dolena allowed herself to be absorbed into the shadows, but Crane turned to look at her, single eye glistening, what passed for a smile twisting his lips. He called her to him with a quick gesture.

"This place meets with your approval?"

"It will not withstand a determined assault by a group of armed men, but it will see us against wolves or brigands."

"More, much more, lives in these forests," Crane said softly. He disappeared into the shadows of the well house and Dolena hesitated in the doorway, unwilling to enter the gloom until her eyes had adjusted to the light. She followed the dwarf's progress by the sound of his voice. "I have seen such sights that would freeze your blood."

"No doubt," she said dryly.

Crane chuckled. "Aaah, but I forget, you are Dolena . . . once called the Pitiless, I believe. In the far south they use your name as an oath; in places, *dolen* or *dolena* has come to mean sudden savage death."

"Those days are over," the woman snapped. She lowered her voice, which had risen enough to draw attention. Brons had stepped away from one of the wagons and was watching her intently. "Long over." The hand on her belt rested close to the hilt of the dagger. "I would prefer if this information went no further."

"It is none of my business." Crane sank to the ground, back against the chilled stone wall and stretched his legs in front of him, straightening his stiffened left knee with both hands. "Forgive me. My people are clannish, we gossip, and we are cursed with long memories. And when we can trade in nothing else, there is always information. However, no one here knows of your previous existence; I give you my word."

"That is good enough for me." Dolena allowed her hand to fall to her side. "I rode into battle alongside Thorking of the High Marches. He was one of the few commanders I trusted without question. His word was law."

"He was related to my sister's husband's family," Crane said absently. "He fell at the Bridge of the Ford."

"I stood with him. I was one of the lucky ones."

"Have you any idea what you saw in the valley earlier?" Crane asked into the long silence that followed. His head was turned so that it appeared he was looking away, though his single eye was fixed on her face.

"No."

"But it disturbed you."

"Yes."

"And now you're going in search of it?"

"I would rest happier."

"Could have been the sunlight sparkling off a pool of water . . . picking out silica in an outcropping of rock . . . the bark of a tree catching the light."

"I can tell the difference," Dolena said quickly. "This *felt* different." She squinted toward the dwarf. He was sitting back in the shadows and she found it difficult to make out his features.

"An excuse," he said eventually. "Admit it, you are curious."

"I will admit that I am frightened. But I would be falling down in my duty if I did not investigate."

"Your duty is to guard this wagon train."

"Why?" Dolena asked boldly. Crouched down on her haunches, she stared hard at the dwarf. "Why do you need a guard this time? You've never had need of guards before. And I know you can take care of yourself."

"You ask too many questions," Crane grumbled.

"It keeps me alive. So, I'll ask you again. Why do you need guards?"

Brons moved slowly through the ruined and tumbled buildings, gradually edging away from the other drovers, noting the positions of Dolena's guards, making his way to the shattered storehouse behind the well house. A quick look over his shoulder, ensuring that no one was watching him, then he ducked into the gutted shell, big-knuckled hand clutching his knife so that it would not rasp off the stones. The voices of the guard and the dwarf echoed off the stones. The drover's thin lips drew back from stained teeth. He had been leading wagons through these mountains since he'd been a youth; his father had shown him this place and demonstrated the acoustic qualities of the walls. Brons had grown wealthy simply listening to some of his wealthy passengers talking: the whispered location of money, the muttered revelations of military and trade secrets, the sniggered revelations of indiscretions. Brons, too, had noted the seals on the bags that never left Crane's side and the unusual presence of armed guards. Whatever the dwarf was guarding must be treasure indeed.

And Brons wanted it.

Lying flat on the dry, dusty stones, Brons pressed the side of his face against the rock and listened.

"You are aware that the earth has shifted recently?" The dwarf's voice was low, made rasping by the stones.

"I've heard stories of earthquakes and upheavals in the high mountains and valleys. An unusual alignment of the moons and planets, I understand."

"Possibly. In places mountains have split, gullies have appeared like wounds through the ancient stone, valleys have disappeared, whole communities have vanished, wiped away as if they never existed."

"I don't see . . ." Dolena's voice was harsh, masculine, arrogant. When the time was right, Brons would kill her.

"New creatures haunt the highlands. Some resemble the creatures of legend and history, but others . . . who knows what has crept from the heart of a shattered mountain? Who knows what has awakened? That's why I hired guards. I'm carrying minerals and salts essential to my tribe's survival. They must get through."

Brons squeezed his eyes shut and bit the inside of his cheek to prevent himself from crying out. It was just his luck to go into high mountains which were acrawl with monsters.

"Do you still want to go into the valley to investigate the light in the forest?

"In view of what you've told me, I've even less choice."

*   *   *

Dressed in her usual worn leathers, but with her face and hands blackened with wet soot, Dolena crept from the camp shortly after nightfall. She had elected to go on foot; riding at night across unfamiliar ground was dangerous, riding through a forest at night was tantamount to suicide. She knew of an island tribe to the west which tied criminals to a rigid frame set onto the back of an oxen and then drove it into a forest. If the victims survived the wild ride through the forest, they were allowed to go free. Less than one in twenty survived; the rest were impaled and scored by low branches.

With the Lady riding high in the night sky, painting the forest in light and shadow, her route was relatively easy. Twice she stopped: once when something that smelled suspiciously like boar lumbered through the underground to her left, and again when a faintly luminescent nightsnake slithered lazily across the path. It raised its flattened head to stare at her with milk yellow eyes before curling away, allowing Dolena to see the distinct outline of a small tree fox lodged in its throat. The guard slid her knife into its sheath and pressed on.

It was close to midnight when she spotted the first glitter of light directly ahead.

Dolena stopped and stepped into the shadows, deliberately looking away from the point of light, judging the height of the Lady in the sky, gauging how and where she would cast her shadows. When she turned her head, the light remained. Touching the knives strapped to her forearms, loosening the short sword on her belt, she stepped out of the shadows and moved toward the light.

She smelled werewolf spoor first, the odor rank and cloying. A few steps further on and she caught the unmistakable stench of orc and the bittersweet perfume of female centaur. Since her eyesight had begun deteriorating, she had come to rely more and more on her other senses, especially her sense of smell, which had always been acute. There were other odors here, some serpentine and unrecognizable, others dead and rotting, like zombies or dullahans. Once she stopped and ran her hand across the shadowed ground; it was pocked with hoof, paw and footprints . . . and all of them were heading in one direction. None returned.

Heart thundering, stomach cramping, Dolena wiped sweating

palms on the legs of her trousers and walked on, nerves tingling. The light was clearer now, though the source was still invisible, lost below a black-edged rise directly ahead. Streamers and tendrils of yellow-white light snaked through the trees and the ankle-high mist that coiled and twisted sinuously across the roots was tinged with alabaster.

Drawing her short sword, she dropped to the ground and snaked her way through the churned icy mud toward the rise.

Tracking the woman was relatively easy. On the few occasions he lost the trail, Brons simply continued in the general direction of the point of light, crossing and recrossing the trail until he picked up her tracks again. Like most drovers, Brons could read a trail, identifying animals and beasts by their tracks, while the depth of the impression and the crispness of the edges allowed him to estimate how much time had passed since the track had been made. He stopped when he encountered the other tracks in the earth. Animals, beasts, were-creatures had all traveled down this narrow path. Most of the prints were days old, though some of the werewolf spoor was fresher, certainly within the day. Brons straightened and unshipped the studded flail as he slowly backed away. He didn't want to meet with any of the creatures that had walked this path. Individually they were dangerous; together they were lethal. He had survived because he had always been cautious—some would have said cowardly, but they were all dead. Let the beasts in the forest feast off the woman.

He was turning away when he caught the brilliant flash of white light. Before it faded it turned yellow, like polished gold.

Greed drew him on.

It looked like stone.

Spear-high, body-thick, with a rounded cap, the white stone was etched with symbols and twisting curling lines reminiscent of the ancient scripts she had seen on some of the island temples. The stone was the color of chalk, but shot through with tendrils of green and gold, black and red. But this was no stone. It throbbed and pulsed with soft white light, and occasionally a shimmering strand of light twisted through it—yellow-white, the texture of gold, ice-white, the color of pearls—and then the light flowed off it, melding with the mist, until it seemed as if the light was rolling along the forest floor.

Dolena felt the radiated power from the stone flow across her skin like marching insects. It crackled through her cropped hair, struck sparks from her metal belt buckle, and danced blue-white along the length of her sword.

This was mana. She wasn't sure if it was an enormous block of solidified mana or some artifact imbued with incredible power.

The ground around the artifact was cracked and broken, the earth split and shattered; the crown of the stone was dusted with earth, and mud was crusted in long streaks along the length of the stone. It had obviously been pushed up from a subterranean vault by the recent upheavals.

Almost unconsciously, Dolena took a step forward.

This was mana. Indescribable, incredible wealth and power. It pulsed green, the mist turning emerald. It flowed across her feet and the woman felt her aches and the scars of old wounds fade. It throbbed blue and soothing, and the sapphire mist laved her feet and legs. Dolena's sword dropped from nerveless fingers as she crouched, dipping her hands into the mist, bringing her damp hands up to rub against her face. The scarred skin on her forehead tingled and itched, but when she touched it again, the flesh was smooth. She blinked tears from her eyes and abruptly realized that the night had become clearer, the stone assuming shape and definition, each pictogram sharp and precise. It had healed her, healed old aches and wounds, repaired scars and faded sight. On hands and knees, Dolena crawled toward the stone.

The studded flail took her between the shoulders, snapping bones, cracking her skull as it drove her face-first into the mud.

Brons stepped over the woman's body.

The Stone of Mana.

The Godstone.

Brons recognized it immediately. It was one of the legends which was told and retold around the camps. But Brons had always dismissed it, relegating it to the tales of the Lost Cities, the Moon Folk, and the Disappearing Islands.

But this was no legend. This was real. The drover could feel the ancient power flow across his skin, easing the ache of knotted muscles and wrenched shoulders, the bane of every drover's life. His skull itched abominably, and when he ran his hand over it, he could feel the rasping fuzz of the hair he had lost in his youth. Stepping closer to the stone, he could feel the flesh on his face tightening, muscles rippling beneath the skin, and when he touched his forehead and cheeks, the wrinkles and grooves around his eyes and mouth were missing.

The Stone of Mana.

Legend had it that to merely stand in its presence was enough to grant a man his heart's desires.

Brons dropped the flail to the ground and stepped up to the stone.

There should be pain.

Dolena had been wounded before. She knew the sickening pain of injury, the burning snap of broken bones, the icy hotness of wounds. The drover had struck her from behind with his flail. She knew her skull was cracked—she had heard the pop of bone—and there was a tingling in her legs that made her suspect her spine was damaged. But there was no pain. Was this what death was like: no pain, merely a gentle warmth that flowed across her skin and settled into her muscles with a soothing heat?

Green and blue mist curled and eddied over her, individual colored droplets standing out on her skin like tiny jewels.

She watched the blackened fingernail of her thumb curl up and drop off, and then, before her eyes, a new nail formed, translucent and perfect.

There was no pain.

And Dolena raised her head, newly knitted bones and repaired muscles sliding easily together.

A touch of the stone, just a touch, would be enough to give him everything he ever wanted. A touch of the stone would grant him power, unimaginable power. He would be more powerful than any planeswalker, the most powerful man in the world.

Brons reached out and touched the stone.

Power—chill, icy, raw power—flowed into his body.

The weight of his four and forty years dropped off him, and suddenly he was young again: young and strong and vital. He ran his fingers through the thick mat of hair that covered his skull, raised his arms to the skies, and cried aloud in triumph.

Dolena came shakily to her feet as Brons reached out to embrace the stone. He saw her from the corner of her eye and turned his head to smile savagely at her. Then he clutched the stone to him like a lover.

Dolena watched the mana flow through the man's body: white and red, green and golden. She saw his muscles fill, his hair coil serpentlike down his head, tufts of coarse black hair sprout on his chest. The man twisted his head and spat, discolored enamel teeth swallowed by the mist, but when he raised his head to snarl at her, she saw that his teeth were whole and perfect.

The stone had made him young again.

"Fear me!" Brons thundered, voice powerful and commanding. "Fear me." Pressing his lips to the stone, he breathed in its very essence.

The stone had made him young . . . and continued to make him young.

From stolid middle-age to prime of life had taken moments, from prime to callow youth took even less, and from youth to child and child to babe, less time again.

By the time Dolena had strode across to the stone, the child on the ground was shrinking, diminishing, losing its human features, losing definition. She squeezed her eyes shut . . . and when she opened them again, Brons was gone.

And Dolena knew then why there had been no beast and animal tracks returning from the stone.

Without a backward glance, she turned away and made her way down the track, reveling in her newfound youth and sight.

*   *   *

"What did you find in the forest?" Crane asked as they broke camp the following morning.

"Nothing," Dolena said shortly.

"More than nothing, surely." The dwarf looked openly at her unscarred forehead, the bloom of youth on her cheeks, the bright sparkle in her eyes.

"Nothing to fear." Dolena smiled.

Dochyel's Ride

David M. Honigsberg

When I was fourteen years old my life changed forever.

I was in the foothills with my friends, playing "Raid the Village." It was my turn to play our hero, Pashalik Mons. Three others were my raiders and ten more took the part of the villagers, trying to stave off our attacks. As usual, the goblin raiders won the day and we began the hike back up into the mountains, heading for the entrance to the caves and to home.

That's when it happened.

We were almost to the mouth of the cave when Carnach, my mother, ran out.

"Get out of the way, Dochyel!" she yelled at me. "Out of the way now!"

We heard a grating sound, stone against stone. One of my friends, Thurka, sprinted to the left. The rest of us followed along at his heels. When we reached the safety of an outcropping, we looked up to see what the source of the sound was. At that moment, the nose of a rock sled came into view. Within seconds it flashed past us, its driver skillfully shifting his body weight in order to maneuver around obstacles in his path. I watched the sled continue down the mountain until it had gone around a bend and vanished from sight. Only then did I look up toward the mouth of the cave. My mother's slender but muscular green form was outlined in the entrance. She looked down at my friends and me, a broad grin on her face.

"Did you like what you saw, boys?"

We all nodded and excitedly scrambled back to the path and then up to the cave entrance. Familiar odors, spawned by centuries of habitation, assailed me and I knew that I was home.

My mother slapped me on the back as I walked past her. "Pretty soon," she reminded me, "you'll have to decide which of the forces to join. I'll be honest with you, Dochyel. If you told me that you wanted to be a sled driver, I'd be very proud of you."

"Really?" I asked, a look of amazement upon my face. I hadn't given much thought to the years I would have to spend in the military, and Mother had never spoken of it before.

"Absolutely," she answered. "Some goblins don't think that driving a sled is as honorable or important as being a foot soldier in village raids, but I've never agreed with them. It takes something special to drive a sled."

"Yeah," Thurka chimed in. "It takes a very crazy goblin!"

I pushed him back against the wall and bared my teeth at him. "I'm not crazy," I insisted. "And I'm going to be the best sled driver ever!"

From that moment on, I dreamt of nothing but rock sleds. Sometimes I woke up well before dawn, the dark comfort of the caves all around me. At those times, my muscles would be stiff and sore, as if I had tensed them over and over again in order to steer around a boulder, or avoid the arrows of a village guard. I began to study with my mother, learning strategies and memorizing the terrain outside of each cave entrance. I listened to the elders talk of ancient battles where sleds had played important roles. I lived and breathed nothing but rock sleds.

I also spent a great deal of time talking to the loremasters. From them I learned that the Rundvelt goblins were the only tribe of goblins who had taken upon themselves the task of teaching the old skills throughout the generations. For that reason, we were the only tribe who used rock sleds and the only tribe who had kept alive the craft of the war drummers. I was astounded when I heard this. Although I had not met goblins from other tribes, I had believed that they all used sleds and drums as part of their warcraft. It made me proud to know that the Rundvelt goblins were different from the others who, through their own ignorance, had become little more than bungling fools.

At first, my friends thought that I was just going through a phase, that I would come to my senses and join up with them again. But as weeks turned into months, I decided that to study to be a real sled driver was more important than to play at being a raider. Thurka and the others slowly drifted away from me until the only friend I had was my pet rock badger, Orshk. He'd sit curled up with me in the shade of the crags, his bulk a solid presence while I'd daydream about what things would be like at the academy.

By the time I turned sixteen, all of the lore of that amazing engine of war had been revealed to me. I knew the names of every famous sled driver and could recite their exploits by rote. Now I could not imagine why I had so idolized Pashalik Mons. After all, it was the Sled Corps that had punched the holes in the enemy's defense which allowed his exploits to grow into legends.

When, thirty days after my birthday, it came time to announce my decision, I told my mother that I still intended to be the best rock sled driver ever.

My parents seemed to glow the day I left for sled school, their belief evident in the emerald sheen of their faces that I would be able to carve out a future for myself in the Sled Corps and bring new glory to the Rundvelt goblins. What's more, because of my mother's importance in the sled testing program, I was allowed to bring Orshk to the sled academy with me. My rock badger, with his habit of nibbling on fingers with his small sharp teeth, and his penchant for making mischief, became the mascot of my class in no time. He quickly learned to tolerate all of the attention he received at the hands of relative strangers, and after a few days learned to anticipate his daily groomings.

My biggest surprise at the academy was the realization that not all of the cadets shared my boundless enthusiasm for sledding. For many of them, the Sled Corps was their second choice, after they had failed to be accepted in one of the raider units for not being good enough on their feet. They didn't seem to care one bit for all of the lore and legends which made the corps so interesting and important to me, and they became indignant when taught that sledders helped make raiders successful.

As for myself, the academy was all that I had expected, and I threw myself into my studies. The difference between me and those failed raiders I shared my barracks with became apparent one day at the end of our tactics class. As usual, I sat in the front row, not wanting to miss one word of wisdom which the instructor had to offer.

On that day, Kovar, the Pashalik who led the class, had been emphasizing the philosophy behind the raids. "Never forget," he told us, "that we raid when we are in need of tools or food or trading goods." His left arm hung limp at his side, the result of an injury suffered years ago during a raid. "We do not kill unless we have to. When would that be?"

I stood up in my place. "We do not kill unless we are threatened, Pashalik Kovar."

"Can you think of another time that killing might be necessary?"

I thought for a moment, unsure how to proceed. "To put fear into the villagers?"

"Exactly," he responded, and addressed the rest of the class. "We never want to the villages to feel more powerful than us. We want them to be afraid. They will certainly defend themselves, even talk to other villages to share their experiences. But terror aids us, for they never know when we will return. There are over thirty villages in the Rundvelt range. We never raid more than five in any given year. There is never a pattern to our attacks. We always keep them guessing."

Kovar's attention returned to me. "Dochyel, come here," he ordered. I did as instructed and Kovar turned me around to face the class. He rested his good hand on my shoulder in a friendly manner as he addressed the other cadets.

"Dochyel is, far and away, the most enthusiastic cadet I have seen in years," he told my fellow sledders. "And I'm not the only one who's noticed, either. He understands sled tactics better than many officers. He knows the histories almost as well as the chroniclers, and his drive and desire to be the best will stand him in good stead in later years. He is what every young goblin sled driver should aspire to be. The rest of you, if you have any hope of doing well here, should try harder to be more like him. He, among all of you, is setting the standard. Class dismissed."

Pashalik Kovar's words thrilled me, but they had a very

different effect on my companions. Later that night, nobody would sit with me at dinner. Nobody spoke to me, either. The next morning, I again ate by myself and I was spoken to only when the need arose. Otherwise, I found myself alone. My classmates even stopped grooming Orshk, as that would entail speaking to me. In a few days I had to admit to myself that, with all my knowledge of rock sleds, extraordinary as it might be for such a young goblin, I was tired of being by myself. I began to help those few goblins who were still somewhat friendly to me better understand their lessons. They, too, began to gain favor with the instructors. Other cadets began to break the code of silence in order to better themselves and Orshk's regular groomings resumed.

At the same time, I sincerely tried to be just another rookie sled driver. That didn't mean I had to become less enthusiastic, but I scaled it down a notch or two. It took a little while, but my eagerness to help, combined with what seemed to others to be a more approachable personality, soon paid off and I was able to turn the envy which had blossomed in the barracks into true friendship. With that friendship, in the firelight of the plebes cave, I found a camaraderie the likes of which I had never before known. Many were the nights when my new friends and I fell asleep to the muffled sounds of war drummers practicing their craft.

We trained for long, grueling days on end. Not a concept was overlooked. I gained hands-on knowledge of things I had only heard drivers talk of in the past. We used old, chipped, training sleds to practice the subtle and not-so-subtle body motions necessary to wrestle the mass of a rock sled around obstacles both large and small. We were taught the basics of sled repair by way of the rudiments of sled construction by masters of the art.

The instructors made it clear that we should never get attached to our sleds. Most of them were used on one raid only, since it was almost impossible to drag them back to the caves. It was more important to destroy the sled if necessary. That way, no village could create a more effective defense against us other than the walls and arrows which they commonly used.

No amount of instruction, however, could have properly prepared me for the day which I awaited with mounting excite-

ment and anxiety—the day I would make my first downhill journey in an actual rock sled. During all of my studies, all of the tac-
tical review, all of the hours I'd listened to tales of past glory, my
mother had never permitted me to do more than sit in a sled
which was about to be tested. Now was my chance to find out if I
really had the stuff legendary drivers are made of.

I held my breath as the sled was pushed further and further
out of the cave's mouth. When it was a little more than halfway
over the lip, it dipped downward and I began my descent. As the
sled gained momentum, the first of the curves came into view. I
instinctively leaned against the sled and was amazed at how
quickly it responded. I was so pleased with my success at the
first curve, that I almost missed the next one. After that, I pushed
all personal thoughts out of my mind. There would be time later
to be giddy with the results of this run. I had to make it to the
bottom in one piece first.

The sled picked up speed. My teeth rattled in my skull. I
had to clench my jaw to stop the sensation. What I couldn't stop,
though, was the shaking of the sled, which made me see double.
Now I understood why instinct was so important to a driver—the
faster the sled went, the harder it was to see anything. A right
turn almost caught me off guard, but I made it through. The next
two lefts were no problem at all.

The angle of descent increased slightly. The sled began to
move faster and faster. I called upon everything I'd ever learned,
leaning this way and that, turning, tilting. My heart pounded in
my chest, and each second seemed like an hour to me as the sled
slid down the test course. When the run was finally finished, I sat
in the sled, gasping for breath, a wide grin on my face. I had
never felt anything so exhilarating in my life. Yet, until the
moment I was hurled down the mountainside, encased in a barely
controllable, carved-out slab of rock, I had never truly known
what fear was, either.

I didn't want anybody to know that I, of all goblins, had
been scared out of my wits. I swaggered out of the sled as if I'd
been driving for years. Those of my friends who had preceded
me down the mountain gathered around, pounding me on the
back. I was so intent on not looking scared that I barely heard
their encouraging words. "Great run," one shouted at me.

"Amazing!" yelled another. "Girga Sul couldn't have done it better, himself," another cried out, invoking the name of one of the greatest sledders of all time. Even my test instructor informed me that he'd never seen anybody take to a sled faster than I.

After that, my progression through the ranks was guaranteed. Within six months I had become an assistant instructor, not only by dint of my fearless sled driving, but, more importantly, because I was a storehouse of knowledge. Orshk and I were soon given new quarters in the officers' caves, something almost unheard of for a cadet to achieve. The difference between my new quarters and the ones I lived in while at the academy was astounding. They were cleaner, more spacious, and had a thick fur covering over the entrance. At the academy, anybody could walk into our quarters at any time, unannounced. Now those who wanted to speak with me had to tell me who they were before I granted them permission to enter.

During my next leave, I decided to visit my parents. When my mother saw the officer's pin on my tunic, she and my father took out a bottle of pag'b, which made the stuff I'd been drinking with my fellow goblins in the Sled Corps taste like poison. We stayed up late that night as I regaled them with stories of my training. The next day mother took me to inspect a new fleet of sleds which had just been delivered and showed me off to everybody at the worksite.

Two months later, I graduated at the top of my class and was assigned to Sled Team 1, the best unit the Rundvelt goblins had ever fielded. It was there that I began to apply everything that I had learned to the practical exercise of raiding villages. It was there, too, that I discovered in what low esteem we were held by other goblin troops. Even though sledders risked their necks every time the call came to raid a village, the foot troops were the ones who claimed all of the glory and most of the spoils. They saw us as nothing more than high-speed battering rams. What's worse, just about every foot goblin seemed to believe that sledders were all crazy—nothing more than egotistical, reckless adventurers. While I was aware that some in the corps fit that description, the majority of sledders I knew were well aware that they put their lives on the line everytime they got into a sled. Some of them even had families and never took unnecessary chances.

I understood that I'd have to do something really special to change the attitude others had about the Sled Corps. I lay awake at night trying to think of something which hadn't been done before, some new way that the corps could be used. I went over everything I had learned and everything I had overheard, hoping to discover a tactic for which the sleds had not yet been utilized.

The problem with this effort was that the Sled Corps' role was very well defined. It was our task to breach a settlement's defenses by barreling through the walls, after which the infantry took over, pouring through the holes we created and taking the spoils from the frightened villagers.

I remembered what I'd been told, over and over again, while still in the academy. Since Kovar had lost the use of an arm, he wanted to ensure that we were all aware of the dangers which every raid presented.

"The problem, boys," he told us, "is that you'll always get to the village before the raiders do. It can't be helped. None of them can run as fast as your sled can go. So, when you get to a village, there'll be a time that you're in danger, very grave danger."

We looked at each other, trying to hide our smiles. We were all trained in the use of daggers and thought that Kovar's warnings were simply the ravings of an old goblin who'd lived past his usefulness.

"When you break through the walls," he continued, "you might be shaken up, even knocked out. A child can kill you if you're unconscious, boys. Don't forget that."

I never forgot his words, especially after seeing one of my friends killed after smashing through a wall that was thicker than usual. With so few sledders killed on raids, though, it seemed unnecessary to do anything differently. Why tamper with something that seemed to work well? Yet my impression was there had to be some way by which the number of sledder deaths could be lowered while, at the same time, infantry goblins could arrive at villages closer to the time the sleds did.

At first I wondered if any advantage could be gained if the number of sleds were doubled. I quickly realized that, although this would grant better odds to the sledders, it would unnecessarily task the resources of the craftsmen who fashioned the sleds and probably increase the number of casualties.

Then I thought of a way for sleds to pull infantry goblins down the mountain using carts or special seats made of hides. I couldn't figure out any way to protect those goblins from serious injury should the towed vehicle turn over or slam into a boulder. I dropped that idea as quickly as I had picked it up. I had to think of something much safer than that. I paced my quarters, Orshk looking up at me quizzically, his dark eyes glinting in the torch-light, as I tried to think of a way to raise the value of the corps in the eyes of the goblin leaders.

Then it came to me, an inspiration so simple as to make me wonder why it had never occurred to anybody before. That it was a new idea, I was certain. I had never heard it mentioned in any of the tales. Even if it had failed—*especially* if it had failed—I would have been told about it. No, this was something entirely different. The problem now was to convince the council of its merit. And that meant speaking before my former idol, Pashalik Mons.

I explained my idea to Pashalik Arngh, my commanding officer, who trusted me enough to take it upon himself to get approval for my appearance. Had I tried to do it on my own, I have no doubt that I would have failed. Even though my family name carried some weight in the Rundvelt, I had no idea of the politics involved with such an endeavor. Arngh, as a ranking officer, was able to schedule a meeting with one of the council member's assistants and she, in turn, was able to arrange for Arngh to speak before the council and present the case for my own appearance. I don't know what he told them, but whatever it was, it worked. He returned from the meeting and immediately began to prepare me for my own experience with the council.

"You'll only have ten minutes," he told me. "If you haven't convinced them by then, there's no hope at all. You have to be ready for any question, no matter how inconsequential it may seem to you."

I nodded in understanding.

"I want you to work on your presentation and we'll talk again in three days. You can go now."

I spent the next three days practicing, hoping that I had con-sidered every possible angle and every rebuttal which could be made. In three days I reported back to Arngh and practiced on him. He was pleased with what I had done and told me that he felt that I was ready for my next lesson.

"Take a look at this," he said as he handed me a slate with odd markings on it. "That's the layout of the council chamber. Each member chooses their own location in the hall. I'll teach you who the most important members are and the ones you'll need on your side in order to have the vote turn out your way. What I can't entirely prepare you for, though, is the manner in which you'll be questioned. Comments may come at you from every side. You'll have to be constantly turning to face your questioners. That's when you'll know if you're really prepared. That's where your idea will float or sink." For the duration of my coaching, Arngh circled me, barking out questions, trying to imitate the cadences and mannerisms of the council members. I studied the chamber layout again and again until I could picture each council goblin in his or her seat. By the time I was ushered into the chamber, I was as prepared as anybody could be.

A fire burned brightly in the middle of the room. Just as I had seen on the slate, the members sat at stone tables, each of a different design, positioned all around the chamber. I addressed my comments to the key members Arngh had told me about.

"The idea is very simple," I explained to them, making it a point to appear as calm and relaxed as I could. I moved as I spoke, making sure I did not linger too long near any one council member for fear that others would see this as blatant favoritism.

"If we were to use slightly larger sleds, each driver would be able to carry one infantry goblin." I picked up a slate and drew the outline of the new sled I was proposing. As the council passed the slate amongst themselves, I continued: "Then, when we push through the walls, the drivers won't have to wait until the infantry arrives. It will be easier for them to fend off any attacks from the villagers. More important, some of the infantry will get into the village immediately. They won't have to expend nearly all their energy chasing behind the sleds as they do now. There won't be room enough for all the infantry, of course, but—"

"It is out of the question, Dochyel. I don't believe that you have thought this all the way through," Halrak interrupted from a seat close to the fire. The constant murmur of assistants and messengers ceased immediately. Nobody wanted to miss a word he spoke. I turned to face him, hoping that he hadn't thought of something I had missed. If he didn't back my plan, I knew it would never be approved. "There's nothing to prevent the extra goblin from being incapacitated in the same way that some of the drivers are now."

"A little extra padding is all we need," I assured him, "a few furs, perhaps. The hardest thing will be to teach the infantry goblins not to clutch at the driver as he sleds down the mountain. If they can be trained to stay toward the bottom of the sled, and if they don't make any unnecessary movements, there should be no problem at all."

"You're serious, aren't you?" Halrak stood up and moved toward me, showing his yellowed fangs. I had never seen so old a goblin in my life. "Do you really think that we can condone the use of infantry in this manner?"

"With all due respect," I replied, while trying to keep the nervousness out of my voice, "the use of infantry will be of great benefit. Any villagers who see us coming will panic due to the size of the new sleds. They won't ever expect that a second goblin is tucked into that larger sled. The element of surprise will be the key."

Halrak spit at my feet to show his disapproval. "It's absurd and reckless, just the sort of idea we've come to expect from the Sled Corps. What you propose, Dochyel—"

"—just might work, Councilmember Halrak," Pashalik Mons cut in, his voice coming from my left and farther back toward the wall of the chamber. "Our young friend here might just have the right idea."

The silence seemed to last forever as all eyes turned to Mons. Halrak stood his ground, but closed his mouth.

"It seems to me that there is much to recommend young Dochyel's plan. Although it pains me to admit it, the sled drivers might well be the bravest goblins in our military. Each year it becomes harder and harder to find recruits willing to take on those kinds of risks. I believe that this plan will do just what he says it will—reduce the danger to the drivers and, at the same time, get some foot soldiers into the villages faster than we've been able to get them there in the past."

He rose from his seat and came over to me. He walked with

a limp and, as he stood before me, I saw that he was both shorter and older than I had pictured him. He had an incredible presence, though, and could still command respect with nothing more than a glance or gesture.

"Dochyel," he said to me, "I know that you have given this idea much thought. I have heard much about you in recent months and have often wished that more young goblins of your caliber were interested in making the military their home. In front of the council, I pledge the use of my own raiders to test this idea of yours. It seems only fitting that the finest raiders join with the finest sled team in these mountains to bring glory to the entire goblin race."

I was astounded. I had hoped that my plan would be accepted by the council, but I never dreamt that it would gain the support of an old raider like Pashalik Mons. Moments after he backed the plan, the council made their decision. The vote wasn't unanimous by any means, but with Mons behind me, and Halrak grudgingly casting his vote in my favor, there were considerably more light-colored stones than dark-colored ones in the ballot box.

In the weeks that followed, I came to believe that my victory in the council chambers had been the easiest part of the plan. The number of tasks which had to be attended to was staggering. New rock was quarried so that the craftsmen could carve out new sleds: sleds which could fit two. After they were carved, a number of top drivers, myself included, had to test them to be sure they were properly balanced and that we could handle them. In each instance, one sledder drove and the other played the part of an infantry goblin, huddled down in the back of the sled, cushioned by furs. It took some time to get used to the way the new sleds moved, but we were all very happy with the new equipment. What's more, the additional weight caused them to go that much faster, especially toward the bottom of the course. When all the test runs were finished and minor repairs made, the next phase began.

This part of the program proved to be much more difficult than I had imagined it would be. That Pashalik Mons had pledged his raiders to our cause was true. However neither he nor I had anticipated the reluctance of the raiders to have anything to do with the Sled Corps. We didn't want to simply order the raiders to get into a sled, as that would undermine morale. Arngh and I came up with the idea of a short class where raiders could learn about sleds without having to set foot in one, a class similar to that given to goblins who were considering joining the corps. If Mons couldn't order his raiders into a sled, he could, at the very least, order them to a class.

The enthusiasm that the drivers showed while talking about the Sled Corps rubbed off on the raiders, and after our presentation, they eagerly joined us to watch a sled run from start to finish. This was a new experience for them, as they were more accustomed to seeing the backs of the sledders as they passed them on the way to a village. This time the raiders stood at the end of a test course and watched as one of the new two-goblin sleds grew from a small speck halfway up the mountain to a full-sized sled at the bottom of the run.

When all was finished, it was still difficult to find a raider who was willing to take a ride. They milled around, looking at each other, wondering who would be the first brave—or foolish—soul to trust his life to the skills of a sledder. Finally, a voice came from a knot of goblins to my right. "I'll volunteer," announced the raider, stepping in front of his fellows. I blinked in amazement. It was none other than my old friend Thurka. Now was my chance to show him that I wasn't another crazy sled driver.

"Come with me," I said with a smile. "We'll show them how it's done."

We trudged up the test course to the mouth of the cave where another of the new sleds awaited its passengers. I showed Thurka the best way to position himself, and he hunkered down like he'd been in a sled many times before. Before he had time to think about what was about to happen, I signaled to the support goblins to get the sled going. They quickly removed the blocks in front of the vehicle and ran around to the back, putting all their strength into the task of pushing the sled out of the cave mouth far enough for it to start the descent of its own accord.

As we picked up speed, I looked back at Thurka. His body was tense, but he seemed unconcerned with what was happening. In no time at all we reached the bottom of the run and were besieged with raiders who bombarded Thurka with question after question about his experience. After he assured them that it was something none of them would want to miss, we had to have the remaining raiders choose lots to determine the order of that afternoon's test rides. It was decided, without hesitation, that Thurka would be the raider I carried when we began the attack. With that hurdle behind us, the combined forces, even the officers, moved into a barracks cave together in order to create a tighter unit.

The drills continued for two weeks. During that time, we in the Sled Corps learned a great deal about hand-to-hand combat. Although we were all taught some close combat techniques, our usual strategy was to rely on our sleds to get us where we were going and then hope for the best. The raiders, however, had always depended on their daggers and spears. Since there would be no room in the sleds for spears, we trained for many hours with new daggers and, when we were finished, each of us could just about hold our own with our raider teachers.

I never trained as hard for any mission as I did for this one. My future with the Sled Corps depended on its success. Pashalik Mons seemed to understand that, and he often talked with me long into the night after raiders and sledders had called it a day. Telling him of my apprehensions made me understand that I had done everything possible to ensure the raid's success. The more we talked, the more I remembered all I had admired about him while I was growing up. As I got to know him better, as he told me stories of his past, he became less an idol and more a real goblin, like any other goblin. Our conversations helped me relax as the day grew closer and closer.

Two days before the raid, raiders and sledders alike made a pilgrimage to the sacred shrine of our ancestors. There we spent the night, not sleeping at all, just as our fathers and grandfathers had done before us as they prepared for special battles. We drummed and we sang; we danced and we drank more pag'b than we'd ever had before. We wrestled and swore, and then drank more pag'b until, when the priests arrived to clean up our mess, we staggered back to our barracks cave and slept the sleep of the dead.

When we awoke, sometime the next afternoon, we felt rested and ready. Falling into place, we began the journey to the cave mouth from which we would launch the sleds. News of our endeavor preceded us and, from time to time, goblins lined our way to wish us luck. We walked silently, but nodded to them, acknowledging their presence. Behind us, pit ponies dragged the new sleds, ten in all, struggling with the unusually heavy load they were forced to pull.

The sun was low when we arrived at the staging cave. I estimated that we probably had no more than one hour of daylight remaining to us. In the distance I could make out wisps of smoke rising from the simple homes of the village we were about to descend upon. By the time we reached them, it would be dark, giving us a greater advantage than that conferred only by surprise.

The site of this experimental raid had been chosen with great care. Ten villages had been scouted before the one below us was selected. The walls were relatively thin, no match at all for our new sleds. There was plenty of tinder available in the form of straw in the unlikely event that we had to put it to the torch. Most important of all, it hadn't been the scene of an attack for almost five years. Unless the memory of the last raid still burned brightly in the minds of the inhabitants, they would be totally unprepared for what they were about to experience.

Slowly and deliberately we settled into the sleds, ten drivers and ten infantry goblins. The remaining fifteen raiders stretched their muscles as they prepared for the long run ahead. Half an hour before sunset, they began to lope down the mountain. Arngh turned over a sand clock. They would get a head start of twenty minutes. We waited in our sleds, not saying a word, watching the shadows lengthen as night came over the land.

When the sand in the clock ran out, the support goblins performed their tasks and the sleds began their journey down the mountain. Thurka huddled in the back of my sled, just as he had been taught, not lifting his head once to look at the scenery racing past us. I took a moment to glance at the other sleds. Each driver was low in his sled, eyes not only on the area in front of him but on areas far ahead, planning the series of body movements which would take him and his cargo past a boulder or around a curve. Only the drivers could be seen; the raiders remained out of sight.

I soon saw the backs of the raiders who had preceded us down the slope. As they heard the approaching sleds, they picked up their pace until, as I passed them, they broke into a full sprint, chasing the sleds as best they could as we hurtled toward the village.

Finally the steep slope began to level out. Steering through a relatively tight turn, I caught my first glimpse of the village. Everything was as our scouts had promised it would be. The only protection was a low stone wall. It would fall easily. The area was quiet. The scent of cooking meat was in the air as the wall rushed toward me. I ducked my head below the rim of the sled as I barreled through the simple defenses.

The momentum of the sled carried me some distance into the village. Behind me I heard the other sleds break through the walls, each driver careful not to use a hole already created. As the sled began to slow, I sat up to get my bearings. As usual, my head was spinning a little from the force of the impact. Directly in front of me was the town's well, a simple contraption with two wooden buckets. Behind the well were a few simple homes constructed of wattle and thatch. All was as it should have been, except for one thing. On either side of the well stood five men armed with farm implements and other crude weapons.

I was surprised to see them. Most villagers run when our sleds hit the wall. Only once in my time with the corps had I faced organized armed opposition. That time, the fear of being beaten had cleared my head quickly. This time, however, it was the villagers who were in for a surprise.

As the men ran toward the sleds, each raider rose from his place, dagger drawn, lips curled back to bare fangs. The villagers hadn't expected this turn of events. Their moment of hesitation was all the raiders needed as they leapt out of the sleds and advanced, menace in their eyes. The villagers brandished their weapons, but I could see that they weren't as confident as they had been a moment before.

Now that things seemed a bit more in our favor, I stepped out of the sled, drawing my dagger as I did so. My fellow drivers followed my lead and we stepped into formation with the raiders, making the odds two to one. The villagers fell back, unsure of how best to deal with this new threat. I could see the faces of women and children peering out of windows. I brandished my dagger in the direction of one of the houses and the faces vanished within.

Thurka took control of the situation, motioning us to join the advance on the frightened men. "Soft-bellied cowards!" he yelled as he approached, punctuating his comments with growls and curses. "We will kill you all if you resist us! We will eat your children and pick our teeth with their finger bones!" None of the humans spoke our language, I'm sure, yet I have no doubt that they understood the threatening tone of his words without a problem. Some of the men dropped their weapons. Thurka growled and cursed at those who didn't.

It seemed that they were determined to be as stubborn as possible until they saw the remaining raiders enter the village through the holes we had made. At that, they threw down the last of their weapons and stood by while we ransacked their homes. They had been beaten, but they weren't defeated. I could see anger smolder in their eyes, and I knew that they would make every attempt to be ready for us the next time we came, whenever that might be. For now, though, we were the victors, and the furs which had protected the raiders in the sleds now became pouches which we loaded full of whatever valuables we could find.

Before we left the place, we threw all of their crude weapons into the well, ensuring that they wouldn't be able to do us any immediate harm. Each of the drivers methodically destroyed the sleds, while Thurka and the other raiders kept a watchful eye on the villagers. Then we vanished through the holes we had made, leaving the piles of rubble as mute testimony to our victory. We headed for home as fast as we could without exhausting ourselves, and the mountains rang with our victory songs.

Two weeks later, after we had been debriefed and attended a large number of congratulatory parties, I decided to visit my home cave. I spent the afternoon with my parents and, as the sun was heading down, I found myself at the cavern entrance where I had seen my first rock sled. I strolled down the mountainside for awhile and enjoyed the breeze on my face. With that breeze came sounds, sounds of goblin children playing in the same area I had played when I was a child. I approached cautiously, not wanting to interrupt their fun. I poked my head around a boulder and was amazed by what I saw.

Two children sat on a slab of granite, one behind the other. A number of cords were tied around the rock and each had a tight hold on one of them. Their bodies leaned to the right and to the left in imperfect synchronization. As I watched, I realized that they were playing sledder and raider, a game I never would have thought possible when I was their age. I moved closer to hear what they were saying to each other.

"Watch out for that rock, Dochyel!" the one behind shouted to the one in front.

"I see it, Thurka!" she yelled back as she threw her body to the left.

After a few minutes of this, there followed a motion imitative of a quick stop. The children dropped their ropes and clambered off the rock, dashing forward to grab imaginary treasure.

By this time, the sun was almost below the horizon. I turned and began to walk back home, content in the knowledge that I had changed more than just the way goblins made war.

Heart of Shanodin

Bruce Holland Rogers

There was no path. The two riders—the heavily armored one astride a great black charger, the gray-clad one upon a horse as leggy and slender as a deer—weaved among the towering trees. They rode parallel, but kept at least a sword's reach between them. The gray rider spoke almost without ceasing, and the armored one not at all.

When the knight for once glanced at his companion, he saw a wisp, a snicker, a joke of a man who hid every thought he had behind a grin. What was Daisilodavi but a self-made mystery? You could not know a man like that, who, for all his talking, never came to utter a serious remark. Yet for all his dither and dance, for all his jabber jabber, for all the distracting whirl that kept the real man invisible, Daisilodavi was efficient at his craft. King Amjad, may his name provoke trembling, found the little man indispensable. That was the thing that nagged the knight most of all, that he should have a rival for his lord's dark heart, and that the rival should be one so airy as this.

Daisilodavi, when he looked at the knight riding beside him, saw a lump, a grunt, an iron statue that hid all its secrets in silence. What was Khairt but a stubborn cipher? A man who would answer no questions about his past was not unknowable. Some things about a man's history might be writ, like ciphers, upon his body. But on Khairt, most such signs were hidden beneath his black chain mail. The ragged scar on his cheek spoke of battle, and what was the surprise in that? There was the grindingly slow way he walked, the grunts he made when he must bend his legs. That might have some interesting cause, but what? Khairt would never say. And if Daisilodavi must have a rival for the patronage of Amjad, may his name cause jaundice, why must it be so unreadable a rival as this? Daisilodavi could tease an opinion or an argument out of the man from time to time, but never anything revealing. Even the knight's accent was strange, such a blend that even the place of the knight's birth remained uncertain.

But soon the knight would reveal something of himself. He would have no choice. Smiling, Daisilodavi rose up in his saddle and waved his hand at the deep forest. "Like stars at the end of time," he said.

Khairt, riding beside him, turned his helmeted head neither to the left nor to the right. He knew what the smaller man was talking about, but he made no reply. Like stars littering the forest floor, spots of sunlight flashed here or there among the black and musty leaves. Such glints of sun had been rare enough when the two horsemen first entered the Shanodin Forest. Now Khairt and Daisilodavi had ridden two days among the enormous trunks, and the trees grew ever taller, the high canopy ever thicker, and sunlight ever weaker with every step that brought them toward the Heart of Shanodin. Scattered spots of sunlight grew still more sparse—stars winking out at the end of time.

"Ah, but such a phrase has too much poetry in it for you, does it not?" said Daisilodavi. "You are all glower and doom and words of one syllable and sentences of one word." He lowered his eyebrows in mock seriousness and scowled. "Aye," he said as deeply as he could. After a long pause, he added, "No." Then he laughed. "And when you have something more than that to say, what is it but some opinion that things are bad and getting worse? You make too much of the name of knight, I think, for you are ever thinking night thoughts. It is daylight! Birds sing! Khairt, don't you ever raise your black eyebrows? Don't you ever open your eyes?"

Still, Khairt said nothing.

"Fah, what a traveling companion you are," said Daisilodavi. "Knight, you're as chatty as a brass man."

It was an apt comparison in more than one sense, for Khairt was armored from head to toe. He was so big that even unarmored he'd have needed a heavy mount. With sword and shield and chain mail, he must weigh three times what his companion did. His black charger was two hands taller than Daisilodavi's mount, and stocky as a draft horse. His raised visor showed but a little of his face, which was dark and blunt, the face of a man accustomed to absorbing, unblinkingly, the shocks of battle. His eyebrows were indeed black.

As everything about Khairt suggested heaviness, so did the other man embody the airiness of an elf. The cape covering his slender shoulders was silvery gray, and it billowed in the slightest breeze. Daisilodavi's hair was yellow near to white. His face, smooth and courtly, was young seeming, though there were fine lines etched about his eyes and mouth, and not all of these came of grinning. There was no sign of any weapon on him, no small dagger at his belt, no odd fold in his tunic where a poisoned needle might be tucked. To most he would seem as harmless as he was talkative.

"Perhaps you are indeed a conjured thing," Daisilodavi continued. "That would explain much, for I have never seen you naked of your iron sheath. Perhaps you are empty chain mail with an enchanted head atop." And he reached as if to rap the knight's metal leg and hear if it rang hollow.

Khairt's gauntleted hand closed around Daisilodavi's wrist like a vice, and only when Daisilodavi winced did Khairt release him. The knight said, "We are watched."

"Of course we are watched," said Daisilodavi, rubbing his wrist. "Eyes have been upon us since the moment we entered the Shanodin, though they are not eyes that have a care for our mission here."

He kicked his horse into a trot, dodging branches as his mount sped him through the trees. "Oh, you watchers!" he cried. "Have you ever seen the likes of me? Has a more graceful rider ever passed among these trees?" And then, with the elegance of a dancing centaur, horse and rider wheeled about and faced Khairt. "Ha!" he cried. "They watch that I might melt their wooden hearts!"

"Take care how you speak," said Khairt.

"Do you fear the ladies of the wood?" Daisilodavi grinned. "Or do you pine for them?" He laughed at his own joke.

Khairt turned his head. "You capering fool," he said, and his voice was as hard and cold as the iron chains that keep Yyelor, the ice giant, bound to the frozen north. Even so, Khairt's voice was not so hard and cold as King Amjad's. Nothing, Daisilodavi thought, was so hard and cold as their lord's voice when he was displeased.

Khairt's gauntlet closed tight upon the pommel of his saddle. "Why does this take two of us? Why did Amjad, may his name be feared, not send me alone to slay this Glinham?"

"Shadowy are the ways of Amjad, may his name cause nose-bleeds," said Daisilodavi. "Though perhaps the answer is obvious. I have been to the Heart of Shanodin before. You have not."

"I can find my way without you bounding at my side like some not-weaned pup. And I don't need your help."

"Indeed. And I hardly need you along to dispatch this Glinham. Do you think I desire your company? Do you imagine that I pleaded with Amjad to send us out together? You lumber like a plow horse and drag your shadow behind."

"All men drag their shadows," said the knight.

"I mean your sulky silence, your dour words, your second skin of black steel. In short, you are as obvious as an ugly assassin. You are the very thing a man fears. The quarry sees you gallumphing from a distance and readies himself for attack. Whereas I come to him with smiles, find him where he is resting, reassure him, encourage him . . ."

A blade flashed in the Daisilodavi's hand, sliced the air before him, then vanished before Khairt could guess where it had come from.

"To ride with you," Daisilodavi went on, "is to send out runners before me crying, 'Beware! Trust not this gentle stranger! He comes in the company of death!'"

"Then depart. Go your own way. I will find the one we seek, and when I have finished him, I will find you by the sound of your prattling."

But neither one could leave the other. Amjad's commission had been explicit. They were together to follow this Glinham to the

Heart of Shanodin—the man had left broad clues of where he meant to hide—and together kill him. But why together? Was there any reason for Amjad to doubt that either of them, alone, could undo this man, this mere merchant? No reason that Khairt could see, and so he was uneasy with a thing he could make no sense of.

The brambles began as a wild rose here, a stem of blackberry there, widely scattered, but as the riders pressed on, the thorny stems grew thicker and more frequent, until all the ground beneath the trees was woven thick with briers. Daisilodavi's horse shied half a step for every step forward.

Khairt dismounted and unsheathed his broadsword.

"We near our destination," Daisilodavi said. "These brambles guard the Heart."

Khairt stepped slowly forward, then raised the heavy sword and swung. Thorn and leaf flew. He took a step and swung the other way, and soon there was a rhythm to his cutting, a march of stroke and step that tumbled prickly stems like waves before a prow. His knees hurt him, but then they always hurt when he was afoot; the pain gave him a focus, helped him to concentrate.

Though the stems grew thicker, higher, and tighter woven as Khairt went, there was pleasure in this work, as there was in battle. If he did not turn around, he could imagine that no one stood behind him but his horse. Every so often, Daisilodavi destroyed the illusion with some loud and foolish joke. "And to think I called you witless! Yet here you deal so cuttingly with the barbs set against you!" But Khairt ignored him, considered him gone, and soon again felt peacefully alone in his labor.

Alone but for the eyes of the forest. Even when he imagined that the assassin was not at his back, Khairt could not help but feel the gaze of the woods upon him.

In the Shanodin, of all the world, a man never walks unseen. That was the saying.

Khairt's shoulders were sore and his breathing labored by the time he broke through the thickest part of the brambles. Now, though, the hewing and hacking grew easier with every step, and soon he was enough into the clear that even Daisilodavi's thin-skinned colt could step between the sparse stems.

Without a word, Khairt leaned a moment on his sword, taking the weight from his aching joints, then returned the broadsword to its scabbard.

"That was well done," said Daisilodavi, "but is not done long."

Khairt did not take his meaning until he turned and saw how the brambles grew and twined to reknit the barrier behind them.

"We've no easier way out than the way we came in, I fear," said the assassin.

"Glinham is trapped. If he is here."

"Oh, he's here," said Daisilodavi. "Rely upon it. He thought this place would save him."

"With so mild a wall of thorns? The man's a fool." Khairt put his hands on armored hips and gazed at the brambles. The stems bore blossoms—white and red and pink. How was it that he had not noticed them 'till now? In the trees above him, a thrush sang sweet a song that minded him of evening, and he found himself thinking of stars crowding in a purple sky. . . .

"Fool indeed," said Daisilodavi, looking hard at Khairt.

The knight, not quite knowing why, dropped his visor before his eyes. Shaking himself, as if from sleep, he took to his horse again. He did not raise the visor until he had ridden a little ways before Daisilodavi, and raised it then only because the forest floor was shot through with flowers. He wanted to see all of them at once.

Above his head, the thrush still sang. Rare sunlight sparkled among the leaves. How had Daisilodavi put it? Like the last stars at the end of time? More like diamonds. More like fires burning on a night sea.

Khairt had slept and at last was waking. For how else to explain what now he saw and now he heard? The world was alive with bird song and blossom. How had he forgotten?

Daisilodavi began to sing, and it was not an unpleasant sound, nor even an irritating one, as Khairt usually found it. The assassin sang of green meadows and bright sun, of a maid with spring flowers in her hair. All of a sudden, the singing stopped.

"So thaws the black ice around Khairt's heart," said Daisilodavi, coaxing his horse to draw alongside the knight. "There's a bit of sunlight ashine within his iron breast."

Khairt lowered his brow. It took some effort. He did not feel stony and distant, but he mastered himself enough that his words tolled like a funeral bell when he said, "More nonsense."

"None at all!" said his companion. "You betray your heart, or shall I say your heart betrays you? As I was singing just now, you were nodding your head in time."

"I was not," Khairt said.

"You were. And in a moment you'd have sprung from your horse to dance!"

"If I spring from my horse, it will be to run you through," Khairt said through his teeth.

Daisilodavi laughed and reined in his horse, letting Khairt again take the lead. Again he began to sing.

This time, Khairt gritted his teeth and concentrated on thoughts of battle in order to block out the song. He tried to remember all the machines of war he knew and consider the weaknesses of each. He thought of tactics for single combat, posing himself questions: if armed with a mace, how to proceed against a swordsman? If unhorsed and disarmed, how then to deal with a pikeman? Caught without armor or weapons, how to close with a dagger-wielding foe? With these thoughts, he ignored singer and song, ignored flower and leaf and dappling sun. He concentrated so well on imagined enemies that a true one was upon him before he knew it.

"Blackguards!" cried the blur that sprang from the bushes.

As Khairt turned in surprise, groping for the hilt of his sword, something struck him high. Had the blow come half a second later, he'd have found his balance and readied himself, but instead he slipped from his saddle and tumbled toward the leafy ground.

"To hell!" shouted the voice. Khairt rolled onto his back as his assailant vaulted over his horse.

"What have we here?" Daisilodavi half sang.

What indeed? thought Khairt. The one who had just unhorsed him was little more than a girl and armed with only a wooden staff. She wore the coarse rags of a scullery maid. A black smudge, as of stove black, marked her cheek.

But the young woman stood in a warrior's stance. She gripped the staff by one end. She swung. The staff arced toward Khairt's unprotected face.

Khairt kicked and rolled in a half-forgotten move. His chain mail slowed him, his left knee throbbed, but the maneuver still worked. The staff struck the earth with a thud, and Khairt was back on his feet by the time the girl was ready for another swipe at him.

"Will you not yield?" she demanded.

"Yield?" said Khairt. "To a girl with a staff? Yield?"

"Or die," the young woman said.

"I rather think she means it," said Daisilodavi, bemused. Still mounted, he had sidled behind the lass, but kept his distance.

To Khairt's eye, there was much awkwardness in the way the girl held herself. As spirited a fighter as she might be, she was unschooled. By shifting her weight, or by standing still too long, she revealed openings, opportunities for Khairt to sweep her from her feet.

Yet Khairt did not do so. Instead, he watched her face. Her hair, though plain and brown, was swept back on either side like folded wings. Her eyes were bright and clear. There was determination in her face, yet little hardness.

She was beautiful, and though he no doubt had looked upon beautiful women often enough, the last time he had looked and *seen* beauty like this had been . . .

Oneah.

He clenched his fists. "*You* will yield," Khairt said. "And you will tell us why you waylay strangers."

"You're no strangers to me," she said. "All about you hangs the stink of Amjad."

"May his name cause head lice," said Daisilodavi.

The girl took a step to the side, trying to keep the gray-clad rider from getting behind her, while still keeping the knight before. "I fight to protect my Lord Glinham."

"Then do I grieve for you," said Khairt, "for Glinham must die."

Resolve flashed in her eyes a moment before she moved, and Khairt knew how she would launch herself and swing her staff. He dove beneath her attack and struck her knee with his forearm. She swayed. He struck again and swept her from her feet.

She did not fall well. He heard a snap that might have been

her wrist as she tried to catch herself. She winced as she rolled aside.

Between the weight of his armor and the creaking of his knees, Khairt could not grasp and pin her. She struggled to her feet, cradling her wrist.

Though Khairt had not even seen the man dismount, Daisilodavi was waiting for her. A needle jabbed the back of her neck before she knew he was near. Before she could turn, he was six steps beyond her, and before she staggered and fell, he had mounted his horse again.

A rictus of agony twisted the pretty face and left it twisted as she died. Khairt looked away.

"That was not needed."

"It was," said the assassin. "She'd never have yielded. Were you to defeat her for the moment, she'd have been hunting us again as soon as she was able. Mayhap she would brain you with a lucky blow, if we let her keep trying."

"She fought like a hero."

"She did," said the assassin, kicking his horse to a walk. "She had the heart of a hero." Over his shoulder he said, "Are you developing a conscience?"

Khairt made himself look at her face again. When was the last time he'd felt the slightest regret in seeing an opponent die? But what he felt was not any pang of conscience. He was only sorry that her face was no longer pretty.

Khairt heaved himself into his saddle again and, at a trot, caught up with Daisilodavi. "If a scullery maid has a hero's heart," he said, "then how much more dangerous must be Glinham's men-at-arms!"

"In the Heart of Shanodin," said Daisilodavi, "expect surprise."

"I always expect surprise."

"Save for the ambuscade of a scullery maid." Daisilodavi winked. "What were you dreaming of, to let her take you unaware?"

"I do not dream," the knight said through his teeth. He called a harsh "Geha!" to his horse and trotted ahead of his companion.

But the question remained. How *had* he been so easily surprised? How was it that he had fallen into a state of bliss, of satisfaction? If ever a man thinks himself satisfied and happy, then does he open himself to wounds. Khairt knew that well, as he knew also that the man who endures is the man who strikes first, who kills without mercy, who sees any garden as a likely battle-ground. What is a hedge but a hiding place? What is a fountain but a place where one's enemies might be drowned?

And yet . . . Even as these hard thoughts came to him, so came to him the gentle rustling of leaves high above, the surprise of bright blossoms in the undergrowth. He thought again of the girl's face, the brightness of her eyes while she lived.

He took a deep breath and drank in the scents of the forest. The black leaves of the forest floor and the black earth beneath smelled as rich as fresh-baked bread. Again, he a heard thrush song and the calls of other birds high above. He felt the eyes of the forest at his back, above, all around.

So it was that, for a second time, he was lost in reverie when Daisilodavi rode up next to him and hailed the man who walked before them. "A fellow traveler," said the assassin. "Did you not see him?" Then, loudly, Daisilodavi called out, "Ho, soldier!" for the man had a short sword strapped to his belt and went along tap-ping the ground with the end of an unstrung bow. "Ho, archer!"

The man did not turn. His clothes were filthy, as if he'd been sleeping on the bare ground.

"Blue and gold braid on his tunic," said Daisilodavi. "This is Glinham's man. Do you see?"

"I have eyes."

"By the look of him, though," the assassin continued, "he may be no one's man at all."

Khairt's hand rested on his sword. "Surfaces deceive."

"Not always," said Daisilodavi with a thin smile. "Not in all places." Then he called again, "Ho, archer! Thou wanderer, ho!"

The man did not stop or look up until the two riders passed him, one on either side. Daisilodavi spun his mount to face him. Khairt rode a bit further, scanning the bushes for signs of another ambuscade. He saw no threat. However, he did notice the butter-flies flitting above the foliage. Their wings were silver on blue— Clouds in Heaven, he'd have called them, were it his task to name them. He leaned forward to see them better.

Stop this! he thought. He was not here for butterflies. He was here to kill a man. With a tug on the reins, he halted and turned his horse.

Daisilodavi was asking the man-at-arms, "And did you not hear us?"

"Aye, whether or not I heard you, that was what I considered," the man said. His hair was tangled and bits of leaves clung to it. "I was thinking, 'Is that voices I hear, and do they hail me?' If I turned to see you, could I then be certain that you existed? What certainty is there in the senses?"

"What's he prattling about?" said Khairt.

"Let him speak," said Daisilodavi.

"I thank you," said the man, "whether you exist or not. As I say, what certainty is there in the senses? Do the mad not see what is not there? Do dreamers not hear and see what they believe to be real? Who is to say that I will not, a moment hence, wake with a start to think what a strange conversation I was having just moments ago in my sleep?"

Daisilodavi smiled. "I take your meaning. And even were you to wake, how could you know that you were not having a dream of waking? Perhaps you are a great sea slug asleep on the ocean floor, dreaming that you are a man, when in truth no such creature as man has ever been."

"Just so."

"Gods and gashes," said Khairt. "I have never heard such nonsense traded." He drew his broadsword from the saddle scabbard, then balanced it on his shoulder. "Answer while you have your head to speak with. Where is your lord?"

"I have no lord," the man said. "I am finished with that life." He lifted his unstrung bow. "Have you considered," he asked, "the impossibility of an arrow's flight?"

"Answer me!" said Khairt, lifting the sword. "Where is Glinham?"

"I can hardly be sure that such a being as Lord Glinham ever existed," the man said, spreading his hands helplessly. "As for where he is now, I do not know, and cannot be sure I would know how I knew if indeed I thought that I did know."

Khairt grew red in the face.

"No need to split his head," said Daisilodavi, smiling. "Put away your sword, knight. He answers you as best he can."

"Nonsense!"

"Hardly nonsense," said the man. "Fundamental questions!"

For the first time, an almost soldierly flash came to his eyes, but he made no move toward the sword at his belt. It was as though he had forgotten he had it.

"Sword down," Daisilodavi said to Khairt. "We'll find neither help nor hindrance here."

The knight rested the heavy blade on his shoulder again.

"You said something of arrows," said Daisilodavi.

"Arrows," the man said. "Yes. That was the end to my soldiering. Consider, before an arrow can fly to its mark, it must fly halfway, must it not?"

"Indeed," said the assassin.

"And from that point, it must fly again halfway further, true?"

"True."

"And from there, halfway again—an eighth—and from there, halfway to the mark once more—a sixteenth. Wherever it flies, from half to quarter to eighth to sixteenth, the remaining space may be divided again by half. And then by half again. And may it not be infinitely divided? Is the space ever so small that it may not be halved again? So the points through which the arrow must pass are infinite in number. And, being infinite, they may not be summed. The arrow will never reach its mark."

Daisilodavi said, "The fletcher's paradox, that is called."

"Is it? I thought I had originated it."

"Nay, it has wrinkled many brows before yours."

"You see now wherefore I leave my bow unstrung."

"I do."

"Do you?" said Khairt. "Do you think an arrow will not pierce a heart because the archer has bethought this muddle?"

"You, sir," said the man, "are a fool."

"*I*, a fool?" said the knight. "I'll show you who's the fool!"

"Come," said Daisilodavi, turning his horse. "We've a task." Over his shoulder, he called to the former man-at-arms, "Here's a thought for you. Consider that an all-powerful demon appears in your dreams and offers you three wishes. Your first wish is that your first wish not be granted. Has the all-powerful demon the power to grant that wish?"

With a snort, Khairt returned his sword to its scabbard. He did not immediately give the former man-at-arms his back. The fellow still had a sword, after all. He might not be so addled as he seemed.

"I wish that this wish not be granted," the man said to himself. He began to chew his lip and rub his forehead.

Khairt turned his horse. When he had caught up with the assassin, he said, "Will you not circle back and poison this one, too?"

"I have poisoned him with a puzzle," said Daisilodavi. "He'll frown upon it until he starves. Or if he gives it up, he'll find another question that wears him down. When he realizes that he is hungry, he'll want a theory of food before he eats. Would that all men were philosophers. Mine would be an easy profession then."

"The world crawls with fools," Khairt said.

"Not fools," said Daisilodavi. "You see not the half of it."

Khairt gave no answer to that. He was already lost in the patterns and variations made by white bark and black, rough and smooth. The very trunks of the trees themselves were a kaleidoscope of shifting geometry as he rode. Only just now had he noticed. As he noticed, he once more felt that his gaze into the trees was returned.

"Not the half," Daisilodavi said.

Dusk light was deepening to gloom when they had ridden far enough to again encounter brambles.

"The far side," said Daisilodavi. "We have ridden the breadth of the Heart of Shanodin."

Shanodin, Khairt thought. It was a beautiful name. There was music to it. But what he said was, "No sign of Glinham himself."

"Oh, there's some sign of him."

"His retainers, you mean."

"No, I mean *him.* Or did you not notice, two or three leagues behind us, a change in the scent of the air? Was there not some unnatural trace?"

Not notice the smell of the air? Why, Khairt had been drunk with it! There were the rich scents of moss and leaf, the musk of a deer somewhere upwind, the sweet notes of flowers, and from some other region of the forest, a subtle scent like vanilla. That was the scent of red-barked Shanodin pines. Nor was that the only spicelike scent. There was a faint trace of attars, as from an alchemist's press—the scent of rose and clove and wanderseed touched with the bite of flame . . .

Khairt reined his horse. "Lamp oil!"

"So you did smell it. And not just any lamp oil, was it? No, someone burns a scented oil, expensive oil. That's the sort of dainty, the sort of luxury, we might expect of a rich merchant, aye?"

"Three leagues back! And you did not stop at once?"

"You were so lost in your dreaming, I dared not wake you."

"Dreaming!" Khairt made a fist, but knew not what to insist or what to deny. He had not been dreaming, exactly, though neither had he been about his business. "Demons and dung!" he said at last. "Now I see why our lord King Amjad trusts you not to do his bidding!"

"Tell me," said Daisilodavi, "what maze of thoughts were you wandering when that scent came to both our noses?"

"Blast you and your lawyerly graces! Blast your slippery tongue! We should turn and ride. Glinham lies close at hand."

"And so will he at the morrow. It grows dark. We'll encamp and wait for light."

"We might have slain him already," Khairt said. "We might be riding home even now."

"And you want to leave, do you?" said Daisilodavi. "I was thinking that you were somewhat drawn to this place."

The knight looked at the dark shadows of the trees. They seemed both lovely and foreboding. "This forest is too like a woman, and I've had naught to do with women since I left . . ."

He caught himself before he named the place. In the service of King Amjad, he had never spoken of his life before, in a court upon the plains. The less others knew of his past, the more free he was of it.

Daisilodavi was leaning forward in his saddle, as if straining for the missing word. When it did not come, he dismounted. "There's no sense in risking our horses in the dark. We'll encamp. Glinham is going nowhere in the meanwhile. He has settled, or why do you think we smelled a lamp burning in the day?"

"A cave."

"Quite so. And we'll find the entrance better by day than by night." Daisilodavi laid a blanket upon the ground and unrolled an oilcloth beside it, then went to see to his horse.

Khairt still did not stir from his saddle.

"Will you sleep ahorse?" Daisilodavi said.

"We are watched. Closely."

"And as we do not profane the trees, the watchers mean no harm. Put the dryads out of your mind, knight. Get down. Sleep. I may make use of your sword arm on the morrow."

"None makes use of me but Amjad and myself. I do not serve you. You make no use of me."

"A figure of speech. Stars in heaven, knight. Dismount and rest!"

Khairt sat a moment longer, lest his immediate response should seem obedience. Then he clambered down, lest his resistance seem only the churlishness of a lesser man. He fed his horse some oats and hobbled it.

The hard tack that had been their meal this week past had passed Khairt's lips untasted day after day. This night, as the last forest light faded, he noticed the fullness of it, the pleasure of so daily a taste as unleavened, unsalted bread.

"Will you sleep sitting up again?" said Daisilodavi. The oil-cloth covered him.

"The sooner to my feet and fighting, this way," Khairt said.

"That's if you wake in time. You slept ahorse today. I do not think you'll stand a vigil any better in the night."

Khairt did not answer.

Daisilodavi closed his eyes, and in the darkness, he smiled. The knight was beginning to show himself. At last, Daisilodavi would see what sort of man it was who stood with him at Amjad's right hand.

For his part, Khairt was troubled without knowing quite why. Yes, the feeling that he was ever watched disquieted him a little. But there was something more. Since he had taken up the sword, since he had come into the service of Amjad, a certain calm had settled over him, though he was always in the midst of murder. Or *because* he was always in the midst of murder. Now that calm had left him. He felt naked. Unarmored. There was something more dangerous about this forest than any line of pikemen he had ever charged.

As his eyes grew accustomed to the darkness, he perceived the ghostly glow of phosphorescence on rotting logs and stumps. On many vigils, he had seen this bluish glow and never fancied it beautiful. Now, as the emberflies and witchbeetles traced lines of red and green light through the black air, he felt as if he'd never seen a greater wonder. Soon he was lost in the weaving patterns of light, and even as his eyes closed, still he saw the lights dance.

He dreamed flowers. He dreamed black tree trunks, and brown, and gray, and white, soaring toward the canopy above like pillars in a great hall. He dreamed of the black swirls and dots and slashes on white birch bark, saw that these markings were lines of poetry he could almost read. His lips, thick with sleep, tried in vain to form the words.

Khairt dreamed of butterflies. He dreamed of brief openings in the canopy, of spots of blue sky glimpsed between the leaves, rare and precious as sapphires.

His arms and legs were leaden. He dreamed of fingers emerging from the tree he slept against, fingers that gently touched his iron rings of chain mail. He dreamed that he sat paralyzed and trusting as more fingers brushed his metal bootguards, worked the hinges of his visor down and up, and tested the weight of his sword.

If this were no dream, his death might be at hand. If these fingers truly played about him, if this being wished him ill . . .

He tried to move. He could not.

With effort, he opened his eyes. Two green witchbeetles hovered before him, not a handsbreadth apart. Fingers gently traced his eyebrows, moved down to close his eyes. *Those are no witchbeetles,* he thought, drifting deeper.

When next he opened his eyes, gray light had returned to the Heart of Shanodin. Daisilodavi, a lumpen heap beneath his oil-cloth, began to stir.

Khairt struggled to his feet. His knees this morning felt filled with broken glass. He grunted.

"And to you, too, a good morrow," said Daisilodavi.

"We had visitors," Khairt said, scanning the ground for tracks. He saw none, but dryads are light upon their feet.

"We're the visitors," said the assassin. "Is it any wonder that they should want to inspect us?"

Inspect they had. Khairt remembered the feel of hands upon his sword. How had he not awakened? How not risen and fought?

Khairt walked stiffly to his horse, sheathed the broadsword, and said, "Let us go and do our killing, then be gone from here."

"Murder, murder, murder. Is pleasure all you ever think of? Oh, thou libertine!"

"I think of getting from this place alive. Arise!"

"Am I a zombie, that you would raise me?"

"From your first words of the day, you prattle."

"From your first words, you are sour. I rise, my knight. Soon we are off to kill. Will you feel better once you have bathed your sword?"

Khairt gave no answer, but bent to unhobble his horse.

As he rode, Khairt concentrated on the purpose of their mission. Yes, the ivy creeping up the trunks was lush, and yes, the trills and chatterings of the birds were rich and pleasing. But he must not think of that. He must only think of spilling blood, of the purifying sweat of battle.

Let Glinham be well armed. Let such men-at-arms who still served him be of great fighting spirit. To fight, to kill, that alone would bring Khairt relief. Damn these butterflies with their vari-colored wings! Let these purple flowers fall and rot! May hawks dine upon these songbirds!

But even as he cursed the beauties of the forest, so too did he enumerate them. He could not help but have eyes and ears.

"We are very near the place," said Daisilodavi, halting. "Back this way, I think." He crossed a brook.

The sound of water rushing by the horse's feet was bright as bells. Khairt grimaced. Eyes half-closed so that he might concentrate on purifying thoughts of blood, he followed.

The entrance to the cave, once they neared it, was obvious. To say that it lay in a clearing would be to suggest an open sky and bright light shining. There are no clearings in the Heart of Shanodin. But for some little space, the trees grew not so crowded, and in the center of that spot was a pile of rocks overgrown with vines and creepers.

Both men dismounted. Daisilodavi rummaged in his saddle-bags for a lamp, flint, and oil rags.

The opening between the rocks was narrow.

"You're too big a rat for this wee hole," said the assassin as he ignited the rags to light the lamp. "Here is where we must part."

"I can get through," said Khairt.

"Mayhap, if you stripped off that chain mail and greased yourself in bear fat. That will take some time. First you must hunt a bear."

"Armor and all," said the knight, "I can get through."

"And then what? Fight with a broadsword where there may not be a shoulder's breadth to swing it? Nay. Stay here. Keep a watch. Perhaps I'll flush the quarry out, and then he will be yours."

"If he is well guarded, what chance have you?"

"I daresay he is not guarded well. No matter how many men-at-arms he brought with him here, I'll wager the one true soldier was that girl we slew. The rest will have deserted him."

"Why?"

"You are ever slow to understand, Khairt. Stand you here a while and think on it." With that, he disappeared into the hole.

Khairt did not stand long, though. His knees ached. He sat on a stone and watched the entrance of the cave, listened for any sound from the assassin.

From the black hole he heard nothing. It was as though the earth had swallowed Daisilodavi up. But all around him, Khairt again heard the music of bird song. He inhaled the forest scents, and all of a sudden the helmet on his head felt like a cramped, confining room. He pried it off. Fresh air against his skin felt as good as it smelled.

Khairt looked again at the cave entrance. The hole might be no deeper than an oubliette. Then again, it might stretch for miles. Daisilodavi could be days in flushing the quarry, if, indeed, he did not simply kill Glinham where he found him.

In an hour, it was clear that the hole was no oubliette.

Khairt knew that he should wait here, helmet on, sword at the ready, like a sentinel. But his hair felt oily, and his skin was sticky with sweat.

He bethought himself, then, of the brook.

The narrow fracture that admitted Daisilodavi narrowed further, until he could just wriggle forward inches at a time. Then the crack widened, grew round, and opened gradually into a wide and level passage. The walls, though smoothed by the tumble of ancient waters, were dry, and the floor was dusty. This cave had long been dead. Here, no waters dripped from the ceiling to grow crystals or stalactites.

The passage gave way to a large room. The sharp smell of guano told of bats crowding the far reaches of the ceiling, beyond the yellow glow of Daisilodavi's lantern. His glow caught the glimmer of something on the floor, and he discovered a little mound of jewelry—a man's heavy golden bracelet, rings set with fine stones. He slipped the bracelet onto his wrist and put the rings in the pocket of his cape.

Then he listened.

Silence.

The tunnel continued on the far side of the room. This passage led to yet another, smaller room. Here, Daisilodavi the assassin sat down to consider, for in this room, with his lamp raised high, the assassin could see no fewer than five openings that promised further passages.

It would do him no good to sniff the air that issued from each. The spiced oil had been burning for some time inside the cave, and the smell had by now bled into every room and tunnel. Besides, the fumes of his own lamp were much the stronger smell. So which way to go?

Then he heard the chanting.

At first, Khairt had only splashed water on his face, rubbed the drops from his eyes, and looked warily at where his chain mail lay spread across a fallen trunk. Nearer to hand was his sword.

When no one crept from behind a tree to fling a stone or rush him with a staff, he dared lower his brow to the running stream. He rose. Cool water ran from his hair, down his cheeks, and onto the back of his neck. His clothes, worn these many days beneath the armor, were filthy.

Not far upstream, an emerald finch landed on the shallow bank, cocked its head to consider Khairt, and then began to bathe in a patch of sunlit water. Droplets rolled from its back and shivered from its wings like diamonds.

Khairt took a deep breath and began to strip. As he laid his black clothes down, as he gave himself over to the open air, it was as though he were laying aside a dream. Naked, he walked downstream until he found a pool deep enough to lie in. First he washed the sweat-crusted clothes. Then he knelt in the current, filled his palm with water, and dribbled it over the flower tattoos on his arms, over the varicolored bird tattoos on his chest.

He sank into the water. The hair on his legs obscured the brown tattoos, but it was still obvious enough that those lines were meant to represent tree bark. "Let my legs be like the oak," he had told the tattoo master. And there had been prophecy in his choice. In every match, his legs had been rooted to the ground. He'd been impossible to move, no matter how the other wrestlers might kick at his knees. Immobile he had stood, waiting for his opening, waiting for the shift that would let him drop and pin his opponent or spin him out of the ring.

Like the oak, he was unbending. And like the oak, when at last he must yield, since he could not bend, he must break. In one match, two body blows to his knees ended his career.

Khairt rolled in the water, letting the stream rush over and around and through. He stretched, luxuriated, and at last rose, dripping.

If before the flowers in the underbrush were colorful, now they were brilliant. If before the thrush's song had seemed beautiful, now it was enthralling. Butterflies danced in vibrant clouds.

"Eyah!" Khairt cried three times, an Oneahn exultation. He shook his head, raining water and delight. He stamped his bare foot on the leaves, ignoring the protest of his knee. "Koy!" he called out. "First approach!" And he stepped across the ground in the first gait of his school, the first balanced walk that he had learned.

"Izza!" he cried. "First turn!" He turned three-quarter turns, always rooted to the ground.

The more complicated moves then came to him as easily as breath, though he had not practiced them for long years. These steps, the Dance That Breaks Bones, were not truly a wrestler's moves. Within the court, they were forbidden, for these moves were not sport but the warrior's art.

Khairt took a running step, leaped into a winged sidekick, and landed on one leg.

His knee quivered. He bit back the pain, but remained standing. He managed to pivot, and then he was into the next move,

the sweeping gestures that made him think of waves. Ah, he was
dancing. He began the Walk of Spinning Pins, turning and turning as he crossed the forest floor. Now he was alive as long he
had not been. Ittono Khairt ni Hata Kan, Grand Champion of the
Court, dances once more, and in his dancing lives the Court of a
Thousand Thousands . . .

Green eyes.

One turn more, and one turn more, and . . .

Green eyes.

He stopped turning. Someone was watching him.

Khairt turned around in the other direction, a little dizzily,
his knees now throbbing with pain.

There. Across the brook, in the shadowed ivy there, between
those trees. Two lights shone like the green glow of witchbeetles,
not a handsbreadth apart.

She blinked, stepped forward, and only when she moved
thus did he really see her. It was as though she'd been invisible,
though now he knew he'd seen her all along, yet not known her
feet from roots nor her arms from branches. He'd not known how
to see her.

The more she moved, the more plainly he saw her. Her arms
did not end in branches at all, but in hands like his. Her feet were
feet, not roots. How had he seen her skin as tree bark, when it
was only tattooed in that pattern, like his legs?

Her eyes, in truth, did not glow like witchbeetles. They were
green, though, and filled with ordinary light. She smiled, and
Khairt did not know if ever he had seen a woman so beautiful.
Not even the courtesans of Oneah had been her like.

Beautiful, yet dangerous, also, should he give offense. He
watched her warily.

She turned a circle, stopped, then looked at him, a question
in her eyes.

Khairt shrugged. She repeated the motion.

"Ah!" he said. "The Walk of Spinning Pins!" He smiled.
"No, no. Not at all like that. Your knee must rise to the level of
your hip. And point your toes, so." And he turned for her, then
watched as she repeated the move. "Yes," he said. "That's better.
Now, mind your hands." He turned for her again, and then she
turned as he had shown her, and soon the two of them were danc-

ing the Walk of Spinning Pins on either side of the brook. They danced as far as the place where Khairt's black clothes lay drying on a bush.

"Gods and gashes!" he cried, remembering his nakedness and snatching up the clothes. At that, the dryad vanished.

Khairt gazed at the spot where she had been. Then he laughed and shook his head. "My apologies, lady of the wood," he said. "I am unaccustomed to dancing without a breechcloth." He tore his wet tunic to fashion one, but she did not soon reappear.

Daisilodavi stopped now and then to listen to the sound of a man's voice as it rose and fell in the rhythms of a prayer chant. The sound had been growing steadily louder, and now the assassin could hear something about the *quality* of the sound. The voice echoed, and not with the sharp echo of a tunnel. This was the resonant, droning echo of a great room.

And he was almost there.

He stopped for a moment to lower the wick of his lamp so that only the tiniest blue flame flickered on the tip, then crept forward a little distance without the light.

At the end of this tunnel, he could just make out an orange glimmer. He went back, raised the wick, and checked to see that all his needles and blades were where they should be. When he continued, he went whistling the tune of a merry drinking song at a much faster tempo than the chant.

The chanting stopped.

Daisilodavi went on whistling. Just before he entered the great cavern, he broke into song:

> *If the maid be merry,*
> *and if the maid be strong,*
> *and if she'll fetch and carry*
> *then I'll marry her anon,*
> *hey, marry her anon.*

Then, as he stepped into the open, he laughed giddily. "Marry her! Sooner drown myself!" Then he laughed again.

The great room was even larger that the first he had passed

through. At the far end of it, high atop a mound of boulders, there burned a lamp, but there was no one to be seen nearby.

"Ho, did my ears deceive me, or did I hear prayers issuing from here? Hey and hullo, is there a holy man about?"

No answer came.

Daisilodavi squinted. He could make out a ledge, a sort of shelf that ran around the great room at the level of the lamp.

"What do you want?" asked a voice. Because of the echo, Daisilodavi could not tell where it issued from.

"I want wine," Daisilodavi said. "I have been *days* without wine. Have you any?"

"'Wine is the bane of reason.' So spake the Prophet Eziir."

"Ah, yes. Well, of course it would be unreasonable to expect you to have any, then. Beer, then? Ale?"

"'Drink not of strong spirits, nor of wine, nor of any fermented drink, lest in body and in spirit ye shall die.'" The voice echoed. "So spake the Prophet Haprina in her sermon to the kings. So accounted are the Words of the Prophets."

"Ah, I see how matters stand, then," Daisilodavi said. "I've little hope of wine. Well, then, Lord Glinham, you'll not object if I ask only to sit and rest, will you?"

"You speak a name that has fallen away."

"Of course, of course. You've a new name now, I suppose. A hermit's name."

There was no answer from the voice. Daisilodavi scanned the ledge above, but he could see no sign of exactly where Glinham might be.

"Why have you come?" asked the voice.

"Would you believe," said Daisilodavi, "to do murder?" And he giggled into his sleeve. "Oh, I found this bracelet and other baubles." He let lamplight play over the gold. "But I ought not tell you, for then you'll want them back, will you not?"

"Those are like the skin of the snake, shed with a former life. I do not want them."

"Turned ascetic, have you?" Daisilodavi set his lamp down on the floor of the cave. "From fat merchant to hermit?"

"'The riches of the earth weigh to a holy man as stones weigh in the pockets of him who drowns.' So spake the Prophet Pringle in the Age of the Silver Sun."

For a long moment, Glinham was silent. Then he asked, "Have you still come with murder on your mind?"

"The Heart of Shanodin changes a man," Daisilodavi observed.

"It makes him true," Glinham agreed.

"So spake the prophets."

"In truth, no. The prophets were silent upon matters of the Shanodin Forest. But the Seer Odamulus wrote of this place. 'In Shanodin's Heart,' wrote he, 'a man lives his heart of hearts and follows the path that he wills not or dares not. In Shanodin's Heart, all hearts are revealed.'"

"And thus, when you offended Amjad, may his name be cause for drinking, you came here. Whosoever Amjad would send must become his true heart in the Heart of Shanodin. A wise choice. A merry choice. A strategy worthy of toasting!" Daisilodavi looked about the floor of the cavern. "Did you not, perhaps, discard some wineskins as you discarded your jewels? Is there nowhere hereabout a drop to drink?"

"No wine," said the priestly voice of Glinham. "And as for the wisdom of my choice, aye, there is wisdom to it, but folly as well. Here I have discovered my true heart as a man who would walk the path of the prophets. But what do the prophets demand? 'From him who has seen the light, let shine forth the light, that it may fill not his eyes alone.' Thus spake the Prophet Eziir."

"The words of the prophets are too subtle for me."

"It means that I must shine forth. I must go out into the world and show the light of the prophets to others. But if I leave Shanodin, my former nature will be reborn. Out in the world where I must bear witness to the light of the prophets, my eyes will dim again. My concerns will return to gold and sweetmeats and silken clothes."

"I see," said Daisilodavi. "As the pendulum swings from side to side, so do you swing between prophets and profits."

Glinham did not laugh. "Outside of Shanodin," he said, "I shall be no more priestly than you shall remain a wine-thirsty harmless fool."

With that, Glinham stepped out of the shadows. He had been near his burning lamp all along. He wore a silken tunic, the edges ragged where he had torn away the fine embroidery. There was deep gloom in his voice when he said, "If I leave, I cannot remain true to the prophets. Yet if I would remain true to the prophets, I must not stay."

"'Tis sad, this puzzle," said Daisilodavi. He sighed loudly. "None but the Shanodin-enchanted for you to preach to. No one to hear your holy words." He sighed again. "Sorrow was always best washed down with wine. Not a drop, are you sure?"

"What did you say?"

Daisilodavi brightened. "Ah, so you *do* have wine!"

"No, no. Before that. About the Shanodin-enchanted. Why, there's *you,* of course! I have *you* to preach to!"

Daisilodavi picked up his lamp and began to back away. "Not if there's no wine-drinking in your sanctuary. No, no words of the prophets for me, thank you!"

As Daisilodavi turned to flee, Glinham scrambled awkwardly down the tumbled boulders. "Wait! Wait!" he cried. "Prayer is better than wine! You'll see!"

When his knees would bear no more capering, Khairt sat beneath a tree, facing the brook. The forest's sounds, its musty perfumes, its wind-shifted light filled his heart, and ere long he was dancing again, though only from the waist up. As he sat, he let his arms twine in the figures of the Dance That Breaks Bones, and then in other forms he knew. Then he improvised, letting the light and shadow of the forest or the teasing call of a jay suggest a ripple of his great arms, a curling and uncurling of his fingers.

In the brush and shadows across the brook, he saw a branch wave in time with his arm. When he fluttered his fingers, leaves rustled in imitation. He smiled. Still sitting, he swayed from side to side and twisted, and a tree trunk seemed to do the same, although, a moment later, it was no tree trunk at all, but her. Her eyes blazed green again, and then were only mortal eyes. She lifted her leg and danced, mirroring what he did with his arms.

"Lady, lovely lady, lovely maid," said Ittono Khairt ni Hata Kan. "Of all the tapestries that hung in Oneah, none there was to match your forest ivy. Of all the musicians that played before the kings of a thousand thousands, none could bring forth the notes of the thrush. Lady, of all the maids I ever bowed to, of all the ladies ever I loved, none was such as thee."

If she understood, she made no sign. She only danced on, even after Khairt's arms grew suddenly heavy and he paused to watch. His breathing grew slow and deep. She danced to the very bank of the brook, and only when his eyelids grew heavy and began to close did he see her smile.

There was something more he wanted to say then. There was some line of poetry he wanted to recite, but his tongue lay heavy in his mouth and would not move. *Do I sleep?* he wondered. *Let me not sleep. Let me not miss, by sleeping, a moment of her presence.*

But if he was sleeping, at least he was dreaming that she was near, for he felt fingertips tracing the birds and flowers of his tattoos. Gently, gently, in his dream, fine fingers traced the lines of bark that decorated his legs.

There was pleasure in her touch, but he bethought himself in danger, too. Should she mean him harm, he was helpless to defend himself. Was a dryad not a creature of the forest? Like a bear, might she not turn from curious to fierce?

He willed his eyes to open. They would not.

And still he willed it. He was a man who had stayed within the ring to finish his final match, though one knee already would not support him. With strength such as that, he willed his eyes to open.

Green lights.

Gently, she made him close his eyes.

Glinham stared at the blood pooling in his palm.

Daisilodavi's dagger glinted in the yellow light. "There's slow poison on the tip," he said. "It seemed a mercy. Though you'll endure some pain, at least you've an hour or so in which to make your peace, to find your consolation in the prophets."

In the assassin's other hand, a needle appeared. "I can give you the quick, if you prefer. Still more pain, but then it's over in an instant."

Tears welled in Glinham's eyes. "H-how?"

"By which you surely mean," said Daisilodavi, "how do I escape the Shanodin's effects? After all, the Heart has made a holy man of you, who before worshiped only gold."

"Not so! I loved the words of the prophets, but only feared to live by them." He clutched his wrist. "How it burns!"

"Howsoever. All of your retainers were changed, and my own companion, who awaits me, is becoming something else, not the brute slayer of men my Lord Amjad so loves. So how do I escape? How does Daisilodavi remain Daisilodavi? Is it really so hard a riddle?"

Glinham looked again at his wound and bit his lip. His hand began to shake, and he closed his fist.

"True, you've other matters to think upon, and so I will solve it for you. You see, Amjad himself brought me here once, for he would know the hearts of those who closely serve him. And he said it thus: 'As thou art poisonous and merry without, so art thou poisonous and merry within.' Or to put it another way . . ."

The assassin leaned close to the wincing Glinham. "I act. I lie. I pretend. I change my seeming in a blink of an eye. So what lies beneath? What is the true nature that I guard by my dissembling?" He smiled. "I am an actor. A liar. A pretender. My single nature is that I have no single nature."

"To greet the eye of heaven, that is sweetness," groaned Glinham. "So spake the Prophet Niptea as she burned."

"Did she really?" marvelled Daisilodavi.

"The quick poison!" Glinham pleaded. "Give me the quick!"

Khairt heard him coming. Or, rather, he heard the silences of the erstwhile singing insects, circles of silence that moved as the assassin moved. Khairt knew when Daisilodavi stood regarding his chain mail, knew when he was looking at the mound of black clothes. Long before Daisilodavi stood over him, Khairt felt his presence.

"Oneahn," Daisilodavi said. "So that's it. A lover of beauty in the Court of Oneah. No wonder I didn't know your accent. That race of men is all but dead."

Khairt opened his eyes.

"We've finished what we came for," said the assassin. "Our lord awaits us with still more bloody deeds."

"I am staying here," Khairt said.

"Knight, you've no choice in the matter. You are sworn to Amjad's service."

"Go. He has deadly enough hands in those two of yours."

"Ah, but we are not the same. Mine are the hands that strike unseen, but he needs yours, too. He may not always strike by stealth."

"I am no longer his."

"You would be," Daisilodavi said. He looked around him. "You would be, were the curse of this place but lifted."

"It is no curse. I am come home. Please, leave me, Daisilodavi." He took a deep breath. "In this forest even *your* name has music to it." He said the name again.

"And you accuse *me* of prattle," said the assassin.

"Once I lived at the center of the world, Daisilodavi, for such was the Court of a Thousand Thousands. I thought that I lived at the heart of beauty. To wrestle was beautiful. To stand in the glimmering court beneath the Roof of Lights was beautiful. And the women of the court . . ."

"That is long since past."

"Aye. For me it was passing with the strength of my body. But I thought it would yet stand beautiful forever, before the Goblin War."

Daisilodavi looked away. "You need speak of it no more."

"Why? Is this not why Amjad bade you bring me here, so that he might know my heart? Listen, that you may tell it well. When the Cities and Court of a Thousand Thousands fell, I thought I would never look upon beauty again. Thought I, if all things come to dust, then shall I be the ally of dust. That is why I wandered far until I found a master who would teach me the art of broadsword. Edged weapons were forbidden in Oneah. Sin resides in steel. I no longer cared. I designed to be as black of heart as any goblin." With that last word, his voice shook. With fury, he said, "Let Amjad look upon me, even Amjad, and fear!"

"That's the Khairt I know!"

Khairt laughed. "No longer. I have looked again upon beauty, and I conclude thus, Daisilodavi: beauty, even more than dust, shall endure."

"Nay," said the assassin. "All things come to dust."

"Not the song of birds. Not sunlight. Leave me. Leave me to the gaze of the forest."

"You do not fear the dryads, then?"

Khairt smiled. "One may know fear, yet not be mastered by it. Only a fool would not fear her."

The assassin nearly said something, then checked himself. "I see," he said. He took a few steps away, then stopped to say over his shoulder, "Dust shall conquer thee, Khairt. Even more than beauty, dust shall endure."

Then he was gone.

Khairt danced and practiced in the last hour of light, and though she did not appear, he knew she watched him.

"Green, more rich than gold, my heart is green," he said. That was the line of Oneahn poetry he had meant before to recite to her. He wished he could remember the rest of the poem, but it was gone. Gone, as all Oneah was now gone.

He must not think of what he had lost. Those were the thoughts of his dark and damaged self. Thoughts of death and ruin did not belong in this place. The Heart of Shanodin was life itself.

When the gloom deepened, he rested against a tree to wait for her. His arms, as before, grew heavy. As before, he could not keep his eyes open.

Near. She was very near.

Feather-light, she touched his skin.

After this dream, his waking dream of her, he dreamed of flower-covered prairies, the sweet plains of his youth.

He woke to a familiar voice.

"High time you were stirring," said Daisilodavi. He was sitting on a log. "It's past first light. We've a long ride today to get out of this forest!"

Khairt rubbed his eyes and stood. "I thought you gone."

"I was gone," Daisilodavi said. "I returned." He threw black rags at Khairt's feet. "Dress. You'll not want to sit ahorse naked. And put your armor on. We may have a fight anon, if we do not ride hard."

"I have no enemies here," Khairt said.

"You do now," Daisilodavi said. "We both do." And as he rose, Khairt saw the shape of the log he'd been using for a bench—the curved calf, the flaring hips, the shoulder.

Khairt groaned, not believing. He rose, knees cracking, and went to turn her, to see the contorted face in the wood.

"Her sisters will not care for details," Daisilodavi said. He grunted as he saddled Khairt's horse. "When they miss her, they'll find this place. There is no judiciary of dryads, no appeal. They'll overnumber and destroy any mortals they soon find near this murder spot."

Khairt gave no warning. Had he moved like the knight Daisilodavi knew, the assassin might have dodged him. But Khairt crossed the ground in the sprinting dance of Ittono Khairt ni Hata Kan, and his knees did not betray him. In half a blink, his hand was at the assassin's throat, and he had the man bent backward across his other arm. From the corner of his eye, Khairt saw the needle poised in Daisilodavi's hand.

They looked into each others' eyes. With a squeeze of Khairt's hand and a shift of his arms, Daisilodavi's throat would be crushed and his back broken. With a dying jab of his hand, Daisilodavi could kill the knight wrestler.

"Why?" Khairt said through his grimace. "Do you hate me as your rival? But I would be your rival no longer! Why? You killed her to destroy me!"

Daisilodavi, choking, managed to gasp out, "No. To keep you."

Khairt looked into the man's eyes, then let him drop to the forest floor. Without a word, he picked up the black rags, shook them out, and began to dress.

North of Shanodin, on the Plain of Suns, the grasses waved in the wind.

There was no path. The two riders—the armored one astride a black charger, the gray-clad one upon a leggy horse—weaved among the grassy waves.

They rode parallel, not a sword's reach apart. Neither looked to the left nor to the right. They did not speak. Not even as the plains gave way to marshes, then to swamps. Not even as they reached the foul and blighted bogs of their Lord Amjad.

May his name cause silence.

Animal Trap

M. C. Sumner

Kolli pushed through the curtained doorway and wrinkled her nose at the acrid stench. The shop was narrow, dirty, and its oiled paper windows let in only a muddy light. Pelts of a dozen beasts hung from the rafters, turning the interior into a maze of hides.

"A good morning to you," called a rough voice from behind the skins. "What can I do for you today?"

"I'm looking for Morl," said Kolli. She saw heavy boots and thick legs approaching from under the screen of pelts.

"I'm Morl." A last skin was pushed aside, and the bearded face of a broad-shouldered man poked through. He didn't see her at first, a smile frozen on this thick lips as he looked left and right.

"Down here."

Morl's bearded face turned down, and the smile faded as he surveyed Kolli's ragged clothing. "Who're you?"

"Dason sent me."

Morl rubbed at his rheumy eyes with one sausage-fingered hand. "Dason? Well then, why'd he send you?"

"He said you were having some trouble with—"

Morl turned and walked away through the swinging pelts. "Go back and tell Dason to send someone old enough lace his own clothes."

Kolli pushed through the skins after him. "I'm fourteen and I'm plenty—"

"Girl, you aren't big enough to make a good breakfast. Go an' get your older brother."

"I've worked with Dason on—"

Morl turned back to her. "This is not taking the change from some beggar's tray. Tell Dason to send someone else."

"Will you let me finish a sentence!" Kolli shouted. "I don't have an older brother. And Dason isn't going to send anyone else because you aren't offering enough to hire anyone else." She planted her hands on her narrow hips. "And you don't need anyone else. I'm the one you want."

Morl's brow furrowed. "Are you now?" He walked around and sat behind a stout table that was covered in scraps of loose fur and spotted with dark stains.

"Yes," she said.

"Did Dason tell you what the job is?"

"Doesn't matter," said Kolli. "I'm the one to do it." She came to the edge of the table and leaned over it, her hands on the rough wood. "What do you need stolen?"

"Careful there," said Morl. "You'll not be wanting to put your delicate little hands in anything nasty."

Kolli flicked her gaze to the discolored table, but she didn't move. "What do you want stolen?" she repeated.

"What I need is a secret."

"How can I steal it if you won't tell me what it is?"

Morl waved a beefy hand. "I don't mean that, girl. I mean it's information I'm after. Somebody else's secret that I need stolen."

"Whose secret?" she asked.

"Kalenth Ush," said Morl, lowering his brows as he said it.

Kolli frowned. "The trader from Keldon? The one who lives out in the woods?"

Morl nodded. "The very one." His thick lips turned up in a smirk. "You're not so sure of yourself now, are you?"

"I've never worked outside of the city," said Kolli. She hesitated for a second. There had been stories of terrible things happening outside the city. In just the last few days, several people had gone missing. "I'll manage. What is it you want to know?"

The big man leaned across the table until his craggy face

was almost touching Kolli's. "I need to know where Kalenth Ush is getting silver wolf hides."

Kolli frowned. "I would suppose he's trapping silver wolves. You don't think so?"

"Not here," Morl said with a shake of his head. "I never heard of a silver wolf within a hundred leagues of this place. But Ush keeps turning up with the things." He leaned back, picked up a scrap of fur, and rubbed it between his fingers. "There's nothing else like silver wolf fur: soft, warm, takes well to dye. And there's no animal in the world so tough to trap: big as a man, mean, and only comes out at night."

"I don't get it," said Kolli. "What's the difference where this Keldon gets his furs?"

Morl snorted. "When silver wolf is plentiful, every other fur turns cheap. Why buy rabbit or common timber wolf if you can get silver wolf? Things keep up like they're going, and every trapper, tanner, and fur trader in town will be out of business."

"I'll find out where he gets the furs," said Kolli. "You have my word."

"Well," said Morl, "I can't say as I find that so very reassuring. Run along, girl, but be careful how you play your games with Ush. He's not much nicer than a wolf himself."

Kolli knew every crooked alley and bird-spattered rooftop of the city, but the woods were a mystery to her. Compared to the densely packed houses and tangled streets, the thick boles of the ancient trees provided scarce cover. Kolli hugged herself tight against the rough trunk of an oak, hoping that her colorless clothing would blend with the lichen-spotted bark. A dozen steps away along a dusty path was the home of Kalenth Ush.

The peaked roofs of several ramshackle buildings showed over a tall fence of sharp-topped poles. There was a narrow gate on the side of the fence facing the road, but it was closed. A length of cloud-gray fur that flapped from a tall staff like the banner of a army served as the only advertisement of the Keldon's business. A trail of smoke rose from one of the buildings and brought the scent of burning pine to Kolli's nose. Ush was home.

The plain fact that the trader felt confident enough to build outside the city walls said a lot about the man inside the fence. The woods around the city weren't known for their kindness. Bandits, giant spiders, and sword-clawed grizzly bears were all common under the dark trees, and basilisks were not unknown.

Kolli had not much fear of the bandits—she'd lived her life among such as them, but the animals . . . It was all she could do to keep from running back to the city when the reddened sun fell to the horizon. A few minutes later, she heard the horns of the city guardsmen. Then came the distant groan of timbers and clanking of heavy chains as the gates were closed for the night.

She waited until the sky had gone a bruised purple and the night birds had started their songs before she released her grip on the tree and moved toward the Keldon's compound. Rubbing her stiff arms, Kolli stepped through the narrow band of woods and hurried across the dusty road. She pressed her face to the rough-hewn palisade and searched for some seam wide enough to look through, but Ush had chinked the gaps with mud.

Kolli's thin fingers slid over the wood, finding every knot and crack. Her arms pulled and her soft boots left the ground. She climbed easily. It took only a few seconds before Kolli's face peered between two pointed poles at the top of the wall.

The largest building was the closest. Smoke came from a hole in the center of its roof, and Kolli could hear the cracking of cedar knots in the fire pit. A series of small sheds lined the back of the compound. Each shed was surrounded by its own stout fence. The gates on two fences hung open, but the others were barred with thick lengths of wood. A small pen just below Kolli held a heap of scythed grass and a trio of mangy sheep.

She wrinkled her nose in thought. What did Ush keep in the sheds? They weren't large enough for cattle, and there was none of the noise and offal that came with poultry. Surely, the palisade itself provided all the protection his animals might need from the creatures of the forest. So the sheds weren't strong to protect what was in them. Maybe they were strong to keep what was in them from getting out.

A smile spread slowly over Kolli's face as she looked at the sheds. She dropped from the wall and trotted back toward town to see if the city's walls were as easy to breach as those of Kalenth Ush.

*   *   *

"Raising silver wolves!" shouted Morl.

Kolli nodded. "He's keeping them in sheds out there. He's even got sheep to feed them."

The fur trader ran a hand across his shaggy hair. "Raising them. I'd not believe it. How could you ever manage them? For that matter, how did he ever catch them and bring them here?" He stopped and looked sharply at Kolli. "You saw these wolves?"

"I saw the sheds."

"Sheds! Sheds could be anything. I'm not paying you to find out if the man has sheds."

"If he's not raising wolves out there," Kolli said calmly, "then how do you explain the news I got from the city guard?"

"What news?" asked Kolli.

"You've heard about the missing merchants and woodsmen?"

"I have, and it's surely the work of bandits."

"That's what everyone's been saying. But last night, some men on horseback were attacked by a beast."

"A hellcat. They'll attack anything."

Kolli smiled. "By a beast that looks like a giant timber wolf."

"Giant timber wolf," Morl said slowly. "Yes, I suppose that's how someone around here might describe a silver wolf. There's more difference than just size between them, though; silver wolves have hands like a man and hell's own meanness."

"Some of Ush's pens were empty," said Kolli. "I figure some of his wolves escaped and are taking care of travelers."

A thoughtful look came to Morl's deep-set eyes. "Perhaps I'll rig a few traps. Couldn't hurt my business to offer silver wolf fur of my own."

"Good idea," said Kolli. "Now, if you'll just pay me, I'll be on my way."

Morl's hand was halfway to his pouch when he stopped and asked, "Suppose you're wrong?"

"I'm not wrong."

"I don't know that. Besides, even if Ush did have silver wolves in those pens, they might have all been killed or got loose by now." He shook his head. "No, I need to know what Ush has in those pens now."

"I've done what you asked," said Kolli. "If you want more, you'll have to take it up with Dason."

"An extra silver."

"Two."

"Done," said Morl. "But only if he's got silver wolves in those pens. No wolves, and I give you nothing."

Kolli remembered the heavy wooden bars across the doors of three of the sheds. Whatever was in there, it was something that Ush didn't want to get loose. And if she was very clever, she might keep Dason from finding out about the extra payment. "Done," she said.

She was careful to climb the fence at a spot as far as possible from both the sheep and the wolf pens. Kolli let herself drop to the weed-choked ground inside the fence and sat still for several minutes, waiting to see if there was any response from the house.

No lamp showed from inside the ragged building, only the reddish glow of the fire pit. For the moment the night was clear and dark, but Kolli had just an hour to complete her work. Already the radiant spark of the lesser moon was high in the black sky, soon the greater moon would join it, and the night would be too bright for Kolli's comfort. She had to move now. She planned her steps carefully, moving from the fence toward the first shed in the line with quick, light steps.

The pens were filthy. The heavy railings were almost as tall as the palisade around the compound, and gnawed and gouged all the way to the top. The sheds showed signs of frequent patches and reinforcement. The wood of the doors was thicker than Kolli's palm. Scraps of light-colored fur were stuck on the rough wood.

At the third shed, she heard a muffled noise. The sound came again—a soft whine.

I just have to see it, Kolli told herself. *I only have to look in, count the beasts, and get out of this fearful place.*

She pressed her face against the rough boards at a spot where there was a finger-width gap. It took some time before her eyes adapted to the almost total darkness in the shed, and even more time before she could interpret what she saw. It was a man. He was tied hand and foot to the opposite wall of the shed. His mouth was covered by a strip of untanned hide. The ragged clothes that hung in ribbons from his body might once have been the garments of a well-to-do traveler. He was staring right at Kolli.

She gave a soft cry and stepped back from the shed. The man tried to speak, his words an animal whine under the gag. Kolli went back to the shed and whispered, "I'll get you out. Don't worry."

A hand clamped around her neck and lifted her from the ground. She clawed at the hand and kicked with her feet, but found only air. Slowly, she was turned to face a fierce visage with eyes blacker than the night and a smile filled with long, sharp teeth.

"Worry," said Kalenth Ush.

"I won't tell anyone," said Kolli. The leather straps from which she hung were chaffing at her wrists, and she couldn't quite turn her head far enough to see what Ush was doing. The fire was only a few feet away, and the room was lit red by the flames. On a small table was a heap of gold and silver—undoubtedly taken from the pockets of the missing travelers, as well as from Ush's trade in silver wolf hide.

Kolli swung her legs, trying to turn her body toward the Keldon. "Really. I've had trouble with the guard, they wouldn't believe me even if I did tell them."

Ush stepped back into view. The man was so tall that his head almost brushed the ceiling. Despite the coolness of the night, his face was bathed in sweat. "Tell them what?" he asked in a voice full of guttural Keldon accent. When Kolli didn't answer, he gave a grunt of disgust. "You have seen it all, but you still don't know. Do you?"

"It's you who's killing the travelers."

"Is it? And why would I do that?"

"You're stealing their money, then feeding the travelers to your silver wolves," said Kolli.

The Keldon snorted. "You foolish southerners don't even know what a silver wolf really is." He stepped closer and ran a rough-nailed finger down Kolli's cheek.

She did not flinch, would not allow herself to flinch.

"What do you know of the skin trade?" asked Ush.

"Nothing. I know nothing. Let me go and I won't say a thing about what I've seen."

He ignored her offer. "In this work, there is always a trade-off. With an older animal, you get the largest pelt. But not the finest pelt." Again, his hand reached out to Kolli's cheek. "The softest pelts come only from the young."

Quite slowly, quite deliberately, he leaned toward Kolli and pulled her jerkin away from her shoulder. Then he bit her. Hard. She cried out; she couldn't help it. The Keldon trader's mouth seemed as hot as a furnace against her skin.

He leaned back, smiling at her over bloody lips.

Kolli took a hard grip on the leather thongs, then she pulled her feet up and planted both heels square in the trader's smiling face. As he staggered away, Kolli whipped herself back and forth until she was able to swing her feet through the smoke hole in the center of the roof. A cloud of embers came up with her, swarming around like an army of fireflies. The heat from the flames below was terrible, searing her legs and back. But relieved of her weight, the leather straps at her wrists grew looser, and she struggled free. Her head swung toward the fire.

Ush screamed something that Kolli couldn't understand and stepped into the fire pit in his effort to grab at her. Sparks and smoke surrounded her as Kolli pulled herself completely through the smoke hole and rolled away across the roof. She felt broiled from head to mid-thigh. Her breeches were scorched and she could smell the sickening odor of her own charred hair.

The door crashed open, and Kalenth Ush rushed into the yard. Orange sparks and smoke followed in his wake. He was beating at his smoking legs and still screaming in some foreign tongue.

Kolli blinked away smoky tears, crawled to the edge of the roof, and sprang toward the palisade. Her palms were torn by a hundred splinters as she caught the top of the fence. For a terrible moment, her feet could find no purchase, but then she was up and over the sharpened logs. She hit the ground hard, stood, and ran doubled over, with a hand against her aching ribs.

It was almost a mile through the dark woods to reach the city walls. Even if she reached them, she'd have to find a way past the guards—the story she'd used the night before was not likely to work again. The sky was turning gray. Any moment now the misty orb of the greater moon would clear the horizon. Kolli had feared it rising before, now she only hoped it would give her enough light to see the path.

Then her bones caught fire.

Kolli fell into the brush. She wanted to scream, but her throat was burning, too, burning white-hot. She could feel each vertebra in her backbone being twisted; her muscles flowed over her melting bones like ice before a furnace wind; her tunic and breeches shredded against her twisting flesh. Then the fire ended, and Kolli lay panting on the trail in the cool night air.

She tried to stand, but her knees bent the wrong direction. In the cold light of the moon, she saw that her arms were covered in silver fur and each finger of her hand ended in a curving claw. Trembling, she lifted one clawed hand to her face and felt at the muzzle that jutted from where her mouth had been. She screamed. It came out as a howl.

Another howl sounded through the woods. It should have been the wordless call of a beast, but it wasn't. Kolli understood every chilling note of that howl. Kalenth Ush was coming.

Kolli found that her hind legs were too short to do more than an awkward shuffle. All fours was more comfortable. It took her a few strides to get the rhythm, then she was running faster than she ever had before, running so fast that the trees around her were nothing but a blur.

Ush was still following. She could hear him on the trail behind her. He was growing closer with every long stride. Kolli turned a corner and caught sight of the torches burning on top of the city walls. She had no idea of what she would do when she reached them, but anything had to be better than being caught by Ush.

The ground underneath her exploded in a spray of leaves and dirt. For the second time that night, Kolli found herself hoisted in the air, this time in a stout net of rope. The net swung only inches above the ground, held up by a heavy hawser. As Kolli bounced and twisted in the net, a cheer sounded from the treetops above her. She twisted her head back and saw Morl climbing down the trunk of a heavy oak.

Kolli tried to talk. Tried to tell him who she was, what had happened. All that emerged from her snout was a series of whines and growls.

"You're about the scrawniest silver wolf I ever did see," Morl said as he walked around the net. From a sheath across his back, Morl pulled a wide-bladed sword. "But small pelts are usually the best." He raised the sword over Kolli.

A gray shape sprang out of the woods and sent Morl sprawling. The sword flew from his hands, falling into the leaves under the net. Morl screamed.

Kolli reached through the net and clawed at the ground, trying to get a grip on the sword. Her transformed fingers were more suited to slashing than gripping, but at last she had it.

One blow, and the net fell to the ground. It took several more hacks for Kolli to cut herself free. Lurching across the clearing, unsteady on her hind legs, she went after Kalenth Ush.

Morl was on the ground in the middle of a black circle of blood. Ush leaned over him, worrying the dead man's neck like a dog shaking a squirrel. He turned toward Kolli and howled, bloody foam spraying from his fangs.

Kolli swung the sword with both hands. Ush dodged easily. A backhanded blow from one of his clawed hands sent Kolli flying. She rolled into a rocky stream. Cold water matted her fur.

Ush stood on the bank, his shaggy form silhouetted against the rising moon. Kolli saw cold moonlight reflected from his silver eyes. With a snarl, he came for her.

It was Kolli's turn to dodge. As Ush hit the water beside her, she lashed out and caught his side with her new claws. His painful cry was rewarding. Kolli jumped away, looking for an opening.

Ush was faster than she thought. The pool of water exploded into spray. Claws tore into her shoulders, and she was hurled down. With one hairy arm, Ush held her in the stream. He opened his long jaws, exposing teeth as curved and sharp as the instruments in Morl's leather shop.

Kolli's clumsy fingers searched across the stream bottom, looking for a stone. What she found was the sword.

Her desperate swing struck Kalenth Ush's furry neck like an ax biting into a tree, and stuck there. The silver wolf fell away screaming.

Kolli struggled to her feet and stepped back, then dropped to all fours and bounded into the trees before turning to look. Ush pulled at the sword, but the hilt was slick with gushing blood. His short arms could not get a grip. He snarled one last time and fell.

She was slow to approach the body. Only when the blood had stopped flowing and her new nose detected the odor of death did Kolli step forward. She pulled the sword back and forth to work it free. Then she struck over and over, until the silver wolf's snarling head rolled among the bloody leaves.

The first light of morning brought the fiery pain of transformation. This time, Kolli welcomed it. When it was over, she was happy to find that all the wounds she had received in the night were gone. But that joy was nothing compared to finding her own face back where it belonged.

She looked at the still form of Kalenth Ush lying among the ferns at the side of the bubbling stream. Would this thing end with his death, or would she again become a monster when the moon rose? Kolli didn't know, and she was too tired to worry about it.

She stood up and started to walk, not toward the city, but back toward Kalenth Ush's compound. There were prisoners to set free. She might need their help if she ever had to explain the death of two of the city's best known fur traders.

And there was a pile of gold in Ush's house. Kolli would set that free as well.

The Theft of Bayende, Heart and Soul

Billie Sue Mosiman

"The magic of first love is our ignorance that it can ever end."
Benjamin Disraeli

Rain fell like silver ribbons all over the land of Kieve. Mist, thick and impenetrable as lengths of rope, rose from the swamps and stalked inward from the sea.

Thane, ruling wizard and proud father-to-be, stood in the shadows cast by the fire. His wife thought that he handled the sacred amulet, Blue Realm, praying his evening prayers, but he had already finished them. Now he found himself simply standing, watching Bayende, drinking in her presence as he would a fine mead.

She sat at a distance from him near the hearth in the murk of the dying day. A shawl of gossamer white lay about her shoulders and a gay multicolored scarf covered her long golden hair. She sighed at intervals while painstakingly sewing the tiniest of satin bows and seed pearls on the infant's gown lying across her lap. It had been foretold their child would be born within a fortnight during another gray rain-washed day. Bayende insisted she would give their son a splendid name so that he could rise above the season of his birth and become as gentle and bright and lov-

ing as his father. What that name might be, Thane did not know. It
was a game between them—he trying to ferret out the secret, she
giggling in protest that he would not know until the birth day. "It
is not your name," she had said, teasing him. "A boy who is the
son of a wizard must have his own name. I have decided on a
powerful name so that he might never fear danger."

Thane watched her now, and his heart swelled with such
emotion that he feared he would rush over and fall before her, at
her knees, and frighten her with an outpouring of his love. How
had he gone all these long years without a woman? Without
Bayende? She had come to mean more to him than all of his
powers, than the comfort of a peaceful land, more than his own
life. He thought himself truly undeserving of such wild luck. For
she loved him, too, and now they were to have a family.

He rolled the turquoise stone, Blue Realm, in his hand and
then clenched it tightly in a fist. He prayed one more prayer, a
selfish one. He silently asked that nothing come between him and
Bayende. He prayed that his son, to be born in the rains of Kieve
when the moons rode high in the sky and the sun barely made a
visit without storm clouds, would succeed him as wizard and
protect the land from the planeswalkers that tried to invade from
other worlds. He prayed for continued peace, for sustained love,
for life uncomplicated and serene.

"Have you finished and could you put your hands on my
back?" Bayende paused in her sewing as if reading his thoughts
and disturbed by them.

Was it wrong, Thane wondered, to wish for perfection in a
life where there was no such thing possible?

He moved from the shadows and entered the flickering light
and warmth. He put away Blue Realm into a pocket of his
trousers. Bayende leaned forward across her knees and he
reached down behind her to massage the tight muscles low in her
back just at the swell of her hips. Touching her excited him, but
he refrained from pressing forward. "Does that help?" he asked.

She groaned with pleasure. "You have magic in your hands.
If you had no other magic at all, that would be enough for me to
love you." She twisted a bit and his hands slid around the sides
of her waist to massage the bunched muscles there. He could see
her profile lit by firelight and watched the gravity of long hours

of work falling from her features as he manipulated the soft flesh all up and down her spine. Her skin glowed pink and her blond lashes feathered her high cheeks like the tiny fans of fern that grew on the roots of old trees.

Now she straightened and he moved back, withdrawing. She rested her hands on her swollen belly and looked up at him with grateful eyes. "I should prepare your dinner," she said. "Time passes so lethargically during the rains that I forget my duties."

She set aside the sewing on a stool and he helped her rise. He wanted to fold her into his arms, but she would protest. She had more work to do before the day was over. He would only annoy her if he tried to touch her too often or too much. They told him, the midwives, that it was a condition of her pregnancy and not a turning away from him. She was necessarily turning into herself, nourishing new life, and he must be patient until the child was born before resuming a normal mating relationship with her.

Thane had never been accused of being a patient man. But with Bayende he thought he was learning. He wanted to learn. He wanted to give to her selflessly. If temporary denial must be a part of love and the making of a family, he would learn that lesson.

While she cooked his dinner, he would consult his books in the library to see if he might find a spell to hurry him along the patience path. It was imperative that he know as many secrets as he could. How would he teach a son what he did not yet know, what he had not yet mastered?

The silver rain fell like ribbons along the eaves of the stone house, and its music accompanied Thane into a colder room where he could concentrate and study until Bayende called him to the table.

Noranda-Zang had been searching through many lands for more than ten long terrible years. Thane must be somewhere and he would find him. It was said Thane was one of the very few minor wizards who had managed to create an ultimate haven where there was peace and plenty.

Well, that would change! Noranda-Zang would not be defeated in the War of Thanopolis without recompense. Had not Thane laughed in his face and thrust a sword through his heart, the laughter twisting his lips even as he twisted the handle of the sword, ripping Zang's heart in two? Had it not been for the preparations Zang made before battle, he might never have returned to himself and taken a new body.

Oh, he would find Thane and he would rend him into bits; he would scatter his hide to the four winds and watch him disappear. Then he would bring down the land Thane ruled, ordering a horde of revenge-seeking skeletons to ride their bony horses through the streets until those streets ran with the blood of the enemy. He would bring forth brainwash creatures to cause the people to trust him and then loose upon them banshees and elves of deep shadow.

When he stumbled from the long path between worlds across the sands of Kieve Beach, he halted and immediately summoned a rogue frozen shade who called himself Caskor. Caskor materialized, cloak wrapped close against the drumming sheets of rain. "What land is this?" Zang asked. "And is there a population?"

Caskor turned slowly, his red eyes scanning from the beach to the sloping land and the forests and rising mountains beyond. Zang waited, peering as much as he could through the velvet mists toward the land before him. It might be a dead world where only creatures walked. If it was, he had no time for it. He had all the creatures he needed at his command, enough and more to entomb Thane when he found him.

"Well," Zang asked, "have you lost your voice or your wits? Do you perceive a people and is there a wizard present? A name, I want the name of this forsaken place!"

Caskor turned back to him slowly and a wicked grin split the lower half of his face. He was the only creature Zang knew who could appear to be amused and haughty all at once.

"I have come at your bidding, master, but I might be more forthcoming if you did not speak to me as you would one of your slaves in Everlorne."

"I will speak to you as I wish, Caskor. Remember who rescued you that time when a witch held you captive in her locked and hidden jewelry box. Had it not been for me, you'd be rattling around in the dark with rubies and diamonds for company." Zang moved in perilously close to the wraith, close enough they stared into one another's fiery eyes. "Well? Shall I cast you to the Outer

Reaches where you wander alone, the way you should be even now and for eternity?"

Caskor turned to a statue and no longer smiled his grim smile. "There are cities and fiefdoms and castles and farms here," he said. "There is a wizard who rules over all. This is the land of Kieve."

"Who is the wizard?"

Caskor blinked slowly and the smile crept back to his thin lips. "Yes, that is a fine question," he said. "'Who is the wizard here?'" And then he vanished.

"Damn you!"

The rain pummeled Zang, soaking him through, making him shiver.

"Damn you, if I see you again," he screamed to the water-laden heaven, his curse carried on a wisp of fog back to sea.

There was nothing to do but trudge inland and find the wizard.

Let it be Thane. A mantra carried through the corridors of a mind for ten years: Let it be Thane who is the wizard here.

Whipping aside the crusty moss-hung branches of trees and parting sharp-toothed fronds, Zang slogged his way into the forest. It would be night soon and he would have to climb a tree to sleep so as not to be sucked into a swamp or carried by a flood toward a raging river. He had not come all this way, through all these years and adventures, to lie drowning in a pool of froth and debris.

Let him be here, he thought, drawing his sword and battering nature aside so that he might enter deeper into the arms of green darkness that protected the inland cities from the rage of the violent and capricious sea.

Thane woke with his wife in his arms. He curled against her back, his arm curved over her waist and burgeoning stomach. He thought he felt the babe kick and that was what woke him. His other arm looped above her head and his hand rested on the crown of her silken hair. He sighed in astonishment that he had seen the beginning of another day with this delicious creature at his side. It grieved him he must rise and leave their warm, fragrant communal bed.

He eased his arms from her and slid from the heavy covers. He shuddered in the chill morning air and hurried into his trousers, long-sleeved red blouse, and a cape embroidered with gold stars and black half-moons. The cape had been given to him on the occasion of his becoming a full-fledged maker of magic. One day he would pass down this cape to his son, and then he would sit idly next to his beloved Bayende for the rest of his blessed days. Forgetting strife. Forgetting dealing justice and righting wrongs and diplomatically bringing people together for their own good.

The city marshals asked for him to come mediate a minor dispute between farmers over the distribution of a crop of hay they had grown together as partners. If he was quick, he could dispense true justice and be home again in time to breakfast with Bayende.

He leaned over her and tucked in the covers to keep a draft from her back. Let her sleep, he thought. She is too tired to rise with the dawn and there is no need for her to work like a peasant in the last days of her confinement.

He shut the door on his way from the room and bounded down the stone steps to the lower level and the double oak doors. He turned back, remembering he should lay a fire in the hearth to warm the house before his love woke.

If he was not always in such a hurry, he would remember to be a better husband. None of his prior study had told him how to calm the adrenaline in his veins or how to slow down enough to remember all the small details that made up an orderly domestic life.

"I'll be cursed," he mumbled, and returned to the great room. Before long he had a roaring fire going and again raced out the door, this time forgetting to place the key in the lock and secure it against intruders.

Noranda-Zang used artifice to make himself look weak and decrepit. He gathered a shabby coat around himself and left the swamp mud on his black boots. He hung his head and let his face wrinkle into a scowl so that he appeared aged. He walked with a stuttering limp, grabbing onto posts and railings and walls to keep himself upright. Villagers moved out of his way, and some of the more pious and intuitive crossed themselves as he passed by.

Zang inquired of an innkeeper where he might find Kieve's ruler; he had business to conduct with him.

The directions were simple and led Zang on a heady trip through the stalls where food was being grilled in the open air and cooks squatted around charred timbers to stir pots of steaming vegetable and sea creature soups. Tantalizing scents of lemon and ginger and garlic almost overcame Zang, but he would not eat, not now. He would not sleep again, either, until his mission was completed. He would not even think of congress with others until he reached his destination. For he had learned the most exciting information from the innkeeper: not only the location of their ruling wizard, but his name.

Thane Du-Moriss IV. Lord and master. Patron and ruler of the land of Kieve. He had found him, found him out, and would now strike the killing blow.

The food stalls gave way to merchandisers with their gaudy trinkets. A wooden pen owned by a woman wearing antler headgear held a giant bear with a collar of pearly shells latched around his neck. There were jugglers, tricksters, hagglers, thieves, beggars, and more consumers than Zang had seen in many a land. This was a prosperous place, indeed, but how would it fare without its wizard? It would fall into disarray and despair. Zang would devastate and lay waste to everything Thane had created, so help him. If need be, he would call upon the misshapen fetuses he raised on clotted blood in the swamp regions. He would call for a ring of fireworms to roll over the bridges, burning and taking down to ashes every fiber of wood in its way.

At the door of the wizard's address, Zang raised his fist to pound the wide planks of oak, but his ever present invisible companion, Gloom, appeared as she always did when she might be of help. She whispered at his ear. "It's open, master."

The gray cloud surrounding Gloom seemed to be a column of the mist that hung over the village. Gleaming droplets of jeweled moisture clung to her cheeks and nose and fell from her lips like untasted tears. "Let us enter," she said, pressing against the door and passing partway through it.

It was as if a stiff breeze pushed at the oak and it opened on leather hinges that needed oiling, for there was a series of crackling and creaks that made Zang cringe. He frowned, following Gloom inside. He kept his hand on the hilt of his sword. He would call upon the fearsome creatures at his command if need be, but he hoped to punish Thane first with his own strength.

Down a dank hallway glided Gloom with Zang in the rear, breathing harshly, his rage fueling a sudden fear that he might have been tricked or subdued or made spellbound. He could hardly believe he would lay eyes upon his enemy after so long a journey.

The hall opened into a great room with a wide uneven staircase leading upward. No one seemed to be around. Where were the servants? Was Thane one of those strange men who thought it uncomely to ask others to work in his stead?

There was a fire snapping in the hearth, but there appeared to be no one home.

Gloom turned to whisper to him: "Upstairs, master, lies the woman."

"What woman? I have not come for a woman. I want the wizard Thane."

"Ssshhhh," Gloom hissed. Her ghostly presence shimmered brightly a moment then dimmed again to dull pewter. Zang smelled her fetid gases and held his breath while he listened. "It is the mistress of the house of Thane," Gloom said. "She is with child."

Zang stood rooted to the spot, his hand clenched fast and knuckles white around the hilt of his sword. Woman? With child? Thane had taken a woman. It was not forbidden, of course. Why, he had done the same, though his precious Celia had died giving birth, but only a wizard with power to spend could take unto himself a family and still wield enough power to protect a land. He had not thought it possible Thane could be of a caliber to do this.

"Let's take her, master," Gloom whispered in a lustful voice. "Let's make her die weeping she ever knew her husband's name."

Zang waited until he knew this was the path he should choose. Yes. Yes, if he did such a terrible deed as murder a wife gravid with child, no greater harm could be done a wizard. In one bold stroke he would be stealing from Thane not only his love but his kingdom's heir. It said in the gramarye that the way to fell a wizard is not always through his physical body. You could attack his mind, his spirit, his soul. Or you could sweep his loved ones, if he was strong enough to have them, into the void, thereby sweeping away the wizard's heart along with them. It was a crippling blow that no power could undo.

"Yes," Zang shouted, rushing up the stairs, his footsteps ringing out like bells of doom. "Yes! Let it be done. Come with me, Gloom, and devour her flesh, scour her bones. We will roll her eyes in our cups tonight."

> The profession of magician, is one of the most perilous and arduous specialisations of the imagination. On the one hand there is the hostility of God and the police to be guarded against; on the other it is as difficult as music, as deep as poetry, as ingenious as stagecraft, as nervous as the manufacture of high explosives, and as delicate as the trade in narcotics.
>
> William Bolitho

Thane knew the first touch of trepidation when he came home to find his door standing open to the ribbons of new morning rain. Water sloshed over the threshold, into the stone entranceway, and produced a shining, shimmering pond that reflected his magical cape. The stars and moons from his shoulders rode the water through ripples caused by a stray breeze.

What have I done? Thane wondered. My heart races. My blood beats against the cymbals of my ears. Something is wrong, so wrong.

It was true there were no sinners in the land of Kieve who would be willing to harm his Bayende, but locks were made to keep out wandering spirits and wardens of evil who searched for a host or a new home. Now he recalled his impatience to get to the town meeting and conduct judgment so he could return to Bayende and a breakfast of sausages and scones. He knew he had failed to fasten the door behind him.

Fool.

And now something was wrong. He sensed it all through the nerve endings of his body, felt it creep along the hairs at his scalp, felt it turn over like a restless sleeping misery in the depths of his heart. Oh my lord, my lord, he prayed, not disaster, please.

Not disaster. Please. I will give you all my treasure and give up my magic. I will give you my kingdom and my fame and my glory. I will give you my arms and legs and be a beggar at the gate if you do not let me witness disaster. . . .

He ran through the standing moon-and-star water, through the empty hallway, past the great room with its now smoldering fire in the grate, and took the stone stairs two at a time, calling, "Bayende, Bayende, Bayende."

At the door he stopped.

His gaze filled with horror at the scattering of blood and raw flesh and golden hair red and wet as the skinned skull it came from. All over the bed. All over the floor. The walls, the walls, the walls were scarlet with the lifeblood of his darling.

Where . . . ? His child . . . ? Torn asunder and half-eaten it lay like a small ball of refuse beneath the leaded window.

Bayende!

Thane fell to his knees and covered his stricken face with his trembling hands. He wept for hours, wept until day turned to night to day. He did not move from his position at the portal to the slaying of his beloved until his physical strength leaked from him and left him lying prostrate in the hall outside the door, his cheek resting against the icy stone, his gaze now turned inward and shrinking to a pinpoint of light.

> Indubitably, Magick is one of the subtlest and most diffi-
> cult of the sciences and arts. There is more opportunity
> for errors of comprehension, judgement and practice than
> in any other branch of physics.
>
>   Aleister Crowley

Thane had been traveling the pathways between the lands for seventeen years. He had lost weight and muscle, but not power. The thinner he grew, the more powerful his morbid thoughts. The deeper his despair, the more his magic asserted itself to balance the equation. In each new land he investigated the secrets of the mountains, the islands, the forests, plains and swamps. He moved swiftly, always on the move, never resting. He walked the planes without having the title of planeswalker. He scurried out of sight when the true gods passed him by. It had taken every drop of his knowledge in order to travel the way he did, but it was worth it. Or it would be, just as soon as he found Zang.

His land he put into the care of elders who sent him reports periodically that Kieve prospered. When told of trouble, Thane sent troops of faceless angels who so frightened instigators that they dared not misbehave in their master's absence.

It had been a long lifetime since he had lost his dear Bayende and unnamed son. He kept them alive in his mind and in his prayers. He had not forgiven himself his thoughtlessness the day evil found his Bayende for slaughter. His sin lasted and burned like a torch in his chest and gave him little rest.

If only he had locked the door. If only he had come back sooner. If only life were not so drear and unpredictable and fearsomely unjust.

But justice was for the brave and he would have it. He devoted himself to seeing Noranda-Zang punished. The law did not protect Zang for such baneful deeds, and there was no one to come to his aid if Thane ever happened upon the monster's land.

In the pale nowhere between lands, Thane stared at the road before him and moved fiercely down the path, taking this turn, avoiding that one, favoring this, ignoring that. Time stood still between the universes as he searched, often lost and without bearings. He frequently felt a wetness on his cheeks and reached up to discover tears he hadn't known he'd cried. How had he come to this hell place that was worse than any prison or torture? Was it really of his own making, a design brought down upon his head for his rash, hasty spirit which had made him exit the house that day without care?

These and other unanswerable questions dogged him through the days and nights, worrying him, eating away his soul into tatters. Over and over he muttered her name—Bayende, Bayende, my Bayende.

His feet stumbled, indication he had moved beyond a path into a new plane. He stood on a deserted beach, the blue mean sea at his back. In front of him stood crags blackened with a carpet of dying mosses. Above the crags scudded clouds bloated with the fever rain that comes in the season of heat and harm. Thane could smell burning offal and bitterweed. Stinging gnats swarmed around his face and stung his flesh. He swatted them away and cast a spell to hold them clear so he could take a breath without sucking in insects.

This place was either a disguise to ward off planeswalkers, or a land where evil crouched on haunches in the darkness at the behest of a savage wizard.

From the south a whirlwind blew suddenly into being. It bore down toward Thane. In the wind's belly swirled tentacles holding mighty swords that were as long as Thane was tall, as sharp as January ice and February whistling glass.

Thane grasped Blue Realm in a fist and shook it at the whirlwind. From out of his fist rose a pair of Nightmares on their winged horses. They brayed, falling back on their heels, then raced forward down the beach toward the clashing swords swung by a dozen-tentacled beast. It was a horned octipus, summoned from the sea.

Thane prayed for victory and saw his two Nightmares slash through the twirling lightning strikes made by the swords. It was a battle that produced thunder enough to shake the ground where he stood. In minutes it was over, the whirlwind dissipated, the swords dropped, the horned octipus flattened and bleeding black fluid into the waves lapping over it from the sea.

Thane called back his Nightmares and had one let him mount so that he could ride over the craggy summit to the land beyond. He would find out who ordered this world and why so many protective measures had been set up. In his experience, when a wizard set traps, he had too much to hide.

Over the black crags Thane flew, holding to the Nightmare's mane, the other nightmare following. He could see green forests in the distance, as forbidding as had been the crags. Beyond that he flew and found towers, an entire line of towers, like a fence or a barricade against marauders. Soldiers saw his approach and shot poisoned arrows into the sky, but Thane laughed and flew ever higher, until the wind was chill enough to mold his face into a mask.

Beyond the towers he spied a soft yellow-green plain with a majestic stone fortress in the center of it. All around the outside lay thatched huts and modest cottages. "There," Thane ordered, and his Nightmare took him earthward to the land, settling just outside the town proper along with its companion Nightmares.

A villager dressed as a beggar ran up and bowed before him. "Master, you are in grave danger here. We have seen no planeswalkers. They are not welcome. You are the first I've seen since I was a child."

Thane blessed the beggar without explaining he was not truly a walker of the planes, not one of the gods, but a mere wizard from a small unimportant land that went beneath notice. Instead he said, "What is the name of this land and who is the wizard?"

"We call this Everlorne."

"Yes? And the wizard? Speak up, man, I haven't all day to spend talking."

"I . . . am not permitted . . . to tell you, master."

"What do you mean you can't tell me?" Thane bellowed, his forbearance as thin as ever. After losing Bayende, he had given up trying to practice patience.

"We can be killed if we speak his name. I'm sorry, sire, but though I own nothing and I am but a poor soul who lives off the charity of others, I would rather keep my skin on my back today."

Thane's natural compassion responded to the ragged man, to the dark fear in his eyes. He took out a coin from his pocket and handed it over. "Never mind. You're a good man," he said. "Pardon my foul manner. My excuse is that I've been on a seventeen-year journey. I'm afraid I've been wandering the pathways so long that I have forgotten civility."

The beggar bowed and stepped back, bowed again and again as he returned to the village confines by walking backward.

Thane glanced up at the imposing structure of the fortress castle. That's where the thaumaturgist will be hiding, he thought. The wizard with an unspeakable name. The most high personage who ruled this dreary kingdom with fear and the flaying of innocent flesh.

Let it be Zang.

Let it be Noranda-Zang, I pray, he thought, gazing up the ramparts to the top of the gray stone fortress. I am weary and growing old. I am heavy with long mourning. There has been no justice for me most of my life.

Just let it be the monster I seek.

He wandered into the lane that led between the small homes of Everlorne's people. They shied from him, fearful of a stranger and what he might want. No one would meet his gaze; men turned aside and women raised their skirts to cover their faces. Where was the color in this land, the cheer, the hope of a better tomorrow? The villagers dressed as if for a funeral, and it was clear from the fear that seized them upon his arrival that they enjoyed no adventure in their lives.

He came to the road crossing over to the castle. Armored guards stood ready at the barred door. Thane took in a deep breath and clutched Blue Realm in his hand. He had left his Nightmares at the city's edge, and now he called for them to fly to him. He also called to the spirit of the pastureland, the green-gold land lying around the edge of the village, and from that grassy plain rose hordes of locusts bearing razor teeth. They came at his command, aiming for the guards. The sentries saw the black mass of deadly locusts and, screaming for mercy, ran from their positions and into the streets of the village.

Thane smiled. He raised a hand to halt the locust storm. They wavered in the air like a blanket of spurs, hovering, clicking their hind legs, grating the razors of their fine teeth.

A Nightmare stood on either side of Thane, pawing the ground, snorting fire from great nostrils.

Thane went up to the huge barred door and, casting another spell, had it open for him. The heavy wooden log rose and fell to the side with a jarring crash. The door opened outward. Before him lay a cobbled courtyard ringed by stunted juniper trees and twisted holly. In every limb and leaf Thane could see pernicious destruction at work. Nothing good came from here. Nothing wholesome.

Surely the wizard had been alerted by now. He would have the power to know when an intruder came onto his property. A man who knew when his people spoke his name would be a mighty wizard indeed. He might not even be one another wizard could kill. Hadn't he killed Noranda-Zang once before, on Thanopolis? Only to have him return to extract unholy vengeance. If this was the abode of Zang, what good would it do to kill him a second time?

Passionate fire leaped in Thane's heart, causing him to let out a gasp. He did not care if he must kill Zang repeatedly down through all time. He would do it and do it again when necessary. He would find him over and over, march across heaven's shores and hell's abyss to strip life from his nemesis. If he had to take the monster's mortality from him a thousand thousand times, he would do it. For to do anything less was failure in light of what had been taken from him.

Bayende, Bayende.

Across the courtyard strode a giant specimen of a man; his face would have frightened a wolf into turning tail. His hair was raven, his eyes aquamarine and piercing. When he spoke, his teeth glistened like old river rocks. "Who goes there? What business do you have with my house? You are trespassing."

Thane called out, "I am Thane of Kieve. I search for Noranda-Zang, who I owe a debt."

"You speak my father's name without fear for your very life?"

Thane felt something lurch in his chest and send him spiraling into a gray dizziness that passed only after some moments of forced concentration. Before him stood the son of a madman. Where was Thane's son? In the belly of a beast, a meal for a demon. All these years Zang had had the comfort of family while Thane walked crooked paths and through brambled lands alone.

Alone and all alone and dreadfully alone.

Thane took his hand from his pocket, the one holding tightly to Blue Realm, and he shook his fist at the younger man, who still came toward him in a menacing stride. Hatred radiated from his raised fist. Thwarted passion joined hatred to form a dense black cloud that advanced toward the human in its path. Within that cloud fumed Thane's loneliness, his grief, his heartbreak. Seventeen long years of it.

"I repudiate you and your existence," Thane roared. "I swear by all that is holy that you are the whelp of evil and the spawn of corruption. I force you from this life. I take your breath as my own, I take your strength into my loins, I take your youth into my mouth, and I cast you down forever."

The young man stopped and looked shocked. Before Thane had finished speaking his death spell, the other man threw back his head and bayed as if he were a wild animal trapped. His throat pulsed as if he would speak yet could not. His long black hair swung away from his shoulders; his arms reached out to heaven.

Then he fell backward as if brought down by a stormy wind.

Knocked to the earth by the force of Thane's fury and power, ripped of his life by Thane's spell.

He lay on his back, a last convulsion causing his eyes to hemorrhage in their sockets. Blood freely flowed from his full lips in rivulets that stained the front of his white silk blouse. He lay still. He lay dead.

The black cloud of Thane's fury seeped into the wind and was borne aloft in the teeth of the horde of locusts.

Thane went to the body and knelt. He looked down on the product of his revenge. He felt no pity or remorse. He hoped only that Noranda-Zang loved the boy. That he adored him. That the son's death would wound him to the quick and never let him find peace again. There would be no heir to perpetuate this horrid kingdom, not now.

Just as Thane passed out the courtyard gates, he heard behind him a voice crying, cursing, calling his name.

It was a father, calling in grief, "Thane, Thane, Thane, no no no, Thane, no, not my son, not my only son!"

Thane did not stop or turn. He did not need to see Zang to know he had taken from him all he ever loved. He had heard it in the voice calling at his back and knew it came from the depths of a soul stretched on the rack of despair. But he could not smile or feel triumphant, for as vicious as he had been in the murder, he was not proud of the deed.

Now there would be two wizards who would live bereft and sorrowful the rest of their days. Now there would be two of them forever at war when it was evident, at least to Thane, that there was nothing more left worth losing.

Not when one had already lost his small beating heart.

Bayende. Bayende.

Had already lost his small pitiful soul.

Bayende, my love.

Lost without hope of retrieving either this side of eternity's vast borderland.

Thane adjusted the worn mantle over his shoulders as he trudged away. The moons and stars that decorated the frayed cloth blinked softly in the falling twilight. They blinked like fireflies drifting lazily across the plains of Everlorne to safely light the way of a vagabond spirit through the encroaching night.

Wellspring

Cynthia Ward

This is the tale she tells, the gray-haired elf-woman *who is not old, the tale she tells to some twoscore elves— men, women, and children—who huddle shivering around a fire stirred to ragged red sheets by the wind in the pass.*

Love is the cause of our despair and our exodus. *So the elf-woman begins her tale.* Love was the genesis of the Wizard Tyrant, the love of Anaki and Turul.

You know who Anaki and Turul were, and you know that they fell in love. But do you know why they fell in love? Do you know of the beauty of Anaki, whose eyes shone black as obsidian, whose ears swept up to shapely points, whose hair flowed to her waist like a torrent of black ink? Do you know how handsome Turul was, with muscles an idol-maker might have carved in sandstone, with hair like curly black fleece? Do you know that Anaki and Turul grew up together from the age of nine, when they were set apart from the other children by their apprenticeship to Anaki's mother Inasha, the wizard of Eredok? For all these reasons, they had to fall in love.

Because they were in love, they often sought privacy in the forest. So love brought them, in their sixteenth summer, to a place they should not have been, a stream said to be the abode of demons.

In terror they looked for demon-sign. The trees about them were neither stunted nor splintered, and the earth neither barren nor burnt. Green grass, ferns, and moss grew to the edge of clear water. The stream formed a pool at the base of a high stone cliff, and the waterfall which plummeted into the pool resembled a delicate white curtain a hundred feet tall, save where it touched the pool, exploding in a thunderous fountain of spray. The pool was otherwise placid. It was also fifty feet broad—and utterly clean. Can you picture it, you children of the swamps? Can you imagine an open body of water so vast and pure?

It was not because clean water was a rare sight that Anaki and Turul stared at the pool; they were the children of plain and forest. No, they stared because they yearned to bathe. Hot and sweaty, they'd followed the sound of running water, thinking they would come to the Great River which in those days flowed past Eredok. They had come instead to the forbidden stream.

"The elders' tales are not always true," Anaki observed.

"I know," Turul said, and he removed his clothes and broke into a run.

"Don't!" Anaki shouted.

She was too late: Turul dove into the pool. His muscular brown body sliced the water as cleanly as a knife. Anaki sucked in her breath; she had not forgotten how dangerous it was to dive headfirst into unknown waters, demon-haunted or not.

Turul surfaced, grinning with delight, and he yelled and gestured, urging Anaki to join him. She released her breath, profoundly relieved that her beloved had not struck his head on a submerged stone. But she would not dive; she was neither as careless nor as headstrong as Turul. She stepped cautiously into the stream.

Turul screamed and vanished in an eruption of spray.

"Turul!" Before the water could begin to settle, Anaki dove. She sank through the painfully cold water with her eyes open, but could see nothing for the clouds of disturbed mud. Eyes stinging, she forced her way to the bottom, to find nothing but silt and stone. Lungs bursting, she planted her feet and snapped her legs straight, hurling her body upward like a spear. When she broke the surface, she gasped in a huge breath, and she shook her head violently and blinked rapidly, clearing her eyes.

She saw Turul. He was being dragged by the leg by something submerged save for a long row of tall, sharp, triangular blades which cut the water like swamp-sharks' fins.

Anaki struck out in pursuit. She was a fast swimmer, but not nearly as swift as the water-creature. And what could she do if she did catch up? Yet she followed.

If only she had turned and fled!

Neither she nor Turul cast a spell, of course. They couldn't. A wizard's hands must be free to gesture, to pull forth strength, to shape and direct the power expended. Even the Wizard Tyrant cannot cast a spell while trying to swim.

In Anaki and Turul's day, and for all our history before their time, being a wizard was a very different thing than it is now. A wizard's effectiveness depended entirely on how strong, healthy, and well fed she was at the time of spellcasting. Her greatest spells we would consider weak, for a spell was powered solely by the strength of her body. And because of this, the wizards of the past died of old age in their thirties.

How we wish we lived in those simple times! How we curse the souls of Anaki and Turul! Not that it matters. If Anaki had not, another would have discovered the knowledge which turned a witch into an immortal tyrant and the Great Plains into the Great Waste.

When Anaki raised her head for a breath, she saw Turul disappearing beneath the waterfall. She swam to a boulder, which rose from the pool at one side of the fall, and scaled its slippery side. She had to blink repeatedly against the stinging force of the waterfall's white spray, but she thought she saw the edge of a cave mouth behind the curtain of water. There had to be an opening; where else could the creature have taken Turul?

Anaki swam to the ledge of stone between pool and cliff and found there was truly a cave behind the fall. She ran toward it. Its mouth opened higher than Anaki was tall and three times wider than its height. It was as black as a night of storms.

Anaki forced her mind to the calm necessary for magic-making and cast a simple spell, creating an insubstantial globe of pale green witchlight. With the globe floating at her shoulder, she entered the cave.

What terror Anaki felt! There was indeed a demon, and it

had taken her beloved. How could she save him from a demon? Could she save even herself, now that she had entered the demon's lair? Perhaps Turul was already dead. Perhaps he was undergoing fiendish tortures. Whatever happened to Turul would be her fate also, of that Anaki had no doubt—but she advanced without hesitation to rescue Turul or die with him.

Anaki moved slowly through a black tunnel, walking carefully on damp uneven stone the witchlight barely touched. A draft blew into her face, painfully cold on her bare wet skin. After what felt like leagues, the tunnel widened and faint light appeared ahead; Anaki extinguished her witchlight. Moments later she shrank back against the wall, for the tunnel yawned suddenly, like a gigantic mouth bristling with stone fangs. The fangs overhead dripped water like venom. The tunnel floor rolled like a vast tongue into its maw: a huge cavern. The cavern walls gave off an eerie glow which was almost as strong as the larger moon's light, yet the cavern was so enormous that the far wall, if there was one, could not be seen.

Some ten feet away, the demon crouched on four powerful legs, with one webbed and clawed forepaw resting on Turul's chest. He lay still as a corpse. The demon's long lean body and tail curved protectively around a cluster of ten or twelve eggs, each the size of an elf's skull. The eggs had dark gray shells, and four or five were rocking; had they been motionless, Anaki might have thought them a pile of water-rounded stones.

The moment she realized they were eggs, she knew that Turul had been dragged into the cave to nourish hatching demons.

The demon's sleek body was twice as long as Turul, with a barb-tipped tail even longer than its body. The demon looked like a huge blue salamander, but from its back rose a tall, reptilian crest, serrated like a Kreshite sword, which stretched from skull to tail-tip. The creature opened its lizard-snout and exposed long sharp snake-fangs, but no lizard or snake ever made a sound like the metallic screech which burst between the long narrow jaws and echoed horribly in the vast cavern.

The demon turned its cold gray eyes on Anaki. It rose and started ponderously toward her, exhaling a plume of red fire. Anaki had never seen anything remotely like this beast, but we know this monster now. It is one of the creatures which the Wizard Tyrant numbers among the slaves of his magic. Anaki faced the water dragon.

Turul was probably dead. Anaki had a slight chance of escaping if she turned and ran. The Wizard Tyrant, tapping mana, can easily dispatch a water dragon; but the strongest elf, unaided by mana, possesses not a quarter of the strength needed to spell-slay a water dragon. Anaki had no chance of success.

Yet she began the most powerful death spell she knew.

Behind the demon and the eggs, beyond a ripple in the stone floor, another water dragon rose into sight. It was three times larger than the first and moved even more ponderously, but it advanced upon Anaki with equal determination.

Anaki's fear increased, but she did not falter. A second demon could not make the odds any worse. She had the concentration necessary for spell-casting, yet her body shook with unsuppressible emotions. This was a new experience, one which went against everything she had been taught; no one knew why, but everyone knew allowing emotion to dominate magic-making was dangerous. But Anaki had no choice; she had no time to enter a calming trance. She wove the spell while trembling with hate stronger than she had ever felt before, while quivering with the searing pain of the heat which reached her from the dragon's fiery breath, while experiencing her love for Turul with exquisite sharpness, and feeling profound terror for his life and her own.

She neither saw nor sensed her magic affecting the demons. Her innate strength was draining away uselessly, like water out of a shattered bowl. But she would not betray her beloved by falling senseless before she completed the spell.

As the heat radiating from the water dragon's flame tickled Anaki's arms with agony, her spell ended, and she felt something snap in some indefinable area in the center of her being—it was as if something had cracked in her soul—and suddenly there was no end to her strength.

Using one's innate strength to make magic feels the same as using it to run or swim. But the fresh energy infusing Anaki's spell felt like a river of force rising from some immeasurably potent wellspring outside herself, surging through her like flood-waters from the world's heart. It was a power unmistakably alien.

Shaped by her spell, that energy flowed over the monsters. They burst into green fire. It extinguished their red flames. Their screams of pain were as harsh as iron on rusty iron, but they did not stop advancing. Blazing as they walked, continuing their frightful advance upon Anaki, the water dragons were ghastly tributes to the unnatural vitality of magical creatures.

From two body-lengths away, the smaller dragon lunged toward Anaki. She tried to leap aside. She fell. The impact knocked the breath out of her, and very nearly her senses as well. But the power continued to flow through her, and she clung to consciousness and stared at the creatures she considered demons.

The green fire blazed suddenly bright as the sun; then it disappeared, and the water dragons were gone with it. Anaki went limp with exhaustion and disbelief. She didn't understand what had happened. Her body curled up in a ball, and her mind almost slipped beyond thought—it would have, had she not remembered Turul. She rose slowly, her legs shaking like those of a colt standing for the first time; she fell like a colt, but could not rise again.

She crawled on her burned hands and her knees to the side of her beloved. She found him lying very still, his eyes closed and his lips parted; he did not appear to be breathing. She pressed her ear to his breast. She heard a heartbeat. After what seemed an eternity, she heard a second. Turul's heart was beating faintly, irregularly.

Turul had been dragged through the water by his legs; Anaki looked at them, and saw that they lay in a pool of blood. Turul's left calf had been shredded to the bone; the tattered flesh was black where not covered with blood, and purple streaks stretched up his brown thigh like bruises. Turul was not dead, but he was dying, poisoned by the water dragon's fangs.

Though Anaki was exhausted and did not know how she had summoned the power that killed the demons, she began the snake-venom spell, the only healing spell she knew that might possibly save Turul. She found no strength to draw upon, but she continued, gesturing weakly and chanting hoarsely, risking the guttering candle flame of her life. She *must* save Turul!

Again she felt the strange snap, as if something had been twisted to the breaking point in her soul, and again the impossible power poured through her. She *would* save Turul!

The spell and the power ended together. Light flared momentarily over Turul's injury, a blinding green flash. When Anaki's eyes cleared, the discoloration had faded from Turul's flesh and the wound had healed without a scar.

Anaki laid her hand gently on Turul's chest; she found his heartbeat, weak but regular. Relief filled her as fully as the alien power had. Then her exertions caught up with her and she lay motionless on cold stone.

Anaki awoke suddenly, her heart pounding. Something was shaking her. She sat up violently, afraid the water dragons had somehow rematerialized, and almost struck her head against Turul's. He was kneeling beside her, leaning close.

They shouted each other's names, and embraced, and spoke the words of lovers, which I need not repeat. Then Anaki told Turul what had happened. He was amazed and more than a little frightened by the alien power she described.

"Before we leave," Anaki concluded, "we must destroy those things." She pointed. Turul gasped to see the huge eggs. All were rocking now, and some were cracking, near to hatching. "I must find that strange power again. We cannot allow one demon to remain alive so close to Eredok!"

Anaki began the death spell. She immediately felt the curious twisting snap and the incredible surge of power. Her body was learning to tap the alien magic. The dragon eggs burst into green fire. Anaki shivered.

"Gods, Anaki," Turul said hoarsely. "What is this power?"

"I don't know!" Anaki said. "Let's *go!*"

As they ran down the tunnel, Anaki noticed by the glow of her witchlight that Turul was not limping. That incredible power had healed him fully.

When the lovers emerged from the tunnel, Turul stopped and stared at the shadowed inner wall of the waterfall. His lips moved, but Anaki could hear nothing except the thunderous roar. She put her head next to Turul's and shouted, "I can't hear you!"

Turul put his lips to her ear and spoke in his loudest voice. "When the monster dragged me under the waterfall, the water struck me so hard I lost my senses! When I regained my wits, I found you lying beside me as still as death!"

He embraced Anaki fiercely.

They stepped out from behind the waterfall. They froze in horror. The trees around the pool were bare and stark, and a mat of brown leaves covered earth and water.

"Oh, gods," Anaki whispered. "What has happened?'"

But they could not guess the truth we know to our sorrow.

When they had recovered a little from the shocking sight of the devastation, Anaki and Turul swam to where they thought they had left their clothes—it was difficult to be sure, with their surroundings so changed—and walked ashore. Plants and fallen leaves crumbled underfoot, and a fine pale dust coated their calves. The last few leaves on the branches were letting go, disintegrating as they fell, powdering the earth and the lovers with dry brown snow. Skeletal tree shadows barred the stricken earth.

"The death of the demons must have released some virulence," Turul guessed. "We are fortunate we weren't struck dead!"

Before Anaki could respond, she stumbled on a loop of cloth. They shook the powdered leaves off their tunics and got dressed. The cotton clung uncomfortably to their wet skins.

"Anaki," Turul said. "You must teach me how to summon that power."

Anaki's face was drawn and her eyes were dull. "Not today."

"Of course not."

They started home with slow steps. Some hundred paces from the stream, the forest changed dramatically. The undergrowth became suddenly lush, the trees abruptly green-cloaked. Anaki and Turul looked around with wide eyes.

"Turul," Anaki said, "we must tell no one what has happened today."

"I agree. No one must know. My father would kill me if he knew I'd been near the forbidden stream!"

"Someday we should tell my mother of this power," Anaki said wearily. "We must tell her, but not today. Not today."

Years would pass before they told anyone what had happened.

Only a day passed before Anaki tried to teach Turul something she did not herself understand.

For secrecy they went to the forest at the edge of the Great

Plains. Their village was hidden by distance and tall grass. Anaki explained her experience as best she could, then watched Turul cast a number of harmless but draining illusion spells, trying to break through to the river of power she had described. Soon he leaned wearily against her, a short stocky boy resting his brow on a tall thin girl's shoulder.

"I cannot do it," he gasped. "I have drained all my strength and not found any more. It is your power only."

"It is not," Anaki said. "Try one more time."

"I do not think I can."

"You must!"

Anaki rarely raised her voice. Turul jumped back, startled, and began another spell. His voice was faint and his gestures uncertain, yet when the spell ended, a boar burst out of the forest. The illusion was convincing, from the powerful reek of the gray body to the earthen clots torn up by cloven hooves. It was, in fact, no illusion, but they did not know that the external magic gave them the means to bind a nearby creature and summon it.

All around the boar, which they still thought an illusion, the grass was losing color, withering, dying. Turul cried out and the power stopped flowing. The boar vanished, for Turul's hold upon it had been no firmer than an illusion. And the lovers found themselves standing in a vast circle of dead grass and trees.

Anaki had discovered the way a wizard uses the vital force of forests or plains as if it is the strength of her own body. She had discovered mana.

But she had not discovered how to *control* the use of mana.

When Anaki and Turul regained wit enough to talk, Anaki said, "We are committing murder! We kill trees or grass whenever we use this external magic."

"My father says a hunter kills only when necessary," Turul said.

"Yes," Anaki said. "We can use this power only to save lives. And we must tell no one what we can do!"

They did not tell anyone, and they did not tap the mana again until more than a year had passed, and Anaki's mother, their master Inasha, lay dying of the premature old age that ended wizards' lives in those days. Anaki and Turul fought to save Inasha, fueling powerful healing spells with great quantities of mana, killing crops as well as plains grass in a bad growing season; but still Inasha was taken by the Hunter of Souls. Guilt filled Anaki and Turul as strongly as their grief.

Yet within six months they tapped the plains again, while struggling to save a mortally wounded hunter. This time they succeeded. The external power did not make them omnipotent, but it did sometimes preserve a life which otherwise would end.

The young wizards kept their vow to tap the plains and forest only when necessary, which in their village of three hundred was not often.

Anaki and Turul wanted many children, but for all their attempts and prayers they had only one. They rejoiced in their son, and Akkurdal grew up in the center of his parents' world, receiving not only their undivided love but their constant attention. For unlike the farmers, hunters, and craftsfolk of the village of Eredok, the wizards did not need to leave their child in the elders' care as they carried out their duties.

This is not to say that young Akkurdal did not spend time with other children. In those carefree days, the children of Eredok had much time for play, and Akkurdal played with them, because he was not yet nine years old, not yet apprenticed to his parents. And because he insisted upon it.

Before he was five he had realized that the other children were frightened of his parents, and therefore of him. So the next time he was touched in tag, he denied it. His playmate Seg asserted truthfully, "I tagged you!"

Akkurdal said quietly, "Are you calling me a liar?"

"Liar, liar, liar!" Seg hotly replied.

"I'm not a liar," Akkurdal said. "I'm going to tell my parents you called me a liar."

"No!" Seg cried, chill with sudden fear.

"My parents don't like liars. They put spells on boys who lie about their son—"

"Akkurdal!" cried one of the older children, a sensible seven-year-old girl named Unekti. "Your parents are healers. They don't cast evil spells!"

"Maybe they won't put a spell on Seg," agreed Akkurdal. He was nimble-witted even at that early age and lied as readily as a child seeking to avoid punishment. "But I know lots of spells!"

"You're not a liar!" Seg cried. "I was jesting! I'm your friend, Akkurdal! Don't hurt me!"

Having Seg in his power filled Akkurdal with pleasure, and he wanted the pleasure to continue. He smiled and replied, "Maybe I won't—if you eat this pile of dog dung."

Seg begged and groveled, and the other children screamed and groaned, but Akkurdal did not relent, and finally Seg did what Akkurdal had directed.

The children always did what Akkurdal directed. And some even became Akkurdal's servants, his enforcers, to enjoy a share of his power over the children of Eredok, so his lack of magical knowledge was not exposed.

Of course, eventually the parents of Akkurdal's playmates learned what was going on, and finally a small, nervous delegation came to Anaki and Turul and told them of Akkurdal's bullying. Astonished, Anaki and Turul turned to their nine-year-old son and asked, "Akkurdal, are these things true?"

"No," Akkurdal said.

Anaki and Turul sent the adults away with admonishments not to believe everything their children told them, while neither interrogating nor investigating their own son.

And they formally apprenticed Akkurdal, as they had been at the age of nine. Oddly, they took no other apprentices; perhaps they still hoped to have more children, though they were nearing their thirties, which in those days was old age for wizards. Akkurdal learned quickly—quickly enough to stay the master when the other children, grown older and wiser (and more desperate), tried to overthrow his tyranny. He had guessed that the healing spells could be twisted to inflict pain and injury, and he was proved right.

When Akkurdal was sixteen, the age at which Anaki had discovered the external power, his parents taught him how to supplement his innate strength by employing that of plain and forest. They emphasized the necessity of responsible use. They wasted their breath.

They had been adults at sixteen; Akkurdal was a child. His first unsupervised use of the power was a spectacular illusion intended to awe and frighten the youths and children of the village. He succeeded in his goal. He also destroyed acres of trees and all of Eredok's crops by draining away the mana from the land beneath them. And he killed many of the onlookers, for he had not summoned an illusion, but actual land leeches.

Akkurdal was astonished by what was happening, but pleasure filled him like sweet strong wine as he realized that he had just greatly strengthened his already considerable power.

The dying children's screams brought scores of villagers running, among them Anaki and Turul. They banished the land leeches, realizing at last that the boar which Turul had summoned years ago had been no illusion.

They ordered their son home and, in the privacy of their hut, they spoke to Akkurdal sternly, harshly, angrily; they spoke to their son as they never had before. He did not respond, and finally they were reduced to shouting at him.

"You knew what you were doing!" Turul cried. "Why did you destroy the crops? Gods, we need them to survive the winter!"

"You killed your friends!" Anaki cried. "You endangered everyone in the village! Don't you care?"

"No," Akkurdal said. "Why should I?"

His careless response shocked his parents into realization of what everyone else in Eredok had long known about Akkurdal's character. The discovery moved Turul to his first use of physical punishment. He was aged now, his blows were weak, but they roused in Akkurdal a vicious anger which inspired the youth to try something that had never occurred to his parents. He reached out, seeking sufficient energy for his dark new idea—and as the mana surged into him, he tasted a new, rank power.

He slew his father and mother, and in the act, made them his slaves.

They were dead. Yet imbued with magical vitality—and utterly subservient to their evil son's will. *Zombies.*

Even in those days of clean water and forest and plain, swamps dotted the length of the Great River. Akkurdal had found the mana which suited him.

And he had not drained the life from the swamps he had reached. In his search for a suitable power, he had chanced to tap mana without draining it away, and thereby learned that he could use mana without destroying its source.

And now Akkurdal was the only wizard in Eredok.

The villagers had not failed to connect the young wizard's flashy, deadly "illusion" with the destruction of their crops. Not knowing the fates of Anaki and Turul, the leading citizens of Eredok came to speak to Akkurdal. Knowing Akkurdal's nature, and seeing Akkurdal's parents nowhere about, the citizens addressed Akkurdal in quiet, placating tones. Akkurdal mocked and reviled them, and told them that from now on they would do as he ordered. They grew frightened and angry, and the chief hunter drew his knife of Lugulite iron and leaped at the wizard. He was young and quick, and close to his target, but he hadn't a chance.

A gesture, a spell, and the chief hunter lay dead.

Then he rose up a zombie and pointed his knife at the men and women who had been his allies.

They were silent, stunned and horrified.

Akkurdal said, "You cannot harm me. Bow to me! I am the headman of Eredok now, and my will is your law. You shall do as I command, or you shall all die!"

Then he declared that the men and women of Eredok must take up their knives and spears and seize their neighbors' lands. The representatives of Eredok protested. Anaki and Turul appeared. The villagers screamed at the sight of their good wizards turned to walking corpses. The dead wizards and the dead hunter—the zombies—tore the terrified villagers apart.

Then Akkurdal turned the dismembered bodies into intact, animate, regenerating skeletons.

So began the reign of the Wizard Tyrant.

The rest you know. Akkurdal's need to dominate and lust for land drove him to conquest, and no wizard nor any number of soldiers could defeat him, for only he knew the secret of tapping mana. And now he is bored after his conquest of the Great Plains, and amuses himself and terrifies his subjects with the wanton displays of power which have turned the Great Plains into the Great Waste, a vast expanse of foul swamp and badland that reaches over a thousand leagues in every direction.

Now you know how the love of Anaki and Turul created a monster and ended our world.

To flee the monster, we slipped out of Eredok to seek a pass through the Mountains of Shenggor, which no one has ever crossed.

We have found a pass, and you will find a new land, new plains or forests, to be your home.

But I shall not go with you.

The elf-woman pauses in her tale, for her ragged, shivering audience shouts in surprise at her revelation. Their cries echo off the sheer basalt cliffs of the pass.

And then, above the shouts and echoes, one elf-man cries: "How do you know all this? How can you know all this?"

How do I know all that I have told you? I learned it from my father, who learned it from his father, the Wizard Tyrant.

Now two-score elves shout in astonishment and fear.

My father tried to kill his father, but he did not have Akkurdal's experience, and so he died at Akkurdal's hand. He is Akkurdal's servant now, the Wizard Tyrant's dreadful Zombie Master.

But Akkurdal, even the mighty Wizard Tyrant Akkurdal, did not know that his son had a daughter. A wizard who knows everything he does about the manifold uses of mana. A wizard who has learned, in this flight to the mountains, that mountains too are a source of mana, and of frightful creatures which can be bound by that mana. A mana which is unknown to the Wizard Tyrant. A magic as powerful as his own.

She rises to her feet, the gray-haired elf-woman who is not old, and the night wind catches her hair and flares it like silver fire, and her eyes gleam red and hot as stars. Her face is hard as granite, set in lines of determination as fixed as mountains in the flesh of the world.

And she raises her fist and cries:

I vow by my father's soul, and by the souls of Anaki and Turul, to destroy the Wizard Tyrant, my grandfather, Akkurdal!

The elves rise up cheering and do not hear her softly spoken conclusion, her most solemn and heartfelt vow:

I shall redeem my evil heritage.

Dryad's Kiss

Morgan Llywelyn

From the bottom of the hollow, the tree reached with leafless fingers toward the larger of the two moons that glimmered above the encircling hills. It was a slender tree, deeply rooted and graceful, bedecked with fragrant blossoms in spring and mantled with green leaves in summer. But on this cold winter evening it was a barren and lonely figure.

Another lonely figure stood on the lip of the hollow, gazing down. Telier wrapped his tattered cloak around him to keep out the icy wind as he surveyed the scene below. The nacreous moonlight made the hollow almost as bright as day.

Once there had been a lot of undergrowth around the tree, woody brush that cut easily and was not difficult to carry away. Then Telier had cleared out all the brush in order to feed his fires. Only the tree itself remained. He was an aging man with tired bones. He did not want to attempt to chop down an entire tree. The task would undoubtedly defeat him, and he had been defeated too much already.

But where to find firewood? From the top of the slope, Telier stared down at the tree and wondered what to do. Perhaps he might take some of the branches. He could throw a rope around a dead limb and break it off. But were there any dead branches not too far above the ground? Live boughs would be much harder to break.

Thinking back, he did not recall ever having seen dead branches on the tree. It always looked so healthy, a health he envied. Recently he had developed a cough, and the cold of winter seemed to bite more deeply into his bones this year than ever before. If he grew ill, with no one to look after him, he would die. Die alone and forgotten, a foolish old man . . .

He went back into his hut and soon emerged with a coil of rope around his shoulder and a handax thrust through his belt. Moonlight glinted off the streaks of white in his hair and beard.

With a weary sigh, he began picking his way down toward the bottom of the hollow. The winding path he followed was footworn and muddy, and he was afraid of slipping. If he fell and hurt himself, no one would hear his cries. He had deliberately sought out this site far from any human habitation.

Magic, he insisted, required solitude.

Not, thought Telier grimly, that any magic was happening. He had devoted his life to the pursuit of mana, spending what money he had on books and lessons, sitting at the feet of the great sorcerers and drinking in their words against the day he would start to practice himself.

In his youth, sometimes he had—almost—felt the tingle of mana in his fingertips. But when that happened he was secretly frightened. The possession and practice of using mana was a huge responsibility. He assured himself that he would be ready for it someday, someday soon, just not quite yet . . . there was so much more to learn, so many preparations to make. He must be older, wiser, stronger. Or so he thought when he was young.

Time had passed. Telier grew older and stronger, but no wiser, no closer to becoming a skilled practitioner of magic. Years flew by as he went from one teacher to another, seeking the one who could open the door for him. And—occasionally— he thought the door did open just a crack, thought he glimpsed a beam of golden light from inside. Thought he heard the distant roar of the minotaur, or the harsh laugh of the jackal-headed being. His heart would begin to race and his palms to sweat. And he backed away.

Afterward, at night in his bed, he tossed and turned feverishly.

Tomorrow, he promised himself. Tomorrow he would be more ready. Tomorrow, when the crack appeared, he would thrust himself through it. He would hurl himself gladly into the realms of magic, the kingdom of mana.

So he continued the pursuit of his dream until time diminished both his fear and his eagerness, and left him only with dogged persistence.

Yet it never quite happened. The mana never became solid and tangible for him, the door never swung wide to receive him. People began to look at him with pity in their eyes.

That was when he shunned the society of his fellows and began living in lonely places with only the trees and the sky for company. The solitude he claimed he needed was an excuse. But he redoubled his efforts to learn magic because he had left himself with nothing else.

Telier sighed; stopped to catch his breath. Below him the tree was waiting. It would be a shame to chop it down, he thought. Its shape was unusually beautiful, graceful and slim, with the branches as pleasingly arranged as if an artist had designed them. The removal of even a single limb would destroy the symmetry of the tree.

But the fire in his little hut had long since gone out, and the winter was growing colder. He must have heat. He must have light. The bottom of the night was the best time to practice and he could not practice in the dark.

He could not practice if he was so cold his joints stiffened and his fingers would not bend to make the secret signs or draw the symbols of power in the waiting air.

He found himself talking aloud to the tree, explaining his predicament. "I hope I am . . . I believe I am close to achieving my goal," he said in a voice rusty with disuse. "Just a little more effort and surely I shall break through. The mastery of mana does not come easily to anyone; it requires great sacrifice. I have given up everything—home, family, friends. I never married, I have no children to inherit my books. And I possess nothing else, except the clothes I wear and that wretched hut on the lip of the hollow.

"But if once I succeed in working magic, everything will change. What is left of my life will shimmer with silver and gold. Beautiful women will come to me eagerly, not seeing me as gray and wrinkled. Mana will make me handsome to them; mana will make me as virile as a boy. All the hardship of my days will be forgotten."

His throat burned with longing. For so many years he had hung on to that one promise. When he was lonely, or hungry, or weary, he had comforted himself with his dream, imagining how it would be. Denying himself pleasure in the present, taking all his pleasure from the future.

He was no longer fearful. He had outgrown the terrors of youth and the timidity of middle age. All that remained of emotion was the overwhelming desire to realize his dream before he died.

He resumed picking his way down the slope, step by careful step. Once he turned and glanced back toward his hut overlooking the hollow. The dilapidated timber shack was not far away, yet already he was dreading the climb back. "I am getting old," he murmured aloud. "I don't have much time left."

He was not talking about the search for firewood.

Reaching the bottom of the hollow, he scuffled through drifted leaves to the base of the tree. The bark was very pale, almost white, resembling flesh in the moonlight. He touched the haft of his ax with his fingertips, but could not bring himself to withdraw it from his belt and bite into the trunk of the tree. No, his other plan was better. A rope slung over a low branch, a powerful tug downward . . .

Powerful. Telier's lips twitched. Summoning any power to his aging muscles would be an act of magic in itself. Tilting his head back, he gazed into the branches. The lowest was near enough for him to reach with his hand if he stretched up. Drawing a deep breath, he took the coil of rope off his shoulder and prepared to throw one end of it over the branch.

But as he concentrated on the rope, something touched his shoulder. He glanced up again, startled. A wind had begun to blow and the branch directly above him was moving, creaking, bending down until its outermost twigs brushed his shoulder with a dancing caress.

Mana! Telier thought, but at once he knew better. He could not summon a branch down to him. Tears of self-pity burned in his eyes as he admitted the bitter truth. He could not do even that much magic—after a lifetime of trying. To believe otherwise was only lying to himself.

"What's wrong with me?" he asked the tree softly. "Others succeed. Others have only to try, and it is accomplished. They turn the right corners, meet the right people, make the right choices. Yet whatever I do seems to be a mistake. Years ago I should have given up the pursuit of mana, but I was stubborn. I could not admit that I had made the wrong choice for my life.

"Once there was a woman who would have loved me—but she was not the woman of my dreams. Once there was a little farm I could have bought for us—but I had not planned to spend my life as a farmer. I was too stubborn. I had told everyone I was going to be a sorcerer, so I continued as I had begun. And if I do not succeed now, I shall have thrown my entire life away."

Telier's shoulders shook with a dry sob. For a moment he did not feel the twigs brushing him again. When he did, he took it as an omen. He was meant to break off the branch for firewood, and this night—this very night!—might see his breakthrough. Might see his stiffening fingers shape the signs properly and his drying lips form the words correctly, so the mana would come to him at last.

He gave a loud cry to hearten himself and lend strength to his arm, then hurled the rope. It snaked upward through the air and over the branch. Telier caught the other end and drew it to him. But when he tugged, though the bough creaked loudly, it did not break. He tugged again. No success. The taste of failure was as dry as dust on his tongue.

Finally in desperation he knotted both ends of the rope around his waist so he could bring his entire weight to bear. Then he threw himself down on the ground, shielding his head with his arms, expecting to hear the crack of wood above him.

Nothing happened. All he heard was the wind.

"No!" he cried in frustration. "Please no! Let this one thing, just this one thing, go right for me. I cannot bear it anymore, I cannot! There must be magic . . . for me . . . somewhere, somehow. I cannot live like this any longer."

His pain and longing had never been so intense. They burned like fire through his bones. Burying his face in the dead leaves, the man called Telier wept bitter tears.

Their moisture seeped into the leaves. The winter wind played its songs on the harpstrings of the tree branches.

Mana shimmered along the silvery bark.

Like tender arms, the branches reached down for Telier. The nearest touched him as he lay huddled on the earth. Its twigs closed on his shoulders like gripping fingers, lifting him to his knees. Another limb encircled his waist, gently tugging him to his feet.

He was startled, then alarmed. With an oath, he struck out at the branches. Then, as he fought his way free, he felt it; felt it for certain this time: the unmistakable tingle of mana.

At the same moment he heard again the roar of the minotaur.

The air above filled with the wings of immense black birds, blood dripping from their talons. From close behind him came the rattle of bones, the brittle music of skeletons dancing. A wave of panic swept through Teriel. He gazed wildly around, uncertain which direction to flee.

Before he could take a step, the ground opened at his feet to reveal a yawning chasm filled with flames. Tongues of fire leaped hungrily upward until he felt their heat against his skin. And all the time the tingle was running through him, the rippling, dizzying excitement that was mana.

He could not fight back; he was too old and too weak. Teetering helplessly on the brink of the chasm, Teriel expected the next moment to be his last.

Then he realized the mana was coming from the tree beyond the chasm. The tree who was still holding out her branches to him, waiting to gather him lovingly to her bosom.

The panic left him then. The failure of the bitter years fell away from him. In a flash of wisdom, he knew that mana had never come to him because some tiny part of himself had always resisted. But he would resist no longer. With a foolish, hopeful smile, he gathered what little remained of his strength and leaped forward across the chasm, into the embrace of the branches.

Even as he soared over it, the fire faded and the chasm closed.

The tree drew him to her trunk, which was as soft as flesh, as warm as life in the winter's night. The light of the moon beamed down, flooding the scene with beauty. Telier felt as virile as a boy with fresh young sap flowing through his veins. The tree bent over him. He became aware of her desire, the desire of a creature of magic for the one special, unique individual who was worthy of the gift of her love.

"Me?" Telier whispered, hardly daring to believe. "Me?"

Using a gentle but persistent strength, the branches drew him closer. He knew what the tree wanted. As if she spoke to him, her thoughts entered his mind. He could refuse, he knew. Until the very last moment, he could turn away and she would let him go. What was happening was not rape.

But it was magic.

With a glad cry, Telier surrendered.

No one came looking for him until the spring. When he did not come into the nearest village to restock his meager supplies, tradespeople began wondering. It took them a long time to decide something must be wrong. They were not callous, or neglectful; they merely had their own lives to lead and he had deliberately separated himself from their world. But eventually they became concerned, and a search party set out.

When they found his hut empty and collapsing from neglect, they enlarged their search to include the surrounding area. At the bottom of the hollow they found one lone tree covered in a massive cloak of bright green leaves that hid the interior of the plant from view. They parted the leaves and peered at the earth under the tree, but it was devoid of body or bones.

Eventually the search party gave up. "Telier must be dead," they told one another. "Poor old man; his life was a failure and he has come to some tragic end." They went home to their wives and families and mundane worries and forgot about him.

The tree grows in the hollow still. In the spring it is fragrant with blossom; in the summer it wears a mantle of green leaves. In all seasons, however, it is radiantly beautiful, immortal with mana.

The Lament

S. M. Stirling

Sauruven Hellwald tilted the last drop of wine out of the flaccid skin. It was thin and sour; he spat into the roadway, making a spray of black spots in the hot white dust, out beyond the drippings of sweat from his horse. He wiped his wide mouth on the cuff of linen that edged his chainmail sleeve, cursing the heat and the caked dirt that smeared to mud on his face. It clung gray-white to the black tabard across his chest, almost covering the crossed runic thunderbolts of his order, the *Schwartzritterein,* the Black Knights.

His narrow dark eyes surveyed the wide mountain valley before him with distaste. The road clung to the steep slope. The river Synar drained this section of the Gurdurngs, and it rushed through a steep canyon impassible to boats or feet. Below him was small lake that fed the angry waters, looking cool and blue and calm. His skin itched to bathe in it. Beyond he could see a centaur farmer harrowing his field, the wide rake strapped to his equine shoulders raising a cloud of dust behind him. A short distance from the farmer's holding was a small village, quaint and tidy; many of the buildings were centaur-built, long barnlike houses with swinging doors. He spat again.

Horse's asses. He hoped he wouldn't have to trade with

them. *Count your fingers afterwards.* Centaurs were notorious
for being tight-clutched with money.

It was demeaning for a knight to barter, anyway. You gave
with an open hand, or took at the sword's edge; nothing in
between. His mouth quirked. At least, that was how it worked
when you were a landed knight with peasants toiling to support
you, or given arms-and-maintenance in a lord's fighting-tail.
When your pouch went light, you bargained, or you took the risk
of turning robber and being strung from a tree by the king's men.
With luck there would be humans in the village—some of the
buildings had a more natural look—or even dwarves, something
that walked on two legs. It looked a fair enough spot; square
fields around the lake, fallow or yellowing wheat or green corn,
pasture beyond, orchards of apple and peach and terraced vine-
yards on the lower slopes. Beyond all of that and best of all, at
the western end of the valley a mountain rose like a giant granite
fist thrust defiantly into the heavens. The land's answer to the
uncaring sky.

His horse whickered at the smell of water, and he stroked its
neck. The three packhorses raised their drooping ears as well.
Time to rest, time to eat. Time to sleep. But first, time for a bath.

He brought his eyes back down to the valley. With a sigh he
touched a heel to its ribs and his black stallion started off toward
the village below.

"Welcome to Kvardalen," the innkeeper said. "What is your pleasure, noble sir?"

"Wine," the knight said.

The innkeeper coughed discreetly into a hand. "Ah, sir
knight—best not. Not while . . . "

He indicated the centaurs clumped around the other end of
the common room. It was open to the air on two sides, thatched
walls held up by poles could be lowered in cold or inclement
weather to make the place more comfortable. There were no
chairs in that section, naturally, since the centaurs would hardly
use them, although there was a rail where they could comfortably
prop a hoof and tables high enough to suit them. The bar was an
L-shaped affair that met the standing walls at two ends. The door

to the kitchen was behind the bar. The scent of baking bread wafted through it, almost overpowering the sweet scent of the beer.

Sauruven shrugged and took a stein of the local barley brew.

"Mules can't take it, eh?" he said—not loudly, but in his normal voice.

The innkeeper—he looked human, save for a suspicious point to his ears—made frantic shushing motions. Centaurs hated being called mules; it implied they were hybrids. Which they were, if you listened to wizards, which most didn't.

"Smell drives 'em crazy," Sauruven went on. "They forget if the tail's got a tail to it, from what I hear."

The bearded faces of the centaurs looked over at him, slow anger kindling under their heavy brows. A few clenched fists on the high tables, or around the wooden mugs that held their liquor.

Give them their due, though, he thought, raising his tankard, *they brew a grand beer.*

He grinned back at them, letting the cloak fall away from his side. His left hand rested on the cross-hilt of his long sword; they froze at the sight and at the oiled gleam of metal links from his mail hauberk.

"Wait."

Another centaur stallion had entered the inn's common room. This one had a belt at the waist where his human torso joined his spotted equine body; he carried a short sword. A double-curved bow and quiver were strung over his upper shoulders. He looked at Sauruven narrowly.

"You've come?" he said suspiciously. "Already? The message must have traveled swiftly." A shrug. "Well, that's the way of wizards. I'm the lord's reeve and forest warden here, and—"

The knight let his hand drop from his sword-hilt. *Wizards?* he thought, then cursed silently.

It would be just like his master Thomil to guide his footsteps here and tell him nothing. Nothing at—

Then, through the afternoon sunlight like an unwelcome guest came a low and mournful song. Deep timbered, sounding like a mountain grieving for some irretrievable loss, the voice echoed across the valley and gradually faded.

Centaur heads came up and their eyes and nostrils widened.

But they clamped their jaws and made no comment, swishing their tails and moving their hooves uneasily.

Sauruven lowered his tankard slowly and closed his open mouth.

What in blazes is a Hurloon minotaur doing here? he wondered. Then shook his head. *Need you ask?* he scolded himself. No doubt the poor bastard had been dropped here like a discarded toy by some wizard who'd used the minotaur to fight his battles for him.

I don't mind, thought Sauruven. War was his trade, fighting his only profession, the only skill he had. Thomil gave him plentiful opportunities to exercise it, and the rewards weren't too miserly; if nothing else, the odd bit of plunder. But the Hurloon were different; they had close ties to their people and their mountains. Abandoning one here alone was sheer cruelty.

He laughed. The others in the common room jerked their attention away from the hills, looking at him in alarm. He schooled his face; no sense frightening the locals when he had more serious matters to attend to.

"Just laughing at myself," he said soothingly.

Well I might. Sauruven Hellwald criticizing another for cruelty, of all things. What next? Dragons landing and telling travelers to bury their campfires for fear of forest fires?

"How long has that been going on?" he asked, indicating the mountain with his tankard.

The mule's nostrils widened and Sauruven glared. He never knew how to interpret that. Usually he took it as an insult, in this case, though, he sensed it signified unease. The reeve fingered the hilt of his sword.

"Started yesterday," the centaur told him. "Went on all night and most of today." He pointed at the mountain. "See that spire of rock?"

After a moment's study, Sauruven nodded.

"That's the horn," the bartender continued. "It's coming from there. But he won't stay up there."

The knight chewed his lip thoughtfully and ran his broad hand across his short dark beard. That was true enough. Hurloon minotaurs might have the heads of bulls, but they ate meat—and they weren't generally too fussy about what the meat had been while it was breathing, either. More than one king kept a mino-taur as an entertaining way of disposing of enemies.

"I won't need your damned room," he told the innkeeper shortly. "I'm going up on the mountain."

The horse put a hoof forward and then pulled it back, snorting and shaking his head until the bridle's curb-chain rattled. A rock clattered away down the near-vertical slope to the right, breaking into fragments with a crack like miniature thunder as it struck a crag. The air was cooler than it had been down in the valley; he was higher than the mountain pass to the east, nearly to the flat hornlike plateau three-quarters of the way up the mountain. High enough that the air seemed thin in his chest. The Hurloon lament echoed wildly here, booming back from the steep gorges.

Sauruven dismounted and soothed his warsteed with an absent hand. The horse was well trained and sensible; he trusted it to know what was safe footing. He looped its reins back to the pommel of his saddle and unstopped his shield, taking off the covering of waxed canvas to reveal the glossy black surface and the lightning blazons of the Schwartzenritterein. His helmet went on next, the familiar feel and smell of the sweat-soaked cork and sponge lining clamping his head under its weight of steel, vision shrinking to what he could see through eye-pieces of the three-bar visor. The wire-bound sharkskin of his long sword was com-forting and familiar in his palm; he shrugged to settle the hauberk on his shoulders and began to walk upward along the trail. Stone and gravel crunched beneath his feet. He carried the shield up and forward, the sword slanted backward over his right shoulder.

The trail narrowed steadily, until he moved along on a nar-row shelf, his chest pressed against the wall of a cliff, his back pressed against the west wind.

The song, when it came, surrounded him, echoes beating back and forth from the flat planes of the mountain. He could feel it humming along his bones and the hair on his neck lifted at the eerie sensation.

Cautiously rounding a bend in the narrow track he was on, Sauruven came upon a broad uneven surface. He saw the body of a young female Hurloon laid upon a pyre, her booted feet tidily bound together, hands crossed on her breast. Upon her brow was a grass wreath entwined with such pale flowers as grew this high in the mountains at springtime. The knight halted, the tip of his sword slowly lowering until it touched stone.

Before the pyre a male minotaur knelt. His hide was purest white, and the elaborate tatoos on his bull muzzle and bronze-tipped horns of his brows marked him as a war leader; so too did the great oak club that lay by his feet. His head was thrown back, mighty hands clenched against his brow, his massive throat throbbing with passionate song.

If I had never before seen grief, Sauruven thought, *I would know it now.* Decision moved in him.

He'd made no sound, but suddenly the young minotaur sprang to his feet and confronted him, eyes blazing redly, menace in every line of his body. Muscles rippled beneath his skin like ship's cables.

"I will fight you," Sauruven told him, knowing he would lose, "if you feel that would honor her." His nod indicated the young female. "But I came to help you sing the Lament."

It was like watching a fire go out. The minotaur's shoulders drooped and he took two steps backward, offering his hands palm-out in a gesture of peace.

"Thank you," he said sadly, almost in a whisper. "A hymn is better with many voices."

Sauruven moved forward, sheathing his weapon, to take a kneeling position in front of the pyre. He brought out a waterskin and offered it to the Hurloon, who knelt beside him and took it with a gracious bow.

After the minotaur drank, he passed it back and said, "I am Eumenes, of the Hurloon Mountains. This," he said indicating the form on the pyre, "is my wife, Eurynomous. That means 'far pasturing' in our tongue. Indeed," he continued in a voice strained with tears, "she came far from her home to die." Eumenes's eyes closed in pain and he bowed his head, beating his hand against his breast.

"How did she die?" Sauruven asked.

This was the first part of the ceremony: the deceased's life would be told backward, from the moment of her death through childhood to her birth.

"We were seized by a wizard's wind. Suddenly we were far from home, far from our own ranges and herds. A rock giant slew her. He came upon her and flung her from the mountain; she was broken in the fall." Eumenes flung back his head and sang. Sauruven sang the descant.

His exhaustion seemed to fall from his broad shoulders and his voice was fuller as he extolled Eurynomous's virtues in the songs he sang of her. And Sauruven sang with him.

Dawn? the knight thought. *How long . . .*

Memory returned. Three days, here in this icy upland amid the boulders. His throat was raw with the effort, but his mind felt at peace; something he'd seldom experienced in all his years and wanderings.

"I must light the pyre," Eumenes said, even his great throat hoarse with effort. "The fire of these mountains is strong; I feel the mana in their bones."

He made a gathering gesture with both hands. Flame exploded from the pyre in a white heat that drove Sauruven stumbling backward, raising his hands to protect his eyes. There was none of the usual evil stink of a cremation, only a brilliance like the heart of a star. Eumenes endured the heat that singed his tear-streaked eyes.

"You're a wizard," Sauruven said uneasily. His eyes went cold.

"No!" Eumenes snapped. "Never that! I have only the one spell. But I can't leave Eurynomous's body to be raised as a zombie to fight some wizard's battles." His eyes flashed with pain and fury in the firelight and Sauruven held his tongue, knowing that neither agreement nor sympathy were welcome.

By sunset, the pyre was cool enough to allow them to gather up the ashes and scatter them on the winds that blew unceasingly from the mountain's summit. Then they stood awhile in sad, companionable silence, staring down the craggy slopes into the centaur's pleasant valley.

"Come with me to my campsite below," Sauruven said at last. "We'll have ourselves a funeral supper, as is proper."

* * *

Eumenes nodded numbly and followed the knight down the trail.
When they camped, he looked around; it was as if he saw the
shield and black armor, the great warhorse, for the first time.
Guarded surprise flickered in his eyes; they moved sideways to
the huge brass-bound club that he'd brought and propped care-
lessly against a tree.

"You're of the Schwartzenritterein," he said.

Sauruven nodded, poking the fire. Pieces of salt pork sizzled
on sticks near it. "Yes," he said shortly. "The Black Knights . . .
There's a cask of beer on the second packsaddle."

The minotaur returned with it, casually staving in the end
with one huge fist. The knight filled his cow-horn goblet and
gestured. Eumenes lifted the small oak keg to his own muzzle
and drank deeply, the Adam's apple working in his great throat.

"I could say that few have heard much good of the
Schwartzenritterein," he said meditatively

"Or of the Hurloon minotaurs," Sauruven replied. He spat to
one side. "But nobody thinks well of wizards—least of all their
servants."

The minotaur's face wasn't constructed for human smiles,
but the way his tail lashed and the razor-tipped bronze points of
his horns tossed conveyed irony enough.

They ate in silence. After he leaned back and wiped his
mouth with the back of his hand, Sauruven said:

"What will you do now?" After a second's pause he added:
"My friend."

The long bull-muzzle nodded. "My heart is torn," the mino-
taur answered. "I want to go home, to be among my own people.
These mountains are too young and harsh to please my eyes. But
I also wish to avenge Eurynomous's murder."

He shook his head and pounded a fist into the ground. It
echoed like a drum to the blow.

"The stone giant didn't have to kill her; she could do him no
harm. It was pure malice on his part. He laughed at the scream
she made. And had I not hoped that I could still help her, I would
have tried to slay him then. But when I returned, he was gone
and I had to prepare her for her funeral."

The minotaur stopped speaking and stared into the fire.

Sauruven felt more uneasy before Eumenes's obvious

shame than he had in the face of his grief. It would do no good to assure him that it wasn't really his fault: the minotaur knew that. Shame needs less cause than grief, but is just as powerful.

"You could return home and gather some friends, then come back here and hunt him down," Sauruven suggested.

Eumenes was shaking his head.

"No, some wizard might summon him and pull him far from this place, then I would never find him. I must do it now."

"Shall I help you?"

"You are generous," Eumenes said with a slow smile. "I have always heard that you Black Knights were good fighters. I have been told that it's what you live for. Generosity I did not expect."

Sauruven laughed shortly.

"I'm a warrior, not a madman. Fighting's the best part of my life, but not the whole of it. Anyway, I'm offering to help you fight—my favorite thing—so it's not so generous after all. Is it?"

"I welcome your aid," Eumenes said with a grin, offering his hand.

Sauruven took it. "I'll take first watch," he said. "You have more cause to be weary."

"No!"

Sauruven shouted in involuntary protest as he came awake. There was no mistaking Thomil's summons, even when it came in the midst of sleep. The wrenching sickness was always the same, the driven rags of mist that covered his sight until their clearing marked some new field of battle. Nor could he mistake the unholy sorcerous strength that vibrated through him, until he felt like the plucked steel string of a war-harp. The world cleared until it was as sharp-edged as glass cut by a diamond. He felt alive, as he never was except in battle—but the exultation of the wizard's battles was more than human flesh could bear.

As the summoning sickness cleared and the disorientation drained away, he opened his eyes to view the battleground. He found himself on a bare plain, a place so flat that a gentle rise not far off seemed a hill. Short grass whispered in a dry breeze. Startled hoppers flicked from the ground before his feet, arching high, to disappear into the grass farther on. The place smelled of dust and heat, and wild thyme.

At first he thought himself alone. *Where is my enemy?* he thought. The crystal clarity of his vision was tinged with red now. Battle-madness was the wizard's gift, and none better for a knight of the Schwartzenritterein.

Then a familiar figure came over the low rise before him. The hard pounding of his heart seemed to falter for a moment, and he felt a great sickness.

Eumenes stopped when he was ten feet away and bowed.

"This is not the battle I imagined us fighting, my friend." The minotaur tried to smile and failed. "If I could, I would not do this," he said. "But the geas of the wizard is upon me."

Thomil! Sauruven screamed in his mind, *I ask a boon, the only one I have ever craved. Do not make me do this. Release me, I beg of you, this creature is my friend.*

There was no answer; and whether the wizard couldn't hear him or chose not to, the results were the same. The rage at the edge of his mind ate inward until he chewed the edge of his shield and screamed with the pain of fighting it. Eumenes moaned, slaver dripping from his taurine lips, flying in strands as he shook his head and bellowed with a sound that shivered in Sauruven's gut.

The brass-bound club swung high. "Kill!" the minotaur screamed in a voice like rocks in torment.

"The knights of the order should have no friends," Sauruven's sword master had told him often enough. *This is the penalty for breaking that rule,* Sauruven thought in the brief seconds before the minotaur was upon him.

The ugly wind of the club's passing fanned his eyes. His training reacted, letting one knee go loose, and his weight moved him around. The backstroke was not quite so powerful; he moved in and caught the club on his shield, angling it so that the club struck below its head. Even that was enough to drive him to his knees, and he heard the crack of the shield's lindenwood frame breaking. His shoulder went numb; the bones would have shattered themselves without Thomil's strength in his veins. Eumenes roared and raised his bludgeon two-handed above his head. Nothing could survive that stroke; it would crush the steel of his helmet and the skull beneath like eggshells.

But the move left the minotaur exposed—and even as he struck, Sauruven knew that Eumenes had intended that, and let the killing rage take him completely and leach away the training and skill that might have saved him. The yard-length of razor-sharp steel sank into the minotaur's body with a soft, heavy resistance that ended in a wrist-jarring thump on bone. It angled up through his stomach and behind the great hoop of the minotaur's ribs, through veins and lungs.

He stayed upright for a moment, rigid with pain and shock. Then Sauruven withdrew his sword and Eumenes fell, an endless toppling like some huge tree under a woodsman's axe. The ground shook beneath the knight as his foe's body hammered into the turf. The club was cast aside; the minotaur's big hands clutched at his death wound. Blood bubbled from it and through lips drawn back from big square teeth.

At that moment, compulsion left them, along with the unclean strength that had made the knight's victory possible. Sauruven fell to his knees beside his friend and threw his sword aside, cradling the horned head in his arms.

Eumenes' eyes rolled back and then focused on Sauruven's face.

"You were a worthy opponent," he gasped, and fumbled for Sauruven's hand. "This is not so bad a thing. I didn't have to suffer the loss of my Eurynomous for long." He grinned up at Sauruven. "I wish she was here to sing me to rest."

That was all. The great head sagged and the large brown eyes half closed. Eumenes, war leader of the Hurloon minotaurs was no more.

Sauruven threw back his head and sang the Lament.

"It is done," said a rough, sly voice beside him.

Sauruven dropped a gold thaler into the small, dirty hand the goblin held out. Behind them, the dawn sun broke over Kvardalen, but the mountain slopes were still in shadow. Snow flecked the wind; it was winter, and a long journey past.

Ended now, Sauruven thought, looking up the mountain slope. This was where it had begun; not far from where his horse had balked seven months ago and he'd gone on foot to meet Eumenes.

"Five," the goblin insisted. "You said a gold piece—surely meant one for each of us." It smiled with a gap-toothed grin. Behind it its fellows grinned, too, and fingered the curved saw-edged swords thrust through their belts. One hefted his broad-bladed stabbing spear.

Sauruven looked down into the goblin's face. His own was expressionless as a mask, and his black eyes flat pools, like windows into nothing.

"Hah! It's a joke!" the goblin said laughing. "You should laugh, it's a good joke. Five! Hah!"

With a gesture, the goblin gathered his followers. They disappeared into the gray stony wasteland. For a moment he could hear the soft scuff of their hide moccasins before they vanished into the fitful snow. He waited, waited until he was sure they were gone.

Tools, but treacherous ones, he thought coldly.

Sauruven moved slowly over to the vantage point from which he could watch a cave down below. He picked up a length of stout rope and wound it around his broad hands, giving him a good grip. He yanked on it experimentally and was pleased by the sound of sifting earth.

The sun cleared the horizon and the rich golden light reached into the cavern as he watched. A loud groan emerged, followed by the sound of heavy footsteps. A massive, bearded creature emerged into the early sunlight and stretched languidly, muscles rippling like waves along his arms and chest. The stone giant hitched up his bearskin kilt and yawned, baring enormous yellow teeth clear to the back of his skull.

Sauruven pulled on the rope, his muscles straining until he could hear them crackle in the cold.

Right where you are, he thought with deadly concentration. *Stay right where you are.*

Beside him the pine-log prop bent sideways, its tip sliding along the bottom of the wooden pallet above it. Above that the load of boulders shifted and gritted against each other—nobody like goblins for setting traps.

The stone giant looked up, stupefied. Astonishment covered the bestial face, eyes bulging under the heavy shelflike brows, long jaw dropping until it almost rested on his gray-skinned chest. Then he gave a single scream of terror.

"Scream, you swine!" Sauruven shouted. It was not in the code of the Schwartzenritterein, but the sound welled up out of him. "Scream as Eurynomous did, you coward!"

The avalanche roared over the giant. When the dust cleared, only its head and part of one arm protruded from the cone of rubble that covered the entrance to the cave. Sauruven hawked and spat to clear his throat of dust and drew his sword, descending cautiously over the uncertain footing. The cave mouth was covered, but some of the carrion reek still clung about it. Amazingly, the stone giant was still alive; blood bubbled from its lips, but the red-and-yellow eyes swiveled to take him in.

"You!" it tried to shout; it came out more like a breathy whisper. "You, knight! I will fight you! Let me free, and I will kill. Kill! Kill!"

"You're not worthy of death in battle," Sauruven said. He sheathed his sword and unslung a long club of brass-bound oak from his back. "This is a death sacrifice."

The giant screamed again as the bludgeon hammered down, and once more. Then there was silence, save for the splintering sound of the blows.

When the thing was done, Sauruven walked to the edge of the cliff. He raised the club and threw it out into the echoing space, watching as it pinwheeled down toward the snow-clad valley.

For one last moment, the Lament of a Hurloon minotaur sounded over the slopes. Then the Black Knight turned on his heel and walked away, down toward the waiting path.

Airborne All the Way!

David Drake

Crewgoblin Dumber Than #3 stared with his usual look of puzzlement as labor goblins unrolled Balloon Prima. He scratched his chain mail jockstrap and said to Dog Squat, the balloon chief, "I dunno, boss."

Dog Squat rolled her eyes expressively and muttered, "Mana give me strength!" She glanced covertly to see if Roxanne was watching what balloon chiefs had to put up with, but the senior thaumaturge was involved with the team of dragon wranglers bringing the whelp into position in front of the coal pile.

Dog Squat glowered at her four crewgoblins. "Well, what don't you know?" she snarled. "What is there to know? We go up, we throw rocks down. You like to throw rocks, Number Three?"

"I like to bite them," said Dumber Than #1. "Will we be able to bite them, Dog Squat?"

The plateau on which the Balloon Brigade was readying for battle overlooked the enemy on the broad plain below. The hostile command group, pulsing with white mana, had taken its station well to the rear. White battalions were deploying directly from their line of march. Gullies and knolls skewed the rectangles of troops slightly, but the formations were still precise enough to make a goblin's disorderly mind ache.

"But boss," #3 said, "how do we get down again?"

"Getting down's the easy part!" Dog Squat shouted. "Rocks aren't any smarter than you are, and they manage to get down, don't they? Well, not much smarter. Just leave the thinking to me, why don't you?"

"I really like to bite them," #1 repeated. He scraped at a black, gleaming fang with a black, gleaming foreclaw. "After we throw rocks, will we be able to bite them, Dog Squat?"

Dog Squat tried to visualize biting from a balloon. The closest she could come was a sort of ruddy blur that made her head ache worse than sight of the serried, white-clad ranks on the plains below. "No biting unless I tell you!" she said to cover her ignorance. "Not even a teeny little bite!"

The large pile of coal was ready for ignition. The metal cover sat on the ground behind for the moment. Instead of forging a simple dome, the smiths had created a gigantic horned helmet. To either side of the coal was a sloped dirt ramp so that labor goblins could carry the helmet over the pile and cap it when the time came.

Balloons Prima and Secundus were unrolled to either side, and the three wranglers had finally gotten their dragon whelp into position in front of the pile. The other unfilled balloons waited their turn in double lines. It was time to start.

"All right, Theobald!" Senior Thaumaturge Roxanne said to the junior thaumaturge accompanying her, a mana specialist. "Get to work and don't waste a lot of time. We're already forty minutes behind schedule. Malfegor will singe the skin off me if we don't launch an attack before noon, and I promise that you won't be around to snicker if that happens."

Roxanne strode over to Dog Squat and her crew. The balloon chief tried to straighten like a human coming to attention; she wobbled dangerously. A goblin's broad shoulders and heavy, fanged skull raised the body's center of gravity too high unless the hips were splayed back and the knuckles kept usefully close to the ground.

"Everything ready here?" Roxanne demanded. The senior thaumaturge in charge of the Balloon Brigade wore a power suit with pin stripes of red, Malfegor's color. Her attaché case was an expensive one made of crimson belly skins, the sexual display markings of little male lizards. Very many little male lizards.

"Yes, sir, one hundred percent!" Dog Squat said. She frowned. She wasn't very good on numbers. "Two hundred percent?" she offered as an alternative.

"Yes, well, you'd better be," Roxanne said as she returned her attention to the dragon-filling.

The dragon whelp was no bigger than a cow. The beast didn't appear to be in either good health or a good humor. Its tail lashed restively despite the attempt of one wrangler to control that end while the other two held the whelp's head steady.

Junior Thaumaturge Theobald stood in front of the whelp with a book in one hand and an athame of red copper in the other. As Theobald intoned, a veil of mana flowed into the whelp from the surrounding rock. The creature's outlines softened.

Purple splotches distorted the generally red fields of force. The whelp shook itself. The wranglers tossed violently, but they all managed to hold on.

Dumber Than #1 bent close to Dog Squat and whispered gratingly in her ear. The balloon chief sighed and said, "Ah, sir?"

Roxanne jumped. A goblin's notion of a quiet voice was one that you couldn't hear in the next valley. "Yes?" the senior thaumaturge said.

"Ah, sir," Dog Squat said, "there's been some discussion regarding biting. Ah, whether we'll be biting the enemy, that is. Ah, that is, will we?"

Roxanne stared at the balloon chief in honest amazement. The four crewgoblins stood behind Dog Squat, scratching themselves but obviously intent on the answer.

"You'll be throwing rocks," Roxanne said, speaking very slowly and distinctly. She tried to make eye contact with each crewgoblin in turn, but a goblin's eyes tend to wander in different directions.

The senior thaumaturge tapped the surface of the plateau with one open toed, wedge-heeled shoe. "Rocks are like this," she said, "only smaller. The rocks are already in the gondola of your balloon. Do you all understand?"

None of them understood. None of them understood anything.

Dumber Than #3 scratched his jockstrap again. Roxanne winced. "Isn't that uncomfortable to wear?" she said. "I mean, chain mail?"

The crewgoblin nodded vigorously. "Yeah, you can say that again," he said. He continued to scratch.

"But when is she going to tell us about biting?" #1 said to Dog Squat in a steamwhistle whimper.

The dragon whelp farted thunderously. A huge blue flame flung the rearward wrangler thirty feet away with his robes singed off. The veil of inflowing mana ceased as Roxanne spun around.

"Sorry, sorry," Junior Thaumaturge Theobald said nervously as he closed his book. "The mana here is impure. Too much ground water—we must be over an aquifer. But she's full and ready."

"Carry on, then," Roxanne said grimly to the remaining dragon wranglers.

The leading wrangler crooned into the whelp's ear as her partner stroked the scaly throat from the other side. The whelp, shimmering with newfound power, bent toward the pile of coal and burped a puny ball of red fire. Roxanne frowned.

"Come on, girl, you can do it," the wrangler moaned. "Come on, do it for mommy. Come on, sweetie, come on—"

The dragon whelp stretched out a diamond-clawed forepaw and blasted a double stream of crimson fire from its nostrils. The jets ripped across and into the pile of coal, infusing the flame through every gap and crevice. The wranglers directed the ruby inferno by tugging their charge's head back and forth with long leads.

After nearly three minutes of roaring hellfire, the whelp sank back exhausted. It seemed to have shrunk to half its size of a few moments before. The two normally robed wranglers clucked the beast tiredly to its feet and walked it out of the way. The third wrangler limped alongside. In place of a robe he was wearing a red gonfalon borrowed from a nearby cavalry regiment.

The coal pile glowed like magma trapped deep in the planetary mantle. "Come on!" Roxanne ordered. "Let's not waste this. Get moving and get it capped!"

The capping crew was under the charge of two novice thaumaturges, both of them in their teens. In response to their chirped commands, the four labor goblins lifted the gigantic helmet by means of crosspoles run through sockets at the front and back of the base. They began to shuffle forward, up the earthen ramps built to either side of the pile of coal.

The porters were goblins chosen for brawn rather than brains. The very concept of intellect would have boggled the porters' minds if they'd had any. In order to keep the crews moving in the right direction, the novices projected a line of splayed, clawed footprints in front of the leaders on either ramp to carefully fit his/her feet into.

The goblins on the rear pole set their feet exactly on the same markings. They didn't put any weight down until they were sure the foot was completely within the glowing red lines. The cap's rate of movement was more amoebic than tortoiselike. Nevertheless, it moved. Senior Thaumaturge Roxanne drummed fingers on the side of her attache case in frustration, but there was no hurrying labor goblins.

The leaders paused when they reached the last pairs of footprints at the ends of the ramps. The porters stood stolidly, apparently oblivious of the heat and fumes from the coal burning beside them.

The novice thaumaturges turned to Roxanne. "Yes!" she shouted. "Cap it! Cap it now!"

The novices ordered, "Drop your poles!" in an uncertain tenor and a throaty contralto. Three of the porters obeyed. The fourth looked around in puzzlement, then dropped his pole also. The helmet clanged down unevenly but still down, over the pile. The metal completely covered the coal, shutting off all outside air.

The horns flaring to the sides of the giant helmet were nozzles. Thick hoses were attached to the ends of horns. The novice thaumaturges clamped the free ends of the hoses into the filler inlets of Balloons Prima and Secundus. Adjusting the hoses was hard work, but the task was too complicated to be entrusted to a goblin.

Roxanne personally checked the connection to Prima while the junior thaumaturge did the same on the other side. "All right," she said to the novice watching anxiously from the top of the ramp where he'd scrambled as soon as he attached his hose. "Open the cock."

The novice twisted a handle shaped like a flying dragon at the tip of the horn, opening the nozzle to gas that made the hose writhe on its way to the belly of Balloon Prima. The senior thaumaturge stepped away as the balloon began to fill.

The balloons were made from an inner layer of sea serpent intestine. The material was impervious to gas and so wonderfully tough that giants set bars of gold between layers of the stuff and hammered the metal into foil.

Prima bulged into life, inflating with gases driven out of the furiously hot coal in the absence of oxygen to sustain further combustion. The four drag ropes tightened in the clawed hands of labor goblins whose job was to keep the balloon on the ground until it had been completely filled and its inlet closed.

"You lot!" Roxanne said to Dog Squat and her crew. "What are you waiting for? Get into your gondola now!"

Dog Squat opened her mouth to explain that she'd been waiting for orders. She forgot what she was going to say before she got the words out. "Dumber Thans," she said instead, "get into the little boat."

The wicker gondola creaked as the five goblins boarded it. The balloon was already full enough to lift off the ground and swing in the coarse steel netting that attached the car to it. A light breeze swept down from Malfegor's aerie, ready to waft the brigade toward the enemy on the plain below.

The floor of the gondola was covered with rocks the size of a goblin's head. Many of the missiles were delightfully jagged. #3 patted a piece of chert with a particularly nice point.

Balloon Secundus lifted into sight from the other side of the helmet. It was sausage-shaped, like forty-nine percent of the brigade's equipment. Prima was one of the slight majority of balloons which, when seen from the side, looked like a huge dome with a lesser peak on top. The attachment netting gleamed like chain mail over the pinkish white expanse of sea serpent intestine.

Dog Squat picked up a rock and hefted it. A good, solid chunk of granite. A rock that a goblin could really get into throwing, yep, you betcha. Dog Squat had heard some principals would try to fob their crews off with blocks of limestone that crumbled if you just looked crossways at it, but not good old Malfegor. . . .

"Shut off the gas flow!" Senior Thaumaturge Roxanne called to the novice on the ramp above her. She released the catch on the input herself. When Prima wobbled, the hose pulled loose, and Roxanne clamped the valve shut.

"Cast off!" she ordered the ground crew.

Three of the goblins dropped their ropes. The fourth, an unusually powerful fellow even for a labor goblin, continued to grip his. His big toes were opposable, and he'd sunk his claws deep into the rock of the plateau.

Balloon Prima lifted at an angle. The gondola was nearly vertical, pointing at the goblin holding the rope.

"Let go!" Roxanne screamed. "Drop the rope!"

She batted the goblin over the head with her attaché case. He looked at the senior thaumaturge quizzically.

"Let go!" Roxanne repeated. "Don't you understand what I'm saying?"

The goblin blinked. He continued to hold onto both the rope and the ground. Balloon Prima wobbled above him.

Roxanne looked up. Dog Squat peered down at her. The balloon chief wore a familiar puzzled expression. The crewgoblins were stacked, more or less vertically, on the back of their chief. A gust from the wrong direction and the contents of the gondola would tip out promiscuously.

"You!" the senior thaumaturge said. "Hit this idiot on the head with a rock. A hard rock!"

Dog Squat looked again at the rock she held, decided that it would do, and bashed the handler goblin with it. The victim's eyeballs rolled up. He dropped the rope and fell over on his back.

Balloon Prima shot skyward, righting itself as it rose. The rope the goblin dropped whipped around Roxanne's waist and dragged her along. The senior thaumaturge weighed scarcely more than any one of the rocks in the bottom of the gondola, so her presence didn't significantly affect the balloon's upward course.

Dog Squat looked over the side of the gondola at Roxanne and blinked. The senior thaumaturge, swinging like a tethered canary, screamed, "Pull me in, you idiot!"

"I didn't know you were coming along, sir," the balloon chief said contritely. She rapped her head hard with her knuckles to help her think. "Or did I?" she added.

"Pull me—" Roxanne said. The rope, kinked rather than knotted about her, started to unwrap. Roxanne grabbed it with both hands. Her attaché case took an obscenely long time to flutter down. At last it smashed into scraps no larger than the original lizard pelts on the rocks below.

Dog Squat tugged the rope in hand over hand, then plucked the senior thaumaturge from it and lifted her into the gondola. Roxanne's eyes remained shut until she felt throwing stones beneath her feet rather than empty air. .

"Are we . . . ?" she said. She looked over the side of the gently swaying gondola. Because of its heavy load, Balloon Prima had only climbed a few hundred feet above the plateau, but the ground continued to slope away as Malfegor's sorcerous breeze pushed them toward the enemy lines.

"Oh, mana," Roxanne said. "Oh mana, mana, mana."

"Boss," said Dumber Than #2, "do you remember when I ate that possum the trolls walked over the week before?"

"Yeah," said Dog Squat. Everybody in the crew remembered that.

"Well, I feel like that again," #2 said.

He did look greenish. His eyeballs did, at least. He was swaying a little more than the gondola itself did, come to think.

"Where did you find a dead possum up here, Number Two?" Dog Squat asked.

"I didn't!" the crewgoblin said with queasy enthusiasm. He frowned, pounded himself on the head, and added, "I don't think I did, anyways."

"Oh, mana," the senior thaumaturge moaned. "How am I ever going to get down?"

"Getting down is the easy part!" Dumber Than #3 said brightly. "Even rocks manage to get down! You're probably lots smarter than a rock, sir."

Senior Thaumaturge Roxanne took another look over the side of the gondola, then curled into a fetal position in the stern.

"Did you eat a dead possum, too?" #2 asked in what for a goblin was a solicitous tone.

Balloon Prima had continued to drift while the senior thaumaturge considered her position. The battalions of white-clad enemy troops were by now almost directly below. They didn't look the way they ought to. They looked little.

Dog Squat frowned. She wondered if these were really the people she was supposed to drop rocks on.

"Boss, are we in the right place?" #4 asked. The gondola tilted thirty degrees in its harness. All four crewgoblins had leaned over the same side as their chief. "Them guys don't look right."

"They make my head hurt to look at," #3 added. "They're—"

Goblins didn't have a word for "square." Even the attempt to express the concept made lights flash painfully behind the crewgoblin's eyes.

In a fuzzy red flash, Dog Squat gained a philosophy of life: When in doubt, throw rocks. "We throw rocks!" she shouted, suiting her actions to her words.

The goblins hurled rocks down with enthusiasm—so much enthusiasm that Dog Squat had to prevent Dumber Than # 1 from tossing Roxanne, whom he'd grabbed by a mistake that nearly became irremediable. When Dog Squat removed the senior thaumaturge from #1's hands, the crewgoblin tried to bite her—probably #1's philosophy of life—until Dog Squat clouted him into a proper attitude of respect.

The gondola pitched violently from side to side because of the repeated shifts in weight. The entire balloon lurched upward since the rocks acted as ballast when they weren't being used for ammunition. The crew of Balloon Prima was having as much fun as goblins could with their clothes on (and a lot more fun than goblins have with their clothes off, as anyone looking at a nude goblin can imagine).

They weren't, however, hitting anybody on the ground, which was increasingly far below.

The tight enemy formations shattered like glass on stone as Balloon Prima drifted toward them. That was the result of fear, not actual damage. The goblins could no more brain individual soldiers a thousand feet below than they could fly without Prima's help.

That didn't matter particularly to Dog Squat and her crew. Throwing rocks was a job worth doing for its own sake; and anyway, the collapse of ordered battalions into complete disorder fitted Dog Squat's sense of rightness. The universe (not as clear a concept as it would have been to, say, a senior thaumaturge; but still, a concept in goblin terms) liked chaos.

White-clad archers well to the side of the balloon's expected course bent their bows in enormous futile efforts. The altitude that made it difficult for the goblins to hit targets on the ground also made it impossible for archers on the ground to reach Balloon Prima. The arrows arcing back to earth did more damage to other white-clad troops than the goblin-flung rocks had done.

Malfegor's breeze continued to drive Balloon Prima in the direction of the enemy command group. The hail of missiles from the gondola stopped.

"Boss?" said #4. "Where are the rocks?"

Dog Squat looked carefully around the floor of the gondola. She even lifted Roxanne, who moaned softly in response.

"There are no rocks," Dog Squat said.

Dumber Than #3 scratched himself. "I thought there was rocks," he said in puzzlement.

"Can we bite them now, Dog Squat?" #1 said.

Dog Squat looked over the side again. She hoped there might be another thaumaturge or somebody else who could tell them what to do.

There wasn't. Dog Squat checked both sides to be sure, however.

The enemy had made preparations against the Balloon Brigade's attack. Two teams of antiballoon ballistas galloped into position between Balloon Prima and the white command group. The crews dismounted and quickly cranked their high-angle weapons into action.

A ball nearly the size of the rocks the goblins had thrown whizzed toward the balloon and burst twenty feet away in a gush of white mana.

"Oooh," said Dog Squat and three of her crewgoblins.

The breeze shifted slightly, driving Balloon Prima in the direction of the white blast. Malfegor was hunting the bursts on the assumption that the safest place to be was where the immediately previous shell had gone off.

"Ohhh," said Dumber Than #2, holding his belly with both

hands. "The more we shake around, the older the possum gets."

Sure enough, the next antiballoon shell flared close to where Prima would have been if she'd continued on her former course. The breeze jinked back, continuing to blow the balloon toward the command group below.

The hostile artillerists cranked their torsion bows furiously. They were also trying to raise their angle of aim, but Balloon Prima was almost directly overhead and the ballistas couldn't shoot vertically. By the time Prima was in the defenders' sights again, the balloon would be directly over the command group.

Dumber Than #4 nudged Dog Squat and pointed to the tightly curled senior thaumaturge. "Can we throw her now, boss?" the crewgoblin asked. "Seeings as we're, you know, out of rocks?"

Dog Squat pursed her lips, a hideous sight. "No," she decided at last. "Throwing rocks is good. Throwing thaumaturges is not good."

At least she didn't think it was. They ought to throw something, though.

"Can we bite them, then?" said #1.

Dumber Than #2 vomited over the side with great force and volume, much as he'd done after the never-to-be-forgotten (even by a goblin) possum incident.

The huge greenish yellow mass plunged earthward at increasing velocity. It was easier to track than a rock of the same size because it was slightly fluorescent. For a moment Dog Squat thought the bolus was going to hit one of the antiballoon ballistas. Instead, it glopped the ballista's captain, who fell backward into his weapon.

The toppling ballista fired its shell straight up. Though the glowing white ball missed the gondola by a dragon's whisker, it punched through the side of the gas bag above.

The top of the balloon ruptured with a loud bang. The blast of mana expelled and ignited the bag's contents in a puff of varicolored flame—a mixture of hydrogen, carbon monoxide, and methane, all flammable and dazzlingly pretty.

"Oooh!" said all the goblins in delight. #2, no longer holding his belly, had a particularly pleased expression.

Ex-Balloon Prima dropped, though not nearly as fast as the rocks thrown earlier. The gas bag had burst, but the steel netting still restrained the tough fabric of sea serpent intestine. The combination made an excellent parachute.

There was wild panic on the ground below. The enemy commanders had realized Prima would land directly on top of them.

Dumber Than #1 looked at the lusciously soft enemy officers, coming closer every moment the air whistled past the gondola. He asked plaintively, "Please, boss, can we bite them?"

Dog Squat glanced at Roxanne—no change there—and made a command decision. "Yes," the balloon chief said decisively. "We will bite them."

Dumber Than #3 scratched himself with the hand that wasn't gripping the edge of the gondola. He gestured toward the senior thaumaturge and said fondly, "Gee, it must be something to be smart enough to plan all this. She's really a genius, ain't she, boss?"

"She sure is," Dog Squat agreed, preparing to jump into the middle of the terrified enemy at the moment of impact.

Senior Thaumaturge Roxanne whimpered softly.

Not Just Another Green World?

Peter Friend

"**L**ook," called little Kilian. "**I found an animal.**"

He was some distance away, and all I could see was a long pale shape in the snow by his feet. A floryndine was my first guess, or perhaps an ice snapper.

"Get back, Kilian! Now!" I shouted. Mirindil and I dropped our bundles of firewood and ran toward him.

"I think it's dead," he said, but stepped back obediently.

He was wrong. It wasn't dead, and it wasn't an animal. It was a man, of sorts, curled naked in the snow, breathing in faint gasps. His body was bruised and burned, not by flames but by the crueler heat of magic. I touched him gently, and he mewled in pain.

"Run back to Big Tree," I told Kilian. "Tell Sharlory we're bringing a sick man back." He nodded and bounded off.

"Are you sure he's human?" asked Mirindil. "He has arms and legs and a head, but look—there's hair growing on his chin and on his chest. Such long thin legs. How could he stand upright? And that skin color—don't tell me that's just from the cold."

I looked down again at the long tangle of limbs, and wondered if she was right, if this was merely some strange wild animal that had wandered over the mountains in search of food.

"Cold," repeated the creature faintly.

Mirindil shrugged her wide shoulders. "He talks; that's good enough for me." She took off her cloak and carefully placed it over him. "Should I give him Forgetfulness of Pain? He smells of broken bones."

I nodded. She stretched out her arms and fingers and started mouthing a chant. I, too, reached into the air, hunting with mind and fingertips for the right lines, weaving them into Fireside Glow. Together, we cast our spells and watched his breathing deepen, felt his skin warm. His eyes flickered and tried to focus on us.

"Green magic," he croaked in surprise, and passed out.

Together, Mirindil and I hoisted him onto our backs. For all his size, he weighed no more than one of us.

"What did he mean'—green magic'?" asked Mirindil as we trudged back over the hill. "What other color could magic be?"

By the time we reached Big Tree, it was already crowded; everyone offering help, stretching their necks and jostling for a glimpse of the stranger. Even the twig dragons woke and peered down from the rafters at all the noise. With difficulty, we pushed our way through to the hearth table and laid the man out on the warm granite.

"Out!" shouted Sharlory as she clambered down Scripture Trunk. "Everyone except magic weavers, out now!"

Grumbling, they filed out, leaving two dozen of us in a semicircle around the hearth.

"He don't need magic," said old Guineren, peering at the stranger. "His arm at least is broken, and he's burned and banged around some, but it's nothing a bit of nursing wouldn't cure. Could speed things up with a Spring Morning Sun spell, I s'pose, but—"

"It's not his wounds that concern me," interrupted Sharlory. "He has lines. Feel them. Carefully."

They stretched out their hands toward him, all except me. Sharlory stared at me.

"He's a magician," I said, nodding. "I sensed it when I first touched him, out in the snow. But . . . not like our magic."

"What did you expect?" asked Guineren. "He's foreign. From over the Dark Sea maybe. I don't recognize none of his lines neither."

"Yes, yes, different spells. But look where they point," said Sharlory patiently. "Up, every one of them, away from the land. So tell me, where are they pointing to?"

"Is he a mirror demon, do you think?" suggested someone. "Should we cast him out and let the winter eat him?"

"He's a traveler, that's obvious. From another world perhaps, like it says in scriptures," said Mirindil, earning a glare from Sharlory. "We have never refused aid to any traveler in need."

There was a rumble of agreement.

"We must be careful," said Sharlory. "I do not trust him."

"Well, I'm not afraid of him," said Guineren.

Sharlory smiled. "Then you can take care of him."

It had been a long dull winter, and Guineren and the stranger quickly became the center of conversation. She found this much to her liking and took to drinking red tea each noon inside Big Tree, recounting the stranger's progress to an appreciative audience.

On the second day, she announced he'd regained consciousness and started swearing at her in an atrocious accent.

On the third day, he claimed to be a mighty wizard called Alzarakh and threatened to turn her into a swamp hog.

"And did he?" a young magic apprentice said, grinning, to general laughter.

She spat at him good-naturedly. "Oh no, claims he mustn't. Says he'll spare my life—for just now. Says he's such a magnificent wizard that some jealous wizards tried to kill him, and he only just escaped here with his life. Reckons that if he was to even shoot a few sparks out his fingertips, they'd spot his magic and be down here like a scurry of grindles."

"Sounds like a mouth wizard to me," said someone, to more laughter.

We'd all known mouth wizards—apprentices boasting of half-learnt lore, old magicians hiding fading powers behind loud bluster. The proof of the spell is in the casting.

On the fourth and fifth days, Guineren told us he sulked in silence and drank a great deal of her hot quizzle soup. Sharlory spent both days poring over crackly old dellskin scrolls and muttering to herself.

"He's just another lost traveler," I told her. "We had three last winter."

"From Bardwa Tree and the Sleen. People like us," she said, and unpeeled another scroll.

On the sixth day, he appeared in person, limping toward Big Tree on his ludicrous thin legs, supported on one side by Guineren, who barely reached his waist.

He was the first person who'd ever had to crouch to enter Keyhole Doorway. As he straightened up inside, there was a collective gasp, and he found himself looking down at two hundred upturned faces.

In the bright firelight, he looked stranger than ever. His bruises and scars were healing well, as was his forearm, covered in a softrock cast. But his skin was so thin you could see the muscles moving beneath it. His neck was so short he couldn't even turn his head to the rear, and his nose so small he couldn't move it at all. Tiny claws, like a newborn baby. Small blunt teeth, so pale they were almost white. Eyes the color of ripe draylobes, staring back at us. Perhaps we looked just as strange to him.

Guineren led him to High Stone Seat, the traditional place for honored visitors and storytellers.

Sharlory looked down from Scripture Trunk and waited for the crowd to quieten. "Welcome to our Tree, Alzarakh. Rest your bones at our hearth," she announced at last, a little coldly I thought. Any magician is due respect from another.

He cleared his throat and peered around. "Thank you," he said in a deep rumbling voice, oddly accented but clear enough, and sat down.

An expectant silence.

"Tell them," Guineren prompted. "Tell them what you told me."

"Yes, Alzarakh," said Sharlory. "Tell us."

He talked for over an hour. And then, refreshed by a flask of musk wine and our encouragement, he continued for an hour more. It was a wonderful story, of a world with only two moons, where magic came in many colors and wizards fought glorious duels with spells we had never heard of. It somehow surprised none of us to be told that he himself was the noblest of all these wizards, the hero of continents, and respected by queens, priests, and scholars.

I didn't believe a word of it, and didn't care. It was the best tale I'd heard in years, and I joined in the stamping and chirping whenever he paused for breath.

Even Sharlory had to grin at some of his boasts, although mostly she just scribbled on a bark memory and scowled a lot.

As I climbed to my weaving class the next day, I heard shouting and found two of my apprentices in the middle of a fight.

"Mouth wizard!" shouted Ramion, baring his fangs.

"Is not!" shouted Tyndryn back, lunging at him with fully extended claws and nearly falling from the branch.

One of the other children saw me and chirped a warning, and the whole class turned and quickly clambered to their places.

I stared at them silently. Ramion was bleeding slightly from a small cut on the side of his nose, and Tyndryn had two new toothmarks on her left ear. They all stared back at me as if nothing had happened.

I sighed, lay back on my branch and gazed up at the roof. Two twig dragons grinned back at me.

"We magic weavers are very privileged," I began, turning my head back to the apprentices. They sighed loudly and drooped their noses.

"Half of our people will never know enough magic to help a flower bloom or scare away a fritch bug. Of all our children, only you here have shown any signs of one day controlling magic, weaving it into something powerful. Even some of you will fail."

Some of them glanced quickly at Ramion and Tyndryn.

"Tyndryn actually believes Alzarakh," Ramion sneered. "She thinks the pompous old fool can summon thunderstorms and walking trees and trolls."

"Trolls are imaginary creatures," said one of the twig dragons.

"Go back to sleep," I snapped at it.

"Why shouldn't he be telling the truth?" asked Tyndryn defiantly. "He has nothing to gain from us but the food and shelter we'd give him anyway. Why should he bother lying? To impress us?"

"Perhaps he wishes neither to deceive or impress us," I suggested. "Perhaps he's simply trying to entertain his hosts with his lively imagination."

"That's what you magic weavers want everyone to believe, isn't it?" Tyndryn said. "And I know why—you're jealous. He's got five colors of magic to your one, and hundreds of spells more powerful than any you've ever known."

Shocked silence.

I breathed deeply, inhaling the gentle scent of inner bark and old sap.

"It snowed again last night, Tyndryn. Our Tree's outer branches are heavy with snow, hiding the hungry leaves from the sun. Perhaps you should spend the afternoon helping the leaf brushers. As you're so wise in things magical, I'm sure your spells will be of great assistance to them."

She curled her nose angrily and leapt down Avenue Trunk, thumping every branch and clawhold as she went.

"And perhaps you would like to like to help her, Ramion," I added, and watched his grin disappear.

"One of the children asked me if I had a spell for shaking snow off branches," Alzarakh told me.

"And what did you tell her?"

"Her? Oh, I didn't realize; you all look much the same to me. Well, I suggested an extremely small tornado, or a very polite walking tree. And then I'm afraid I laughed, and she scrunched up her snout and ran off on all fours. Did I hurt her feelings?"

"No doubt. She's an apprentice magic weaver, very young, very bright, and very impatient. She wants to throw lightning bolts and summon bowlidders, and all I teach her is—"

"How to sprout seeds?" he suggested, and laughed. He laughed a lot, we'd noticed. Too much, some said.

I bared my teeth. "You think our magic's a joke, don't you? Just because we don't summon earthquakes or slaughter each other with giant ogres."

"And now I've hurt your feelings, too. I'm sorry, really," he said, trying to keep his face straight. "I'm seven hundred years old. I've lost count of the number of planes I've visited. I've seen entire cities built by magic, and the same cities destroyed by a wizard's spite. I've seen fireballs that could turn this great tree of yours into ash in a second. So, yes, I watch you people carefully casting spells to raise a crop of grain, and frankly it all seems rather . . . domestic."

"Perhaps you should count your words with more care," said Sharlory, dropping down beside us from a higher branch. "We've yet to see you sprout even a single seed, let alone a whole crop."

He smirked, as if this was a great joke. "I know, I know. I hear everyone calling me 'mouth wizard' behind my back. And when I'm healed, I'll just disappear in a puff of smoke, and you'll think no better of me then."

"The sooner you do leave, the better I'll think of you," said Sharlory, and dropped off to another branch.

"Soon, I promise," he said to me. "I'm getting stronger all the time. Both my body and my magic. Your land is one of the richest in mana I've ever seen—it's quite fascinating. My new mana lines keep stretching, breaking. My spells, they're the same—I wake up each morning and they're drifting away in all directions. It gets worse each day. But I can't leave for a few weeks yet. In the meantime, I'll try to behave."

His smile was lazy, his eyes hard and bright.

He kept his word, we had to admit. His stories changed to long humorous tales about enchanted birds and mud fairies, and magicians were barely mentioned. He loudly praised Big Tree, insisting he'd never before met a people so clever they built most of their village inside a single tree. He admired our winter harvest of needle corn, and politely asked Guineren for her quizzle soup recipe.

And he spent an afternoon lecturing my apprentices on the dangers and difficulties of magic. He showed them all his old wounds, from the jagged black scar behind his ear to the missing toes on his left foot, and explained how he received every one of them. He showed them all his spell lines glowing up toward the sky, cheerfully describing their effects in bloody detail that impressed even Tyndryn and Ramion.

From nearby branches, all the magic weavers watched and listened in silence. And again, I didn't believe a word he said, and didn't care. He was an arrogant patronizing braggart, but I still thought him harmless. Only Sharlory and a few others continued to frown suspiciously whenever they saw him.

"You got your wish," said Tyndryn. "Guineren says his arm's all healed; she's chipping off the softrock cast right now."

"You sound almost pleased. I thought you two had become friends the last couple of weeks. Didn't you spend most of yesterday morning in the forest with him?" I asked.

She smirked. "Just helping him. His lines keep floating away. It's not like that on his world—there your spells stay where you leave them. And they have real dragons, too, ones that breathe fire, not stupid little ones like here that just eat wood. He's taught me a lot. Things you could never teach me," she added, and bounded off, neck and nose held high.

I climbed out of Big Tree and down a cablevine toward Guineren's budhouse. Alzarakh was sitting on the roof, blinking in the early spring sunshine and flexing his healed arm carefully.

He saw me and grinned. "Come to bid me a fond farewell already? I'm touched. But I'm not going quite yet. Just a little more mana to collect, and I've mislaid one of my spells."

"Mislaid?" I repeated incredulously.

"Mmm, a couple of days ago. They drift around—I mentioned it before, didn't I? Something about this world; all the green mana I suppose. Not to worry—I'm sure it will turn up somewhere." He grinned again, but would not look me in the eye.

The sky rumbled and flashed green. We turned and saw a bright emerald line piercing the clouds, reaching down to a nearby clearing, where a small figure turned somersaults and shouted for joy. Beside her, a vaguely treelike shape began to condense from the air.

"She actually did it," he said in amazement. "That's my spell—your little Tyndryn has just summoned one of the Ironroot Treefolk."

All around us, people swarmed out of Trees, pointing and shouting at each other.

I grabbed Alzarakh by his arm and dragged him toward the green line. "Stop it. Stop her. Do something. That creature could kill her."

He grabbed onto a thick branch and held on grimly. "No, no, you don't understand. Forget the treefolk. She's used a spell linked to another plane—they'll see it for sure. We have to get back."

The sky pulsed white, blue, black, several shades of red, then black again. Half a dozen shadowy figures flickered into existence, hurled colored lines towards Tyndryn, then vanished.

She screamed and was swallowed by a ball of cold rainbow flame. The huge tree creature shuddered and crumpled back into nothingness and the green line disappeared. Lightning bolts hailed down, and the ground beneath us buckled and groaned.

At last, silence. Where Tyndryn had been, there was only a circle of smoking blackened rock.

"That was meant for me," said Alzarakh in a small voice.

"Yes. I wonder why the other wizards hate you so much. Perhaps it's because you're the type of person who deliberately lets a child die to save your own life," I said loudly. People started to gather around us. I tore his grasp from the branch and dragged him toward the black circle, my claws pressed firmly into his flesh.

"That thieving brat stole my spell! Is that my fault?" he asked.

I growled deep in my throat. "You spent weeks filling her head with envy for your magic. You made sure everyone knew about your supposedly drifting spells. And then you left that spell somewhere you knew she'd find it and couldn't resist casting it. You knew the other wizards would see it and think they'd found you at last."

"Let me go, you stinking animal," he shouted, tearing at my hand with his small fingers. "I'll kill you. I'll kill the lot of you."

"You think you're safe now," I said. "Your enemies believe you dead. It would be easy to slip away from this 'domestic' little world and back to your old life. Wouldn't it?" I released his arm and pushed him onto the still smoking black ground.

"Yes," he shouted, "right after I teach you impudent beasts a lesson in respect." He raised his arms and opened his mouth.

Guineren cast Wooden Tongue on him. He choked and reached for his mouth, and Mirindil wrapped him in Crown of Thorns. He fell to the ground, the barbs slicing his skin. I reached into the air and wove Acid Sap, and watched him writhe as his own blood burned him inside.

Sharlory crushed the air with her hands. Tiny green shoots appeared from his nostrils, mouth, ears and eyes. A few minutes later, there was only a small, oddly twisted tree growing in the blackened earth.

"Magic is green, wizard," she said. "Green and powerful."

The Going Price

Sonia Orin Lyris

Melelki forced herself awake, blinking weariness out of her eyes, and pushed herself out of the warm blankets. Struggling to her feet, she dressed and stamped outside the tiny cabin into the autumn sun.

"Daylight to you," she said, greeting her daughters.

"Morning, Mama," Tamun said, sounding entirely too bright. She stood by the clothesline near a basket of wet clothes.

Sekena was sitting on the step. She groaned. Melelki sat down next to her. Her own arms and back were aching, which meant that Sekena, at only fifteen, would be feeling even worse from the long night's hard labor. But it was only once a year.

For this year, at least, the danger was past. Icy high rocks and long drops, and all by lamplight. Fortunately, they were all good climbers. Dangerous as it might be, it was better to risk the mountain in darkness than chance running into a men's mining group during the day. The miners would not appreciate what the women were bringing down from the mountain.

Hard work, indeed. But now, she thought with a smile, they had sixteen eggs in the basement. And that meant gold.

Tamun pinned to the line clothes and sheets of linen so thin that the tree-splintered sunlight shone through them onto the flat, small stones beneath their feet. The linen was for sewing pictures onto, but they didn't do much of that these days, except in the winter, when it was too cold to do anything else.

But Tamun, getting up so early after what they'd done the last night—she must not have slept at all. And that after carrying more than her share of the sixteen eggs down the steep mountain trail last night, from the high cradle to the cabin. Still she had so much energy. Unfortunately, there was only one explanation.

Next to Melelki, Sekena sat, exhausted. Melelki put an arm around her youngest daughter. "You were so strong last night."

"Thank you, Mama."

She tilted her head close to Sekena's, enough to mix their wild strands of dwarf-streaked straw brown hair, and whispered, "Look at Tamun. See the blush? The color under her eyes? The red on her ears? Notice how little sleep she wants? First heat, that's what it is."

"No," Sekena gave back in whispered shock. "She's too young."

Melelki snorted softly. "Ta! You're the one to ask, eh, child? Fifteen years and you're an elder wisewoman?"

Sekena blushed, scowled. "She's too young," she said, insistent voice tinged with fear. "Isn't she?"

"If you're going to talk about me," Tamun said from the line, "speak up so I can hear you."

Her mother sighed. "You look to me to be going into first heat."

Tamun's hands froze on the line. She looked distant. "That would explain some things, wouldn't it? But I'm only nineteen."

"Ta, it doesn't come to everyone in the same way, my eldest flower. Rare as early as you, but also rare as late as twenty-seven, like my sister Belkena did a few years ago. Remember? She's got three now, two of them girls, and won't stop talking about them."

"Hope it never comes to me at *all*," murmured Sekena.

Her mother cuffed her lightly on the head. "Ta," she scolded. "Then what will you do, steal Belkena's extras? I can have children as well as those stones now, so you'll get none from me. You have to take it when it comes, because you won't be getting more than a few years of your heat. Don't wish for idiot things."

"But I don't want—"

"Hush," Melelki said, putting an arm around her daughter's

broad shoulders. "It's fun, you'll see. You'll be as strong as the strongest of the men, but that won't matter, because they'll not be able resist your charms. They'll come and bring gifts. Jewels and pretty things forged—"

"Swords?"

"Perhaps, if that's what you want. And then. Well. You'll see."

"I'm strong enough to carry dragon eggs, Mama. Isn't that strong enough?"

"Hush," Melelki said quickly. "Only talk about that inside, child, I've told you that. Someone could be coming up the path. Even the trees—"

"Mama, in the years we've been—"

"Magic can hear," Melelki insisted.

"But that's silly—"

"I said *hush*," Melelki said, her voice turning sharp as the needles with which the three of them sewed pictures into the fine linen. With that she stood, brushed down her trousers, and went to help Tamun hang clothes.

"We've got a lot of sewing to do for the fine ladies up in the big houses. Isn't that right?"

"Yes, Mama," Tamun said enthusiastically.

"Ta," Sekena exhaled, threw her hands wide in disgust, and went into the house.

Tamun snorted and softly said, "Does she want to go back to dyed fingers and bloody pin-sticks? Not me. We could even stop sewing, maybe move back into town, don't you think, Mama? Seems like it gets colder every winter."

"Oh, it's not so bad. And the village isn't far."

"But it gets lonely."

"Ah, there is that, especially now, with you—"

Her daughter blushed a little, frowned, stared at the ground.

It would be good to go back to live with the others, with family and friends, to not have to walk an hour there and an hour back to go to market. Up here they had lots of privacy and were closer to the mountaintop. Closer to the cradle.

The gold seemed so much each year, but each year there was less left of it than she had expected. It wasn't that they spent too much, it was that the pictures didn't sell as well as they used to, and things cost more.

Or maybe it was more that they didn't work as hard, knowing that the eggs would be there next autumn. They'd gotten used to living in a clean place, without rats and bugs and crawling slime.

Their poorer days seemed long ago. Then Melelki's only luxury had been the mountain. She went to climb, just because it was fun. The rock was a sort of question, and everytime she climbed it she found a different answer. It was fine luck the day she found the cradle, fine luck and a strange scent that caught her attention, led her up and up, past outcroppings and long drops onto sharp stones to a small opening between two high peaks of ice-crusted rock.

And there it had been: a cache of large white eggs, sparkling, hinting of rainbow colors against the sun's touch. Like goose eggs, they were, but much, much bigger. Each was longer than her forearm. There was only one thing they could be.

Dragon eggs.

Some would have run. Not Melelki. She walked around the eggs, her heart crashing inside her, but too fascinated to leave until she had run her fingers over the hard shells.

Dragons would come out of these, she thought. Dragons.

She'd seen them before, from a distance. Every now and then during the harvest there would be one, flying so distantly it looked like a bird, except the shape wasn't right. Everyone would stop and point. At night there'd be tales of dragons feeding on virgins and lining their nests with babies.

Melelki grinned. There were no babies here. Maybe it wasn't true about the virgins, either.

Dragon eggs. Her mind had moved in new directions as her eyes flickered over the sparkling eggs. She and her daughters were mud-poor. Humans and elves made jewelry from the shells. And tips of weapons. What might a whole egg be worth?

And who would buy it?

That summer an arrogant, thin human with blue eyes and stringy hair had come prancing into town, spending money, buying up weapons from the high-house smiths. For human soldiers fighting orc rebellions to the east, he said.

The next day, swallowing her distrust of humans, she found the human at the Squat Duck, bought him an expensive drink, and asked him what he knew about dragons.

"I recommend avoiding them," he had said.

"Well, what if someone were to find some eggs? Would they be able to sell them?" she asked. "Usually my daughters and I just sell our cloth pictures, but if—"

His look was intent. Softly he said, "Take care in discussing such things. Such items are worth much, but are dangerous, too."

"Because of the parents?"

"No. The females lay in the high mountains, in cradles of ice and snow, but they're lousy parents. Too horny to stick around. The females drop the eggs and fly back to the warmlands, because that's where the males are. Then they screw until the next time they have to lay again."

"They don't guard the eggs at all?"

"No need. The shells are hard as metal, and the hatchlings can take care of themselves."

"The hatchlings—what do they eat?"

"Children and virgins." He watched her eyes widen and then laughed, making her scowl. "Nothing bigger than they are, if they can help it, and they're about as big as a large village mutt. Sure, they'll attack if they're scared, but they prefer small prey, and they can eat just about anything. Grass, leaves, pine cones, fallen branches, rotting trees. Garbage. Anything. Just like orcs."

"They only lay in autumn?"

He nodded. "They drop eggs every autumn for a few years and then they—vanish. There are legends of elder dragons—" He exhaled. "Which I hope stay legends, because the whelps start out mean and just get meaner every year. But the adults only make babies during those few years. Just like your kind, dwarf-lady."

"Dragons are beasts," she said coldly. "Is that what you think we are?" So thin, he was. She could break him in half so easily. Just grab and twist and pull, and he'd pop.

His gaze slid away from hers, quickly around to see who might be listening, then back down to stare at his beer. "I didn't mean it that way." He brushed long strands of black hair out of his face, then leaned forward. "I'm interested in your—your pictures. No one has quite the eye that you dwarves have for form and perspective."

She snorted her amusement at his absurd compliment. He meant the eggs, of course.

"Listen. I'll buy as many as you can lay hands on. How many and how soon can you have them?"

Melelki thought of the one egg she had managed to take back with her, stashed in the forest. She had almost run into a group of men transporting iron from a mining route on her way back from the cradle. They would have to move the eggs at night. She was already weaving transport slings in her head.

"How much?"

"Two gold each."

He said it so easily, as if he spoke such numbers every day.

She caught her breath. Fourteen eggs. That was a lot of gold.

So they had agreed on where and when to meet, she with her eggs, and he with his wagons. And his gold.

After that first night of climbing and pulling and lowering, she and her daughters were so sore they could barely move. But with the gold the human had paid for the eggs, they had been able to pay off their debts and buy new winter clothes. In the spring they built themselves a little cabin halfway up the mountain.

Closer to the eggs that they hoped would be there the next year, that indeed *were* there the next year. And the year after that, too. For five years they sold the human their sparkling, rainbow-tinted dragon eggs. They had lived better than they ever had before.

And now—

Tamun snapped a wet rectangle of fabric out onto the breeze and then hung it on the line. Melelki thought about her offspring, Sekena hinting at her adult size, Tamun warrior-strong and quickly becoming quite, quite distractible.

The eggs lay in the cellar, carefully surrounded by thick straw that they didn't need, only because the three of them could not bear to put such expensive and dangerous things on hard brick.

The eggs would be hatching in a few weeks, based on the mottling that got thicker as they got closer to their time. But it was all guesswork, and there was no room for mistakes where dragon hatchlings were concerned.

And so, tired as she was, she readied herself for the hike into town, where she would send a message to the blue-eyed human and get him to come with his wagons to bring them gold and take the growing eggs. Before they hatched.

*   *   *

But the blue-eyed man had sent her back a message, not that he would meet them at the cabin, but that he wanted to talk with her at the traveler's station along the mountain trail.

So it was days later when Melelki woke at dawn, put on an oil-soaked cloak and wrapped herself against the slushy, falling rain, and hiked along the ice-encrusted mountain trail. She passed by the village at the base of the mountain, close enough to see the smoke from the forges. She trod upward toward the falls.

A while later she opened the creaking wooden door, shook the water off her cloak, and stepped into the small traveler's station.

The room stank of wet human. He sat on the wooden bed in the middle, long dark hair falling over his shoulders and into his face across those startling blue eyes. Melelki nodded at him.

"Wet out there," he said, which she supposed he meant as a greeting. Of course it was wet outside. It was raining. It was late autumn and nearing winter.

"Yes," she said, not knowing what else to say. "I have the— embroideries for you." They didn't talk about actual eggs, even now, even miles away from the village, in case someone might somehow be listening.

But "embroideries" was such a human word. She knew human words, but they were a struggle to use. They were such long, slippery things, and they always somehow meant something else. Why couldn't they just say "pictures" and be done with it?

Of course, they weren't talking about pictures at all, but eggs. Dragon eggs.

"How much?" he asked.

She stifled her tension beneath an impatient exhale. "Same as always."

He waited, eyebrows raised in question.

"Two gold for each," she said, irritated. Perhaps he would like her to dance for him, too?

"I don't think so."

"What? Of course it is. It always is."

"Not this time. My employer thinks that your price is too high. He offers you less."

She felt panic rising inside her. How could he offer less?

"Last year—"

"Last year is last year."

"And the last five years!"

"The past is past."

"How much less?"

"Two gold for as many as you have."

She was stunned. "Human-crazy. That's absurd."

"That's the offer."

"But—*why*?"

"I don't know. Maybe he doesn't need them anymore. Maybe he's found another source."

"I don't believe you."

He shrugged. "I'm only a messenger."

Something about the way he said that made her suspicious. But then, he was a human, and all his answers made her suspicious.

She thought fast. What did his employer do with the eggs? In the last five years she had thought on it and had decided that the employer was a wizard. Who else would want dragon eggs? Who else would know how to handle the whelps once they hatched?

But what would he do with that many dragons, year after year? It must be the battles to the east, which kept the dwarvish village forging weapons and hired many as mercenaries. Who knew what a wizard could do with dragons? Maybe he did have enough of them.

But then, why would Blue-Eyes be here talking with her at all?

No, he wanted them, he just thought he could get them for less. And if he wanted them, then he needed them. He just didn't want to pay for them.

She snorted her amusement. "I could make far more than the usual by just selling the shells." She didn't care about who overheard now. Maybe someone would overhear and make her a better offer.

His eyes met hers, locked. That blue, that unnatural blue, like living ice. That must be it—humans had ice in their eyes, ice in their minds. Ice didn't think.

"Go for it," he said. "Good luck with the whelps."

She shuddered inside.

About nine years ago a dragon hatchling with a broken wing had wandered into the village and tried to eat sausages off a marketeer's cart. The whelp had bloodied the half-dozen men who tried to tackle it barehanded—dwarvish men, as usual braver than they were smart. Only when those with weapons gathered, mostly women, and put spears and swords into the little beast had it stopped moving. Who would have thought something so small could be so nasty? There had been a great deal of tale-telling that night to go with the dragon whelp stew.

Melelki did not like the idea of sixteen hatchlings, all hungry at once.

Could it really be that someone else was selling eggs? It was hard to imagine that anyone else's luck, nose, and climbing ability would be as good as hers had been that first time.

She decided. "Ta, too bad," she said, as if she were only mildly disappointed. She ignored the voice inside that said he was more used to these games than she was and could probably see right through her pretense. "I guess I'll have to sell my cradle to someone else."

His chuckle made her feel very cold, because he sounded purely amused at her words. It shook her resolve a little, so she fueled it with her anger at him, at his cheating bluff, at his making her wait so many days to be told this.

She shook the water off her coat and onto the floor, twirled it onto her shoulders, fastened the laces, then glanced back at him. He seemed thoughtful, but with a human, who knew?

"The offer still stands," he said, fixing her again with that ice-cold stare.

"Two gold, to take them all away?" She laughed derisively, letting her anger overwhelm her fear and sore temptation.

They would find another way.

She turned and left, closing the door hard enough to shake the whole small building.

Melelki thought dark thoughts about the human as she trudged through muddy puddles along the trail home. Part of her wanted to go back and tell him, yes, she would take the two gold if he would only come with his cart and take away the dragon eggs.

She had that part of her under control, though, bound and gagged and shut away in some corner of her head. She had a valuable cache: sixteen dragon eggs! Surely someone would want them, would pay as well as he had for them. She would have to buy a cart, of course, without raising questions. She'd need money, and that would take most of what little they had left. Then she would need to find another buyer, and quick, because the whelps would hatch in just a couple of weeks, and—

And there was no time for all that.

She was an idiot. All these years, assuming that Ice-Eyes would want them, would pay for them, instead of— Of what? Instead of finding someone else. Instead of finding out what they were *good* for.

So much for dwarvish curiosity, she thought viciously to herself. Where was that curiosity last year, or the year before, when the weather was good, when she could have gone wandering to the east to see what the blue-eyed human did with the dragon eggs he bought from her? Instead she had spent the year climbing around on the mountain, sitting around with her daughters, telling tales and weaving baskets and sleeping late. And occasionally sewing pictures.

Never again. From now on she would find out everything.

But first she had to get rid of the eggs before they hatched. And not to him. Not to that arrogant, blue-eyed, smelly human. Not for two gold, not for four. Not even if she had no other choice but to take them back to the cradle before they hatched.

She exhaled slowly, her breath like smoke in the cold air.

That's what they would have to do. Take them back up the mountain and put them back in the cradle. There just wasn't the time for anything else. Not this year.

And that was a bitter thought, because it was getting to be winter and everyone got stingy at market during the cold months, and they needed that gold. She was glad she had some money saved from previous years, but it wasn't much. It would see them through until spring, if they were very careful, and then they would find something else to do for money. Maybe they could sell the pictures again. At least their house was well built to hold against the snow and cold. They would simply huddle down and sleep a lot.

She thought wistfully of an enormous cauldron, of hard-boiling every single dragon egg. They'd eat well all winter, at least. But probably the shells were too thick, or something else awful would happen.

She did not relish the thought of climbing back up the mountain, dragging each egg along in a sling, hoisting them up the slippery edges of the high crags.

Then again, she wouldn't have to return them to exactly the same place, would she? Just far enough away from the cabin. And away from the mines. If whelps got loose in the mines—

Far away.

She stamped her frustration into the puddles of mud, ignoring her cold feet, the wet rain on her face, and the memory of the human laughing at her.

Sekena stood in the dark, tiny basement, the sixteen eggs flickering in the light of her lamp. The straw-covered floor was barely big enough for them all. Upstairs Mama and Tamun slept, while Sekena, restless, had quietly got up and slipped downstairs.

They would take the eggs back to the cradle this year. None of them were happy about it, but Mama was right, and there was no other choice.

The storm had other ideas, though, and there was no way up the mountain in this night's driving snow, so they had to wait until the storm passed. Maybe tomorrow.

Sekena was disappointed. It wasn't just the work, the awful, cold-numbing, arm-aching labor of climbing all over again, but to take the eggs back . . . ! To lose them and all the gold, too.

How strange that the human didn't want to pay for them. There had to be more to it than that. In any case, if the eggs were going back to the mountain cradle tomorrow, Sekena had to see them tonight.

Hands trembling, she crouched down and ran her fingers over one of the mottled white, iridescent shells. Smooth as glass, hard as iron. In some places, they made jewelry and weapons out of the brilliant white shards of dragon eggs.

Weapons. She wanted to see those.

Mama said it was just like humans to make jewelry out of eggs that someone else had gotten for them. It made them feel brave, as if they had somehow broken open the eggs themselves. As if they had been brave enough to watch them hatch. Few would really want to be there when that happened.

Sekena did. She would dream about it at night, about how the whelps would look when they came out. Who had ever seen dragons hatch? She had missed the one in the village years ago, but had heard all about it, over and over. To *see* it, that would be something.

All those nights with the eggs down here, for all the years they had gathered them, Sekena had been unable to sleep. She would lie awake and fight the temptation to come down and try to break one open. Sometimes she grabbed the edges of her bed, hoping that her sister and mother would wake up in time to stop her if the craving got to be too much, terrified that they wouldn't, desperate not to find out.

It was her dwarven blood, of course, the strange curiosity that drove her kind. The same curiosity that had led Mama to poke about up in the high crags of the mountains and find the cradle, that had Tamun exploring the forest floor, collecting dead animals that she cut open, dried, and added to her collection of bones.

Sekena looked at the marvelous sparkling eggs, inhaled the wild scent of them, deliberately making the temptation as cruel as possible. Curiosity burned inside her like a forge fire, but she fought it and won. She was no child to be thrown about like a leaf in a storm, but nearly an adult now. So she would stand here, burning all the way through, and not touch a single egg.

Mama would be proud of her, if she ever found out, but Sekena would never tell. This was Sekena's own battle, her private triumph. This was the sort of woman she would be. Not like Tamun.

Watching Tamun's feverish actions filled Sekena with dread. Her older sister hardly slept and talked obsessively about going back to the village, about houses, about children and men.

Sekena shuddered. She would keep her own secret: she had already decided that when she reached her heat, she'd become a dwarvish mercenary. They took women then, when they were in heat, because they were stronger than the men, but only if they promised not to get pregnant. She could make that promise. No matter how her passion drove her, she would never let it control her.

And so she stood there, testing herself, her fingers aching to touch the eggs, to take a hammer to them and see just how strong the shells were. The ache was so strong it was like hunger, but she controlled it and not the other way around.

Today she proved herself with the eggs, but someday it would be with a fine dwarvish sword in battle. She could see it clearly in her mind. Light armor, so she could move and favor her natural speed. And the sword—she could feel the grip, the weight of it swinging, the *chunk* as it sank into a squealing orc, the ugly creature going down, its dark blood feeding the land.

So vivid was the vision, so clear the sounds, that she barely noticed the new sound that came from the cellar.

She blinked when she heard it again. Breath left her as the sound came again. It was a ripping, crunching sound. There, on a far egg, was something she thought she'd never see.

A crack.

She took the stairs three at a time.

Melelki led them downstairs, each of them carrying a lamp.

There it was, in the far corner: an egg with a small, jagged line through it.

In the dim light she checked the rest of the eggs, stepping lightly around them, furiously stoking her curiosity so that it would be stronger than her terror. The mottling on the cracked one was much thicker than on any of the others. The darker splotches of iridescence supposedly told how close they were to hatching. It was only the cracked one that seemed that way. It wasn't much of a relief.

The three of them stood in silence for long moments, listening, watching. Then the sound came: a muffled, crunching sound. The sound of something alive, something trying to get out.

"Up," Melelki said shortly, and they went back into the house.

"I'll barricade the door to the basement," Tamun said.

Melelki nodded. "Sekena. Pack us food and bring cloaks and lamps to the door."

Sekena ran for the kitchen.

With both of them gone, Melelki allowed herself a deep breath and a ragged exhale. The eggs were not supposed to hatch for weeks. She shut her eyes tightly, tried to guess how long it would take the whelp to break out of the shell. Was there anything they could do to prevent it? She just didn't know.

Should they try to kill it?

A memory of bloodied dwarven men flashed across her mind.

No. She and her daughters would simply not get in its way if—when—it broke out. The human had said that they did not attack unless they were scared, that they did not eat animals larger than themselves. So the three of them were not in danger as long as they did not get in its way.

She hoped the human had been telling the truth.

Everything was urge. Everything was the pain of hunger trying to break free.

Out, out, sang the song of his blood, the beating of his heart. He bit and kicked and howled at the hard, dark world that tried to keep him enclosed.

Determination burned. He fought, he struggled, he stretched with everything he was. At last sounds came. Good, rewarding sounds.

Free sounds.

The sounds of freedom cut the smoothness of his world. His prison cracked, became sharp-edged. He had broken it.

He was free.

He lay on the pieces of what had been his prison, gasping. Exhausted and cold and hungry, but the sweetness of escape washed over him above all else.

Free.

When enough strength at last came to him, he looked up and around. He opened his mouth to taste the air.

Something was wrong. Something was missing. Where was the sky? Where was the breeze? He needed things. Need rushed through him as if it were fire. His discontent returned.

The things he needed were supposed to be here. Of that he was sure.

Fury kindled inside him.

Somewhere was the sky and the breeze. The things he needed. He would find them.

Out, out, sang the song of his blood.

And up, up.

He began to climb.

The sun had just risen when the sounds began to come from the basement, chilling Melelki all the way through. The whelp had broken free of the egg, that was certain, and now it sounded as if it were breaking the very stones and beams that held up the house.

"Out," Melelki said, and they grabbed their packs and lamps and cloaks and piled out into the thick snow that covered everything, then ran toward the trees, where they stopped and turned to watch the cabin.

"Do you think it's safe here?" Sekena asked.

"I don't know."

"We can't just leave," Tamun said.

"No."

It was curiosity and fear and something else that kept them from fleeing to the village. They had built that cabin with their own hands—it was theirs. And those in the basement were their eggs. Theirs.

As they waited, the sun came up in a blueing sky. The storm had passed.

"At least the weather's clear," Sekena said softly. But in the light of day they could all see that the trail up the mountain was thick with snow and impassable. There would be no returning the eggs today.

If it even mattered.

The house shook as the whelp somehow bashed around inside, over and over. Such a lot of power for such a small creature, Melelki thought.

The beam that supported the corner of the house nearest to them rattled, then snapped in half. Melelki felt it like a blow to her own body. Should she take them back down the trail? She could not leave. Not yet. None of them could.

Tamun clenched and unclenched her fists. "Mama—"

Melelki put a hand on her older daughter's shoulder. Tamun was tense, her body fired with the power of her full heat, which she had come into fast. Melelki gently patted her back, trying to keep them all calm, starting with herself.

The house trembled again. There was a repeating slamming sound.

Sekena nudged her and pointed away from the cabin, far to the right. A figure hiked out of the trees.

"Ta, by the moon," Melelki hissed. It was the blue-eyed human.

Fury surged in her, and she fought it down. He looked at the shaking house and slowed.

"Human scum," Melelki yelled at him, unable to stop herself. "You said they would not attack. Look!"

Another corner beam of the cabin snapped and one whole side of the house sagged. There were now tearing sounds coming from the cabin, like trees and rocks being pulled across each other.

Tamun's eyes were wide and furious. Melelki gripped her shoulder tightly.

"It's destroying our home!"

"Ta," she said to her daughter. "I know, flower, I know."

"What does it want? Food?" Tamun sputtered. "What? Stupid beast."

The human was as close to the house as they were now, and he stopped. "I think it's trying to get out."

Tamun's face was red. "Get *out*?"

"Yes," he said. "It wants to get out. To get up onto something and throw itself off. That's how they learn to fly."

Some part of Melelki's mind stored the information for later. Right now, though—

"Make it stop," Tamun told him harshly.

He laughed once, a short laugh. "Make a dragon whelp stop?"

A window shutter splintered open. A green nose poked out.

"There it is," Sekena whispered, more fascination in her voice than fear.

The nose disappeared. More crashing sounds issued from the cabin. Melelki winced.

"You must know how," Tamun insisted.

"Not without—" He shook his head.

"What are you doing here?" Melelki asked.

"I thought you might have reconsidered my offer."

"Ta," Melelki hissed. "Did you make the egg hatch just to try to convince us?"

"No," he said. "No. It's hatched early."

"We can't let it finish," Tamun said through clenched teeth.

"We'll have nowhere to live," Sekena added. Then more softly, "We've got money saved, right Mama?"

"A little, my flower. A little."

The roof of their cabin trembled, buckled, and fell in with a loud crash. Pieces of wood flew out from all the collapsed walls, landing and plowing up little rains of snow.

Tamun yelled, a deep, long yell, like a battle cry. Melelki and Sekena both grabbed at her at once, but she shook them off without effort and took off at a dead run toward the cabin.

Melelki started after her, but Sekena grabbed her arm, pulling her back, her face twisted in pained determination. "No, Mama!"

"It'll kill her," Melelki howled, struggling full against her younger daughter's surprising strength. Sekena pulled her to the ground, where they wrestled for a furious moment. Then they both stopped, turning to watch Tamun.

The human was yelling at her to get back, that she was stupid, all sorts of things that at any other time Melelki would have found outrageously insulting, but at the moment she entirely agreed with. He reached down, picked up handfuls of snow and dirt, and hurled them into the air after her.

Crazy. Human-crazy.

Just like it was crazy to store dragon eggs in the basement. Dwarf-crazy. And now Melelki would pay dearly for her stupidity.

Tamun was only halfway to the cabin, but that didn't matter. It was too late to do anything but watch her run straight to her death. Heat-driven and heat-strong as Tamun might be, she was no match for a dragonling. It would snap her like a dry twig. Melelki wailed her grief and agony, but had to watch.

It was odd how many details she noticed, and all at once: Sekena's white fingers still pressed against her arm, Tamun's hushed steps in the snow, the human's chanting as he threw dirty snow at the remains of their cabin.

Odd, the things that made this horrible moment stretch into a very, very long, horrible moment. She could not believe that in heartbeats her eldest daughter, her Tamun, her flower, just now in first heat, would soon be unmoving meat. Alive in this moment, dead in another few. How could that be? If she could somehow freeze her daughter, freeze the whelp, freeze them all, if only, if only—

Thunder fell upon them. The earth shook. Melelki was slammed against Sekena and her ears rang. She struggled to her feet, but Sekena had rolled over and was already standing.

The cabin was completely flattened into rubble, every piece of timber and stone charred black and scattered in a circle outward. Tamun lay in a heap halfway there. Melelki was already running toward her, but the human arrived first, kneeling on the ground next to her. She gripped his shoulder, tossed him backward without a glance, and dropped down next to her daughter.

The irritating creature was back again in a moment. She growled at him, deep and guttural.

"I'm trying to help, you stupid woman!"

"I'll kill you if you touch her," Melelki said in one breath.

"Curse you, I just saved her!"

The words meant nothing, not now, not with Tamun lying there. Melelki bent down to listen at her daughter's mouth, holding her own breath until the other's sounded clear in her ear. With it, a deep, vast relief washed over her.

"She breathes," Melelki said, swallowing a sob.

The human sat back on his haunches. "I'd like to tell you that she'll be fine, but if you won't let me near her—"

"To hell with you," Melelki said softly, stroking her daughter's streaked hair gently.

"I guess it's too much to expect a little gratitude from a dwarven woman."

"Gratitude?" she growled.

"The dragon whelp is dead," he said, saying each word clearly, slowly, as if she were some stupid creature that might not understand.

Indeed, the words barely made sense. She looked over at

their flattened cabin. Sekena was walking around it, toeing pieces
of it with her boot.

"Where did the whelp go?" Sekena asked.

"It's in there," he said. "In small bits. Very, very small bits."

Melelki looked at him. He looked almost angry.

"Do you want me to look at her or not?"

Grudgingly she motioned him closer. He dropped down next
to Tamun, touched her neck, pulled back an eyelid.

Melelki thought through the last few minutes, then thought
them through again.

"You're the wizard," she said.

He nodded.

A chill worked its way down her spine.

"What kind of wizard?"

"Elemental," he said. "Not—not the other kind."

She exhaled slowly. "A mud wizard," she said, relieved. Not
the sort who could plow under whole villages with a word or
summon hoards of zombies with a gesture. That was good.

"Mud wizard," he echoed sardonically. "But wizard enough
to turn a whelp into a piece of thunder. She'll be okay. What did
you call her?"

"Tamun."

He bent down over her and said her name softly, again and
again. Tamun opened her eyes.

"Praise land and sky," Melelki exhaled.

"Did I kill it?" Tamun asked, struggling to sit up, brushing
away the human's attempts to help her.

He laughed once, a short laugh. "In a way."

"It's dead? Then the cabin—"

"No," Melelki said, "flower, the cabin's—destroyed."

"Destroyed?" Her tone was pained. "The eggs—"

From the ruin came Sekena's voice. "I found one," she said,
hurling a piece of wood to the side. "And here's another. The
whole place came down on them and they're not even *scratched*."

"Dragon eggs," the human said, nodding. "The one was
early, but the rest are probably still a couple of weeks away.
Check them for dark spots. Mottling. Check for—"

"You," Melelki said, her anger rekindling. "You foul stinking human parasite—"

He exhaled and stood. "Even an orc would consider thanks, woman."

"Thanks? For offering us nothing for our cradle, for leaving us to this—this monster?"

He turned away, brushed the snow off his cloak. "Thanks for your daughter's life, maybe. But not from a dwarven woman. Of course not. Heartless, selfish bitch. You'll make good parents to those whelps."

She stood, came around him to block his way, staring up into those cold blue eyes.

"Ta, you're the one to say, trying to cheat us and leave us to the hatchling's fury!"

"At least I would have taken them. Then this wouldn't—" He waved his hand, made a frustrated sound and a dismissing gesture. He tried to walk around her, but still she blocked him. His eyes narrowed.

"You ought to be a little afraid, woman. Even a mud wizard is dangerous."

"Ta, you ought to pay for what you ask for."

"I can't pay with what I don't have," he said through clenched teeth.

"Don't have?"

"Money. Gold. I don't have any."

"But— why not?"

"Inquisitive creature, aren't you." He smirked humorlessly. "But I'm not here to discuss my fortunes. Or lack."

Tamun stood just behind him. "The eggs," she said suddenly. He turned, momentarily startled at how close she was. She fixed him with her dark eyes. "What do you do with the eggs?"

For a moment he returned her stare, then he glanced at the cabin where Sekena was throwing more pieces of wood to uncover the eggs. "That."

"That?"

"I pump mud magic into them. If I get it right, they explode."

"But why do you do it?"

"Why should I tell you?"

She reached out her hand and put it on his chest. He started, uncertain of what to expect, looked down at her hand for a long moment, then back at her.

"What are you doing?"

"Why do you do that, with the eggs?" Tamun asked him again.

"The eggs," he said slowly, "they're weapons. I—" He stopped, swallowed. "What are you doing?"

Melelki had seen that expression before, the one the human now had on his face. Where had she seen it?

On the faces of dwarven men was where.

Oh.

"Tamun," she whispered. "No. Not a *human*."

Sekena quietly joined them.

"The eggs," Tamun prompted, ignoring her mother's plea.

"There are battles to the east. You've heard. Orcs and humans. But it's not just that. Havenwood hired me—" He shook his head. "You're doing something to me."

"The elves hired you. Go on," Tamun said.

One of his hands, shaking, came up and hovered over hers. For a moment Melelki thought he would grab her hand and pull it away. Instead he gently pressed his palm on top of her fingers.

"Havenwood hired me to attack both sides, to make it look as if it were the other side's work. I convinced human scouts that the restless orcs were planning an invasion. Then I sneaked across the lines and helped the orcs develop battle plans against—against my own people. All the while I set attacks on both sides."

Melelki and her eldest daughter exchanged quick, worried glances. Sekena was staring at her feet with a look of intense concentration.

"But why would the elves want this?"

"Because—" He shut his eyes tightly, his breath coming harder, his hand still on Tamun's. "Because the elves want to have orcs and humans fighting each other, instead of coming farther east to Havenwood."

"The elves had you start a war for them," Sekena said.

He opened his eyes, exhaled. "Yes."

"Then why did they stop paying you?"

His tone was bitter. "Because I succeeded. The war has begun."

Melelki snorted. "Ta, I'm not surprised. Elves hate to get their hands dirty, don't they? But they love their little shows. Now it makes sense, why they've been buying up so many weapons and armor, coming here to hire us to guard their borders. Disgusting creatures."

"Then what—" Sekena asked "—what did you want *these* eggs for, if the elves have stopped paying you?"

A slow smile crept over the human's face. "I thought I might give Havenwood a bit of their own show. I thought they might like to see it up close."

Tamun returned his smile with one of her own, bright, with teeth showing. "Aha! Wonderful. We will come with you."

Melelki turned on her daughter. "What?"

"Yes, of course," Sekena agreed, grinning.

"Are you crazy?" Melelki demanded. "Is this mud magic at work, stirring your minds into garbage soup? We have nothing. *Nothing,* you hear? Maybe a few gold pieces, somewhere under the rubble that used to be our home. Maybe. Probably not."

"Yes, Mama, exactly," Tamun said. "Rubble, fifteen dragon eggs, and two weeks. That's our entire fortune. So let's go visit those honorable, worthy elves. I wonder how they'll like the sort of entertainment *we* can offer them." She let her hand fall from the human's chest. His hand followed hers, as if it had a mind of its own. Their fingers entwined.

Sekena's face was alight with anticipation. "Maybe we can get them to fight among themselves."

"Or buy our dragon eggs, instead."

"Or both."

"At the start of winter?" Melelki demanded. "Has the cold frozen your minds?"

"We'll be moving fast, Mama. We'll stay warm. And besides, we've only got two weeks before they hatch, then we'll be done."

Melelki had a feeling that if they went on this trip, it would take a lot longer than that.

"If we get cold we can start a fire," Sekena continued. "Or we can always have the human blow up one of the whelps."

The wizard made a sound. "I don't remember inviting you all along."

Well, Melelki thought, it wasn't as if they could bring their cabin back by wishing. And besides, hadn't she resolved to find out everything she could about dragons?

"Two gold," he went on, "and I'll take them away, but all of you—"

"All or none," Melelki told him.

He looked at her, then Sekena, and longest at Tamun, who brushed thick strands of streaked hair back from her glowing face.

He clenched his free hand into a fist, looked away, looked back. "What are you doing to me, woman?"

She laughed.

"Tamun—" Melelki said in warning, then exhaled. There was nothing for it, not when a dwarven woman went into her time of power. But a human? It made her feel funny to think about.

Sekena rubbed her hands together. "Let's get going. I want to actually see one of the dragonlings. All we've seen so far is a nose. Besides, all this standing around talking is just making me cold. Now, human—"

"I have a name."

"Yes? So say it."

His eyes were still on Tamun. "Reod. Reod Dai."

"Strange name."

Reod snorted, glared at the other two. "There are no songs sung about dwarvish tolerance."

"Reod Dai," Sekena said, pronouncing the words carefully. "Where are your wagons?"

"Down the trail."

"There's still a price to figure," Melelki said, "for our eggs."

Reod's mouth dropped open. "You astound me, woman."

"Ta, you won't get them for nothing."

"Then let's go get my wagons. If you must, you can haggle en route."

"Mama," Tamun said, "Sekena and I will stay here and bring up the eggs from under the house."

Her eldest's daughter's look told her that she would also be searching for their stash of gold coins while they were there. While Reod Dai was not.

Reod gave Tamun a look that was part worry and part something else. She gave him a reassuring smile and at the same time gently disconnected his hand from hers.

"Come on," Melelki said to him, keeping her amusement hidden. But who should she be amused at? The human or Tamun? And who would have thought it? She shook her head.

She and the human walked down the trail together. The sun was climbing higher, warming them both.

"Price," she reminded him.

"Price," he snorted. "What price? I have nothing to give you."

"I'll take the two gold, and—"

"And?"

"And I expect all the protection you and your mud magic can give us every step of the way. And—"

He laughed, incredulous.

"And if we manage to make any money on the eggs, we take three-fourths of it."

"Three-fourths? I don't think so. A quarter at most."

"Half."

"Half. All right. You were never so difficult to bargain with before."

"I've learned. From you, human. Reod Dai. Or do you still think we dwarves are as dumb as beasts?"

"No." He hesitated. "About Tamun—"

"Ah, yes, that's the other thing."

He made a frustrated, dismissive gesture. "I'm not bargaining with you for the affections of—"

"Of a dwarven woman."

"Yes, a dwarven woman."

"I wouldn't be so stupid. But you have to understand—she's going into her first heat. It makes her—strong in many ways. It's not the same as what you humans do."

With a wry smile he said, "I've noticed."

"And, still, she interests you?"

"She does."

The sun streamed down between the trees, and Melelki found that despite all the terrible things that she and her daughters had faced, there was a brightness on the air, the promise of new things, as if in answer to her dwarven curiosity. As if there were a new mountain to climb.

And her eldest flower was in full bloom. It was a good time. But, she thought with a wince—a human?

"It seems odd to me, Reod Dai, that you, with all your wizard's ways—mud ways though they may be—and all your knowledge, would be seduced by a simple dwarven woman in her first heat. Surely you've seen that and worse before. Being human and a wizard on top of that, I'd think that you'd be able to resist Tamun entirely."

For a few moments the only sound was their boots crunching on the sparkling, white snow.

A smile came to his lips. "Well, there is that about seduction magic, you know. It doesn't work if sent only in one direction."

Melelki pondered that a moment, then stopped. Reod turned to face her, their feet making triangular patterns in the new snow. He was downhill from her on the trail, but he was still taller, smiling down on her with that same cocky smile she had seen years ago.

"What are you saying?"

"It's never entirely just one side's doing."

For a long moment she looked him over. Tall and thin. Very thin. Easy to break.

But not, perhaps, as easy as she had once thought.

She began to walk down the trail again, and silently he fell into step beside her, glancing over at her. In his look was something beyond arrogance. Hope, perhaps.

It occurred to her, as she took a deep breath of cold air, that the human didn't smell so bad after all.

At last she spoke. "And I expect you to keep us all from freezing to death."

He laughed, and Melelki thought she saw relief just beyond his amusement.

"I think I can manage that."

She smiled a little. "I expect it of you."

"Of course you do. I'm fortunate that there's plenty of mud in the world."

"You're fortunate to have such good company."

"Yes," he said softly. "That I am."

About the Authors

Carla Montgomery is a writer and freelance journalist in North Carolina where she lives with her husband, Carl, and two telepathic cats. She recently finished a Masters at Duke University in chaos theory and the nature of change in scientific thought. In previous incarnations, she has been a dancer, groom, bingo hall usher, science museum teacher, marsupial breeder, and cop reporter.

Montgomery despises shoes, enjoys dabbling in photography and art, and is inspired by the outdoors, music (from McLachlan to Mozart), and close friends. Currently she dreams of buying a Harley and returning to her native home in the Southwest.

Michael A. Stackpole is an award-winning game and computer game designer who was inducted into the Academy of Gaming Arts and Design Hall of Fame in 1994. His fiction includes nine *BattleTech* novels and the epic fantasy *Once A Hero*. He is currently writing four *Star Wars* X-wing novels for Bantam; the first, *Rogue Squadron,* is set for publication in January 1996. Until writing this bio piece, Stackpole had forgotten that like his hero, Loot, he suffered amnesia due to head trauma. It figures.

Hanovi Braddock was born in Tucson, Arizona. He did not spend years fishing on an Alaskan trawler, fighting oil rig fires in Texas, sailing a small boat alone across the Atlantic, or teaching agronomy in Gabon. He wishes he had, because that's the sort of thing one is supposed to include in a writer's biography. Instead, he went to college, changed his major five times, and finally settled for a B.A. in Humanities, which was the next best thing to a degree in Major Undecided. Two decades later, he still doesn't know what to specialize in. Braddock's previous stories have appeared in *The Leading Edge*.

S. D. Perry has authored three books for Dark Horse Comics—*Aliens: The Female War, Aliens vs. Predator: Prey* (both with her father, Steve Perry), and the novelization of *Timecop*. Her first short story, "The Key" (*Pulphouse Hardcover*, Issue #11), won honorable mention in *The Year's Best Fantasy and Horror* (fifth annual, ed. Datlow/Windling). This is her second short story sale.

Perry lives in Portland with her artist boyfriend and their dog, H. P. Lovecraft. She is currently working on her own horror novel, *Woodland Creatures*, about a necrophile and his friends.

In 1990 **Mark Shepherd** began collaborating with Mercedes Lackey on the *SERRAted Edge* urban fantasy series with the novel *Wheels of Fire*, available from Baen. Also available from Baen is another collaboration with Lackey, *Prison of Souls*, and in 1995 Baen will publish a solo project, *Moonrise in Roksamur*. These novels are both tie-ins based on the best-selling roleplaying computer game *Bard's Tale*. Shepherd's first published solo work, *Elvendude*, is an elves-in-the-mall urban fantasy set in Dallas, Texas. Within weeks of its release it appeared on the *Locus* bestseller list. In the works is a sequel, *Spiritride*, which takes place six years later in Albuquerque, New Mexico.

Shepherd lives in Oklahoma in the aerie known as Highflight, along with Mercedes Lackey and her husband Larry Dixon, their ten tropical birds, miscellaneous raptors in rehabilitation, and three cats: Gizmo, Max, and Mutant.

Ben Ohlander was born in Rapid City, South Dakota on July 16, 1965. He has lived in seven states and three countries. His family is split between Colorado and Ohio. He attended military school in Virginia and lost an appointment to the Naval Academy when his sponsor committed suicide. Ohlander then joined the Marine Corps, where he spent six years as an analyst, serving such tours as Cuba and Panama. He went on to receive a degree in International Studies in 1994.

Ohlander writes, fences, and dabbles in music and fine wines. He currently resides in the Midwest with a cat, dog, and bad weather. His first novel, a collaboration with David Drake, will be available for purchase in early 1996.

Dublin-born **Michael Scott** began his career as a bookseller and dealer in antiquarian books. An omnivorous reader, he was soon drawn to the related areas of Irish history and Celtic mythology, and he is now considered one of the leading experts in the folklore of the Celtic lands.

Scott began writing fifteen years ago, and has published such diverse works as a critically acclaimed fantasy trilogy entitled *Tales of the Bard,* the best-selling historical novel *Seasons,* the non-fiction guide *An Irish Herbal,* the definitive *Irish Folk and Fairy Tales* series, several collections of folklore and ghost stories, and a number of highly successful books for children. His horror novels are considered classics of the genre. He and author Morgan Llywelyn are currently collaborating on a three-volume epic fantasy entitled *The Arcana.* Volume One, *Silverhand,* will be published in 1995.

David M. Honigsberg lives, works, and writes in New York City. His short stories have appeared in *Elric: Tales of the White Wolf* and the upcoming *Sorcery: Magicks Old and New.* With Mike Stackpole, he has also written the *CHAOSWORLD Campaign Book* for Hero Games, and he periodically reviews games for *Science Fiction Age.* A student of Jewish mysticism, he teaches courses in Kabbalah at the Theosophical Society in Manhattan. Honigsberg has appeared as a singer/songwriter/guitarist in Greenwich Village and as a disk jockey in Hartford, CT. His scholarly pursuits include Arthurian studies and Judaica.

Bruce Holland Rogers writes fiction across the spectrum, from fantasy, SF, and mystery to literary and experimental. His work has appeared in an unlikely assortment of publications: *Fantasy & Science Fiction, Quarterly West, Woman's World, Century, The Quarterly, Ellery Queen's,* and *New Mexico Humanities Review,* among others. Rogers has taught creative writing at the Universities of Colorado and Illinois, but now limits his teaching to writers' conferences. His mystery story, "Enduring As Dust," was a 1994 nominee for the Edgar Allen Poe Award. That same story later won the Jonny Cat Litter-ary Award. The award from the Cat Writers' Association—we're not making this up!—is sponsored by the Excel Mineral Company, which manufactures cat litter.

M. C. Sumner is the author of a number of thrillers, including *Deadly Stranger* and *The Dark.* He is also the author of the upcoming cowboy fantasy *Range.* In addition to his novels, he has written many science fiction and fantasy short stories, a number of computer games, and a regular magazine column on games of all sorts. He is an insatiable, fanatic game player who is always ready to lose a round of **Magic: The Gathering** to anyone. He currently lives at the edge of the Ozark Plateau, along with his wife, son, and a menagerie of critters.

Look for M. C. Sumner's **Magic: The Gathering** novel, *The Prodigal Sorcerer,* from HarperPrism in Fall 1995.

Billie Sue Mosiman is the author of the Edgar-nominated *Night Cruise.* She has published more than eighty short stories in various magazines, including *Realms of Fantasy* and twenty-three anthologies such as *Tales From The Great Turtle.* Her newest novel is *Widow.* She lives in the country with cats, wandering deer, a pug named Ringo, and a shar-pei called China.

Cynthia Ward was born in Oklahoma and has lived in Maine, Spain, Germany, and the San Francisco Bay area. She now lives in the Seattle area with her husband and their Maine coon cats. She blames Ken St. Amand and Greg Allen for introducing her to **Magic: The Gathering**. She has stories published or forthcoming in *Asimov's SF, Tomorrow Speculative Fiction, Galaxy, Offworld, The Ultimate Dragon, Sword & Sorceress* (vols. 8, 9, & 11), *After The Loving,* and elsewhere.

Morgan Llywelyn originally intended to raise horses for a living, and spent many years showing jumpers and dressage horses. Only after she narrowly missed being on the Olympic Equestrian Team did she turn to writing. Her first historical novel, *The Wind from Hastings,* was published in 1978, to be followed by the international bestseller *Lion of Ireland.*

Since then, Llywelyn has published a total of nine historical novels focusing on Ireland and the Celtic culture; these have been translated into a total of twenty-seven languages. She has also published a non-fiction biography of Xerxes of Persia for City College of New York, and an environmental fantasy entitled *The Elementals.* Her short stories have been published in magazines such as *Weird Tales* as well as various anthologies, and the first collection of Llywelyn short stories will be published in 1995 under the title *The Earth is Made of Stardust.* She and author Michael Scott are currently collaborating on a three-volume epic fantasy entitled *The Arcana.*

Stephen Michael Stirling was born on September 30, 1953 in Metz, Alsace, France (or Germany, depending on whom you ask). His father was born and raised in Newfoundland, of Anglo-Scottish background; his mother was born in Lancashire, England and raised in Lima, Peru, and Halifax, Nova Scotia. He is descended from Border relatives on both sides.

Stirling has lived for several years each in France, England, Canada, the U.S., and Kenya. Previous temporary residences include Italy, Israel, Tanzania, South Africa, Spain, and Mexico.

His hobbies include history, literature, and anthropology. He has a brown belt, second dan, in Tao Zen Chuan karate.

Stirling has an honors B.A. in History and English from Charleton University and an LL.B. from Osgoode Hall. His previous employment included farm and secretarial work and a stint as a bouncer in a recreational establishment. Due to moral scruples, he has never practiced law. Since 1988 he has been a full-time novelist and the husband of Janet Catherine Stirling.

David Drake was born in Dubuque, Iowa in 1945. He graduated Phi Beta Kappa from the University of Iowa, majoring in history (with honors) and Latin. He was attending Duke University Law School when he was drafted. He served the next two years in the Army, spending 1970 as an enlisted interrogator with the 11th Armored Cavalry in Vietnam and Cambodia. Upon his return, he completed his law degree at Duke and was for eight years Assistant Town Attorney for Chapel Hill, North Carolina. He then drove a city bus for a year and, since 1981, has been a full-time freelance writer.

Drake has a wife, a son, and various pets. He lives in a new house on twenty-two acres in Chatham County, North Carolina, where he feeds sunflower seeds to birds.

Peter Friend is a New Zealander who writes a lot of humorous articles and depressing short stories. The articles tend to sell better for some reason, but he's had fiction published in *Aurealis* and *Interzone* magazines. He also draws, paints, and animates cartoons in the vain hope of becoming a living art treasure one day. In real life, he's a computer analyst.

Ignoring friends' warnings and her own good sense, **Sonia Orin Lyris** picked up her first **Magic** deck in August '94—a black and white deck, of course. She quickly became an addict, and now plays all colors, currently favoring Christmas.

Lyris's science fiction and fantasy has appeared in *Asimov's SF* magazine, *Pulphouse,* and *Expanse,* as well as the anthologies

Infinite Loop (ed. Larry Constantine), *Cyberdreams* (ed. Gardner Dozois and Sheila Williams), and Greg Bear's forthcoming *New Legends*.

Lyris has finished a fantasy novel called *The Seer,* which is still searching for a publisher, and is now at work on a cyberspace novel.